*His eyes raked her with a look
that left her trembling.*

"I've said before—and I still believe—that you're a very capable young woman. But just how do you propose to handle the herding and branding and other work required to care for a herd? I propose we make a deal."

She eyes him warily. "What kind of deal?"

"Turn your herd in with mine. I will brand them with your mark and drive them to market next spring. Let me have that section bordering the property I already own."

The fact that his proposal was reasonable did nothing to lessen her dismay at having been bested. "You came here today planning to make that proposal, knowing I'd have no choice but to agree," she said. "Now you can go home and gloat about how you got the better of me."

"Don't suppose you can know my thoughts, Miss O'Connor, especially where they concern you." To her astonishment, he closed the gap between them and took her chin in his hand. "If you could truly read my mind, you would know that I find you one of the most aggravating, perplexing, *intriguing* women I've ever encountered."

A rush of emotion shuddered through her. How could she both detest and desire one man so?

Patchwork Hearts

CYNTHIA STERLING

JOVE BOOKS, NEW YORK

A QUILTING ROMANCE is a trademark of
Berkley Publishing Corporation.

PATCHWORK HEARTS

A Jove Book / published by arrangement with
the author

PRINTING HISTORY
Jove edition / February 1999

The Penguin Putnam World Wide Web site address is
http://www.penguinputnam.com

ISBN: 0-515-12446-X

A JOVE BOOK®
Jove Books are published by The Berkley Publishing Group,
a member of Penguin Putnam Inc.,
375 Hudson Street, New York, New York 10014.
JOVE and the "J" design
are trademarks belonging to Jove Publications, Inc.

PRINTED IN THE UNITED STATES OF AMERICA

10 9 8 7 6 5 4 3 2

To Jim

In the midst of life's uncertainties,
Your love is always a sure thing.

Patchwork
Hearts

1

TRACE KNEW THE WOMAN was watching him. He'd felt her gaze on him ever since he'd stepped through the door of the mercantile. The hair on the back of his neck prickled the way it had at Appomattox, when he'd realized the sniper was tracking his progress through the woods.

He stood for a moment just inside the store, brushing the rain from his slicker and pouring half a cup of water from the crown of his hat. Out of the corner of his eye, he studied the woman. She was young, with dark hair and a pretty, intelligent face—the kind of woman who made a man think of polishing up his manners and his boots and getting to know her better. The way she was watching him, he might even have thought she'd welcome such attention; but then, he'd been fooled by beauty before.

As soon as he raised his head to look at her directly, she turned away, pretending to examine a bolt of cloth. But he hadn't missed the spark of real interest that sprang from her green eyes. The knowledge made him more uneasy than the open hostility from the three old coots gathered around the potbellied stove in the corner.

"Howdy, stranger." A gray-bearded man in a white apron rose from a chair in front of the stove. "Nasty weather out, ain't it?"

"Yes, sir, it is that." A nudging at Trace's knees urged him further into the room. He glanced behind him and saw the boy, Josh. Ever since they'd crossed the Red River, Josh had refused to let Trace out of his sight, fearful of being scalped by Indians or lynched by angry rebs.

Trace walked over to the stove, concentrating on moving with no hint of a limp. The leg only bothered him when he was tired; today he was bone weary. He stretched his hands out to the warmth while Josh hovered in his shadow. The two men still seated by the stove looked from him to the boy. If they thought it odd that a white man and a black boy traveled together, they didn't air their opinions. But even the blazing stove couldn't melt the frost in their eyes as they watched Trace.

One man's leg was missing from the knee down. He propped his wooden peg on the stove fender, as if to warm the foot that was no longer there. The other man wore a patch over his eye, the rest of his face crisscrossed with scars. Trace followed the men's gaze to the faded yellow stripe that ran down the leg of his own Union uniform trousers. Ah, that explained the chill in the air.

He turned his back on the old soldiers and addressed the storekeeper. "I need to buy a few supplies, and then I need directions to Hiram Fischer's place."

"Hiram ain't here." The man with the peg leg rose to confront Trace, glaring at him with bloodshot eyes. He huffed out a breath heavy with the smell of whiskey. "He ain't made it back yet from the fightin'."

Trace ran his thumb along the worn brim of his hat and nodded. "He won't be coming back either." He waited for questions, but none came. He didn't have to tell these men why Hiram wouldn't be returning; most likely they'd known the truth even if they hadn't been willing to admit it yet. How many other local sons and fathers had never "made it back" from that awful war?

"So why do you need to know where his place is?" the one-eyed man asked. "Far as I know, Hiram didn't have no kin, leastways not here."

"He deeded his property to me." Trace looked at each man in turn, letting them see that their animosity meant little to him. He'd lived with worse before. "I plan on living there."

He let that sink in—the idea that they'd have a Yankee soldier for a neighbor. The silence grew thick, the only sound the crunch of a log falling to coals in the stove, and the whisper of the woman's footsteps down the aisle.

In all this time, she hadn't stopped watching him, and he had never stopped being aware of her. Her gaze was like a physical caress that he both welcomed and resisted. He'd been alone a long time now, but he didn't need trouble. Like Eve in the garden, this woman with the bold eyes would be sure to vex him.

"Hiram's place is a fur piece from here." The storekeeper spoke up at last. "Too far to travel on a night like this. You're welcome to stay in the stables out back and get a fresh start in the morning."

"No, thanks, I'll—"

Josh sneezed, cutting off his words. It was one thing for him to push on to Hiram's place in the darkness and rain; he'd traveled in worse these last five years. It was another to expect a ten-year-old boy to do the same. He nodded to the storekeeper. "Much obliged, sir. I'll do my shopping in the morning before I leave." With a nod to the three men, he turned to go, Josh shuffling in his wake.

"My name's Nate O'Connor," the storekeeper called after him. "If you need anything during the night, just knock on the back door."

He paused at the door and looked over his shoulder. "Pleased to meet you, Mr. O'Connor. I'm Trace Abernathy." He nodded to each man in turn, still pretending he hadn't noticed the woman, though every part of him was aware of her. Then he replaced his hat on his head and headed back out into the dark and the blowing rain.

∞

LUCY O'CONNOR WATCHED TRACE Abernathy disap-
pear behind a curtain of rain, the little black boy hurrying
along behind him. She turned away from the window with
an odd feeling of emptiness. It felt as if ten men had left
instead of just one and a boy; there was that much more
room in the store now.

"Just how do you think a Yankee soldier got ahold of the
deed to old Hiram's place?" Bill Pollard sank back into his
chair and propped his wooden leg on the stove fender again.
He took his pipe from his pocket and began to fill it.

"Maybe he's not really a Yankee." Lucy crossed the
room to stand beside Uncle Nate. "Maybe he took those
clothes off a dead Yankee. Maybe he and Mr. Fischer were
comrades in arms, and Mr. Abernathy took care of Mr.
Fischer before he died."

"You've been lettin' that girl fill her head full of romance stories again, haven't you, Nate?" Zeke Early
shaped his mouth into a grimace Lucy knew was meant to
be a smile. "Sounds like your imagination run away with
you, Lucy girl. Real life ain't like those stories you're always scribblin'."

She pinched her mouth shut but said nothing. Mr. Early
wouldn't be so quick to dismiss her writing as "scribbling"
when those Eastern publishers started paying for her stories.
"Mr. Abernathy didn't *sound* like a Yankee," she said,
remembering the gentle drawl. "He didn't sound like a
Texan either—his accent was softer, more refined."

"Maybe our Lucy's taken a fancy to that handsome
stranger." Mr. Pollard took a long pull on his pipe and
pretended to smile at her. She knew as soon as her uncle's
back was turned, Pollard's smile would transform into a
leer. She'd learned quick enough not to let herself be caught
alone with old man Pollard.

"Good to see young men moving back to the county."
Uncle Nate picked up a cloth and began polishing the

counter. He didn't use adjectives like "strong" and "healthy" to describe their visitor, but Lucy added them in her head. Plenty of young men had come limping back to town after the war, missing parts of their bodies or spirits. Even the whole ones seemed old before their time, bent and gray as grandfathers.

Trace Abernathy, with his broad shoulders and coal-black hair, radiated strength and health. In that brief moment when his brilliant blue eyes met hers, she'd felt a shiver run through her, as if she'd been awakened from a trance by a bucket of ice water. And then, when she'd turned away, she'd felt his eyes still on her, warming her through.

"Did you see that colored boy with him?" Pollard asked. "The kid was sure light skinned. Reckon that's one from the wrong side of the blanket?"

"Now, Bill." Uncle Nate gave Pollard a warning look and cut his eyes toward Lucy. She flushed and looked away.

"Lucy, why don't you take some of that good stew you made out to our guests?"

Uncle Nate's request surprised her. "Are you sure? I mean, what if he *is* a Yankee?" Her heart fluttered nervously. Despite his courtly manners, Trace Abernathy had a dangerous air about him.

"The war's over, child. Remember your Christian charity." He nodded toward the back door and the stable beyond. "Leave the door open when you step out. I'll hear if there's any trouble."

Heart pounding, she walked to the kitchen in the living quarters behind the store. How could Mr. Abernathy mean anything but trouble? He hadn't been in town half an hour and already he'd stirred up the old men by the stove more than anything since Lee's surrender at Appomattox. She fumbled with the ladle as she filled a crockery bowl with stew. He'd stirred something in her, too—a restlessness and longing for excitement outside her familiar, never-changing small-town world. Pushing aside that thought, she inverted a plate over the bowl and dashed across the yard to the stable door. Rain beat on her back and splashed on her skirts, but she shielded Mr. Abernathy's dinner with her body to keep it dry. She arrived at the stable damp and breathless.

Sheltering under the eaves, she pounded on the rough wooden door. "Mr. Abernathy! I've brought you some supper!"

"I'll be right there."

A moment later he opened the door, still buttoning his shirt with a free hand. "Come in."

She stepped past him into the feeble glow of a lantern hanging from a beam. In one glance she took in the basin of water, bar of yellow soap, sacking towel, and the damp triangle of hair showing at the open neck of Trace Abernathy's shirt. The subtle perfume of the sandalwood soap hung in the air. She'd caught their visitor at his bath. The knowledge made her grateful for the deep shadows that hid her blush.

"I brought you some stew." She offered the dish.

He took the bowl, his gaze locked on her as he lifted the plate. "Smells good. Did you make it?"

She nodded. His bold stare made her uncomfortable. There was a hunger in that look for something besides the stew. She scanned the stable for something else on which to focus, and spotted the boy. "What's your name?" she asked him.

He ducked his head and addressed the stable floor. "Josh."

"Hello, Josh. I'm Lucy O'Connor."

"The storekeeper is your father?" Trace spooned half the stew onto the plate and handed the bowl to Josh. The boy took the dish and disappeared into the shadows.

"He's my uncle." She knew she should go now; she had no business standing here alone in this stable, talking to a man who might have recently been her enemy. But her feet seemed rooted to the floor.

"Ahh. Are you just visiting or do you live with him?" His voice had a caressing quality, like velvet.

She hugged her arms across her breasts, as if to fend off the softness of that voice, to protect herself from the wild emotions this man kindled in her just by speaking. "I live here." She forced herself to look at him, ignoring the way her heart sped up when their eyes met. She'd never known a man with eyes so blue—bright Federal blue, the color the enemy wore. But they weren't enemies anymore, were they? "My father died when I was six. My mother passed on three years ago."

"I'm sorry for your loss."

She'd heard the stock phrase enough times in the last three years; Trace Abernathy actually sounded as though he meant it. The knowledge that this Yankee soldier might feel sympathy for her rankled. "You've been asking all the questions—I ought to ask you some." She gave him a challenging look.

He leaned against the ladder leading up to the hayloft and scooped up a spoonful of stew. "Ask. Although I might not necessarily answer." He sounded amused, which made her all the more indignant.

"Why are you wearing that Yankee uniform?"

"A man wears the clothes he can afford."

She frowned. "What is that supposed to mean?"

"It means, just because the war's over doesn't mean I should throw out a good pair of pants."

"You don't talk like a Yankee."

"I'm from Virginia."

"If you're from Virginia, how could you—"

"How could I fight for the Union?" He shrugged. "I did what I thought was right."

"How could betraying your own home state be right? How could—"

He straightened and set the plate aside. "I won't refight the war with you. It's a battle no one can win." The corners of his mouth lifted in the beginnings of a smile. "Besides, I'd hate to spoil the chance for future conversations."

"You, sir, are impertinent."

"Yes, ma'am." He chuckled, and she felt her face burn anew.

With a cry of disgust, she turned and ran from the barn, away from Trace Abernathy's laughter and piercing blue eyes, away from the strange longings his presence stirred within her.

∽

"YOU THINK SHE'S PRETTY, don't you?" Josh emerged from the shadows and handed Trace the empty bowl.

Trace looked toward the closed door, behind which Lucy O'Connor had fled. "Yes. She's pretty."

"You gonna court her?"

Trace sank down onto a pile of hay, suddenly too tired to stand. It had been another long day in a series of long days. He put his hand in his pocket and rubbed his thumb along the smooth pewter watch case there. The gesture always soothed him. "I'm past courting anyone."

Josh folded himself up cross-legged on the ground. "You talk like an old man. You not that old."

"Sometimes I feel old, though."

The boy picked up a stick and began to trace patterns in the dust of the floor. "You like her, don't you?"

"What makes you say that?"

"You ain't said more than three sentences to nobody since we left Virginia. You spent a whole half hour jawin' with her."

"It wasn't that long." Trace shrugged. "Besides, you heard her. I'm just another damn Yankee to her."

"What about that bunch by the stove?"

"What about 'em?"

"No young bucks in that bunch. Didn't see any on the way in, either. Before long, ever' woman for ten miles around will hear there's a new man in town—one with both legs and all his own teeth. They'll be on you like a duck on a june bug. Might be Miss Lucy will think differently then.''

''I guess it's a good thing I've got you to scare them off.''

Josh grinned. ''See, I told you you wouldn't be sorry you brought me along.''

''I didn't have much choice, did I? Seeing as how I didn't know you *were* along until we hit Tennessee.''

''I had to hide out until we was far enough from home you couldn't take me back. I knew I'd never get to come with you any other way.''

''You knew Theresa wouldn't let you come.''

Josh's face clouded at the mention of his mother. No doubt she was wailing her eyes out by now over her missing boy. ''We'll write her and let her know I'm all right, once we're settled,'' he said.

''That won't be long now. You heard the man—he'll give us directions to Hiram's place in the morning.''

''Your place now.''

His place. It had been a long time since he'd had more than a bedroll to truly call his own. He stood and blew out the lantern. In the sudden darkness, one of the horses whiffled and stomped. ''Let's get some sleep.''

Trace wrapped himself in a blanket and lay down in the loose straw, hat pulled low over his eyes. The little shiver of excitement he felt at the thought of tomorrow surprised him. He'd told himself he was past caring where he laid his head, but the promise of a place to call his own again seduced him like a sweet-voiced woman.

Lucy O'Connor's voice was sweet enough, with a hint of vinegar to keep it from cloying. Ah, but she'd taken his measure and found him wanting, hadn't she? Just as well; he'd had his fill of headstrong women. For all their beauty and spirit, they'd bring a man nothing but grief.

He rolled over and pulled the blanket tight around his shoulders, smothering the twinge of pain that stabbed at him. He had nothing to gain from brooding over the past. Better to think on the future, on the cabin he'd build and the cattle he'd raise. Tomorrow he'd begin life all over again. He wouldn't make the same mistakes this time around.

∞

THE SUN SHONE BRIGHT the next morning on a world washed clean by last night's rain. Trace waited on the front porch of O'Connor's mercantile, pretending not to notice the covert stares of every person who passed by. The town was small, with not more than half a dozen businesses lining the one main street, but he would have sworn the entire population had come out this morning to get a look at the Yankee in their midst. A few of the men nodded to him, and more than one woman cast him a coy glance from beneath her bonnet. He wouldn't exactly call it a friendly reception, but at least no one was recruiting a lynching party just yet.

"Good morning, Mr. Abernathy." Trace turned as the storekeeper walked out onto the porch and propped open the door. "I trust you slept well."

"Warm and dry, thank you. And well fed." He followed the older man into the store and held out the plate and bowl, which he'd washed this morning. "Please thank your niece for me."

O'Connor nodded and stowed the dishes behind the front counter. "Warm and dry and well fed. I reckon a man can't ask for better than that."

"No, sir, I don't believe he can." He pulled out the list he'd written on a scrap of paper. "I need to stock up on a few supplies before I head out to Hiram Fischer's place."

O'Connor took a broom from a peg and began sweeping the area around the stove. "I knew Hiram Fischer. Kind of a quiet man—but clean, and a hard worker. Good German stock. Surprised me when he said he was going to sign up to fight. Most of his countrymen tried hard to stay neutral." He paused in his sweeping and looked at Trace. "How did you come to know him?"

"We were in the same company." He waited for some protest—shock or outrage—when the storekeeper realized Hiram Fischer had joined the Yankees.

"I wondered." O'Connor hung up his broom. "I remember he was pretty upset when word came about those Germans being lynched down in Comfort because they wouldn't support the Confederate cause. I was upset myself. Every man's got a right to stand up for his convictions, even if they don't agree with mine." He looked Trace in the eye, the way a man looks at an equal. "Now, what was it you were needin'?"

Trace handed over the list, silenced by a sudden tightness in his throat. In that brief exchange, Nate O'Connor had let him know that, no matter which side of the war he'd supported, O'Connor would now support him. He hadn't realized before now how much he needed that support. He'd been fighting his battles alone for too long.

"Uncle Nate! Uncle Nate!" Footsteps pounded across the porch, and the door blew open to admit Lucy O'Connor, skirts held up with one hand, slim ankles flashing as she raced across the room. With the other hand, she waved an envelope like a signal flag. "It came! It finally came!"

O'Connor caught her by the shoulders. "Slow down, child. What is it? What has you so excited?"

"It came, Uncle." She shoved the envelope toward him. "The letter from *Leslie's Illustrated Weekly*. They want to buy my story."

O'Connor unfolded the sheet of stationery and read it through. A smile lit his face. "Lucy, that's wonderful news."

"Congratulations." Trace leaned on the counter and nodded to her.

She stared at him, as if she were only now aware of his presence. Pink suffused her cheeks, the delicate color of sunrise. "Thank you, Mr. Abernathy."

"What is your story about?" he asked.

"It's . . . it's a romantic adventure. About an exiled Russian princess who falls in love with a Confederate colonel

from Texas. She uses her family jewels to pay for his release from a Yankee prison, then she nurses him back to
health, and they discover a cache of Mexican silver buried
on his plantation, which saves them from bankruptcy.''

"No doubt a very realistic tale," he said drily.

She glared at him. "It's not meant to be realistic, Mr.
Abernathy. The world is full of hardship and bad news. I
want to entertain people. Some people must like it." She
held up the envelope. "*Leslie's Illustrated* is willing to pay
me twenty-five dollars."

"What do you intend to do with the money?" her uncle
asked. "You could order some new dress goods. Or some
fabric to finish your bridal quilt. We've got those new cal-
icoes that come in, though they're still pretty expensive."

"Bridal quilt?" Trace blurted the words before he realized he'd spoken. The thought that a woman so young and
full of life might already be engaged to marry one of the
old or infirm men he'd seen in town pinched his gut.

She shot him a puzzled look. "It's just a quilt every girl
makes in anticipation of getting married *one day,*" she said.
"It doesn't mean she necessarily will."

"At the rate she's going, Lucy will be stitching hers on
the eve of her wedding. She refuses to allow any of the
other young women to help her." O'Connor gave her an
indulgent smile. "Your mama now, she was one for quiltin'. I reckon when the time comes, you can always use
that trunk of coverlets she quilted that's up in the attic."

A hurt look flickered through those emerald eyes, a pain
that sent a jolt of recognition through Trace. "I'm not like
Mama," she mumbled, turning away.

Trace searched for some words of comfort to offer her,
some verbal balm to soothe the ache that shuddered through
them both. But before he could speak, she took a deep
breath and turned back to face them, her bright expression
in place once more. "Don't you want to hear what I've
decided to do with my money?"

"By all means, do go on," O'Connor said.

She smiled triumphantly. "I'm going to buy cattle."

"I can't think you'd get many cattle for twenty-five dollars," Trace said.

He regretted the words as soon as he saw the way they made that joyous light in her eyes dim once more. She straightened her shoulders. "It's a start," she said stiffly. "I'll sell other stories."

"Now, don't get your hopes up too high, darlin'." O'Connor patted her hand. "Remember how long you had to wait for just one check." He shook his head. "What do you want with a bunch of cattle, anyway? They're not worth much, even if you sell them for their hides."

"But up North they're worth a lot more. You remember the newspaper article I showed you—about the cattle drive to Missouri?"

"To Sedalia, wasn't it?" Trace asked.

She glanced at him. "Yes. How did you know?"

"I read the same article. It's why I decided to come to Texas."

That news didn't seem to please her much. She frowned and turned back to her uncle. "The men on that drive plan to sell their cattle in Missouri for forty dollars each!"

O'Connor let out a low whistle. "Forty dollars. That is a lot of money. 'Course, it seems to me a lot could happen between here and Missouri. Might be none of the cattle even make it to Sedalia."

"They will. They survived the war pretty much untended, didn't they?" She nodded as if to answer her own question. "I've already spoken to Mr. Gibbs, and he's going to help me pick some out."

O'Connor turned to Trace. "Sterling Gibbs owns land bordering Hiram Fischer's place, so you're bound to meet him one of these days soon."

"Cattle raising and story writing. You sound like a very industrious woman, Miss O'Connor," Trace said.

"I just know what I want and work to get it, Mr. Abernathy."

Her expression dared him to dispute her. A shiver ran up his spine, along with the feeling he'd had this conversation before. Only then, he hadn't known the wisdom of keeping his mouth shut. No more, it seemed, than he knew enough to exercise that wisdom now. "It sounds as if you and I will be in the same business," he said.

She looked wary. "What business is that?"

"I intend to raise cattle, too." He straightened and plucked a peppermint stick from a display on the counter, watching her out of the corner of his eye. "If you should ever need assistance, I'd be happy to help you."

The look she gave him could have lit fires. "Women learned to do a lot of things for themselves while the men were away fighting," she said. "I'm sure I'll be able to handle things fine on my own."

"I never said you couldn't." His stomach churned. He didn't have to be a prophet to see Lucy O'Connor was headed for trouble. The peppermint stick snapped in his hand. *It's none of my business,* he reminded himself. "Just add this to my bill." He stuffed the broken candy into his shirt pocket.

"Lucy, dear, if you'll excuse us, I'd better get to filling Mr. Abernathy's order." O'Connor nodded toward her letter. "I suppose you'll be wanting to tell Twila the good news."

"Yes, I was on my way over there now."

"That reminds me. I've got something for you to give her." O'Connor reached under the counter and took out a small card, which he handed to Lucy. Trace thought it looked like the fancy engraved calling cards ladies sometimes exchanged with each other. "Lady came through here yesterday afternoon, said she was interested in buying quilts. I thought since Twila's so handy with a needle, she might want to talk to the woman. Maybe they could help each other out."

"Mrs. Thomas Sorenson," Lucy read from the card. "I've never heard of her."

"Sure you have. She's the Swedish lady lives in the big rock house over toward Birdtown."

Lucy shrugged and slipped the card into her pocket. "I'll tell Twila."

"You be careful, then."

"It's all right. I saw Mr. Pollard drive past here a good hour ago." She darted a glance at Trace and flushed. "Twila will be grateful for the company."

"Well, don't stay away too long."

"I won't, Uncle." She nodded to Trace. "Good day, Mr. Abernathy."

"Good day, Miss O'Connor."

Both men watched her cross the room and exit at a more sedate pace than the one at which she'd entered. "Lucy has always been a very independent young woman," O'Connor said when she'd left them alone. "I worry about her sometimes but don't see the profit in trying to change her nature."

"No." His stomach burned, all the old pain welling up inside him once more. He didn't want to think about those things, let alone worry about a woman he scarcely knew. He shoved his hand into his pocket, feeling for the watch, rubbing his thumb across its smooth lid. "How far did you say it was to Hiram Fischer's place?"

O'Connor cleared his throat. "It's about an hour's ride. I'll draw you a map." He took a piece of paper from beneath the counter and smoothed it out in front of him. "Guess you're anxious to see the place, huh?"

Trace nodded. Anxious to see his new home, anxious to stop wandering, to stop moving—to stop fighting the past and turn his face once and for all to the future.

LUCY WALKED SEDATELY DOWN the street toward
Twila's house, past the blacksmith's forge and the log
church and the wood yard; past the whitewashed school,
with the sounds of an arithmetic lesson drifting from its
open windows. She crossed the street to pass the town's
two saloons, which sat side by side in friendly competition.
At this early hour these buildings were silent and empty;
still a lady wouldn't dream of even walking on the same
side of the road of such sinful places.

To anyone passing by, Lucy would certainly have presented a picture of a proper young lady, her sunbonnet
shielding her face from the hot sun, her steps slow and
decorous. But inside, she felt like skipping—running and
jumping—even shouting. The letter and the check from
Leslie's were proof to all who'd ever doubted her "scribbling" that she was capable of producing saleable work. It
was the first step in her dream to have money all her own.
She'd never again be beholden to a man for the clothes on
her back and the food on her plate. Not that Uncle Nate
ever made her feel as if she were a burden to him, but
others would not be so kind.

"If it weren't for me, you'd be out on the street." The

words rang in her memory, painful even at the distance of three years. Her stepfather had reminded her mother of this "fact" every day Lucy could remember. As a widow with a young daughter, Mary O'Connor had accepted an offer of marriage from a man she scarcely knew because it was the only way she could see to keep herself and Lucy clothed and fed.

Until the day she died, Lucy's mother had protested that her husband was not cruel. After all, he didn't beat her. But Lucy saw the greater cruelty of his words; he had stolen Mary's spirit. He had turned a vivacious beauty into a stooped, fearful woman, grown old before her time.

Lucy wasn't like her mother. She would never let herself fall into that trap. No matter where her life led, she'd always have her own money to care for herself.

She shook off the shroud of grief and turned down a side street that led to a row of small houses on the edge of town. Twila and Bill Pollard had moved here after the war, when Pollard, unable to work his farm, had been forced to sell the land. Twila never complained, but Lucy knew times were hard. She suspected Twila's family helped out with some of the bills. Now maybe Twila could sell some quilts to this Mrs. Sorenson and bring in a little extra cash.

She turned in at a whitewashed wooden gate and picked her away along a rock path that wound through clumps of flowers and herbs. More pots of flowers filled the narrow porch of the house. A wreath made of dried grapevines and artfully arranged seed pods and cones adorned the front door. She knocked, then stepped back to admire the wreath. Twila could do more with odds and ends like this than anyone she had ever met. She and Lucy had been friends since second grade. Twila was the only girl in Lucy's circle of friends who had actually achieved the coveted "baker's dozen"—twelve different quilts in her hope chest and an elaborate bridal quilt to grace the marriage bed.

The door opened, and Twila greeted Lucy with a wan smile. Blond and blue-eyed, she reminded Lucy of a bisque doll. "I was just thinking about you," Twila said. "I was hoping you'd come for a visit."

Lucy stepped inside and gave her friend a hug. "You don't have to wait for me to stop by, you know. You're welcome to visit me at the store anytime."

Arm in arm, the two women walked toward the parlor. "Mr. Pollard doesn't like me to leave the house when he's away," Twila said.

Lucy pinched her lips together to keep from blurting her opinion of Bill Pollard and his likes and dislikes. How could Twila ever have married that odious man?

"Besides," Twila continued, "I'll be showing soon, and then it won't be proper for me to be out and about." She smoothed her apron across her barely rounded belly and blushed a deep pink.

"Twila! You mean you're going to have a baby? When?" Lucy grabbed her friend's arm.

"Sometime in the fall, I think. October." She smiled. "I haven't even told Mr. Pollard yet. I wanted you to be the first to know."

"Congratulations." Lucy squeezed her hand and kept hold of it as they walked into the parlor. Twila had used her skill with a needle to transform the simply furnished room into a place of beauty and warmth. She had sewn bright curtains, embroidered pillows and samplers and covered the sofa with an intricately woven blanket. But even here Pollard intruded, the stale odor of his pipe tainting the air.

They sat side by side on the horsehair sofa. "So tell me everything," she said. "How are you feeling?"

"A little queasy of a morning—that's what made me think it might really be true. I'd only suspected before. But then I talked to my mother, and she confirmed it."

"Then this couldn't have come at a more perfect time." Lucy slid the calling card from her pocket and put it into Twila's hands. "This lady came by the store yesterday wanting to buy some quilts. Uncle Nate thought maybe you might have some to sell to her."

Twila turned the card over and over in her hand. "Well, I don't know. . . ."

"You're so clever with a needle, you could make whatever she wanted in no time at all."

Twila sighed and returned the card. "I can't."

"But why not?"

Twila worried her lower lip between her teeth. "I'm sure Mr. Pollard would never allow it," she said after a long while. "It wouldn't do to make him angry."

Lucy almost screamed in frustration. "Hang Pollard! He doesn't have to even know about this if you don't tell him. You could earn your own money for you and the baby."

Twila laced her fingers together and rested her hands in her lap. "It wouldn't be right for me to deceive him. Especially now, when I have a child to think of." She stared down at her folded hands. "I know you never approved of me marrying Mr. Pollard, but don't you see—this makes it all worthwhile."

Lucy winced. "I know it's not my place to judge, Twila, but you're so pretty." She reached up and touched the thick blond hair that curled softly around Twila's face. "You could have had your pick of men—and Pollard's so much older than you and so ill-tempered."

"You'd be ill-tempered, too, if you lost almost everything you had in the war—including your leg." Twila shook her head. "You're sweet to say I'm pretty and could have my pick of men, but don't you see? There aren't many men left to pick from—and not nearly enough for every single woman to wed." She searched Lucy's face, pleading for understanding. "I didn't want to be one of the ones left alone, depending on the charity of relatives—just because I'd been too particular."

"Like me, you mean?" Lucy held up her hand to still Twila's protest. "It's all right. I know I'm not likely to marry, and that suits me fine."

"Lucy, you don't really mean that." Twila folded one arm across her belly and looked sad.

"There's no need to feel sorry for me. I've no intention

of ending up some pathetic old spinster, beholden to Uncle Nate for every handkerchief and hatpin.'' She slipped the envelope from the pocket of her skirt and smoothed it across her knees. ''I'm going to make my own fortune, and this proves I can do it.''

''Your own fortune? How?''

''*Leslie's Illustrated Weekly* just bought my first story.'' A thrill of excitement ran through her as she passed the letter and the check over to her friend. ''And they say they want more. I'm going to use the money to buy cattle. With the war over, people are going to need beef, so I could stand to make a lot of money.''

Twila's stricken expression didn't change. ''But what about children?''

Lucy tried to hide her hurt. Was this all Twila had to say about her first sale of a story? She shook her head. ''Having children isn't enough of a reason for me to marry without love. Children grow up and move away, and you're still married to a man you have no feelings for.''

''We can't predict the future, Lucy. All I know is, for now having children is worth whatever small sacrifice I have to make.''

Lucy frowned. She didn't consider marriage to a hard-drinking, foulmouthed man like Bill Pollard a ''small'' sacrifice, but then, she and Twila had always seen things differently. Twila could look at a pile of broken pots and discarded tins and see the makings of a flower garden; apparently she could see the good in Bill Pollard as well.

''Now, don't go looking so down in the mouth.'' Twila patted her hand. ''Just because I can't accept this Mrs. Sorenson's offer doesn't mean you can't.''

''Me? Twila, I haven't even finished one quilt.''

''You could make a fine quilt if you'd put your mind to it.'' She straightened and turned to face her. ''I've been thinking of hosting a quilting bee. I want a new quilt for the baby, and even if you don't want to work for Mrs. Sorenson, isn't it about time we finished your bridal quilt?''

The bridal quilt again! As if finishing that quilt were all

that stood between her and happily ever after. She shook her head. "You don't need to go to all that trouble. I'll get around to finishing it myself one of these days."

Twila's eyes grew round. "Lucy, you can't do that!"

"Of course I can. I know I don't sew as fine a hand as you, but I can make my own quilt."

"No—I mean, you can't do all the work yourself. They say a young woman who makes her bridal quilt all by herself will never marry."

Lucy didn't know whether to laugh or cry over the horrified look on her friend's face. "It's just a superstition," she said. "How could sewing on a quilt really affect my chances of marrying?"

Twila nodded and smoothed her hands along her thighs. "Well, even if the superstition isn't true, you *do* need help with that quilt. The last time I saw it, you weren't even halfway to finishing it. At the rate you're going, you'll never be through. And I don't care what you say, you want to be ready when the right man comes along."

"You said yourself this area's not exactly crawling with eligible bachelors—so I don't have to be in any hurry."

"Oh, I don't know about that." Twila gave her a teasing look. "Mr. Pollard tells me there's a handsome stranger in town."

So that's where all this was leading. "Mr. Pollard told you Trace Abernathy was handsome?" Somehow that didn't sound like Twila's husband.

"You know his name? No. What Mr. Pollard said was that a Yankee had showed up in town—an arrogant young upstart. He said he had a colored boy with him." She grinned. "It was the 'young upstart' that gave him away. I could hear the envy in the words, even though Mr. Pollard would never admit to it." She leaned forward. "So am I right? Is Mr. Abernathy handsome?"

Lucy nodded. "Trace Abernathy is definitely handsome." She thought of his piercing blue eyes, those broad shoulders, and the crisp curls she'd glimpsed last night in the open neck of his shirt. Her stomach fluttered at the memory.

"Where's he from? And what's he doing here?"

"He's not really a Yankee." She forced her thoughts from contemplating Trace Abernathy's physical attributes. "He's from Virginia."

"You do know quite a bit about him, don't you?" Twila's eyes sparkled. "How did you find all this out?"

"I talked to him when I took him supper last night." She carefully smoothed out a wrinkle in the blanket that covered the sofa.

"Then what's he doing here? Mr. Pollard said he claimed to have the deed to Hiram Fischer's place."

"He says he's going to live here and raise cattle." She frowned. "He seemed to find it amusing when I said I planned to do the same."

"Most likely he was flirting with you."

"Flirting?" Her breath caught in her throat. Why would a stranger she'd only just met want to flirt with her? "He wasn't flirting. He was being impertinent."

Twila laughed. "Sometimes it's the same thing. Now, tell me, what's he like?"

Lucy sat back. How could she describe Trace Abernathy? "He's the sort of man people pay attention to, I think," she said after a moment. "The minute he walked into the store last night, the air almost vibrated with a kind of tension. Zeke Early was there, and he and Mr. Pollard were glaring at that Yankee uniform he wore, but Mr. Abernathy didn't appear to take much notice of them."

"But he noticed you, didn't he?"

Lucy flushed. "What makes you say that?"

"You said you took him his supper. He talked to you. He *flirted* with you."

"I told you, he wasn't flirting." She shifted, restless. "We were just making conversation."

"How old do you think he is?"

"It's hard to say. . . . Not too old. Maybe . . . thirty?"

"Only eight years older than you. About right, I'd say." Twila put her hand on Lucy's arm. "You just forget all this nonsense about not wanting to marry and set your cap

for this Virginia Yankee," she urged. "There's no sense
being alone when you could have a handsome *young* man
for a husband. You've already caught his eye."

Lucy pulled her arm away. "I told you—I intend to raise
cattle and be independent."

Twila shook her head. "You can raise cattle with *him*.
Cattle and *children*. Don't you want a family?"

Lucy caught her lower lip between her teeth. A part of
her longed for a husband and children and a little house to
call her own. But a greater part of her warned that the price
of such things could be too great to bear. She straightened
and held her head high. "One day, when I've made my
fortune, I'll be able to have my pick of men. Maybe then
I'll marry. I can't afford to right now."

"I don't think you can afford to let a man like this slip
by you," Twila protested. "You know once word spreads
that he's in town, every single female from eight to eighty
will be makin' eyes at him."

"Twila, you make it sound so predatory!"

"I suppose in a way it is." Twila looked thoughtful.
"Courtship is a kind of competition, after all. The war has
just made things worse." She sighed. "You're my best
friend, Lucy. I don't want to see you lose out on a chance
for happiness."

Lucy folded the letter from *Leslie's* around the check and
slid it back into the envelope. "This letter and this check
make me happy today, Twila. And unlike a man, I can be
pretty sure they won't make me *unhappy* tomorrow."

She stood, and Twila rose also and followed her to the
door. "Come to my quilting bee, Lucy. And bring your
bridal quilt," she said. "Give Trace Abernathy a chance.
You don't want to look back one day and wonder if you
made a mistake." A troubled expression stole into her eyes.
"It's not a pretty view. I know."

Lucy hugged her friend close, then turned and hurried
down the steps before Twila could see her tears. Her mother
and Twila were cut from the same cloth—she couldn't
think of one without remembering the other. The two

woman had taught her one lesson: Life as a spinster was preferable to years in a prison of one's own making. She might sleep alone every night under a bridal quilt fashioned with her own hands, but she'd sleep soundly and happily, satisfied in her own work.

She put her hand in her pocket and wrapped it around the envelope containing the check—her first money earned with her own hands. If only it were more than twenty-five dollars. Mr. Abernathy was right, it would take her a long time to build up a herd at this rate. If only she had a way to earn more money—guaranteed. She clutched the letter tighter and felt the slick hardness of the calling card beneath her fingers.

How much would Mrs. Sorenson pay for a quilt? she wondered, slowing her steps and drawing the card out to stare at it. Everyone said the old Swedish woman had money from the old country. If Lucy could sell her a quilt or two, she could get started on her herd right away, instead of waiting no telling how long to sell another story.

Her shoulders sagged, and she shoved the card back into her pocket. Who was she trying to fool? It would take her forever to sew an entire quilt. She'd been working on her bridal quilt for more than a year now, and it wasn't anywhere near finished. She'd told the truth when she said she wasn't like her mother. She certainly hadn't inherited her talent with a needle.

Her mother! She stopped in her tracks. Why hadn't she thought of it before? She had a whole trunk full of her mother's quilts in the attic. Maybe Mrs. Sorenson would want to buy one of them. Maybe she'd want to buy more than one. There might even be enough quilts in that trunk to pay for the cattle and supplies and everything else she'd need to secure her fortune.

Excitement welled up inside her, and she practically ran the rest of the way back to the store. Scarcely nodding a greeting to Uncle Nate behind the counter, she took the stairs two at a time to their living quarters, then raced along the hall and up the ladder to the attic. The trapdoor groaned when she shoved against it with her shoulders, then slowly swung up on creaking hinges.

Standing on the ladder with her head and shoulders in the attic, Lucy remembered she should have brought a lantern. But as her eyes adjusted to the dim light streaking through dirt-encrusted windows in the gables, she spied a stub of a candle on a saucer and the tin of matches by its side.

She took the last few steps up into the room and crawled over to the candle. The match flame sputtered, then caught at the candlewick, illuminating the low-ceilinged room in a golden light.

The attic was as orderly as the store, with everything assigned to its own area. Old store fixtures and furniture crowded one end of the room, a broken-back rocker next to a rusting birdcage and a sagging baby carriage. The middle of the room was reserved for items they might need more often—Christmas decorations and traveling trunks filled with out-of-season clothing.

Bending over slightly to avoid bumping her head, Lucy carried the candle to the far end of the room, to a corner occupied by a few trunks and barrels. The first trunks held Aunt Cora's, Uncle Nate's wife's, clothes. Uncle Nate had shown them to her once before, when he'd given her one of the dresses to cut down to wear to a party. That was back during the war, when even ordinary calico was impossible to get, much less fancy materials for a party dress.

She found the trunk she wanted at the very back. The sturdy, curve-topped trunk was trimmed with silver, now tarnished with age. She wiped the dust from the top with her sleeve and saw the initials there in fancy script—MJB. Mary Jane Bridges.

She stared at the letters for a long time, pain clenching her stomach. This had been her mother's hope chest, designed to hold her trousseau—her hopes and dreams. The hopes and dreams were gone now, reduced to the contents of this trunk.

She didn't want to look. She didn't want to remember

what she'd spent so long trying to forget. "Coward," she whispered. She'd never realize her own hopes and dreams if she didn't get the money she needed to buy cattle. Uncle Nate had said there were quilts in here, quilts she needed to sell.

With trembling hands, she grasped the hasp and lifted the lid. It stuck at first, wood swollen with age, then broke free and fell back. The scent of lemon verbena wafted up to her, bringing sudden tears to her eyes. Her mother had worn this scent until the day she died.

Stop it, she silently commanded herself. She hadn't come here to indulge in such maudlin thoughts. She had work to do. Blinking back the tears, she held the candle aloft and stared down into the trunk at the tumble of bright fabric within.

The first quilt was a pattern called princess feather, done in bright red and green. She traced her hand across the pinwheels of bright plumes. Even in the attic dimness, the colors shone bright. Mrs. Sorenson would pay a lot for a work of art like this. She set the candle on the floor and carefully lifted the folded fabric from the trunk. On closer inspection, she discovered the quilt wasn't finished. In fact, only one half of the coverlet had actually been quilted. The rest was only basted to the batting and backing. What had happened to interrupt her mother's work on the quilt?

She laid aside the princess feather and took the next coverlet from the trunk. This was a pieced top in a sawtooth-star pattern, unattached to batting or backing, ready to be quilted. Lucy ran her finger along a triangle of brown worsted. She'd had a dress made out of this fabric once and a bonnet to match. Her mother had made them for her to wear at Easter the year Lucy was five. Tears clogged her throat as she recalled how proud she'd been of the outfit. She resolutely forced them back.

The next quilt was only partially pieced, while the rest of the trunk's contents appeared to be cut triangles and squares of fabric, unassembled into any pattern. Lucy stared at the various incomplete quilts around her in dismay. There was nothing here she could offer for sale to Mrs. Sorenson, nothing that would buy her cattle.

Sighing, she began to repack the trunk. The candle flickered eerie shadows across the sloped ceiling, and her head ached from too much time spent in the stuffy confines of the attic. As she replaced the princess-feather quilt in the trunk, she let her hand linger over the finely quilted section of the coverlet. The stitching was all but invisible, especially in this light. She could never do such fine work herself.

Or could she? The idea wormed its way into her consciousness like a needle sliding through the many layers of a quilt. Why couldn't she finish this quilt to sell to Mrs. Sorenson? After all, the most difficult part, the piecing, was done. And she had the pattern of her mother's work to follow.

Her heart beat faster as she stared at the rows of neat stitches. She could do this. She could finish this quilt and sell it. She'd take the money she earned and put it with the money she already had from selling her story and be that much closer to paying her way to independence.

∞

TRACE HAD THE FEELING he'd been down this road before. The narrow, rutted lane, trees closing in on either side, reminded him of a dozen other such lanes across the South. Sometimes the trees were different—pines or dogwood instead of these scrub oaks. Sometimes the dirt was black gumbo or red clay instead of white Texas caliche. But the sunlight shone through the trees in the same way, casting shifting patterns of shadow and light. He'd come to dread those shadowed roads, and the uncertainty of where they would lead.

The sniper had been hidden along a road like this. His leg still ached at times, a reminder of that day. He'd suffered a different kind of wound at the end of another tree-lined lane. That was the day he came home from the war and found his future reduced to ashes—his home burned, his father dead.

He had limped from sunlight to shadow down that long road and seen the scars the war had left on the land. As he walked, he felt as if a fist clenched his heart.

Theresa met him at the gate, a baby in her arms, its skin the color of coffee with cream against her mahogany flesh. A knot rose in his throat when he saw her—the first sign that he'd truly made it home. Then he noticed the tears in her eyes. "Miz Marion's gone," she moaned. "Marse Alan done shot that damn fool horse."

He shut his eyes against the memory that stabbed so deeply. The war had stolen his wife, Marion, from him, too. If he hadn't been off fighting, he'd have kept her away from the cantankerous stallion she'd insisted on riding. He would have found a way to make Marion, who had a will as strong as any man's, listen to reason.

The knot in his throat threatened to choke him. He opened his eyes and stared at the gate, which hung by one hinge. He'd been a fool to think he could find any kind of welcome here.

"Sure don't look like much, do it?"

Josh's comment jerked him from his memories. He blinked at the crooked gate, aware once more of his surroundings. Virginia was a long way behind him now. He was in Texas, staring at his future.

"I seen slave cabins in better shape," Josh continued. He scowled at the log cabin on the other side of the gate.

Trace studied his new home with a critical eye. The simple cabin was missing part of the roof and much of the mud chinking between the logs. The front windows lacked glass, and the door hung by one hinge. But in spite of the disrepair into which the cabin had fallen, he could see that Hiram Fischer had taken care to lay the logs straight and fasten them securely. With a little work, the cabin would make a warm and dry home.

"It sure ain't Belle Haven, is it?" Josh's voice held a challenge.

Trace thought of the plantation where Marion, and Josh, too, had lived most of their lives. That towering mansion, with wide oak-floored hallways, had never felt like home to him. "If you wanted Belle Haven, you should have stayed there." He set the brake and climbed down from the wagon.

Josh scrambled down behind him. "I didn't say I wanted to be back at Belle Haven. I just didn't figure somebody like you, who was used to livin' in a big house like that, would think much of a shack like this."

"I didn't grow up at the mansion like you. My father and I shared rooms behind his law office. And I spent five years living in tents and caves and holes in the ground." He swung open the gate and stepped into the weed-choked yard. "I'd say a log cabin is a move up in the world."

"I reckon you bein' a man and all, it don't make as much difference." Josh followed him through the gate and up a faintly marked path. "Miz Marion shore wouldn'ta liked it none."

Marion would have demanded to be driven back to town rather than spend a single night in this humble place. As the daughter of one of the Tidewater's most prosperous plantation owners, she was accustomed to luxury—the luxury of fine things and of having her own way.

Trace had long suspected Marion's interest in him was due to the fact that he was the first man she'd been unable to rule with a flirtatious look or teasing caress. When her father forbade her to associate with Trace, a common lawyer's son, she accepted the challenge by convincing an admittedly smitten Trace to elope with her.

He'd been no better a match for her self-destructive recklessness than her father had been. Marion had died having her own way, riding a horse he'd forbidden her to buy. Once she'd purchased the stallion, he'd asked her not to ride it, but he might as well have asked a river not to run downhill. In the end, off fighting the war, he hadn't been able to protect her from herself.

He shrugged off the guilt that clung to him like a leg

trap. Marion wouldn't be living in this cabin, so her opinion of it didn't matter. He wasn't responsible for her anymore.

He pushed open the door to the cabin, bracing himself for the worst. "Careful," Josh whispered behind him. "Might be wild animals denned up in there. Leastways rats."

No rats or other vermin scurried away when Trace stepped into the room. A quick glance showed the inside of the dwelling to be in much better shape than the outside. "If rats have been living here, maybe I can bribe them to keep house," Trace said as he surveyed the swept floor, scrubbed table, and neatly made bed.

Josh ran his finger along the edge of the table. "No dust."

Trace walked over to the fireplace, squatted down, and held his hand over the ashes. "Still warm."

"Who you reckon been livin' here?" Josh picked up a tin mug and sniffed at it.

Trace straightened and focused his attention on the iron bedstead in the corner. A faded patchwork quilt covered the mattress, the only color in the otherwise somber room. The mattress sagged in the middle, suggesting the shape of a sleeping man. "Some squatter, I guess." He didn't relish the idea of having to fight some stranger for the land. What if the fellow was a local man, someone who could count on the town taking his side in the dispute? The deed in Trace's pocket wouldn't matter much against the animosity of his new neighbors.

He hadn't even wanted the deed when Hiram had first offered it to him. Two Southerners surrounded by men from the North, they had become friends, patrolling side by side. The same sniper who had wounded Trace's leg had shattered Hiram's shoulder. In the dirty chaos of the field hospital, gangrene had set in. "You should give the place to your relatives," Trace told the sick and obviously dying man.

"No relatives in this country." Hiram pressed the folded paper into his hand. "You take it. It's a pretty place—on a creek, with woods and good grazing. Lots of cattle, probably all gone wild now. Take your *frau* there and be happy.''

He had no frau to bring here now—not that the German word for a young woman suited his proud, aristocratic wife. A picture flashed through his mind of Lucy O'Connor, the way she'd looked when she'd skipped into the store this morning, flushed and smiling. Had Hiram ever addressed her as ''fräulein''?

He'd found himself answering Lucy's smile, his careful reserve cracking under the onslaught of her lively enthusiasm. His physical reaction to the glimpse of her slender ankles surprised him, too. Not too long ago, he'd thought he'd never want a woman again—evidently his body had healed even if his mind hadn't.

Maybe once he was settled, he'd look around town for a sweet, simple woman to take to wife. Not, however, a woman like Lucy O'Connor. He'd recognized the stubborn light in her eyes the instant they met—recognized it as the twin to Marion's own headstrong determination to ignore sensible advice. He'd learned his lesson about women like that. Like a horse who refused to let go of the wildness in its nature, such women could never be taught or trusted.

∽

TRACE WOKE THE NEXT morning to the unfamiliar sensation of a roof over his head. He stared up at the dusty beams in Hiram Fischer's cabin and decided he liked the view. Even with sunlight streaming through gaps left by missing shingles, Hiram's roof was more solid than the tents and caves that had sheltered him for months now. More real even than the delicate muslin canopy of the bed he'd shared with Marion, which seemed almost a figment of his imagination at this distance of time and space.

The door to the cabin creaked open, and he lunged for the pistol in the gunbelt hanging from the bedpost. But the intruder was only Josh, staggering under a load of firewood.

The boy dumped the wood and straightened, brushing bark from his clothes. "There's chicken pens out back, but no chickens," he said. "Garden patch, too—'sparagus all eaten by rabbits."

Trace swung his legs over the side of the bed and stretched to straighten the kinks out of his spine. Mattresses, like roofs, were something he'd have to get used to all over again. "What about cows? Did you see any of those?"

Josh knelt and began piling kindling on the hearth. "Nope." He paused and looked over his shoulder. "How we gon' be ranchers if we got no cows?"

"What's this 'we' business?" Trace dug a clean shirt from his saddlebags and pulled it on.

Josh's shoulders slumped. "You don't reckon on doin' everything by yourself, do you? I can help."

One look at the boy's dejected expression and Trace wished he could take back his retort. He sometimes forgot that in spite of his sharp tongue, Josh was only ten—a little boy a long way from home. If Trace didn't look after him and help him learn to be a man, who would?

He finished buttoning the shirt, then slipped the watch into his pocket. "I'm counting on you to give me a hand." He clapped Josh on the shoulder. "Reckon you can learn to lasso a wild cow?"

Josh straightened and puffed out his thin chest. "Sure I can." He frowned. "Uh . . . what exactly is lassoin'?"

"It means throwing a rope around a cow's neck while it's running away from you. That's how you catch it so you can put your brand on it." He dug a sack of coffee beans out of his saddlebag and poured a handful into the grinder clamped on to the end of the table.

"You mean, we're gonna steal us some cows." Josh nodded and turned his attention back to laying the fire.

"Not steal. Hiram told me he had a small herd here before the war. A lot of them and their offspring will still be here. Then there's lots of wild, unmarked cattle running around out here. The first man to put his brand on an unmarked cow can claim it as his own.'' He cranked the grinder and savored the aroma of roasted coffee. "It's the best way for a man with no money to make a stake."

"Then it's a wonder everybody and his cousin ain't runnin' around after all these 'free' cattle." Josh struck a match against the stone hearth. He wrinkled his nose at the stink of burning sulfur and held his tongue between his teeth as he guided the bright flame to his stack of kindling.

"Just as well for us most people don't want to put in all the hard work required to get those 'free' cattle." Trace located two tin mugs on the shelf by the fire and wiped them clean with his shirttail.

The fire caught, and Josh gave a grunt of satisfaction and stood back. "Never said I was afeard of hard work." He walked over to the saddlebag and pulled out a muslin-wrapped package of bacon. "Biscuits or corn pone this mornin'?"

"Biscuits. And don't burn them like you did last time."

"That was you burnt the biscuits. I scorched the bacon." He cut his eyes to Trace. "Maybe you ought to think on findin' you some woman who can cook. There's bound to be one around here somewheres. I doubt you'd have to do much courtin'. From what I seen, pickin's are pretty slim among the men 'round here."

"I don't have time to do *any* courting. I've got work to do. You'll just have to learn to be a better cook or starve."

"Sure be easier to let a woman do it," Josh mumbled as he picked up the frying pan and headed for the fire.

Trace ignored Josh's grumbling. The last thing he needed right now was a woman to look after. He'd do well to watch out for Josh. No telling what kind of trouble a boy like him could get into without Trace to keep a close eye on him.

After a breakfast of biscuits, coffee, and bacon, he and Josh started in on the list of jobs Trace had compiled while they ate. He set the boy to mending the fence around the house, while he began cutting shingles to fix the roof.

The weathered cypress log he'd found split easily, and he fell into a rhythm. Lift the ax, bring it down, split off another slab of wood, thicker at one end than the other. After a while, he removed his shirt and hung it on a nearby limb. The garment stirred in the breeze like a war-weary flag, faded and worn thin in places. He'd have to consign it to the rag bag before long, not even good enough for quilt scraps.

What kind of material had Lucy O'Connor put into her bridal quilt? He remembered a coverlet his mother had made, composed of scraps from all the party dresses she'd worn before her marriage. Would Miss Lucy have a quilt like that, rich with silks and satins and memories of parties and balls? Or would she and her husband sleep under a coverlet of more practical gingham and calico?

He brought the ax down too hard and cursed as a too-thin slice of wood flew off to the side. What did he care what kind of quilt Lucy O'Connor made? Or who shared the coverlet with her? A headstrong woman like her would be lucky to find any man who'd put up with her. Trace, for one, could tell the man what a mistake he'd be making, to hook himself up with a woman like that.

He brought the ax down again, but he'd lost his rhythm. After a few more desultory strokes, he decided to abandon the chore in favor of dinner.

After a meal of cheese and crackers washed down with creek water, Trace sent Josh to the barn to collect straw to mix with mud for chinking the logs. The boy had not been gone five minutes when he came racing back, eyes wide. "Trace, come quick!" he urged in a loud whisper.

Trace laid aside his hammer and climbed down from the roof. "What is it? Why are you whispering?"

"Shhh." Josh put a finger to his lips. "He might hear you."

"Who might hear me?"

"The man in the barn."

3

THE HAIR STOOD UP on the back of Trace's neck, and he took in Josh's wide eyes and shaking voice. This wasn't some childish prank—the boy was frightened. He put one hand to the gun on his hip. "Who is it?"

Josh shook his head.

Trace led the way to the barn, Josh hovering in his shadow. He paused just outside the open doors and drew his gun, then, every muscle tensed, he stepped into the darkness.

The barn had the familiar smell of all such places—of hay and leather and oats. The lead wagon horse whinnied a greeting and stuck its head over its stall. He gripped the gun tighter and scanned the dimly lit interior. Now that his eyes had adjusted to the light, he saw nothing out of the ordinary. He turned to question Josh and collided with the boy.

"Don't shoot *me*!" Josh protested.

"Then don't stand so close," Trace snapped. "Now, where did you see this mysterious man?"

"Over here." He led the way to the end of the barn, by the feed bins, and pointed to the ground. There, in the loose dirt, Trace saw the distinct impression of a man's brogan.

He holstered the gun and knelt to examine the print more closely. It had been made by a good-sized man, judging from the size of the print and the depth of the impression. "What did he look like?" He looked back up at Josh.

The boy shrugged. "I didn't exactly see *him*. Just that print there." He folded his arms across his chest. "Bet it's the same fellow who was stayin' in the cabin. Likely he's not too happy we run him out. I reckon he was after the horses. Good thing I come along when I did."

Trace frowned. "How do you figure that?"

"Why, I probably scared him away."

"Or maybe this print was from last night and the man is miles away by now. Maybe he was just checking the feed bins for an ear of corn or something else to eat." He straightened. "There are a lot of hungry men traveling around these days. I won't begrudge a fellow food."

"Hmmph! You'll be singin' a different tune when he's done run off with the horses. We ain't gonna be able to lasso no cows on foot."

Trace rubbed the back of his neck. The boy had a point. "All right. I'll sleep in the barn tonight, just to make sure."

Josh's eyes widened. "You ain't gonna leave me in the house by myself, are you?"

Trace didn't know whether to groan or laugh. Humor won over aggravation. "All right, we'll both sleep in the barn." He thumped the boy on the back as he passed. "You'd better get to work now, clearing us out a place to sleep."

"I shoulda knowed you'd find a way to turn this into more work." Josh picked up a shovel and called after Trace. "When we gonna start collectin' them cows?"

He couldn't hold back his chuckle now. "It's not like stamps or butterflies. You don't 'collect' cows. You round up cattle. And we'll begin soon enough. I want the house weathertight first."

Josh started shoveling manure out of one of the stalls. "You said yourself you been sleepin' in the open for years. What difference is a few more weeks gonna make?"

"My days of living like a nomad are over. I want a good, solid house to come home to at the end of the day."

"Next thing you know, you'll be paintin' the house white and servin' mint juleps on the veranda." Josh shook his head. "I'll have to wash up for every meal and wear shoes in the summer and even go to school. Pretty soon, everything'll be just like it was back home."

Not just like it was, Trace thought. The war changed things. It changed people.

It changed me.

∞

LUCY PERCHED ON A stool behind the counter at the store and concentrated on making tiny, even stitches in the quilt top fixed in the hoop before her. She thought she was doing a pretty good job so far copying her mother's work, though it was a lot harder than it looked. She smiled and smoothed her hand over a bright red plume of the appliquéd princess feather. Out in daylight, the design practically shimmered against the stark white background of bleached muslin. Mrs. Sorenson wouldn't find a prettier quilt anywhere in the county.

She bent over her work once more, determined to complete the quilt as soon as possible. She'd worked on it almost every waking moment for the past week. It still amazed her to think her mother had ever done such fine work. The woman she remembered had been so frail and workworn. Her hands had been so rough from washing dishes and clothes and picking cotton that she'd scarcely been able to darn stockings without her fingers snagging in the wool.

"Let's have some service here!"

Pollard's booming voice rattled the feed buckets hanging from the rafters. She dropped her needle and jerked her head up. "I'll be glad to help you, Mr. Pollard," she lied pleasantly. "You needn't shout."

"Hmmph!" Pollard scowled and limped to the counter,

leaning heavily on a walking stick fashioned from a peeled sapling. "What you doin' back there? Got your nose buried in bookwork again?"

Lucy shoved the quilting hoop under the counter. The last thing she wanted was for word to get out that she'd taken up quilting for money. The other women, familiar with her past ineptness with a needle, would make her a laughingstock. No, she'd keep quiet about this until she knew she could carry it off successfully.

"If a body didn't holler at you, the place could burn down around your head, and you'd never notice," Pollard boomed.

She gripped the edge of the counter with both hands and inhaled slowly, counting to ten. No sense letting old Pollard rile her with his criticisms. He considered argument a form of entertainment; she had no wish to oblige him. "What can I do for you?"

"Not me. Her." He jerked his thumb toward the door, and she realized for the first time that Twila was standing just inside, half-hidden in the shadows.

At Pollard's words, Twila moved forward. "Hello, Lucy. I've come to pick up a few things for my quilting bee. You will be there, won't you?"

She stifled a groan. She'd rather have ants walk across her eyeballs than endure an afternoon with a roomful of women who would offer subtle and not-so-subtle critiques of her stitching, her clothing, and her marital status. They'd gossip and gripe and giggle until Lucy's head ached. If she dared to leave early, they'd all talk about her the minute she was out the door.

But she had to attend. Twila was hosting the party, and Twila was her best friend. She sighed. "Of course I'll be there."

"Oh, good. Now come show me this new calico you've gotten in. I haven't seen anything this pretty since before the war."

Leaving Pollard to scowl at a display of tobacco, she went to pull the bolts of calico off the shelf. "I'm sorry we disturbed you when we came in," Twila said softly. "Were you working on another story?"

"Something like that." She hurried to change the subject. "I gave the check from *Leslie's Illustrated Weekly* to Mr. Gibbs when he came in this morning. He's going to let me pay for my cattle a little at a time. Tomorrow I intend to ride over to his place and pick them out." The words bubbled out of her. She'd stayed up half the night working on the princess-feather quilt. She intended to deliver it to Mrs. Sorenson tomorrow, before she visited Mr. Gibbs. With any luck, she'd be able to give the rancher another payment. She'd fought off sleep with the thought of having something as solid and quantifiable as cattle for her very own.

Twila nodded. "That's nice," she said absently.

Lucy suppressed a cry of frustration. Twila couldn't help it if she didn't understand; most people didn't. They thought all a young woman needed to be concerned about was perfecting her recipe for pie crust or making neat stitches in her bridal quilt.

Twila appeared oblivious to Lucy's discomfort. "You won't be sorry if you come to the quilting bee," she whispered as she smoothed her hand over the fabric. "I've gotten Mr. Pollard to agree to host a dance at our home that evening."

Her stomach gave a nervous flutter. Twila looked entirely too delighted at the prospect of a dance. After all, Pollard wasn't likely to twirl her around the dance floor on that wooden leg of his, now was he? "A dance?"

Twila's eyes sparkled. "I'm going to invite Trace Abernathy."

Lucy caught her breath and took a step back. "Why? He's a stranger here—and a Yankee soldier. If you invite him, it'll just be awkward."

"He's a handsome, single man. And I'll wager he's a good dancer. Everyone will come to my party to meet him."

Lucy squirmed. "Does Pollard know about this?"

Twila nodded. "He thought it would be a good opportunity to get to know our new neighbor better."

Lucy glanced over her shoulder. Pollard sat in a chair by the stove, eating from the cracker barrel. He was the kind of man who refused to let travelers so much as water their horses from his well without paying for the privilege. Why would he be anxious to welcome any stranger, much less a Yankee, to his home?

"How much is the calico?" Twila asked, stroking her hand over a bolt of Turkey red with blue flowers.

"Three dollars a yard."

"And to think before the war we could get five yards for a dollar." Twila sighed. "Well, I suppose I'll have to pass. Just give me ten yards of this muslin." She indicated the plainest, least expensive fabric on the shelf.

As she measured out the cloth, Lucy thought about Pollard and Trace Abernathy. There'd been no love lost between the two when they'd met here in the store the other night. By now Pollard had had time to let his animosity fester. What if he'd agreed to this dance in order to set a trap for Trace? Surrounded by his friends—all embittered Confederate veterans—and aided by generous doses of home brew, Pollard might orchestrate all manner of schemes against the unsuspecting stranger. One only had to read the newspapers to know things like lynchings and tarring and feathering still went on.

"Lucy, you can stop now."

She stared at Twila's hand on her wrist, and the yards of muslin puddling on the floor at their feet. "I only want ten yards," Twila said.

"Sorry." Her face burning, she began rewinding the material on the bolt. "Guess I just got distracted."

Twila grinned. "Uh-hmmm. Does this 'distraction' have blue eyes and black hair and a soft Virginia accent?"

Lucy picked up the scissors and slashed a length of material from the bolt, furious with herself for becoming concerned over a man she scarcely knew. She had quilts to finish and stories to write and cattle to raise and a fortune

to make. She had no time for worrying over any man—
especially a man like Trace Abernathy, who ridiculed her
stories and mocked her ambition, all the while making her
heart race and her thoughts scatter with a lift of one brow
or a hint of a smile on his lips.

∞

"VERY NICE WORK. JUST vat I am looking for." Mrs.
Sorenson smoothed her hand over the curving plumes of
the princess-feather quilt. Lucy let out the breath she'd been
holding and felt her shoulders relax. She'd been on pins
and needles ever since she'd turned her horse into the lane
leading up to the Swedish woman's imposing home. Con-
structed of blocks of local white limestone, the house rose
two stories, much larger and more elegant than any other
house around. It had green shutters at every window, and
woven carpets on the floor of every room.

Mrs. Sorenson was every bit as intimidating as her home.
Easily six feet tall, she towered over Lucy, her snow-white
hair wreathing her head like a cloud. Only after Lucy had
extracted the quilt from its protective muslin wrapping had
her severe expression softened. She looked up from the
coverlet and fixed her bright blue eyes on Lucy now. "You
vill bring more, yes?"

"Y-yes." After all, the trunk contained several unfinished quilts or pieces of quilts. The question remained, how
much money would they bring? Enough to buy her cattle?

"Come. We vill haf tea." Without bothering to see if
Lucy followed, Mrs. Sorenson gathered the quilt in both
arms and led the way into a dark-paneled parlor. A heavy
silver tea set sat on a low, piecrust table in front of a red
velvet-covered sofa. Mrs. Sorenson lowered her tall frame
onto the sofa and arranged the folded quilt beside her. Lucy
perched on the edge of a slippery leather-cushioned chair.
She wondered how to tactfully bring up the issue of payment for her work.

"I imagine you are wondering vat I intend to do with

the quilts, yes?'' Mrs. Sorenson handed Lucy a cup of tea and two small cookies covered with powdered sugar.

"Oh. Well, not really.'' What else would a person do with a quilt besides use it on a bed?

"I vill send them back to my home country. I haf a cousin there I am thinking can sell them in his shop. They do not haf quilts there, you know.''

"No, I didn't know that.'' Lucy bit into the cookie. It was brittle, with a strong licorice flavor. The tea was strong, too, and bitter.

"We haf featherbeds. Soft, varm featherbeds.'' She shook her head. "But no quilts.'' She glanced at the quilt by her side. "And vat are you calling this design? My brother vill be wanting to know.''

"Princess feather.'' Lucy set aside her cup of bitter tea and the saucer of crumbled cookies and gripped the arms of the chair.

"It is very lovely. You get it from a book, yes?''

Lucy frowned, then realized Mrs. Sorenson was referring to the design, not the quilt itself. "The pattern belonged to my mother.''

"Your mother must be very proud of your skill with the needle, yes?''

She shifted in her chair and looked away. As far as she knew, Mary O'Connor had been too caught up in her own concerns to give much thought to her daughter, to be proud of her or not. "I really must be going soon,'' she said. "You've told me you'd like to buy the quilt. How much will you pay?''

Mrs. Sorenson's laugh startled her. She glanced up and saw the woman's severe expression replaced by a broad smile. "You Americans, so abrupt. All business. Very well. I vill pay twenty dollars.''

"Twenty-five.'' She'd decided on the way over here that this was the sum she'd ask for. It only seemed fair that she'd get as much for the hours of work she'd put into the quilt as she could earn from a story that would take just as many hours to write and polish.

Mrs. Sorenson arched one brow, but her smile never faltered. "Ah. A businesswoman. Very well. Twenty-five dollars." She reached into her skirt and drew out a green velvet bag. She fished five five-dollar gold pieces from it and pressed them into Lucy's hand.

Lucy slipped the heavy coins into her pocket and stood to take her leave. "You vill be bringing other quilts soon, yes?" Mrs. Sorenson said as she opened the front door for Lucy.

"Yes . . . soon." Lucy thought of all the work she'd have to do to complete the next coverlet.

Mrs. Sorenson watched her climb into the saddle. "You vill be stitching your way to happiness, yes?" She chuckled, as if she found this very amusing.

What an odd thing to say, Lucy thought as she turned and rode down the long drive. Perhaps Mrs. Sorenson had meant Lucy would stitch her way to wealth. She slid her hand into the pocket of her riding skirt. The coins were cool and heavy against her thigh. Completing the quilts was only a means to an end. Quilting might never bring her the kind of wealth cattle would; and sewing certainly wouldn't bring her happiness, would it?

∞

AFTER A WEEK OF restless nights in the barn with Josh, Trace announced a move back into the house. "I've had enough of sleeping with animals to last a lifetime," he said one morning as he spread blankets to air in the freshly trimmed grass in front of the house. "The horses will make a racket if anyone tries to disturb them, and I'll have my Springfield ready. A thief won't get far."

For once, Josh didn't argue. "When are we gonna start huntin' cows?"

"I think today we'll ride around a little, scout out the most likely places for cattle to be hiding out. Then we can pick out a location to set up a camp to work from. We'll move camp every few days, until we've branded as many cattle as we can get hold of."

"I've been practisin' my lassoin'." Josh pantomimed twirling a rope. "I'm gonna catch me a bunch of cows."

Trace bit back his laughter. "I'm counting on you to do just that."

Josh stopped twirling his imaginary rope. "What we gon' do with all these cattle once we get 'em all branded?"

"We'll sell some of them, keep the rest, and breed for a bigger herd for next year."

"And every year we'll have more cattle to sell and we'll get more money and pretty soon we'll be rich—that right?"

Trace shook his head. "I don't think it's as simple as it sounds, Josh. There are probably easier ways to make money."

Josh shrugged. "Way I figure it, it beats pickin' cotton."

They set out a little while later, riding the draft horses. Trace studied his new home, trying the scenery on for size, as his father might have said. The center of Texas looked very different from his native Virginia—fewer trees and more open spaces, the view extending as far as the eye could see in all directions. Rocky creek beds, full from the recent rain, bisected the gently rolling hills, which were painted pale green by a fuzz of new grass. Wildflowers bloomed amid the grass in clumps of brilliant pink and red and blue, like calico patches on an otherwise somber quilt. He breathed in lungfuls of the clear, flower-scented air and nodded to himself. This land would suit him fine. A man could grow to love these open spaces after so much time living closed in—by trees and people and even by ideas. Thirty wasn't too old to start over in a place like this.

"I think I see some cows over there!" Josh stood in the stirrups, pointing toward a clump of oak trees.

Trace leaned forward and squinted in the bright sunlight. Darker silhouettes among the shade of the trees took shape; half a dozen or so cows chewing cud. He nodded and signaled to Josh. They began to walk their horses in a wide circle around the cattle.

As they drew closer, he could make out the mottled hides of the rangy animals. Horns as thick as his arm and spread as wide as bedposts curved up from their heads.

"How we gonna get a rope around those horns?" Josh whispered, his eyes wide.

"I said it wouldn't be easy, didn't I?" Studying the cattle now, he knew nothing short of luck was going to land him very many of these wary beasts. Even now, with Josh and him stationed downwind, their voices never rising above a whisper, the cattle seemed restless, as if they sensed the intrusion into their territory.

Suddenly a red-backed cow rose up on her haunches and snorted. Before Trace had time to fully register what was happening, the cattle bolted, the thunder of their hooves fading into the distance.

"What spooked 'em?" Josh asked, staring after the vanished herd.

Trace turned to look in the direction opposite the one in which the cattle had run. A solitary figure moved toward them, leading a bay horse. He slid his hand into position, resting on the butt of the pistol, and waited.

The figure moved slowly, too slight to be a man. A child maybe?

"It's a girl," Josh said after a moment.

Trace nodded. They could see the long skirts now and the distinctive shape of a woman's sunbonnet. The reason for her slow progress became evident as she drew closer. The horse was limping.

He swung down off his horse and swept off his hat. "Hello, ma'am," he called. "May I be of any assistance?"

She raised her head, and his heart began to beat a little faster as he looked into the challenging green eyes of Lucy O'Connor. "Hello, Mr. Abernathy. I thought that was you."

For a split second, he felt gratified she'd remembered him enough to recognize him at a distance. Then he reminded himself that no one else was likely to be roaming around Hiram Fischer's land with a Negro boy in tow.

"Hello, Miss O'Connor." He nodded to her horse. "When did your horse come up lame?"

"About half an hour ago." She held up a horseshoe in one gloved hand. "He threw a shoe."

He opened his mouth to offer to replace the shoe for her, but the memory of their last meeting held his tongue. If a prideful woman like Lucy O'Connor wanted help from him, then she'd have to ask for it. He began walking, leading his horse, and she fell into step beside him. "Where are you headed?" he asked.

"I remembered the Fischer place—your place now—was over in this direction. I was headed there."

"Oh? Come calling, are you?"

She frowned. "I started there *after* Amigo here threw the shoe."

He pretended to study the horizon, but he was only too aware of the woman beside him. She smelled of lavender. The hard soles of her boots made soft clinking sounds against the rocks as they walked. He held his arms stiffly at his sides to keep from reaching out to steady her. Or was it merely that he wanted any excuse to touch her—to smooth his fingers across her porcelain skin, to feel the softness she guarded with her bristly attitude? He could sense the tension in her, every muscle clenched with exasperation, like an overheated kettle about to explode. He kept his voice light when he finally spoke. "Oh? And why is that?"

"Mr. Abernathy, you are no gentleman!"

He turned to her, feigning affront. "Miss O'Connor, whatever have I done to earn such scorn?"

She raised the horseshoe. He wondered if she intended to hit him with it, and prepared to duck. "A *gentleman* would offer to repair this for me." Her eyes glowed like embers, and a similar glow burnished her cheeks. Lucy O'Connor in a rage was a sight to behold.

He bit the inside of his cheek to keep from laughing. Not at her so much as at the silly game they played. "Why, Miss O'Connor, if you need assistance, you only have to ask," he said. "I'm always happy to aid a damsel in distress."

She didn't exactly wince at his words, but he knew she wanted to. Maybe he was laying it on a little thick. Lame horse or not, Lucy didn't deserve to be lumped in with all the sniveling ninnies who no doubt would have dissolved into tears at the first sign of trouble. Come to think of it, none of them would have been out here alone in the first place.

"Mr. Abernathy—will you or will you not repair this shoe so that I can ride home?" She spoke through clenched teeth, eyes blazing.

He gave a slight bow. "With pleasure."

They walked the rest of the way back to the cabin in silence. Trace wondered again why she had been out riding alone. Didn't that uncle of hers care enough to look after her properly? As her only relative, or the only one around here, Nate O'Connor had a responsibility to watch over his niece.

The thought reminded him of his own responsibilities. He glanced over her shoulder and saw Josh riding some distance behind them. The boy waved. "I'll catch up with you in two shakes!" Josh called. Not waiting for an answer, he turned and rode in the opposite direction.

"Hope he doesn't get lost," Trace mumbled.

Lucy gave him a curious look. "Was Josh your slave . . . before the war?"

"I've never owned slaves."

"Then what is he doing with you now?"

"Now who's being impertinent, Miss O'Connor?" He smiled to soften his words and was pleased to see a blush darken her cheeks at his remark. She clamped her mouth shut and looked away. "Josh belonged to my wife," he said. There, let her chew on that a while.

She pursed her lips, as if trying to keep the words dammed up in her mouth. Stubborn pride won out over curiosity, and she remained silent until they came in sight of the cabin. As they walked into the yard, she looked around. "You've been busy," she said. "Fixing things up."

"You've been here before?" He led both horses into the barn. He turned hers into an empty stall, then led his into the next and began to unsaddle it.

She leaned over the door of the stall to watch him. "I've stopped by to water my horse when I've been out riding."

"Do you often go riding by yourself?"

"Why shouldn't I?"

He heard the challenge in her voice and knew she was baiting him, but he couldn't hold his tongue. "There are a lot of men roaming around these days up to no good— renegades, outlaws. And what about Indians? Aren't they still a danger?"

He turned to look at her. She rolled her eyes. "All Easterners seem to think Texas is crawling with outlaws and Indians. Why, nobody's seen a hostile Indian around here in ages!"

"What about the outlaws?"

She shrugged and patted her pocket. "I'm not addle-brained. I carry a gun and I know how to use it."

"I never said you were 'addle-brained.' In fact, you strike me as one of the more intelligent women I've met."

The compliment apparently caught her off guard. She flushed and looked away. He fought the sudden urge to pull her close. She was a woman deserving of both compliments and caresses, but the careful way she held herself apart from everyone made him think she hadn't enjoyed many of either in her short life.

"You don't need to worry about me, Mr. Abernathy," she said, avoiding his gaze. "I can look after myself."

He turned away, a shudder moving down his spine. *I can look after myself.* Marion's favorite words.

He came out of the stall and began gathering up the tools he needed to shoe the horse. She followed, so close he imagined he could feel her breath on the back of his neck. The sensation left him restless and irritable. "Stand back," he snapped, then attacked the wayward horseshoe, beating it straight on an anvil, the ringing of his hammer echoing from the rafters.

Silence hung thick in the air when he finished. He could feel Lucy watching him, her gaze like a physical touch against his back as he bent to measure the shoe against the horse's hoof. Again the urge to draw her near, to make some physical contact, was almost overwhelming.

"So, is that what you were doing today—just riding?" he asked, hoping casual conversation would dispel the closeness he felt to her.

"No. I went to see Sterling Gibbs. I'm buying some cattle from him. He's going to let me pay him a little at a time, as I get the money."

"Money from writing more stories?"

"That . . . and other things." The simple query seemed to have flustered her. She looked away.

"And have you selected the cattle you want from Mr. Gibbs?"

She turned back to him, excitement flaring once more in her emerald eyes. "I picked out two dozen good heifers and one . . . bull."

He smiled at her hesitation at the word. At least she hadn't substituted the old maidish "gentleman cow." He would have burst out laughing then.

"You think ranching is a foolish occupation for a woman, don't you?"

His smile vanished, and he began filing the horse's hoof. "I think ranching is a dangerous occupation. And a risky one. Not one I'd favor for my sister or wife or daughter."

"Then I'm fortunate not to have a brother, husband, or father to keep me from doing what I wish to do." She sounded assured, but he thought again how alone in the world she was—alone, like him.

He shook himself. Lucy O'Connor wasn't alone. She had her uncle and friends. If none of them were particularly concerned that she chose to buy two dozen cantankerous cows or go riding across the country by herself, why should he care?

"Mr. Abernathy, there's something I need to tell you."

He looked over his shoulder at her and raised one eyebrow in question. She stood at attention, hands folded in front of her as if she were about to sing a hymn or give a recitation of "Captain, My Captain." "Yes, Miss O'Connor?"

"I really feel you should have more concern for your own safety than mine," she said. "After all, you're a stranger here and not everyone in town takes kindly to . . . to your sort of person."

"You mean a Yankee."

"A Yankee *soldier*."

He gave the horseshoe one last tap, then released the horse's foot and straightened. "Are you saying I can expect to have my throat cut in my bed one night, or be ambushed on the way home some afternoon?"

She raised her chin. "I'm saying *some* people might be unfriendly toward you. A little extra caution in dealing with them might be wise."

Was she serious, or was this just some flight of fancy from her story-writer's mind? He thought about the footprint in the barn. Was someone spying on him, plotting mischief? "Well, *you* don't need to waste your strength worrying about *me*, Miss O'Connor. I came here to raise cattle and live quietly. I don't intend to involve myself in whatever passes for the social whirl in Elm Ridge, Texas. So I won't be upsetting people with my unwanted presence in their midst any more than necessary."

"Trace! Trace come quick! Come see what I found!" Josh's shout shattered the afternoon stillness.

Trace exited the stall and strode toward the barn door, Lucy at his side. Josh charged toward them, heels drumming the sides of his horse, which trotted along, a wild look in its eyes. Lucy gasped. Looking past the boy and the horse, Trace saw the reason for her surprise. "What the hell—"

Running along behind the horse, wrapped up like a mummy in several feet of hemp rope, was a burly black man. His heavy brogans made slapping sounds on the hard-packed earth of the yard.

"Whoa, there!" Josh tugged on the reins and brought the horse to an abrupt halt. His prisoner stumbled up beside the boy, a murderous look in his eyes. Josh grinned at Trace and Lucy. "I done caught us a no-good horse thief!" he announced.

4

TRACE STUDIED THE MAN at the end of Josh's rope. Of average height, well muscled, with skin the color of tanned leather, the stranger met Trace's assessing gaze with a keen look of his own. His homespun shirt and canvas trousers had seen better days, and up close Trace could see holes in the toe of one of the stout brogans. He wore no weapon, not even a knife strapped to his waist. Judging by the breadth of his chest and circumference of his arms, this man could defend himself well with his hands when he had to. Even now, his fingers curled into fists at his sides.

Trace stepped forward and tugged at the slip knot that held the loop tight. The loosened rope fell around the prisoner's feet.

"Hey! What are you doin'?" Josh slid from the saddle and hurtled toward Trace. "He'll get away!"

The man stood ramrod straight, chin up. He had a dignity about him, despite his shabby clothing and awkward predicament. "What's your name?" Trace asked.

The man raised his chin half an inch. "Who wants to know?" His voice was deep, the words slow and deliberate.

"You can't talk to Mr. Trace that way!" Hands on hips, Josh scowled at the man.

"Josh, hush!" Trace looked at the man again. "I'm Trace Abernathy."

The man nodded. "I go by Rye Booth."

"So, Mr. Rye Booth—are you a horse thief?"

Anger sparked in Booth's eyes, but his facial expression never changed. "No."

"He is, too! I know he is!" Josh looked on the verge of tears as he shouted his accusation.

"The boy's either crazy or a liar," Booth said.

"I am not!"

Lucy put a hand on Josh's shoulder and bent to whisper something in his ear. He turned and buried his face in her skirts.

Trace watched them, awe and aggravation warring in his chest. Just when he'd written Lucy off as too caught up in her own concerns to care about anyone else, she proved him wrong. Josh cuddled up to her like a puppy to its mother. He'd forgotten how much a boy that age needed petting and cuddling. Lucy had known Josh all of a few hours, and already she was handling him better than Trace ever had.

He sighed and turned back to Rye Booth. "Maybe he's just a boy."

Booth shrugged.

Trace looked down at Booth's worn shoes. "Someone was in our barn night before last. Josh saw the footprints and thought it was someone after the horses. Was that you?"

"I was in the barn, but I wasn't after the horses. I was just after someplace dry to sleep."

"You were the one living in the cabin before we arrived."

Booth hesitated, then nodded. "Nobody else was using it. I kept the place up, ran off the varmints, cleared out trash, in exchange for the roof over my head."

"Where are you from, Mr. Booth?" Lucy stepped forward, one arm still draped protectively around Josh. "I don't recognize your face or the name."

"I come over from east Texas, ma'am. Thought I'd make a new start."

"Doing what?" Trace asked.

Booth looked him in the eye. "Now that you're here, thought I might hire on with you."

Trace shook his head. "I can't afford to hire any help."

Booth let his gaze wander over the yard—past the half-chinked cabin and the dwindling woodpile, over the now-sleeping wagon horse, past Lucy and Josh, and finally came to rest on Trace once more. "The way I see it, you can't afford not to."

The man had nerve, Trace had to hand him that. He said he'd left east Texas—hell, he'd probably been run out of town by a bunch of rebs upset that he wouldn't stay in his place. "How do you figure that?"

"I heard you talking to the boy—"

"My name is Josh!" Two brown eyes glittered from among the folds of Lucy's skirts.

"I heard you talking to *Josh* here about rounding up cattle. It's a hard job for two men. A man and a woman and a green boy would find it mighty slow going."

Trace glanced at Lucy. She was busy rubbing Josh's back, slender fingers making circular patterns down his spine in a way that made Trace hungry for the same fondling touch. Rye Booth apparently thought he and Lucy were husband and wife. The thought burned like lightning through him. What would it be like to have a firebrand like Lucy O'Connor warm his bed each night?

She raised her head, and their eyes met. Awareness arced between them, and she let out a gasp. He jerked his head away, angry with himself for letting his desire show so clearly on his face. He already knew the answer to his question—he'd lived through it once already, and once was enough for any man. Marriage to a woman like Lucy O'Connor would be hell wrapped up in a heavenly package.

"You don't have to pay me cash."

Booth's words cut through the chaos in his head. "What do you want?" Trace asked.

Booth rubbed one hand along his jaw. "I'm willing to make a deal. I go to work for you, and I get one cow for every five we catch for you. I put my brand on my cows, run 'em with your herd. Come next spring, we take 'em north and sell 'em, and I get my cut. With you and me, and your wife here, too, if she's willing, we could do all right for ourselves."

"I'm not his wife." Lucy looked flustered. Trace had a feeling this didn't happen often. "We're not married. I mean . . . I just stopped by because my horse threw a shoe."

"Too bad."

Trace wasn't sure if Booth was referring to the thrown shoe or the fact that he and Lucy weren't husband and wife. Not that any wife of his would ever be riding over half of Texas, roping and wrestling wild cattle.

But another man—with another man to help him, he could more than make up the difference of Booth's "wages." "Can you ride?" he asked.

"I can ride. I can rope and shoot, break horses, do veterinary work, too."

Trace nodded. "I've only got two horses."

"I'm not giving up my horse!" Josh howled.

Booth scowled at him, the menacing look lightened by the laughter in his eyes. "Quit your squalling, boy. I don't want your old nag. I got my own mount."

"Where is it?" Trace asked.

Booth jerked his thumb over his left shoulder. " 'Bout two miles back, where that young'un decided to lasso me."

Trace stepped forward and offered his hand. "You're hired, Mr. Booth."

Booth's handclasp was firm, his palm well calloused. "You won't be sorry, Mr. Abernathy."

"I'll lend you a horse, and you can ride back and get your things." Ignoring Josh's grumbling protests, he handed over the reins to the wagon horse to Rye Booth.

When Booth had ridden away, Lucy patted Josh's shoulder, then reached up to retie the strings of her bonnet. "I'd best be going, too."

Trace followed her into the barn, where she retrieved her horse from its stall. "Thank you for repairing the horseshoe, Mr. Abernathy."

"Wait. I'll ride with you part of the way." He lifted the latch on the door of the stall where his own horse waited.

"That's quite all right. I know the way." She led her horse to the mounting block and climbed onto her sidesaddle.

The words rankled. He grabbed hold of her horse's bridle and glared up at her. "I didn't say you didn't know the way. I was only offering out of common courtesy."

She stared at him. "Then I appreciate your courtesy, but it isn't necessary. I *prefer* to ride alone."

He released the bridle, causing her horse to dance sideways in alarm. His irritation grew as he watched her struggle to bring the animal under control. "What if something on the trail were to spook your horse while you were out riding alone?" he asked. "What would you do then? You could get hung up in those long skirts and dragged to death, or thrown into a ravine where no one would find you for days."

The animal calmed, she turned her attention to him once more. "Really, Mr. Abernathy, you should be the one writing stories. You certainly have an active imagination." She laughed and turned the horse, then touched her quirt to its side and rode from the stall at a fast clip.

Trace stared after her, an old frustration gnawing at his gut. What did he care what that obstinate woman did? It would serve her right if she was thrown. But the thought of Lucy lying by the side of the road, silent and bruised, made cold sweat break out on the back of his neck.

"Josh, when Mr. Booth gets back with his horse, I think I'd better ride into town and pick up a few more supplies."

The boy stared up at him. "You goin' to see Miss Lucy?"

"No! With another mouth to feed, we'd better get more groceries."

Josh shrugged. "When you see Miss Lucy, ask her if she can cook." He gave Trace a sideways grin. "If you're extra nice, she might even let an old man like you come callin'. You play it right, and we could be eatin' like kings." He giggled and ran, narrowly missing a swat from Trace's hat.

∽

LUCY SLOWED AMIGO TO a walk as soon as she was out of sight of Trace's cabin. What was wrong with the man? He'd told her he thought she was smart, yet he still insisted on trying to boss her around. She'd never met a more exasperating person in her life—or a more intriguing one.

She shifted in the saddle, trying to ignore the fluttery feeling in her stomach that still lingered from her encounter with Trace Abernathy. For a moment back there, when they'd been alone in the barn, she'd wanted more than anything to reach out and touch him, just to lay a hand on his shoulder or brush the hair back from his forehead. What would he think of her if she dared to reach out to him that way?

She was twenty-two years old—no belle of the ball, though no stranger to flirtation—and no man had tormented her emotions the way this Virginia Yankee did. When he looked at her in that way of his that seemed to see right down into her soul, she didn't know whether to slap him or kiss him. Neither action was proper behavior for a well-bred young woman, but slapping at least might be defensible. Kissing a man who was practically a stranger was beyond the pale—and by far the more tempting response of the two.

She tightened her hold on the reins and guided the horse down the steep embankment of Comanche Creek. This was her least favorite part of the ride. A sidesaddle didn't give a woman a great deal of control over her mount. But Amigo was surefooted, and Lucy had never fallen. Mr. Abernathy just liked to look for trouble.

She stopped in the creek to let the horse drink. Even after the recent rains, the water didn't reach the bottom of her stirrups. Pecan trees cast deep shade over the water. She relaxed and savored the coolness. This was her reward for negotiating the creek bank—the compensation for a little risk. She liked the analogy. One day she'd receive a big reward for the risk of putting her money in cattle. She'd have her own fortune to spend as she saw fit.

The horse finished drinking, and she urged him up the opposite bank. This was almost as bad as going down, fighting the sensation that at any moment she'd slip off the saddle. But of course, she never had. Accidents like that only happened to careless people, and she wasn't careless.

Trace Abernathy didn't know that. Maybe he was used to weak-willed Virginia belles, who fainted at the sight of a spider and tripped over their hoop skirts running from imagined dangers. She smiled. Maybe Trace wasn't used to tough Texas gals who were accustomed to fending for themselves.

She imagined Trace dressed in a planter's white suit, with a Panama hat and a mint julep in his hand. Did he have a big plantation in Virginia, one with white-columned verandas and hundreds of slaves working in the fields?

No slaves, she corrected herself. Josh had belonged to his wife. A shiver raced down her spine at the word. So Trace had been married. What happened to her? Her imagination examined the possibility—she could have run off with another man while Trace was fighting in the war. Maybe she even divorced him when he chose to fight for the North. Or Trace might have left her. Men came to Texas all the time, conveniently "forgetting" whole families back East.

Most likely she'd died—of disease or childbirth, the way so many women did. She nodded. That was it. Trace had probably come west to forget, still grieving over the woman he loved and the child he'd never seen. She blinked back tears. Yes, surely there was tragedy in Trace's past. He'd returned from the war to find everything gone—he'd kept Josh with him because the boy had been his wife's favorite.

The Negro cowboy, Rye Booth, had thought she and Trace were husband and wife. Imagine that! They'd probably scratch each other's eyes out within a week.

Of course, whoever did marry Trace would no doubt be the envy of almost every girl in the county. He was strong and healthy, with thick dark hair and a smile that could make even her weak at the knees. She knew better than to give in to those feelings, though. She knew about the personality behind that devastating smile. Oh, he wasn't mean or ill-tempered like Pollard or her stepfather. She didn't think a woman would ever have anything to fear from Trace. But, like most men she knew, he expected a woman to bow to his judgment and to stay in her place.

Trace's wife had probably been one of those bisque-doll women—beautiful to look at, but empty-headed. Such a woman wouldn't dream of contradicting her "lord and master." If that was the sort of woman Trace was used to, no wonder Lucy infuriated him so!

Well, Trace Abernathy's opinion mattered little to her. If the right man came along, then one day she'd marry—but not before she had her own money set aside to look after herself and her children. And if she never married, well, she'd have friends and her writing and ranching to occupy her time. She'd be happy, knowing she'd never be totally dependent on any man—especially a man like Trace Abernathy.

∽

DARKNESS HAD FALLEN BY the time Trace reached O'Connor's store. Light slanted through the open door, and as he tied his horse, he heard the low rumble of men's voices in conversation. The men looked up when he stepped in the door—O'Connor and the other two who had greeted him his first night here. "Mr. Abernathy, what brings you out so late?'' O'Connor stood and nodded in greeting.

"I needed a few more supplies." He handed O'Connor his list, then followed the storekeeper to the front of the store and stood with his back to the counter. He nodded to the other two men in turn, then let his eyes scan the aisles. Everyone seemed calm; most likely Lucy was fine. Unless, of course, her uncle thought she'd gone to visit a girlfriend, instead of gallivanting across the prairie. Trace considered this a real possibility. He couldn't imagine a reasonable man like Nate O'Connor allowing his niece to ride out across this rough country without an escort.

"You lookin' for something in particular?" The one-legged man rose and limped over to stand at Trace's side. His tone was casual, but the cold look in his eye made Trace cautious.

"Horseshoe nails." Trace turned to face the storekeeper. "Better add a pound of horseshoe nails to that list."

O'Connor walked over and grabbed up a handful of nails from a bin on the wall and dumped them in a hanging scale. "On the house," he said. "Lucy told me you fixed that shoe for her this afternoon. Much obliged."

Trace let out a breath he hadn't even realized he was holding. "So she made it home all right?"

O'Connor nodded. "Come skipping in here, all excited about the cattle she bought." He chuckled. "Most women would act that way over a new bonnet or dress goods, but Lucy's always been a little different." His expression grew solemn. "Not that she hasn't got her feminine side, too. She can cook and sew and keep house with the best of them."

Trace had the uncomfortable feeling O'Connor was trying to sell him on Lucy's suitability as a housewife—emphasis on the wife. He felt a hot flush rise from his collar. The embarrassment was as much for Lucy as for himself. No doubt she'd be mortified to learn her uncle was praising her homemaking skills like an auctioneer touting the attributes of a brood mare. Besides, he'd never doubted Lucy's femininity. Despite her headstrong attitude, she'd always acted the perfect lady. And one look at her comforting Josh told him all he needed to know about her woman's heart.

He accepted the bag of nails, unable to meet O'Connor's eyes. He felt foolish now, riding all this way to check up on Lucy. Of course she was fine. He really had been letting his imagination run away from him.

He paid O'Connor for his purchases and turned to go, but a heavy hand on his shoulder stopped him. "I want a word with you, Abernathy."

He stared into the one-legged man's eyes. They were a muddy brown, red capillaries painting the yellowed whites. "I don't believe we've met," he said.

The man straightened. "I'm Bill Pollard."

Trace nodded. "Trace Abernathy." Pollard didn't offer his hand. Probably couldn't bring himself to shake hands with a Yankee, Trace thought. His gaze flickered to Pollard's wooden leg. Hell, maybe if he were in Pollard's place he'd feel the same way.

"Lucy tells us you're from Virginia."

He nodded, bracing himself for some comment about turncoats or traitors.

"Mind tellin' us why you had to leave?"

He stiffened. *Yes, I mind.* He forced himself to relax. He'd gain nothing by arguing with this man. "I wanted to start over. Texas seemed a good place to do it."

Pollard nodded. "Lot of folks startin' over after the war. Before I signed up to do my duty for the Confederacy, I had forty acres I planned to put to cotton. When I got back, the market had gone sour, the niggers had run off, and me with half a leg. So I had to start over, too. But I did it right here. I didn't have to go cross country to do it."

Trace clenched his teeth together until his jaw hurt. "Everyone copes in his own way," he said evenly.

Pollard looked him up and down, his expression suggesting he wasn't pleased by what he saw. "Lot of folks curious about you, you know?"

He felt his patience stretched near to breaking. "Is there

something in particular I can do for you, Mr. Pollard?''

"Well, now, it's more a matter of what I can do for you."

Pollard's hand was still heavy on his shoulder. He fought the urge to shrug it off. "And what is that?"

"I'm throwin' a little party Saturday evenin' at my house, and you're invited.''

Pollard's words were friendly enough, but something in his manner made Trace think the only party the Texan wanted to host for him was a hanging party. Or was he letting his imagination get the better of him again? "It's mighty kind of you to offer, Mr. Pollard, but I'm afraid I won't be able to make it Saturday.''

Pollard dropped his hand from Trace's shoulder and reared back. "Texans not good enough to associate with you fine Virginia planters?''

"That's not it at all.''

"Then what is it?''

What indeed? "I've got to chink the cabin" didn't sound like a very good excuse. "I've got a lot of work to do to get the place in shape,'' he said out loud.

"Can't work in the dark, now, can you?'' Pollard nodded, as if this settled everything. "Mrs. Pollard'll be mighty disappointed if you don't come. I'm sure a *fine Southern* gentleman like you wouldn't dream of hurting a lady.''

He flinched at the heavy sarcasm in Pollard's voice.

"This'll be a good opportunity for you to get to meet your neighbors.'' Nate O'Connor leaned over the counter and addressed him. "Let 'em see you're not some two-headed Yankee monster—just an ordinary fellow.''

He relaxed a little. Maybe O'Connor was right. Maybe he should go to the dance and get it over with. When everyone's curiosity about him was settled, they'd leave him be. "Tell your wife I'll be there, Mr. Pollard. Much obliged for the invitation.'' He tucked his purchases more securely under his arm and started for the door. "Good night, everyone.''

"I'll tell Lucy,'' O'Connor called after him. "She'll be

pleased to hear you're coming to the dance. She loves to dance, that girl does.''

Loves to dance, cooks, sews—so why hasn't someone else snatched up this paragon of Southern womanhood before now? He tucked his purchases into his saddlebags and swung up into the saddle. Part of him dreaded coming face-to-face with Lucy O'Connor at Pollard's party. He didn't seem to be able to think too clearly around her. She made him angry one minute and moved him the next. He'd had enough turmoil in his life for any one man. He didn't need a green-eyed tornado like Lucy stirring up his life or his heart.

5

SEWING BASKET IN HAND, Lucy set off for Twila's house on Saturday morning, determined to keep a civil tongue in her head throughout the day, even if she had to bite the end off to do it. She wouldn't waste her words on the disapproving busybodies who looked down their noses at her and her independent ways.

Better to save her strength for the dance tonight, and her next encounter with Trace Abernathy. A not unpleasant shiver raced through her at the thought of that handsome, exasperating man. He didn't approve of her behavior any more than the busybodies, but beneath his disapproval she sensed a grudging respect. Hadn't he told her once she was smarter than most women he knew?

Respect alone, however, did not explain the restlessness Trace Abernathy stirred within her, an excitement that made her heart race and her stomach flutter. When she was small, a boy had dared her to cross Comanche Creek during a flood by walking across a downed tree to the far bank. She'd made the journey with her heart in her throat, every nerve alive to the feel of her bare feet against the rough tree bark and the roar of the rushing water below. No sooner had she reached the other side than she looked back with a sense of longing, a desire to feel that thrill of danger again. Trace Abernathy made her feel the same way, as if she were more alive in his presence than at any other time.

She shook her head at this silly notion. Her feelings were probably just due to the fact that Trace Abernathy was the first newcomer of any interest to arrive in town in ages. Her writer's imagination appreciated the chance to gather new material. That didn't explain the warmth that washed over her when he looked at her a certain way, but she shoved that thought aside.

Buggies crowded the street in front of the Pollards' house. As she stepped through the gate, she noted the Earlys' farm wagon between Ada Russell's phaeton and Patricia Scott's buckboard. A mule wearing a flowered straw hat—Elizabeth Ferry's usual mount—grazed just out of reach of Twila's flower garden. "Looks like a full house," she muttered to herself as she knocked on the door.

"Lucy, I'm so glad you've come." Twila kissed her cheek. She looked very pretty in a ruffled wrapper of blue calico dotted with tiny yellow flowers, a belt of yellow ribbon around her still-slim waist. Fastened to her belt was an ornate chatelaine, with dangling scissors, needle case, thimble holder, and silk tape.

"What a lovely dress," Lucy said. "Is it new?"

Twila smoothed the full skirt. "Mr. Pollard surprised me with the fabric a few days ago. Wasn't that sweet of him?"

Sweet wasn't an adjective Lucy ever associated with Pollard. And where had the old man come up with the money for expensive calico? A dress like that would have cost thirty dollars or more. Twila took Lucy's bonnet, and they linked arms. "Look everyone—Lucy's here. And she's brought her bridal quilt to work on."

The furniture had been cleared from Twila's front parlor and two quilting frames set up. One held a colorful New York beauty, the sawtooth design rendered in red and green and yellow calico. The older women stitched at this frame, while the younger ladies gathered around the second frame, and a Texas star pattern done in shades of green and white.

"This is Elizabeth's bridal quilt," Twila explained.

Elizabeth Ferry smiled at Lucy from her position at the top of the quilt. Lucy returned the greeting. Some people thought Elizabeth was homely, but Lucy thought her wide-set brown eyes and ready grin offset her rather prominent nose and carrot red hair. "I started not to bring my quilt, because I thought we'd be working on yours," Elizabeth said. She nodded at the basket in Lucy's hand.

"No, I'm still piecing mine." She started to take a seat at the frame holding Elizabeth's quilt.

"Oh, no, Lucy. You sit here." Twila ushered her to a rocking chair along the wall between the two frames. "You and I can work on piecing your quilt top. Maybe we can even finish it today."

Reluctantly Lucy settled in the chair and opened the basket. She'd been hoping she wouldn't have to reveal how little she'd accomplished on this cursed quilt. For one thing, she'd been spending all her free time working on the quilts for Mrs. Sorenson. Bracing herself, she drew out a section of fabric barely five foot square.

"Is that all you've done?" Ada Russell's exclamation filled the small room. "Elizabeth there is three years younger than you, and she has several good quilts for her dowry chest. And Twila had more than a dozen quilts completed before her wedding—you'll be lucky to have one."

"You know what they say." Patricia Scott looked up from her work. " 'A maid with no quilt at twenty-one shall never greet her bridal sun.' "

"Maybe I have no intention of marrying." Lucy held her head high and gave the trio of older women a defiant look.

"Not want to marry?" Mrs. Russell sniffed. "Well, you're well on your way to ending up a spinster, the way you stick your nose in the air whenever a man comes near you. It will serve you right if you end up alone."

"Now, Mama, of course Lucy isn't going to end up alone." Twila put a comforting hand on Lucy's arm. "She just has more important things than quilts on her mind right now. She's been busy writing stories. She even sold one to *Leslie's Illustrated Weekly*. She's going to be a famous author someday.''

''Hmmph!'' Sandra Early frowned at Lucy over the top of her glasses. ''I've read some of the scandalous stories in that publication. Fiction is the devil's work. A young woman ought to be spending her time on useful work, rather than filling her head with such nonsense.''

A deadly silence settled over the room at this pronouncement. Twila's hand tightened on Lucy's wrist, as if she feared her friend might run away. She smoothed the quilt top across her knees. ''This is coming along nicely. I believe your stitching has improved of late.''

Hours spent copying her mother's neat, tiny stitches in the princess-feather quilt had indeed improved her skill with the needle. What would Mrs. Early and Mrs. Russell think if they could see that fine piece of work? They certainly hadn't been impressed by anything else she'd ever done. She stared at the carefully pieced quilt top with its design of appliquéd hearts until the colors blurred. To these women she would always be ''that lazy O'Connor girl, head always stuck in a book.'' Even if she did decide to tell them about her work for Mrs. Sorenson, they'd never believe her.

''It's a beautiful pattern.'' Elizabeth leaned over to touch one of the blocks, which pictured four hearts, points together.

''It's called patchwork hearts,'' Lucy said, some of the tension easing from her.

''I've never heard of it,'' Twila said. ''Leave it to you to find something so original.''

''I found it in a magazine.'' She traced the gentle curve of a blue calico heart. The cloverlike arrangement of brightly colored hearts had intrigued her. She'd imagined how cheerful it would look spread across a bed. And what better motif for a bridal quilt than hearts, a symbol of love? True, it wasn't traditional, like wedding ring or Texas star, but then, she'd always been one to go against tradition in most things.

"Hmmph! Not fancy enough for a bride's quilt, if you ask me," Mrs. Early said.

Who asked you? Lucy thought, but she bit her lip and searched for her needle instead. Twila patted her arm and stood. "Just let me thread a needle and I'll help you." She reached for the needle case that dangled by a chain from her chatelaine.

"That's all right. I don't mind working alone."

Twila looked concerned. "But you'll finish so much faster if I help."

Lucy concentrated on threading her needle, not looking at her friend. She'd grown used to working by herself. She'd had to so much of her life.

To tell the truth, she wasn't in any hurry to complete this quilt. She didn't really believe in superstitions, but still, it seemed as long as her bridal quilt was unfinished, she had a convenient excuse to put off people's talk of marriage. She straightened the length of thread hanging from her needle. "You go back to helping Elizabeth. I know she's anxious to get that quilt completed before Dudley Southworth pops the question."

Elizabeth blushed bright red. Lucy grinned. Dudley Southworth was a balding beanpole of a man with three motherless children under the age of five and a hardscrabble farm five miles out of town. Despite all these strikes against him, the shortage of able-bodied men in the area made him a prime catch. Elizabeth had attracted his attention, and a proposal seemed likely in the very near future.

"Maybe you should hurry with your quilt, Lucy." Constance Early, who was Twila and Lucy's age and as yet unspoken for, smiled at Lucy across the quilt top. "I hear that handsome newcomer, Trace Abernathy, has been making eyes at you around the store."

To her annoyance, she felt a blush creep up her throat. She bent her head over her piecework. "I don't know what you're talking about. All Mr. Abernathy is interested in is rounding up cattle.''

"Mark my word, a man Mr. Abernathy's age who has chosen to start over in a new place, once he's settled in, he'll be looking for a wife," Mrs. Russell said.

"What I want to know is how he came by the deed to Hiram Fischer's place to begin with." Mrs. Scott made a row of running stitches along the edges of Twila's quilt. "That's prime property down there along the creek."

"Mr. Fischer *supposedly* gave the deed to Mr. Abernathy," Mrs. Early said.

"Mr. Abernathy was a Yankee soldier, wasn't he?" Constance Early asked. "Maybe he killed Mr. Fischer in the fighting and *stole* the deed."

"Mr. Abernathy would never do anything like that!" Lucy exclaimed.

Every woman in the room turned to look at her. "What makes you so sure?" Mrs. Scott asked.

Her face grew hot. How did she know? She thought of Trace's fair treatment of Rye Booth and the care he gave Josh. "Mr. Abernathy struck me as a gentleman. I don't believe he's a murderer."

"All the soldiers had to kill the enemy in the war, didn't they?" Elizabeth drew her needle through the layers of fabric. "That's not the same as murder, is it?"

"Trace Abernathy *was* the enemy," Mrs. Early said. "I call it a disgrace, a man born and raised in the South, who'd turn coat and join the Yankees. For all we know, he might have been the very one who killed and maimed our men."

Lucy gripped her needle so hard she thought it might bend. A shiver ran down her spine at Mrs. Early's words, and yet, they were true, weren't they? All the soldiers in the war had had to kill or be killed, and Trace was one of them.

"We must leave it to the Lord to pass judgment." Twila's voice floated like a balm over the tense silence. "Mr. Abernathy has chosen to live here now. We must treat him with respect and courtesy, as our neighbor."

"I don't have any trouble *respecting* a man as good-looking as that." Constance Early grinned. "And if you're truly not interested in him, Lucy, I might try my hand at catching his attention. A girl could do worse than a Virginia gentleman with his own land and a *wickedly handsome* smile." Constance and Elizabeth erupted into giggles.

"Is it true Mr. Abernathy is coming to the dance tonight?" Elizabeth asked.

"Mr. Pollard invited him," Twila answered. "We thought it would be a nice opportunity for all of us to get to know him better."

Lucy glanced at her friend. Twila seemed unconcerned that Trace's presence tonight might cause trouble. "Mr. Pollard didn't act very pleased to see him the night Mr. Abernathy came to town," she said.

"That was before he knew Mr. Abernathy intended to live here. After all, one can't be too careful, what with all the riffraff wandering into Texas since the war."

Twila's explanation seemed reasonable, but it didn't put an end to Lucy's suspicions. Even before the war, Pollard had a reputation as a bully; the fighting hadn't softened him any. She could have easier believed he'd taken a temperance pledge than she could accept that he would welcome a Yankee soldier into his home. Especially a soldier who was handsome, charming, and a true Southern gentleman—everything Pollard was not.

"Are you worried Mr. Abernathy won't receive a warm welcome tonight?" Twila asked. "I can understand how some people might be a little reserved when they first meet him, but I'm sure having him here as our guest will help to ease the awkwardness."

"Worried? Why would I be worried?" Lucy stabbed her needle into the fabric. "Whether Trace Abernathy is accepted here or not is none of my concern."

Twila grinned as she bent over her sewing once more. "You forget I know you too well. You always were a terrible liar."

"Not much of a seamstress, either, from the looks of

things." Mrs. Early nodded toward the quilt top in Lucy's lap. "If I'm not mistaken, you've managed to fasten that last strip right to your dress."

Lucy lifted the quilt top and stared in dismay at the patchwork fastened to her skirt while all around her the room erupted in laughter. "I think something besides book-work is distracting Lucy these days," Elizabeth said. She leaned over and handed her the scissors. "Better get to work. Looks like you could be needing that bridal quilt sooner than you think."

∞

TRACE HEARD FIDDLE MUSIC long before he reached the Pollard home. The lively melody floated on the night air, setting his toes to tapping in the stirrups. Though it had been a very long time since he'd been to a dance like this, it seemed his body had not forgotten how.

He found a place for his horse among the other mounts and buggies tethered in front of the house. The music swelled around him, along with the sounds of conversation and laughter. A group of men gathered under a spreading oak in the front yard fell silent and watched him as he made his way up the walk to the porch. Out of the corner of his eye, he watched them pass a jug around their circle. He unconsciously put his hand up to feel for the gun at his side. But he'd ridden unarmed. It didn't seem neighborly to come to a party decked out like the soldier he wasn't anymore.

He stopped in front of the door and took a deep, stead-ying breath. The scent of blooming passion flower filled the air, hot and sweet. A vine climbed up a trellis at the end of the porch, with purple blossoms big as saucers in the moonlight.

"Mr. Abernathy! I thought that was you standing out there." An angelic blond swung open the door and smiled out at him. She offered her hand, and he fought the urge to bow over it. "I'm Twila Pollard," she said. "Do come in."

His first thought was to wonder how an unpleasant man like Pollard had ever snared a beauty like this. "I'm pleased to meet you, Mrs. Pollard." He swept off his hat as he crossed the threshold. "Thank you for inviting me to your home." A Negro man in a white coat appeared at his side to take the hat.

"I'm delighted you could come." Mrs. Pollard took his arm and led him into a large front room that had been cleared of furniture. A three-piece band, consisting of a guitar, banjo, and fiddle, was tuning up at the opposite end. "There's food on through there," she said, indicating another room through an open archway. "Please help yourself." She stopped before an older couple. "Mr. and Mrs. Maddson, may I present Trace Abernathy. He's just moved to the area." She gave him another engaging smile. "From Virginia, isn't that right, sir?"

He nodded and suppressed a chuckle. *Very nicely done,* he thought. *Recall my ties to the old South before anyone mentions I sided with the enemy.* "How do you do, Mr. Maddson, Mrs. Maddson." He nodded to each in turn.

Mr. Maddson squinted at him. "Virginia, did you say? Did you know a family called Elloway? Raised sugar, I believe."

"No, sir, the name isn't familiar to me."

"What part of Virginia are you from?" Mrs. Maddson asked rather loudly.

"Near Portsmouth, ma'am."

She frowned. "What did you say? Speak up, please."

He raised his voice. "I'm from Portsmouth."

The level of noise fell considerably as the others in the room listened in on the conversation, while pretending not to listen. Trace gave a grim smile. Well, this was the whole point in inviting him here, wasn't it—so that everyone could satisfy their curiosity about him at once? He'd better get it over with. "My father was a lawyer," he added to Mrs. Maddson's obvious delight.

"And did you read law also, Mr. Abernathy?"

"Yes, ma'am." He made a bow. "Now, if you'll excuse me, I believe I'll visit the buffet. May I bring you anything?"

"No, thank you. Do go on."

Her murmur of "very nice manners" drifted to him as he made his way into the next room. A long table practically sagged under the weight of the feast spread out upon it—a ham and a turkey, as well as beans, potatoes, deviled eggs, relishes, cakes, cookies, pies, and a silver tureen of punch. He helped himself to a glass of punch and took a careful survey of the room.

Several young women, and some not so young, studied him behind their fluttering fans. Almost every man in the place glanced his way as well, their expressions ranging from avid interest to studied reserve. None looked at him with the open hostility he had feared. He felt some of the tension flow out of him.

"I wondered if you'd really come."

The woman's voice made his heartbeat quicken, even before he turned and saw Lucy O'Connor. She was dressed very smartly in a flowered silk gown with expansive hoops and a wide square neckline that showed off her creamy throat. The dress made him more aware of her full breasts and slim waist than ever before. "Why wouldn't I have come?" he asked, setting aside his glass.

She shrugged. "You made such a point of telling me how all you wanted was to 'raise cattle and live quietly.' "

She glared at him, ready for battle. Apparently she'd like nothing better than for him to get angry and leave. He could see right through that ploy. If Lucy didn't want him here, he'd make sure he was the last one to leave.

He gave her a broad smile. "Ah, but I couldn't pass up the chance to dance with such lovely ladies as yourself." He grabbed her hand and pulled her toward the other room, where the band had struck up a waltz.

"What are you doing?" She struggled to pull away, but he held her fast.

"Dance with me, Lucy," he said, and swung her into the waltz. "Everyone is watching. Show them you're not afraid to dance with a Yankee soldier."

She stopped struggling, though she still held herself stiffly away from him. He grasped her right hand in his left and rested his other hand at her waist, conscious of the warmth of her skin through the fabric of her clothes. Or was that merely the warmth she kindled in him at her touch? He looked around the room, anxious to distract himself. "I see despite the deprivations of the war, the ladies have managed to keep up with fashion," he remarked. "I haven't seen so many elegant dresses since before the war." He looked down at her skirt. "Though I daresay I'm not the only man who wishes these ridiculously wide hoops would go out of style."

She giggled. He looked at her in surprise. "What do you find so humorous?"

She leaned forward. "Promise not to tell?"

He frowned "Tell what?"

She lowered her voice to a whisper. "They're not real hoops."

His frown increased, as did her laughter. "We haven't been able to get steel hoops out here, so my friends and I made our own—out of dried grapevine." She gave an exaggerated thrust of her hips to the side, which made her skirt sway like a tolling bell. "Works pretty well, don't you think?"

He laughed. "You continue to amaze me, Miss O'Connor. Not only are you a writer and businesswoman, but now I learn you're a fashion designer as well."

"Are you mocking me, Mr. Abernathy?" She looked indignant. "Some people seem to think that just because a woman takes an interest in business or a career that she's less of a woman."

"And who might those people be?" His hand tightened on hers. "Not me. I've already sampled your cooking, and your uncle was quick to point out to me that you are a model housewife."

Her eyes widened. "When did you talk to Uncle Nate about me?"

He looked away. "I came into the store the other evening . . . to buy more supplies. The subject just . . . came up."

She flushed and ducked her head. "Uncle Nate was just being kind. Some of the older women think I'm hopeless because I don't have even one quilt in my hope chest, and the one I've started isn't coming along very quickly."

"That would be the bridal quilt your uncle mentioned."

"I imagine your wife had dozens of quilts made before your wedding."

He smiled at this transparent attempt to fish for information. "I don't recall," he said. "If she did, I'm sure she didn't make them. She had slaves for that sort of thing."

"She must have been from a very wealthy family."

"Yes."

She fell silent, and he allowed himself to revel in the feel of a woman in his arms again after so long. Her hip flared enticingly from her slender waist beneath his hand, while above her corset he was conscious of the swell of her breasts. Lucy was tall for a woman, the top of her head coming even with his nose. The scent of her hair filled him, delicate and sweet as the passion flowers blooming outside. The dark locks looked like silk. His fingers ached with the urge to loosen the pins in her hair and lose themselves in the tumbled curls.

"Have you seen Bill Pollard this evening?" Her voice broke the spell his thoughts had been weaving.

"No. I met Mrs. Pollard. A very charming woman."

"Twila is a dear. She's my best friend, and much too good for Pollard."

He'd had much the same thought, but kept this to himself. "I imagine my host will make himself known to me sooner or later."

"It would be better if he didn't."

"Why do you say that?"

"He's been drinking all afternoon. I could smell it on

his breath when he came in to help us clear away the quilt frames."

"I saw a group under the tree outside, passing a jug."

"He was probably there. Did they see you come in?"

He nodded, remembering the feel of the men watching him. "I doubt there'll be any trouble. Pollard made it a point to persuade me to be here tonight. He said I should come so that everyone could satisfy their curiosity about me."

The music stopped, but she stayed in his arms, her hand gripping his tightly. "He's up to something, I'm sure of it. It's not like him to be so friendly with strangers."

"Especially a Yankee."

Her eyes burned, feverish in their intensity. "You think I'm exaggerating, but you don't know these people the way I do. Pollard and his friends all lost something in the war—businesses, homes, family members, even pieces of themselves. They came home beaten and broken. All they have is their pride, and you threaten even that."

"How can you say that? The war's over. I don't have any more than they do."

"You've got the background and the . . . the pedigree most of them only wish they had. You've got your health and your looks and enough money to start over in a new place. And you've got the attention of every woman in this room—*their* women. Don't think there aren't some of them who hate you for it."

"I'll agree I'm probably not the most popular man here tonight, but only because I'm a curiosity. That doesn't mean I'm in any real danger."

She threw her hands up, breaking the connection between them. "Why did I even waste my concern on you? I should have known you'd never take me seriously. No one does." She whirled and darted through the crowd.

He started to go after her, but the eyes of a dozen other people in the room pinned him in place. He made a show of straightening his jacket and strolled in the opposite direction, exchanging greetings with people as he passed.

Later, when they'd both had time to calm down, he'd speak with Lucy again.

He eventually made his way back to the punch bowl and helped himself to another cup of the lukewarm drink. Part of him wished for a shot of whatever liquor had been in that jug—anything to make the evening go faster. He pulled his watch from his pocket and flipped open the burnished pewter cover. Much too early to make his excuses and leave the party. Besides, he still wanted to speak to Lucy again. He closed the watch and rubbed the case with his thumb. *What would you do, Father?* he silently mused. *Am I playing with fire in having anything to do with another head-strong woman like Lucy O'Connor?*

"Mr. Abernathy, I'd like you to meet Constance Early."

He returned the watch to his pocket and looked up to see Twila Pollard at his side with a mousy young woman in a pale green dress. "Miss Early and Miss O'Connor and I were all in school together."

"Though I, of course, was much younger." Miss Early fluttered her lashes and offered her hand.

"How do you do, Miss Early?" Trace bowed over her hand.

"Delighted, I'm sure." She inclined her head toward the other room. "I saw you dancing earlier. Isn't the music lovely?"

To ignore this obvious hint would be rude, and wasn't he here to impress his new neighbors with the fact that he was a perfect gentleman? "Would you care to dance, Miss Early?"

"Why, I'd be honored."

She was an awkward dancer, too stiff and so short he had to bend over uncomfortably to accommodate her. He breathed a sigh of relief when, duty done, he was able to leave her with a cup of punch and her fan. He turned away in time to see Lucy O'Connor slip out the front door.

Thinking she had stepped out onto the porch for a breath of cool air, he followed, intending to continue their earlier conversation in a calmer frame of mind. But he found the porch empty. He stood at one end and let his eyes adjust to the darkness, searching the shadows for some sign of the young woman.

The group under the tree had grown, dark shapes shifting under the canopy of branches. The sound of raised voices, followed by raucous laughter, floated across the yard. Even the latecomers to the group would have been drinking for some time now. Would the liquor ease their pain or aggravate it? Would his presence here—a victor in the camp of the defeated—be enough to incite them to violence, as Lucy seemed to think?

A figure broke away from the group under the trees, darting behind a parked wagon. Trace watched as the man crouched beside the wagon as if trailing something.

Or someone. Curious, Trace stepped back into the deeper shadows against the house, then eased to the end of the porch and slipped noiselessly under the rail. He waited until the man moved forward again, then Trace dropped to the ground. Oblivious, the man darted past, around to the back of the house.

Trace followed. Rounding the corner, he looked ahead of the man and saw a female figure pacing in the shadows between the woodpile and the wash kettle. Lamplight from an open window illuminated her as she passed. He froze as he recognized Lucy's dark curls.

The man he'd been trailing rushed forward and stopped in front of Lucy. Trace waited, tensed. For all he knew, this might be a friend whom Lucy had arranged to meet here. He clenched his hands into fists. The thought of Lucy in some secret lover's arms sent a pain through the pit of his stomach.

She spoke to the man, her voice urgent, too low for Trace to make out the words. The response was harsh laughter, then the man grasped her roughly by the arms and pulled her near.

She scarcely had time to cry out before Trace lunged. He grabbed the man around the throat in a choke hold and wrenched him away, bringing one knee up for a vicious blow to his back. Lucy gave a strangled cry, then snatched the paddle from the washpot and brought it down hard on the man's head. Her attacker slumped in Trace's arms.

"Oh, my God. I didn't mean to kill him!" She dropped the paddle and stared at the man, eyes wide with horror.

Trace eased his burden to the ground. He looked down at the slack face of a boy barely out of his teens. "He's not dead."

"Are you sure?" She came to stand beside him.

"I'm sure." He bent closer, and the odor of raw whiskey made his eyes water. "Dead drunk is more like it." He hefted the young man under the arms and dragged him into the deeper shadow behind the woodpile. "He'll wake up in the morning with a knot the size of an egg on his forehead and he'll wonder what happened." He glanced toward her. "Do you know him?"

She followed him around behind the woodpile and stood staring at the man, arms folded up under her breasts. "His name is Frank Spencer. He was sweet on me once, but I told him I wasn't interested. I never thought he'd . . . force himself on me."

Trace watched her, catching his breath. Now that he knew she was safe, anger boiled up in him. What if he hadn't followed her outside? He swallowed the knot that rose in his throat. "What did you think you were doing, going out alone like that, when you knew men were out here drinking?"

"I wanted some fresh air. Why shouldn't I be able to go out alone?" For all her defiant words, her voice trembled when she spoke, destroying his last defenses.

He held out his arms, and she came to him, burying her head against his shoulder. He could feel her heart beating against his chest, a wild vulnerable sensation, like a trapped animal—but he was the one who was trapped, by emotions he didn't want to name.

The neatly stacked logs reached almost to the top of his head, hiding them from view. For a moment at least, they could enjoy this time alone, without fear of interruption. It wouldn't do a young woman's reputation any good to be caught alone in the dark with a man, especially an outsider like him.

She raised her head and looked up at him, no glint of tears on her cheeks. "I didn't go out alone to deliberately flaunt convention or because I have no sense. I just wanted to be by myself for a moment—to think."

Her face was so close to his, he could feel her breath brushing his cheek. The sweet scent of her hair made him light-headed. Her breasts pressed against his chest, sending a heat coursing through him. All he had to do was turn his head slightly. . . .

He captured her lips beneath his own, softly at first, then more insistently. Even as he savored the kiss, he braced himself for her withdrawal, and the stinging slap, or the more stinging assault of words he was sure would follow.

She moved toward him, not away, crushing her skirts against the growing fullness in his groin, the wide hoops belling out behind her. She sighed, and he slipped his tongue between her teeth, savoring this first taste of her.

She grew still, and again he expected her to draw away. But soon she began to move in concert with him, making her own explorations of his mouth, tentatively at first, then with more enthusiasm. She was a quick learner and a brilliant pupil. She also had no idea of the state into which she was putting him. She writhed against him and, groaning, he reluctantly ended the kiss. "Lucy, darling, we've got to stop before we go too far."

She looked up at him, blinking as if in a daze. *Ah, now she's going to slap me,* he thought, and sought for some remark to defuse the situation. But before he could open his mouth to speak, another voice broke the night stillness.

"Abernathy, we know you're behind there. Come out this instant!"

6

LUCY FROZE, HER FINGERS digging into Trace's arms. Pollard's drunken shout stabbed through the darkness, like a slap jerking her from a wonderful dream. She looked up at Trace and started to plead with him not to respond, but he clapped his hand over her mouth.

"Don't say a word," he whispered, his breath warm against her ear. "I'm going out to talk with them. Don't let them know you're here."

She shook her head vigorously. Trace was crazy to think he could face down Pollard and his friends alone.

"If you don't promise me you'll keep quiet and hide back here, I'll have to tie you up." With one hand, he started to undo the length of silk at his throat.

He'd do it, too, wouldn't he? she thought. He'd leave her trussed up like a chicken while he walked out there and got himself tarred and feathered, or even shot. Telegraphing her anger with her eyes, she nodded her assent. She'd agree to remain silent, but that didn't mean she wouldn't look for some other way to help him.

"Come out, or we'll come back there and get you!" Pollard's voice echoed in the sudden stillness. All music and laughter had ceased, replaced by a thick silence, punctuated by a man's muffled cough, and the scuffle of boots in the dirt.

Trace gave her a last warning look, then released her and walked out to stand in front of the woodpile. "What is it, Pollard?" His voice was strong and even, the voice of a man not easily cowed. Lucy shivered and bent to peer through a gap in the stacked logs.

Pollard stood at the head of a crowd. Lucy counted at least a dozen men from town and elsewhere in the county, all familiar to her as customers of Uncle Nate's store. Like Pollard, they were Confederate veterans, many with visible scars of the wounds they suffered. Farmers and tradesmen, they were men with little wealth and less power. But fueled by whiskey and Pollard's bitter words, they'd found a focus for their frustration and anger. Their faces, some glassy-eyed with drink, looked sinister in the wavering light of the lanterns they carried. "We don't want your kind among us!" Pollard spat. A rumble of assent rose around him.

Trace folded his arms across his chest. "As I recall, *you* invited me here as your *guest*, Mr. Pollard." The posture called attention to his muscular arms and shoulders. Standing ramrod straight, his black suit still crisp, he presented the image of a well-bred, strong, and healthy man. Lucy watched more than one man look from Trace to the men around him, then glance behind him to where the other men and women stood. Did they see how inferior they looked compared to a man like Trace?

"Guests don't go sneaking around on other people's property." Pollard jerked his head toward the woodpile. "What were you doing back there?"

Lucy held her breath. Trace was tall enough that Pollard might have seen his head over the top of the woodpile. Had he seen her also and was just leading Trace on?

"Well, now, I'd rather not say in mixed company." Trace inclined his head toward the women. Lucy was sure more than one feminine heart raced at the gallant gesture.

"What kind of sabotage were you planning to repay my

hospitality, you Yankee dog?'' Pollard took a step toward Trace.

"Let's just say I had a little too much punch and was in a hurry to relieve myself.''

This lie brought a few gasps from the female onlookers. Lucy sighed.

"You lie!'' Pollard's voice rose. "I've known men like you before. You're a traitor to your own people. Why, the great Robert E. Lee resigned his commission in the Union Army to defend his native state, and you ran away to join the enemy. Then you come here to rub our noses in our defeat every time we see you.''

"I came here to raise cattle and to be left alone.'' Trace turned toward Pollard, his profile to Lucy. In the moonlight, his face was reduced to harsh lines and flat planes, handsome still in its masculinity. Pollard looked wrinkled and sunken by comparison. "Now, if you'll excuse me, I'll be going.'' Trace turned as if to walk away.

"Seize him!'' Two burly youths grabbed hold of Trace. He struggled mightily, until Pollard stepped up and laid a gun alongside his head. "Don't think you'd be the first Yankee I've ever killed,'' he muttered.

Lucy bit her knuckles to keep from crying out. Trace ceased struggling and stood between his captors, his arms pinned behind his back. Still holding the pistol, Pollard took a careful step back, bracing himself against the woodpile with his free hand. He was so close, Lucy could see the fraying at the collar of his shirt and smell the whiskey odor that clung to him. "You ever see a man tarred and feathered?'' he asked.

Trace remained silent, glaring at Pollard. Pollard laughed. "Light the fire,'' he ordered. A boy ran forward to light the fire under the nearby washpot. Another boy swung the washpot out of the way and hung a tar bucket over the flames.

"First of all, the tar's hot, so it burns going on. It melts right through your clothes—we'll leave your longhandles on so as not to mortify the women.'' Pollard's words sent icy chills through Lucy. Trace never flinched. "But the tar melts right through the fabric and sticks to the skin. Hurts a good bit, I understand, especially when it reaches certain, uh, sensitive parts of the anatomy."

Nervous laughter erupted in the mob. The laughter gave way to grumbling as a man shoved his way to the front, leading a horse behind him. Feeling faint, Lucy recognized Uncle Nate, with Trace's horse. "All right, Pollard. You've made your point. Time to put an end to the theatrics and let Mr. Abernathy go."

"Stay out of this, O'Connor." Pollard waved the pistol at the storekeeper. Lucy choked back a scream. "You ought to be thanking me for getting rid of this vermin. If you ask me, he's taken entirely too much of an interest in that head-strong niece of yours."

Nate swallowed hard but stood his ground. "I mean it, Bill. This is wrong, and you know it." He reached for Pollard, but two men emerged from the mob to drag Nate away. Pollard turned to Trace once more. The horse wandered off a short distance, reins trailing, and began cropping grass.

"Next we put on the feathers. They stink and add to the humiliation, and make the tar harder to remove." Pollard continued the description of the torture Trace was to receive, obviously savoring the opportunity. Lucy realized her fears had been correct: Pollard had been planning this punishment for a long time. The tar, the carefully laid fire, and even this speech were the work of long preparation. "If you ever do manage to get the tar off and don't die from the burns or from infection, you'll be scarred for life," he went on. "Decent men like us won't have to worry about you distracting our women then. They'll turn away whenever they see you on the street."

"Mr. Pollard, you must stop!" Twila's anguished cry cut through the night. She ran toward her husband, pursued by a man who had apparently been holding her.

"Stay out of this, woman!" Pollard ordered.

"No, Bill, please!" She grabbed hold of his arm, throwing him off balance.

He staggered, his face contorted with rage, then swung the pistol and caught his wife on the side of the head with the heavy barrel. Twila fell back, a dark stream of blood coursing down the side of her face. Her erstwhile captor quickly wrapped her up in his arms. "Take her inside and tie her up where she won't interfere anymore!" Pollard snapped.

Lucy waited for someone else to rush forward, but the rest of the crowd stood immobile, mesmerized by the grim horror of the scene before them. Some of the guests turned and walked away, unwilling to participate, but equally unwilling to stop this evil. The scent of burning tar had already begun to fill the air.

Choking back tears of rage and fright, she pulled away from the peephole in the woodpile and began searching for a weapon. Her eyes fell on the maul used to split firewood. With effort, she could probably lift it over her head, but then what?

She stumbled, almost falling over the prone body of Frank Spencer. He lay sprawled on his back, breathing deeply, fast asleep. With a shiver of apprehension, she knelt and began searching his body for some sort of weapon. Her efforts yielded a pocket knife with a broken blade and a caul wrapped in a handkerchief—a common good luck charm. She could certainly use good luck right now, but she didn't see how either of these things would be immediately useful.

"Stir it up good there, Jed," Pollard's voice called. "It's starting to look ready."

Heart racing, she made another frantic search of her surroundings. Her gaze fell on a thin peeled log, about as big around as a table leg and five feet long. She'd seen Pollard with a similar walking stick before.

The piece of wood was light yet sturdy in her hand. It seemed to her about the right shape and size for a gun barrel. In the darkness, would a drunken mob be able to tell the difference? During the war, Confederate soldiers had sometimes taken logs and painted them black to resemble cannons. These "Quaker guns" had fooled more than one contingent of Yankees.

"Maybe you ought to ladle us up some to test out," Pollard called.

Heart in her throat, she snatched up the walking stick. As an afterthought, she grabbed the sleeping man's hat and crammed it onto her head. Then, as quietly as possible, she dragged a section of tree trunk over to where Pollard stood. Climbing onto the stump, she let just the top of the hat show over the wood, and rested the walking stick on top, "aiming" right at Pollard's head. Deepening her voice as much as possible, she sought to imitate the growl of an angry man. "Let him go, or I'll blow you to kingdom come!" She accented this command with a jab of the "gun" into the back of Pollard's head.

He froze. "Who's there?"

"Never mind that! Let him go." She jabbed the gun again. "Now!"

She'd always thought talk of frightened men shaking in their shoes had been exaggeration, but now she could see that Pollard literally trembled. He let go of the pistol he'd been holding. "You heard the man! Let him go!"

The two men holding Trace stepped away from him, but Trace stood rooted in place, staring openmouthed toward the woodpile. "Get out of here!" Lucy's voice rose dangerously at the end of that command. She was shaking, too, now with fear and frustration.

Trace took two steps backward, then raced for his horse. Swinging up into the saddle, he dug his heels into the animal's flanks and bolted forward.

Lucy jumped down off the stump and dropped her "rifle." Knocking the hat from her head, she gathered up her skirts and ran also, just ahead of the crowd that swarmed around the end of the woodpile.

∽

TRACE LAY LOW OVER the horse's neck and drove the animal for all it was worth, leaping hedges and fence rows, quickly leaving the clamoring crowd behind. When the noise of the pursuit had faded, he swung the horse around in a circle and charged back toward the fray. He wasn't about to leave Lucy to that mob.

Lucy! She fashioned grapevine hoops to conform to the latest fashion, yet cast propriety to the wind and kissed a man who was little better than a stranger to her. She approached kissing like everything else in life, with enthusiasm and passion that more than made up for any lack of experience. The realization that she *was* inexperienced both delighted and dismayed him. What did Lucy O'Connor see in him—what did she *want* from him—that had led her to kiss him with such fervor and abandon? The question nagged at him, even as the memory of their embrace heated his blood and set his heart to racing.

The Pollards' house glowed against the darkened sky, every window spilling lamplight onto the lawn where a crowd still milled. He slowed the horse to a walk and guided it along the edge of the shadows, toward the woodpile. Damn Lucy for putting herself in danger that way! Had the woman no sense?

His conscience pricked him at the thought. What would have happened if he'd been waiting behind the woodpile with a more sensible woman? Would he even now be suffering the agonies of burning tar, the humiliation of a coating of feathers?

He spotted the woodpile and the group of men around it. They were bent over a prone figure, only a pair of scraped shoe soles visible in the press of people. His chest constricted, breathing suddenly impossible. By God, if they'd hurt Lucy, he'd—

He'd what? If only he hadn't been such a gentleman and left his pistol at home!

He leaned forward, straining his ears to make out words in the murmur of conversation that drifted to him on the night breeze. Voices raised in anger. Another voice answered, petulant. The tones were too deep for Lucy, weren't they?

The band around his heart eased as Frank Spencer emerged from the crowd, carried roughly between two of Pollard's minions. The angry host himself hobbled along beside them, fairly vibrating with anger. Trace suppressed a chuckle. He would carry to his grave the memory of Pollard's stricken expression when Lucy jabbed her ''gun'' into the back of his head.

The crowd began to disperse. Pollard and a few others stayed with Spencer, but the remainder headed for the front of the house, where the horses were tied. Time for Trace to leave once again. Lucy appeared to have safely vanished. He could only hope she was home by now, cured once and for all of her yen for adventure by tonight's narrow escape.

∞

LUCY SLIPPED OUT OF the house at dawn the next morning. The sun shone through a heavy veil of mist, like a lamp behind a gauze curtain. Moving as silently as possible, she fed Amigo a measure of oats and saddled him while he ate. She wanted to be away before Uncle Nate woke. He had stayed out very late, hunting for some of the younger men who had followed Trace into the night. He'd returned in the early hours before dawn, gray and weary, with no news of the men or of Trace.

She led the horse out of the barn, stopping at the mounting block by the fence to climb into the saddle, then rode toward Twila's. Pollard would no doubt be sleeping off the excesses of the night before, leaving Lucy free to check on her friend.

Mrs. Russell answered Lucy's knock. ''Twila isn't up yet,'' she said, her face grave. ''You'll have to call another time.''

''It's all right, Mama. I'll talk to Lucy.'' Twila appeared in the hallway, a shawl draped over her night rail. She'd combed her hair forward in an attempt to hide the mark from Pollard's pistol, but it showed through her fair hair, an angry red wound amid a blackening bruise. "You must have come for your quilt." She nodded to the sewing basket that sat by the door.

Lucy slipped past Mrs. Russell and greeted Twila with a hug. "I came to see if you were all right," she said, keeping her voice low.

"Of course I'm all right. Come into the kitchen, and we'll have some tea."

Lucy untied her bonnet and turned to hang it on the hatstand, then saw Trace's top hat hanging there. Her heart gave a lurch, remembering him riding off into the night, Pollard's gang close behind him. Was he all right this morning or lying dead or injured in some ditch? She forced herself to turn away from the hat, and from the grim direction her thoughts were leading, and followed Twila into the kitchen.

"Mother made some batter cakes for breakfast. Won't you have some?" Not waiting for an answer, Twila forked up two of the pancakes and set them on a plate before Lucy, then slid into a chair. Behind her, the kettle on the stove began to steam.

Mrs. Russell moved silently about the kitchen, fetching cups and pouring tea. From time to time, she touched her daughter on the shoulder, a gentle, reassuring gesture.

Lucy sat at the table across from her friend. "Does your head hurt much?"

Twila looked away. "Only a little."

"What are you going to do? You know I'll help you any way I can. If you need money—"

Twila's eyes widened in alarm. "What are you talking about?"

Lucy leaned toward her. "Well, you can't stay here, can you? What if he hits you again?"

Twila bent her head and stirred her tea, liquid sloshing over the rim of the delicate china cup. "Mr. Pollard won't hit me again. Last night was . . . was just the drink. He's had a terrible time since the war. Besides, I . . . I should never have gotten in his way. I'm sure he never meant for it to happen this way."

Lucy stared at her friend, a heavy, sick feeling growing in the pit of her stomach. "Twila, what he did was *vicious*. He could have killed you. He *would* have killed Trace Abernathy."

Twila made a sound halfway between a laugh and a sob. "Of course he wouldn't have done that. He was just trying to frighten him. He thought Mr. Abernathy was . . . was trying to steal something that belonged to us."

"What would he be trying to steal out by the woodpile?"

"Why, I haven't the slightest idea. Your tea is getting cold. Would you like sugar?"

Lucy closed her eyes, sure that when she opened them, this twisted nightmare would be over. But when she looked at Twila again, her friend still bore the ugly mark from last night's confrontation and a patently false expression of unconcern. "I have to go now." She shoved back her chair, almost knocking it over in her hurry to be away. Twila followed her to the entryway and watched as Lucy tied her bonnet strings with shaking hands.

"Where were you last night?" Twila asked suddenly. "I didn't see you after you danced with Mr. Abernathy."

She kept her eyes fixed on Trace's hat. "I went home early," she said. It wasn't exactly a lie. She had certainly retired earlier than some. On impulse, she took the hat from the rack. "I'll just return this to Mr. Abernathy."

"Good-bye, then." Not waiting for a response, Twila turned and walked back toward the kitchen.

Lucy picked up her sewing basket and slipped out the front door. Mrs. Russell followed her onto the porch. "I hope you aren't going to make excuses for Pollard, too," Lucy said. "I won't stay to hear them."

"You're quick to condemn my daughter, but you don't hesitate to come to the defense of a total stranger in our midst." Mrs. Russell folded her arms beneath her ample breasts. "How can you be so sure Trace Abernathy wasn't up to mischief last night?"

Lucy never blinked, willing herself not to blush. "Mr. Abernathy was a perfect gentleman throughout the party. Unlike some others, he didn't spend the evening drinking."

Mrs. Russell frowned. "Did you know they found Frank Spencer passed out behind the woodpile last night? What was Mr. Abernathy doing back there with him if not plotting some wrongdoing? That young man's been nothing but trouble for years—and yet he was the one who came to Mr. Abernathy's defense last night."

Lucy struggled to maintain a blank expression. "What does Frank say about it all?"

Mrs. Russell shook her head. "He doesn't remember a thing. Too drunk, I imagine. But it was definitely him—some of the men recognized his hat, and they found the walking stick he was using as a 'gun.' "

Lucy allowed herself a small smile now. "I imagine Pollard was livid when he found out he'd been fooled by a stick."

Mrs. Russell's frown deepened. "Mr. Pollard is a troubled man. You must try to be more charitable toward my daughter. She has no choice but to stand by her husband."

Lucy clenched her fists at her sides. "Even when he beats her?"

Mrs. Russell glanced over her shoulder as if to make sure Twila was not watching them. "She vowed to forsake all others and she's got to stand by that, for the sake of her unborn child if nothing else."

Lucy held her head high. "When I marry—*if* I do—I'll make sure I have choices. I'll have my own money, so that I'll always be able to look after myself and my children."

Mrs. Russell shook her head. "It would be a rare man who would put up with such a thing."

Afraid of what she might say if she stayed one minute longer, Lucy nodded and hurried away.

She rode out of town at a trot, anxious to be free of an atmosphere she suddenly found suffocating. She had always thought of Elm Ridge as a peaceful, even dull town.

The thought that such hatred festered beneath the peaceful facade sickened her.

She balanced the sewing basket on her lap and handled the reins with one hand while she carried Trace's hat and her whip with the other. The black silk was worn in places, but neatly brushed. It smelled of leather and hair oil, a distinctly masculine scent that made her senses tingle.

She crossed Comanche Creek and pushed the horse to a faster pace as she neared Trace's cabin, her hand tightening on the reins until her fingers ached. She prayed God she'd find him there.

Rye Booth was coming out of the barn when she rode up to the gate. He came out to meet her and to take the reins of her horse. "I wanted to return Mr. Abernathy's hat." She said the words in a rush as she slid from the saddle.

"He's inside there." Rye nodded toward the cabin, then led Amigo toward the barn.

She paused in front of the door to smooth her skirts, then took a deep breath and knocked. In a moment, Josh answered. "It's Miss Lucy," he announced.

"Don't just stand there, boy. Let her in." Trace stepped up behind Josh and opened the door wide. His eyes met hers, his expression cautious. "What brings you out so early this morning?"

She held up the hat. "I came to return this."

"Thank you." He reached to take it, and their fingers brushed. She saw the multitude of feelings she felt reflected in his eyes. The memory of last night's kiss burned there, along with the unspoken longing to repeat the experience, if only to confirm that such sensations could be real.

Trace hung the hat on a peg on the wall. "What's in the basket?"

She looked down at the sewing basket she still carried. "It's my quilt."

"Ah. Your bridal quilt?" He held out his hand. "May I see?"

She hesitated, surprised at his interest. He made a beckoning motion with his hand, and she gave him the basket. "The pattern is called patchwork hearts," she said, surprised at her sudden nervousness. She wanted him to like it, more than she'd ever wanted a man to like anything about her. The knowledge shook her.

He opened the lid of the basket and unfolded the pieced fabric. She and Twila had doubled the size of the coverlet yesterday, though it was still far from large enough to top a bed. Trace smoothed his hand across a square of blue, red, and brown hearts. "My mother used to quilt," he said. "I don't recall seeing one like this." He smiled at her. "It looks like you."

His smile mesmerized her and made her giddy with happiness. "Why do you say that?"

"It's bright. Pretty. Out of the ordinary."

She fought the urge to tell him about the other quilts she worked on—the ones begun by her mother and now sewn by her in secret. Would he appreciate the hard work she was doing and why? Or would he laugh like the women in town, who dismissed her dreams as foolishness? Would Trace understand why she worked so hard to buy her future freedom?

His warm smile seemed to say that he would understand. She looked away, breathless in the heat of his expression. She didn't feel safe, letting one man's opinion affect her so strongly. It was just another dangerously tempting trap.

"When are we gonna eat?" Josh's query broke the spell between them. Trace replaced the quilt top in the basket and returned it to her. They moved apart, Lucy fiddling with the handles of the basket to hide the sudden awkwardness she felt.

"We were just sitting down to breakfast." Trace motioned toward the table. "Won't you join us?"

She set the basket aside and followed him to the table, where rather overdone bacon and suspiciously flat biscuits beckoned. She'd been too anxious to eat before she left the house this morning, and she couldn't bring herself to accept food in Pollard's house; now, even this meal made her

mouth water. "Josh, fetch a cup for Miss O'Connor."
Trace pulled out a chair for her at one end of the table,
then took the seat opposite her. Josh set a steaming cup of
coffee in front of her, then took his own place between
them.

"We already said grace," Josh said. "Do we have to do
it again?"

"What do you say, Miss O'Connor?" Trace looked to
her.

She smiled. "I'd say you've already got things covered." She spread her napkin across her lap and accepted
the plate of biscuits Trace passed.

"I take it you made it home all right last night," Trace
said.

She nodded. "And you?"

"No problems." He paused, then added, "As soon as I
could, I circled back around to make sure you were safe. I
don't want you to think I'd ever have left you to face that
mob alone."

She shook her head. "I would never think that." She
turned her fork over and over in her hand. "I'm glad you
weren't . . . injured."

He helped himself to several slices of bacon. "Only my
pride. Can't say it does much for a man's self-respect to
let himself be taken advantage of by a one-legged drunk."

"A one-legged drunk with a pistol and a crazed mob to
back him up." She clasped her hands in her lap to control
the shudder that raced through her at the memory of the
scene.

Trace glanced at Josh. The boy stared at them, wide-
eyed, his jaws working to chew his biscuit. "Josh, why
don't you take some breakfast out to Rye? You can stay
and eat with him."

"But I want to stay in here."

"Go help Rye."

Josh hung his head. "Rye is mean to me."

"He isn't mean. He just doesn't put up with any of your
sass. You pay attention to him and you'll learn a lot."

With exaggerated slowness, Josh piled biscuits and bacon onto a plate and shuffled out the door. When he was gone, Trace turned to Lucy again. "I guess I have you to thank for saving my hide last night."

His look warmed her through, and she found herself wishing he'd kiss her again.

He leaned toward her, and she caught her breath. At that moment, she wanted nothing more than to be in his arms. The thought both terrified and thrilled her. "What the hell possessed you to pull a crazy stunt like that?" His voice was gruff, like the brush of his calloused hands across sensitive nerve endings. "Pollard would as soon have shot you as looked at you, the mood he was in last night."

She licked her suddenly dry lips and tried to find her voice. "I had to do something. No one else would."

He covered her hand with his own, an intimate, protective gesture. "Your uncle tried. So did Mrs. Pollard."

She blinked back sudden tears. "I saw Twila this morning. She's pretending it all never happened—that Pollard hitting her wasn't wrong."

"I suppose, in her mind, that's the only defense she has."

She looked away, unable to find an answer.

He squeezed her hand, setting her heart to racing. "What are you going to do? Pollard might find out you were the one to help me and come after you."

She shook her head. "No. Everyone thinks it was Frank Spencer—the young man who attacked me. They found him passed out behind the woodpile, with the hat and the walking stick. He, of course, doesn't remember a thing." She raised her head and looked into his eyes. "What are you going to do?"

"Do? I'm going to work my cattle and mind my own business. We should be able to start rounding up mavericks and branding them in a few days, as soon as the corral's finished. And Rye says I need to think about getting some more land so I'll own the water. If homesteaders should ever come in and fence out the cattle, the way they have other places, I'll be protected. I'm looking around while prices are cheap.''

She frowned. ''Do you really think that will happen?''

He shrugged. ''It's good land. I'm not the only one ready to make a new start now that the war's behind us. It makes sense to me; if the cattle business booms as I think it will, then the man with the most land to spread out in will be ahead of everyone else scrambling to find room for themselves.''

She nodded thoughtfully. It did make sense. Maybe she should . . . maybe she should be careful of letting Trace distract her so easily. ''What about Pollard?'' she demanded.

He shrugged. ''This will all blow over soon enough.''

''I don't think Pollard will let it blow over.''

''He's a coward at heart. You saw that last night. A lot of the men who were with him will realize how foolish they were—when they sober up.''

''Some of them will. The rest will have Pollard feeding their fears, blaming you for everything that's wrong—from falling cotton prices to that cheap land you mentioned.''

''I didn't cause those things, and getting rid of me won't make them go away. Sensible men will realize that.''

She wanted to believe him. Looking into his eyes, she could believe almost anything he said. If he kissed her again, she was sure she'd forget all about these things that frightened and worried her. She leaned forward, willing his lips to touch hers. She watched his eyes darken, his lips part, and then his free hand came up to draw her near—

''Trace! Trace!'' The door slammed open, and Josh barreled into the room. ''Wagon coming up the road!''

Trace was out of his chair, reaching for his gun, before Lucy had time to react. ''Stay inside until I'm sure it's not trouble,'' he ordered. He pushed the boy toward her. ''And keep him out of the way.''

The door shut behind Trace, and Lucy turned to Josh. ''Stay inside, and I promise you a piece of licorice a foot long,'' she said, then rushed to follow Trace. The gun in his hand told her he didn't believe his own words about not expecting trouble.

By the time she reached Trace's side where he stood by the gate, he was already holstering the gun. "I thought I told you to stay inside," he said, glancing at her.

"Since when do I take orders from you?" She said the words with a teasing smile, and he laughed.

"No threat there," he said, pointing toward the wagon. It was a rickety affair pulled by a mule. The animal wore a straw hat. As the wagon drew closer, Lucy could see that the black woman who drove the vehicle was young, about her own age. A baby slept on the wagon seat beside her.

The woman stopped at the gate and set the wagon brake. She glanced at Trace, then looked at Rye, who stood a little apart, hat in his hand. A smile came to her lips, broadening as her gaze fell on Lucy. Finally she returned her gaze to Trace, lingering on him longest. "Texas has been good for you," she announced.

The front door flew open, and they turned to see Josh racing across the yard. Arms outstretched, he launched himself at the woman in the wagon. "Mama!"

7

TRACE WATCHED THERESA CLIMB down from the wagon to cuddle the baby with one hand and Josh with the other. The sight made him feel unsteady and disoriented, as if he'd suddenly been yanked back in time. He'd stood at a gate like this before, with the woman in the bright head rag and the baby wrapped in a piece of old patchwork. Any second now, Theresa would look up at him with tear-filled eyes and tell him Marion was dead.

Marion *was* dead, and so was his life back at Belle Haven. But you never could really leave the past behind, could you? Pieces of it, like Theresa, would follow you even halfway across the country.

She raised her head and met his gaze with understanding, not tears, reflected in her eyes. "I decided I better come look after my boy." She rested her hand on Josh's head. "Now that I'm free, I didn't want to live at Belle Haven no more. Nothin' good about that place for me."

Josh clung to her like a burr on a bird dog. "I missed you, Mama." He grinned up at her. "Mr. Trace and Mr. Rye are teachin' me to cowboy."

She nodded to the black man. "You must be Mr. Rye."

"Rye Booth, ma'am." Rye straightened and all but

puffed out his chest. Trace might have laughed but for the serious expression on the cowboy's face. "That's a fine boy you got there, ma'am."

Theresa gave Josh an indulgent look. "I don't call it fine to run away from his mama. I 'bout wore myself to a frazzle, worrying about you."

Josh hung his head. "I wanted to go with Trace."

She glanced at Trace again. "Thank you for lookin' after him. Once I knowed he was with you, I didn't fret so much."

"He was smart enough to wait until we hit Tennessee before he showed himself, or I'd have sent him back. But he's been good company—most of the time." He winked at the boy, then turned to the woman once more. "What do you plan to do now?"

"I'm not sure." She frowned. "Try to get a job, I guess."

"You know you're welcome to stay here as long as you like. I can't pay much in the way of wages, but you won't go hungry, and you'll have a roof over your head until you decide what you want to do."

"I'd be much obliged." Relief easing the worry lines from her brow, she turned to Lucy. "Where do you want me to put my things, ma'am?"

Lucy flushed a becoming pink, and Trace bit back a smile. Apparently Theresa, like Rye before her, had mistaken Lucy for mistress of the house. "This is Miss Lucy O'Connor." He put a steadying hand at Lucy's elbow. "Miss O'Connor, this is Theresa. Miss O'Connor is . . ." He hesitated. What was Lucy, exactly? After the kiss they'd shared last night he could no longer think of her as a mere acquaintance, though they clearly had no future together as sweethearts; their constant clashes proved that.

"I'm a friend of Mr. Abernathy's."

So the independent Miss O'Connor would deign to be known as his friend? Considering the events of last night— *after* their kiss—this was noteworthy indeed.

"I'm pleased to meet you, Theresa," she continued.

"Theresa Washington." She chuckled at Trace's look of surprise. "Do you like the name? I chose it myself once they said we was free."

He nodded. Slaves didn't have formal surnames, though some were known by their owner's names. He wasn't surprised Theresa had elected to shed her old name along with her shackles. "Why don't you bring your things inside?" he said. "I'll bunk in the barn with Rye, and you and Josh can have the cabin for now."

She reached into the back of the wagon and retrieved a small bundle, which she handed to Josh. "I'll see to your mule," Rye offered and stepped forward to take the traces.

She gathered the baby in her arms and offered Rye a brilliant smile. "I'd be much obliged."

"You must have been camped close by last night, to get here so early this morning," Lucy said as they walked up the path to the cabin.

Theresa shook her head. "I drove all night. I took to campin' during the day. Less trouble that way."

Trace frowned. Of course, a woman traveling alone, especially a black woman, whom some Southerners would still think of as a slave, would present a tempting target.

Theresa stood in the doorway of the cabin, surveying her new surroundings. Trace tried to see the place as she must see it. Certainly the cabin was in better shape now, the chinking replaced, the roof repaired. The same faded patchwork covered the bed, which with the table and chairs was the only furniture. He waited for some comparison to Belle Haven, but none came. After a moment, she stepped inside and laid the baby across the end of the bed and unwrapped the swaddling blanket from around it.

Lucy stood beside her, openly curious. She glanced from the infant to Trace, the obvious question in her eyes, then quickly looked away, her face flushed.

Trace stepped over for his own look at the child. He didn't even know if it was a boy or a girl, though it was pretty obvious the baby was half white. He had a good idea who the father was; all the more reason for Theresa to leave Belle Haven once she had her freedom.

"What's the baby's name?" Lucy tenderly stroked one dimpled knee.

"Mar—Mary." She gave Trace a guilty look. He turned away. He was sure she'd been about to say the baby's name was Marion. Theresa had genuinely loved her sometimes difficult mistress.

As if sensing the sudden awkwardness in the air, Lucy hurried to excuse herself. "I'd better get back to town. Uncle Nate will be worried." She collected her bonnet and shawl from pegs by the door.

Trace stepped up to help her with the shawl. "Theresa, did you meet anybody on the road this morning?"

"Only one old farmer on a horse."

"And you didn't have any trouble last night?"

She shook her head. "No. Why?"

"There were some drunks stirring up mischief in town last night, that's all." He took hold of Lucy's wrist as she reached for the door. "Maybe I'd better send Rye back with you, just in case."

She jerked her hand away. "Don't be ridiculous. *I'm* not the one in any danger."

"I don't like the idea of you making the ride alone. It's asking for trouble."

"Your likes aren't my concern," She glared at him, her eyes frosty. Reluctantly he took his hand away. "Good day Mr. Abernathy, Mrs. Washington. I'll have Rye fetch my horse."

He let her go, frustration gnawing at his gut. Lucy O'Connor's temperament was as variable as the weather, blowing hot and cold with maddening unpredictability.

"Sounds like your friend is set on having her own way or be damned," Theresa observed. She clucked her tongue. "I never knew any other woman like that, did you?"

He ignored the remark. "Arrange things however you want. I'll move my stuff out to the barn later." He walked to the table and surveyed the remains of breakfast. "Reckon you could take over the cookin'? Josh and Rye are mighty tired of my offerings.''

"I can handle the cooking." She helped herself to a cup of coffee from the stove and took a long drink, studying him over the rim of the cup. "What was she talkin' about, when she said *she* wasn't the one in danger? Does that mean you are?''

"I'm not in any danger." He crumbled a biscuit between his fingers. "Some of the locals aren't too thrilled about having a former Yankee soldier in their midst, but it'll blow over, long as I lay low.''

"Hmmmph! Miz Lucy didn't seem to think so.''

"I don't give a damn what Miss Lucy thinks." He shoved the plate of biscuits aside and grabbed the rifle from its post by the door. "I'm going out hunting. If you need anything, ask Rye.''

"Don't go huntin' trouble," she called after him. "Listen to a woman for a change." Her gentle laughter followed him out the door, a reminder of home and Marion, and a lot of other things he'd just as soon forget.

∞

MONDAY MORNING, THE GOSSIPERS were waiting on the front porch of the store when Lucy opened for business. They came ostensibly to buy sewing thread and coffee beans and twists of tobacco, and lingered to rehash the events of late Saturday night and early Sunday morning. From her post behind the counter, she listened with growing unease as the townspeople condemned not Bill Pollard's horrible deed but Trace's Abernathy's character and motives.

"Just what was he up to off in the shadows like that?" Sandra Early paused in her examination of a crate of lemons. "And with Frank Spencer of all people. Everybody knows that young man is nothing but trouble.''

"I heard after the party Twila Pollard found a number of valuable items missing from her home." Patricia Scott frowned at the label on a bottle of Hostetter's Celebrated Stomach Bitters. "I believe Mr. Abernathy smuggled the items outside under his coat and gave them to Frank to spirit away. No doubt they planned to meet back up later and sell the items in another town."

"Well, we all know those Yankees would just as soon steal as look at you." Mrs. Scott squeezed a lemon as if she intended to make lemonade on the spot. "They certainly helped themselves to anything they wanted during the war—and the carpetbaggers in Austin aren't any better."

"Listen to them!" Lucy hissed at her uncle as he walked by with a crate of lamp chimneys. "How can they believe such lies? I'm going out there right now and set them straight."

Nate set the crate aside and put a restraining hand on her shoulder. "I appreciate your righteous indignation, child, but it won't do you or Mr. Abernathy any good for you to go rushing to his defense that way."

"No one else is defending him," she protested.

Nate nodded. "Mr. Abernathy strikes me as an intelligent man. He knew coming here that there were bound to be people who wouldn't approve. I wouldn't be surprised if he didn't run into some of the same kind of thing back in Virginia. It may even be why he decided to make a fresh start out here."

"Just because it happened before doesn't make it right."

"No, it doesn't. But if you go flying out there like a hen defending a chick, you'll start even more rumors about your relationship to Mr. Abernathy. Not to mention you'll make him look like a man who hasn't got the gumption to stand up for himself." He shook his head. "No. If he's decided to keep quiet and let all this blow over, I suggest you do the same." He patted her arm, then shouldered his crate once more and moved on.

She retreated to the end of the counter, where Uncle Nate had built a ledge to hold her account books and inkwell. These days, she kept her quilting hoop there as well. Behind the tall counter, no one could see what she was doing. Most people seemed to think she was busy with bookwork. Uncle Nate welcomed her sudden attention to needlework as a sign that his niece was maturing and settling down. He never seemed to notice that she seldom worked on any one project for very long.

This was the second quilt in her mother's trunk, the broken star pattern in shades of green and blue and brown. She'd added a border all around and basted the top to a layer of combed cotton batting and a backing of unbleached muslin. She paused to admire the neat symmetry of color and shape in the design. Who would have guessed her mother was really such an artist? The thought pleased her, but her pleasure was quickly overwhelmed by a wave of sadness. By the time Lucy had been old enough to know her mother well, all the art and beauty and compassion had been beaten or worn out of her. The unfairness of it all made her throat ache.

She took up her needle once more. No sense fretting over a past that couldn't be changed. Maybe if she focused her attention on the needlework she could block out the ugly words swirling about her.

She started outlining an indigo blue triangle of fabric. Trace's eyes were this color. He had a way of looking at her that stole her breath and made her forget everything around her.

Why had she spoken so crossly to him when they'd parted yesterday? She'd been so upset, she'd forgotten all about her sewing basket and left it behind. They'd been getting along so well before . . . before Theresa Washington arrived. Trace had seemed so glad to see her; he'd even given up his cabin for the woman and her baby.

Her stomach twisted. Did that baby belong to Trace? Is that why the woman had traveled halfway across the country to get to him? Of course, he would have been away fighting the war when the child was conceived, but soldiers sometimes came home on leave, didn't they? Maybe he'd gotten Theresa pregnant then. Maybe Josh was his, too.

Stop it! She put her hands to her head, as if to squeeze out the wicked thoughts that churned through her mind. She was as bad as the town gossips, thinking the worst of a situation she knew little about.

"You shouldn't work so hard if it makes your head hurt, dear."

The teasing words made her smile, even before she put away her work and turned her attention to the man with the long white beard who grinned back at her. "Mr. Gibbs! What brings you into town?"

Sterling Gibbs held up a thick bundle of papers. "Rode in to collect my mail and catch up on the news." He glanced around the crowded store. "Sounds like I missed all the excitement when I decided to skip the Pollards' party Saturday night."

Her smile faded. "Don't believe half of what you hear." She kept her voice low. "Mr. Pollard tried to tar and feather one of his own guests, and you'd think he had every right to do so."

Mr. Gibbs leaned over the counter toward her. "I take it you don't agree with Pollard's opinion of this Mr. Abernathy."

"The only thing that's true is that Mr. Abernathy did fight for the Union during the war. But he's not a Yankee. He's from Virginia. And he didn't try to steal anything from Pollard's house. He's a gentleman."

"Even so-called gentlemen have been known to help themselves to other folks' belongings before. What makes you so sure Abernathy's any different?"

"I just *know*." She felt the heat of a blush crawl up her neck. Mr. Gibbs's amused look only made her blush more furiously. "I'm glad you came in today," she said, anxious to change the subject. "I wanted to ask you a question about my cattle."

"Ah. Back to business." He took a twist of tobacco from his coat and bit off the end. "Ask away."

"I was wondering . . . do you think I ought to buy some land so I'll be sure of having, uh, water rights and such?"

She stumbled over the unfamiliar terms, trying to recall yesterday's conversation with Trace.

Gibbs chewed his tobacco, considering this. "What put this into your head all of a sudden?"

She assumed what she hoped was an innocent look. "Oh, nothing really. I, uh, heard some people talking about all the homesteaders that would probably be moving out this way soon, and how they might try to fence the cattle out of their gardens and such, and the next thing you know, there wouldn't be anywhere to graze the cattle."

He nodded thoughtfully. "I think it'll be a long time before anything like that happens. But I can't see as it would hurt anything for you to have a piece of land. Of course, you're welcome to graze your stock on my place as long as you want." He grinned at her. "But if you're interested, I just happen to have a few acres I could part with."

"You do?"

"Not many people with cash these days, dear. You know that as well as I do. If you can come up with the green-backs, I'll sign over the land."

"I don't have the money now. But I will soon." As soon as she delivered another quilt to Mrs. Sorenson.

He nodded. "When you have the money, come and talk to me again." He gathered up his bundle of mail and tipped his hat. "Good day."

She turned back to her quilting hoop, more determined than ever to finish the coverlet and deliver it to Mrs. Sorenson. Of course, if she was going to have cattle, she ought to have land, too.

By the time she rethreaded her needle and found her place in the quilt, she was already speculating about the kind of house she might build on her property one day when she was wealthy.

She became so engrossed in her work that she lost all track of her surroundings, until she was nudged from her creative trance by the unnatural silence of the room. Looking up, she followed the furtive glances and fearful looks of the other customers to a solitary figure making his way down the aisle between the displays of ladies' shoes and barrels of rope. If anything, Bill Pollard looked older and meaner today as he leaned heavily on his walking cane.

"Better watch that stick, Pollard," a voice called from the back of the store. "It might go off."

Pollard's furious glare stilled the crowd's nervous laughter. "So you think it's funny that a low-down Yankee vermin would pull one over on an honest citizen trying to protect his own, do you?" His voice cut through the silence like a sword through flesh. He stalked to the front of the store and faced the gathered townspeople.

"Which one of you didn't suffer during the war?" he asked. "Which one of you didn't lose money and property? Which one of you didn't have kinfolk and friends killed in the fighting? How many of you, like me, literally gave part of yourselves to the cause?" Lucy had never thought of Pollard as eloquent, but now every person in the room focused on his words. Women dabbed tears from their eyes, and men clenched their jaws in hard lines. Her own throat tightened with fear. Every word Pollard had uttered so far was truth; she waited with growing dread to see how he would bend that truth to serve his own purposes.

"What about now, after the war?" Pollard's voice gained renewed strength, so that even those in the back of the room could not fail to hear him. "Are any of you better off now that the fighting is over? How many of you came home to run-down farms and weed-choked fields? And even if you worked from dawn to dusk, clearing those fields and preparing the soil, you can't sell your cotton for even half of what you got before the war. You can't sell your land, neither—not for what it's worth. You can't hardly give it away for twenty or thirty cents on the dollar."

Murmurs of agreement rose around the room, gaining strength as Pollard spoke. "And yet the Yankees—men like Abernathy—are quick to come in and take advantage of us while we're down. They take over farms and buy up the land for pennies and put their brands on our cattle. Over in

Austin, they put the carpetbaggers and even the darkies to govern over us, and they threaten us with prison if we protest. They take food out of our children's hands and give it to swine.''

Lucy gripped the edge of the counter until her fingers ached. Pollard made it sound as if Trace was personally responsible for falling land and cotton prices. He faced the same hardships they did; the fact that he was willing to get out there and work to better his situation, while some of them were not, wasn't his fault.

''I say it's time we quit waiting for folks in Austin to look after our interests!'' Pollard's battle cry brought applause from the crowd.

''It's time we take back our own—show the damn Yankees we won't stand for their thievin' ways.''

''Amen, brother!'' someone shouted.

Pollard thumped his walking stick on the floor. ''I say we start with Trace Abernathy!''

''Let's run him out of town!'' someone cried.

''Let's lynch him!'' shouted another.

Lucy listened, scarcely believing her ears. People she thought she knew, faces familiar to her all her life, were shouting about killing a man who was their neighbor, a man whose only crime was fighting for the winning side in the war.

Heart in her throat, she started to move out from behind the counter. Someone had to speak in Trace's defense.

But before she could make her way around the counter, Uncle Nate pushed past her. ''Hasn't there been enough killing?'' He silenced the crowd with his accusing stare. Lucy had never thought of her uncle as an imposing man, but anger made him seem three inches taller and twice as powerful. ''Listen to yourselves! Do you really propose to kill a man—your neighbor—when you have no proof he's done anything wrong?''

''He's a Yankee. That's all the proof I need.'' Pollard looked to the crowd for confirmation. Several men nodded in agreement.

"He's a citizen of the United States, and as such he's protected by the law." Nate turned his angry gaze on Pollard. "Do you want to bring half the marshals in Austin down on our heads?"

"Since when am I afraid of a bunch of carpetbaggers and niggers?" Pollard sneered.

"What about God? Are you afraid of His justice?" Nate turned to the crowd once more. "What you're proposing is murder. Trace Abernathy is our neighbor. We're commanded to welcome him into our midst as a Christian brother. Every one of you who would allow this *murder* to take place will have blood on your hands."

Many in the crowd looked away. Lucy watched a few slip out the door. "Mr. O'Connor is right." Patricia Scott spoke up. "We don't have to like Mr. Abernathy—but killing him would be wrong."

"The war's over," Sandra Early said. "We have to accept that and get on with our lives."

"She's right."

"Murder's murder. I won't be a party to that."

With comments such as these, the crowd began to disperse. Soon only Lucy, Nate, and Bill Pollard remained in the store. Nate turned to Pollard. "I've got the only store in town, so I won't impose hardship on you and your family by insisting you take your business elsewhere," he said. "But I won't have you inciting people to break the law or spreading your hate-filled ideas here. Unless you can convince me you've had a true change of heart, you're no longer welcome to linger here." With a curt nod of dismissal, he turned and walked back behind the counter.

Pollard stared after his former friend. Lucy shivered at the hate reflected in his bloodshot eyes. Despite Uncle Nate's efforts to keep the peace, she felt as if shots had been fired here today, the first vollies in a war that threatened those she loved the most.

8

TRACE STARED AT THE scattered posts and timbers, the remains of the corral he and Rye had spent most of yesterday constructing. "Looks like they threw a rope around it and pulled it down with a wagon," Rye said. He pointed to a pair of ruts dug by iron wagon wheels.

Trace squatted down beside the ruts, two slashing scars against the thick green grass. Resentment surged through him, fueled by the memory of all the destruction he'd seen in the last few years. His hand involuntarily went for his pocket and the watch resting there. He rubbed his thumb across the smooth surface and struggled to regain control of his emotions. This is what war taught: to tear down and destroy in the name of protecting home and country and all those solemn virtues men hold dear. And while you were off ripping away at the dreams of others, your own treasures lay defenseless.

"Reckon we'd better get to work." Rye hefted the end of an oak post.

He nodded. Anger at something like this was a waste of energy. Better to put his thoughts to accomplishing something useful. He rose and helped Rye drag the post into position, ignoring the pull of muscles that still ached from yesterday's labors.

"Who do you reckon did this?" Rye asked as they tipped the post into a hole and anchored it with dirt.

"Folks from town." He tamped the dirt in place with his boot and moved to the next post. "Could be anybody. Pollard, maybe." They shoved the second post into a hole alongside the first. "It doesn't matter."

"It does if they keep bustin' up your corrals." Rye took up a third post.

"They'll get tired of harassing me and move on." Trace set the fourth pole in place. Now they were ready to rebuild the first side of the corral. They gathered scattered timbers and slotted them between the posts at either end, each timber atop the one before. The resulting wall of timbers, resting between the sets of posts, was strong enough to hold a raging longhorn bull, and cheaper and faster to build than a single-post fence held together with nails. They lashed the timbers together at intervals with rawhide, which added strength and stability.

"By gum, they won't pull this one down so easy," Rye declared, knotting a strip of rawhide around the top pair of timbers.

"I think I might spend the next few nights out here." Trace hefted another pole. "Just in case they decide to come back."

"Yeah, well, another day or two, and we'll be ready to start roundin' up the cattle anyways." Rye paused to mop the sweat from his brow. "If we work the rest of the summer, come fall we ought to have us a good herd."

"And in the spring, we head up the trail north." Trace steadied the pole with one hand and looked toward the horizon. "The herd that left this spring ought to be in Missouri by now, don't you think?"

Rye shrugged. "Could be. If they didn't run into trouble."

"What kind of trouble?"

"Any kind. Floods. Fire. Maybe a bunch of angry homesteaders who don't want a lot of ornery cows tramping through their fields.''

''You think that could happen here, don't you? Homesteaders fencing out the cattle?''

Rye shoveled dirt around a post. ''The way I figure it, a lot of folks lost pert' near everything in the war—money, land, family. And a good many of those people are gonna want to start over somewheres new.'' He straightened and looked around. ''They could do worse than a place like this. But I know one thing—when they come they'll put an end to free-roaming cattle, one way or another.''

''So the answer is to buy up land before they get here.''

''That's what I'd do, if I had the cash. Land's pretty cheap right now.''

Trace bent to pick up one end of a timber. Rye lifted the other, and together they raised the timber over their heads and dropped it between the paired posts. ''I'm planning on riding over to Sterling Gibbs's place later in the week,'' Trace said. ''He's the biggest property owner in these parts, and his place borders this one on the west. I'm thinking maybe I can persuade him to sell me a quarter section or so.''

''It'd be good insurance, if nothing else.''

Trace wished he could find such easy insurance against the townspeople's animosity. Outwardly he shrugged off petty vandalism and idle threats, but inside he couldn't deny the real hatred at the root of some of these acts. One look into Pollard's bloodshot eyes the other night had convinced him that the embittered Confederate would have shot him if given half a chance. Probably the presence of a crowd, and Lucy's quick thinking, were all that had saved him then. Another time he might not be so lucky.

They worked the rest of the morning, setting posts and fitting timbers, until the corral was almost back together. They were erecting the posts for the gate when a child's laughter broke the stillness. ''I'm comin' to help!'' Josh shouted, racing toward them through the tall grass, jumping and leaping like a puppy.

Theresa, baby on her hip, followed at a slower pace. She carried a cloth-wrapped bundle atop her head. "I brought you men some dinner," she said, stopping in the shade of an oak beside the corral.

"Thank you, Theresa." Trace stripped off his gloves and walked over to where she was spreading out a meal of cold meat and cheese. "You didn't have to walk all this way. You could have sent Josh."

"Well, now, maybe I wanted to get out of the house, have a look around." Her gaze lingered on Rye, who was scrubbing his face and neck with a bandanna soaked in water from his canteen.

Trace fought the smile that tugged at the corners of his mouth. In some ways, Theresa took after her former mistress; she set her sights on a man and went after him like a Ketchum grenade. Heaven help the person who tried to interfere.

"Now, don't this look like a fine feast?" Rye towered over the quilt Theresa had spread in the shade. "I declare, Miz Washington, we like to starved before you come along. Now we eat like kings."

She gave him a long, considering look. "You don't look like a starving man to me, Mr. Booth."

The cowboy lowered himself to the quilt beside her. "I'd be obliged if you'd call me Rye, ma'am."

She added a wedge of cornbread to a plate and handed it to him. "Then you'd better call me Theresa. Miz Washington still don't sound quite natural."

Trace moved a little apart and rested his back against the tree. He ate in silence, letting the muted tones of Rye and Theresa's conversation wash over him. A soft breeze ruffled his hair and dried the sweat on his brow. The breeze smelled of green grass and sun-warmed fields. The stench of war—of sweat and gunpowder and the sickly sweet odor of ether and gangrene from the field hospital—was finally fading from his head, replaced by this clean, renewing scent.

He closed his eyes and dozed, to a dream of riding across

green fields. Marion rode ahead of him, dressed in a habit of wine-colored velvet. He raced to catch up with her, but she rode swifter still, jumping her horse over hedges and fences. She galloped toward a wall, higher than any she'd tried before, and he shouted for her to stop, but she raced on recklessly, and launched the horse toward the wall.

In horror, he watched the horse stumble and Marion go sailing over the wall. By the time he reached her, she lay like the fallen in battle, body twisted in an unnatural angle. He knelt beside her and turned her over gently, then gasped at what he saw. The rider he'd been chasing wasn't Marion—it was Lucy O'Connor.

He jerked awake, still shuddering from the horrifying image of the dream. Theresa stood over him, frowning. "Are you all right?" she asked.

He nodded and struggled to his feet. Fighting for composure, he drew in a deep breath. "Fine. I must have dozed off."

She studied him a moment longer, then looked away. "I'm headed back to the house now. I'll take Josh with me so he won't be in the way."

"Awww, Mama!"

"We're almost finished," Rye said. "Maybe the boy can stay and help."

Josh looked at Rye, wary. "I could be a big help."

Trace nodded. "Let him stay. We'll find something for him to do."

Theresa smiled. "All right. Just bring him home in one piece."

When she was gone, Josh puffed out his chest. "What you want me to do? I could help hang that gate."

"You can gather up the limbs we trimmed and the scrap wood and pile them up to burn," Rye said.

Josh scowled. "That's little chil'ren's work."

Rye walked over to stand in front of him. Josh shrank in his shadow. "You look like a child to me," Rye said.

Still scowling, Josh slumped off to gather scrap. Trace watched him a moment, then turned to Rye. "If you'd give him half a chance, Josh would do anything for you.''

Rye picked up a strip of rawhide and began lashing together timbers for the gate. ''I ain't never been around chil'ren much.''

''If you want to please Theresa, you'll make friends with her boy.''

Rye nodded. ''How long you known Theresa?''

Trace butted two timbers together and joined the ends with rawhide. ''Since I married her mistress. About eight years.''

''Uh-huh. She was a house slave?''

He nodded. ''She took care of Marion's clothes, sewed for the house, things like that.''

''So Josh must have been a small boy when she first come to your house.''

''That's right.'' He sat back on his heels and surveyed the work so far. ''After Marion and I married, we moved into a house her father bought for us. He didn't think his only daughter should have to settle for whatever lodgings a lawyer's son could provide.'' It surprised him to find that the memory still rankled. You'd think after all this time, he'd have gotten over the snub. ''Theresa came with us.''

''And the boy?''

He glanced at Rye, not sure if he should tell the next part. But then, the cowboy had probably already guessed the worst of it. ''Josh didn't live with us—not for the first few weeks. Apparently, while Theresa belonged to Marion alone, Josh was considered part of her father's property. So he stayed behind.'' He leaned forward and began lashing another length of rawhide in place. ''I didn't even know Theresa had a child—I thought she wasn't happy because she'd had to leave Belle Haven—Marion's father's plantation. Theresa had lived there all her life. One day I found her sobbing in the pantry, and she told me she was crying for her baby.''

''You bought the boy back for her.'' Rye's voice was a low rumble like thunder.

He nodded. ''Marion's father couldn't understand why I

was so furious. Later, when I had to choose which side to fight for, I remembered that.'' He looked up and met Rye's solemn gaze. ''I never was a pulpit-pounding abolitionist and I didn't think the North was entirely in the right to take away states' rights. But when everyone was making such a hue and cry about 'preserving the glorious South' I couldn't see what was so glorious about a way of life that allowed children to be torn from their mothers.''

''It takes a lot for a man to go against his family and stand on the courage of his convictions.''

Trace's shoulders sagged. ''That's what I've been trying to tell you—badly. I didn't go to war to fight against slavery. Nobody knew when things started that Lincoln would even free the slaves. I just didn't want to be on the same side as my father-in-law and all his cronies.''

''What I said still stands.'' Rye picked up another timber and fitted it into place. ''So what about Theresa's baby— the little girl? She must have been born just after the war.''

''I reckon.''

''Who's that baby's pa?''

Trace stopped work again and looked the cowboy in the eye. ''If you want to know that, why don't you ask Theresa?''

Rye looked away. ''Maybe I will. Later.''

''Why later? Seems to me you two were getting along fine a few minutes ago.''

''We get along. But a man wants more to offer a woman than getting along. A house slave like Theresa, she be used to finer things. I reckon I better get me a stake before I go to courtin' her serious-like.''

''One thing I know—Theresa's not the type to wait forever. If you want her, you'd better come right out and tell her.''

''I could say the same to you.''

He sat back on his heels once more. ''What do you mean?''

''I mean, if you're interested in a woman, you ought to speak up.''

He looked away. "I'm not interested in any woman."

Rye laughed. "You ain't much of a liar, either."

He knotted another piece of rawhide and kept silent. Rye was right; he wasn't even good at lying to himself. But what he felt and what he knew was best were two different things. If he let himself get involved with Lucy O'Connor, he'd only live to regret it. She took too many chances and in the end she'd get hurt; he didn't want to have to watch that happen.

BUCKBOARD BANDIT STRIKES AGAIN

"This is for all the Yankees who think they can prey on a South caught with its pants down." Thus reads the latest message from the mysterious outlaw authorities have dubbed the "Buckboard Bandit." The bandit, who always leaves the scene of his crimes in a farm wagon, struck again Wednesday evening, this time waylaying an agent of the Freedman's Bureau and relieving him of his cash and his weapon. A passing farmer found the agent the next morning, tied to a tree with his trousers around his ankles. The bandit's note was pinned to the man's chest.

The Buckboard Bandit, described as a man of medium height and build, wears a long coat, slouch hat, and a handkerchief tied over his nose and mouth. He targets agents of the federal government—Yankees and so-called carpetbaggers exclusively. His Robin Hood–like character has captured the imagination of young and old. Authorities speculate many may know the man's identity, but are concealing this information in the spirit of Southern solidarity.

Lucy read the newspaper article with guilty fascination. The idea of a bandit in their midst chilled her, but the thought of a modern-day Robin Hood, taking from the rich to give to the poor, held a dramatic appeal. This Buckboard Bandit—even the name had a novel ring to it—sounded like a character from one of her adventure stories.

"What are you studying there, my girl?" Uncle Nate looked over her shoulder and frowned. "Why is it the newspapers feel compelled to make a hero out of a thief and robber? 'Southern solidarity'—hogwash! Why anyone would want to side with a masked outlaw is beyond me."

She folded the paper. "I suppose some people like the idea of getting back at the Yankees and the government."

Nate's expression remained grave. "This kind of bullying isn't any different from the actions of that mob that tried to tar and feather Trace Abernathy. Who gave this bandit—or anyone else—the right to be judge and jury against people whose only crime is where they were born or which side they fought for during the war?" He shook his head. "The war is over. Men like this bandit are only stirring up trouble."

Lucy bowed her head. Uncle Nate's words made her feel ashamed. Of course this bandit's actions were wrong. What if he chose to attack Trace? She hugged her arms across her body in an attempt to still the sudden shiver that raced through her at the thought.

She hadn't seen Trace since the day after the Pollards' party. He'd kept to his decision to lay low until feelings against him died down. Though she'd agreed this was the sensible thing to do, she'd never anticipated how much she'd miss him. Even though she'd chafed at his constant warnings of dangers and difficulties, no one else would even consider talking with her about raising cattle or writing stories, or anything at all interesting. Trace might rebuke her for her daring behavior—no one else even thought she might *attempt* anything adventurous.

She glanced at the bold headline again, then shoved the paper under the counter. Maybe she *would* write a story about the bandit—only she'd make sure he got exactly the punishment he deserved in the end.

She went to the back of the store and began straightening the sewing goods. A bolt of calico sprigged with pink rosebuds caught her eye. She ran her hand over the crisp fabric.

This would be perfect for the backing of her bridal quilt—the quilt she'd left at Trace's cabin. It seemed as though Trace and that quilt were connected somehow. Ever since she'd met him, she'd found herself thinking of the bridal quilt more, even as she worked to sew the others for Mrs. Sorenson. The other quilts were a way to finance her cattle business. The bridal quilt meant more, somehow, maybe because she couldn't think of it without also thinking of Trace.

She snatched her hand away from the calico and began rewinding a bobbin of lace. Her mother's trunk of quilt pieces and Mrs. Sorenson's willingness to buy had interested her in working on quilts again, including the bridal quilt. Trace had nothing to do with it.

The front door opened, and someone came into the store. "I'll be right there," Lucy called, shoving the bobbin of lace back on the shelf.

The customer didn't wait, but started toward her. She froze, heart in her throat. If a man's footsteps could sound angry, then these did, boot heels striking hard against the wooden floor. Had the Buckboard Bandit decided to pay them a visit?

She glanced over her shoulder. Uncle Nate had disappeared outside somewhere. Fine. Hadn't she always said she could look after herself? Taking a deep breath, she smoothed her skirts, and felt the sewing scissors in the pocket of her apron, where she kept them handy for cutting fabric for customers. Fingers curled around the scissors, she walked to the end of the aisle.

And found herself nose to chest with Trace Abernathy. "I want a word with you," he snapped, eyes dark with anger.

She let out her breath with a rush. "Trace! You startled me. I wasn't expecting you."

"You weren't expecting me to follow up on my plan to buy land from Sterling Gibbs, either, were you?" He loomed over her, crowding her against a pyramid of flour barrels. "What did you do, run to him the next day and tell him not to sell to me?"

She put a hand to her throat, unsure if her heart pounded so furiously from the force of Trace's anger or from the physical closeness of his body. The sandalwood-and-leather scent of him over powered her. The heat of his skin warmed her, and his gaze scorched a path to some secret place inside her. She trembled under that gaze, though not from fear. She clenched her hands at her sides to keep from reaching out to pull him close, to feel the silk of his hair beneath her fingers and the press of his lips against her own.

"You won't even deny it, will you?"

She blinked, fighting through the rush of sensation that almost overwhelmed her. "Deny what?"

"Deny that you deliberately set out to cheat me."

She straightened, anger bringing her to her senses like a stinging slap. "I never did any such thing. How dare you storm in here to accuse me!"

He stepped back and crossed his arms over his chest, as if to hold himself back from a more forceful response. "I rode over to see Sterling Gibbs this morning about buying some of his land that borders my place. He told me he couldn't sell it to me because he'd already promised it to you."

She nodded. "That's right. I told him I'd pay him as soon as . . . as I'm able."

"Then you *do* admit it!" He uncrossed his arms, fists at his sides. "I didn't want to believe it. How could you?"

"How could I what? You never said you wanted Mr. Gibbs's land—just that you wanted *more* land."

"Who else did you think I meant to buy from? Gibbs has the only big place bordering mine."

"For all I knew, you could have meant you wanted land in another *state*." She shoved past him toward the front of the store, her pleasure at seeing him erased by his ridiculous accusations. Why, she had practically saved his life that night at the Pollards', and this was the thanks she got.

"Why else did you rush to buy land from Gibbs almost

immediately after I told you of my plans?'' he said, following her.

Reaching the front counter, she whirled to confront him once more. ''You're always so free with your advice, Mr. Abernathy. One would think you'd rejoice to know that I finally heeded your words. After all, *you* were the one going on about the benefits of owning cattle *and* land to graze them on. Or does that only apply to *male* cattle raisers?''

He scowled. ''I wasn't giving you advice that day. I was only telling you my plans. I never thought about whether or not you should own land, too.''

''Exactly!'' She threw up her hands. ''Raising cattle is unsuitable for a woman, so you just put it out of your mind.'' Oh, that wound cut deep—the knowledge that Trace Abernathy held no more respect for her abilities than any other man.

His eyes raked her with a look that left her trembling. ''I've said before—and I still believe—that you're a very capable young woman. But just how do you propose to handle the herding and branding and other work required to care for a herd? I expect Rye and I will be pressed to do it all.''

She raised her chin. ''I've thought of that, of course. As soon as I'm able, I plan to hire help.''

''Then you'll lose half your profits to pay wages.''

''I suppose you have a better idea?''

He hesitated, then nodded. ''I do.'' He folded his arms across his chest and stared at the floor a long moment. ''I propose we make a deal,'' he finally said.

She eyed him warily. ''What kind of deal?''

''Turn your herd in with mine.'' He looked up. ''Rye and I will brand them with your mark and drive them to market next spring.''

Her stomach twisted with apprehension. ''And what do I have to do for you in return?''

''Give up your claim to Gibbs's land. Use your money to buy another place somewhere else if you like. Let me have that section bordering the property I already own.''

He was right, but that admission galled. With cash in hand, she'd have little trouble finding other land to buy. And she'd have more of that cash come next summer if she didn't have to pay wages to hired help. Still, she felt as if she'd swallowed a stone. The fact that his proposal was both reasonable and mutually beneficial did nothing to lessen her dismay at having been bested. "You came here today planning to make that proposal, knowing I'd have no choice but to agree," she said, hiding none of her bitterness. "Now you can go home and gloat about how you got the better of me."

"Don't suppose you can know my thoughts, Miss O'Connor, especially where they concern you." To her astonishment, he closed the gap between them and took her chin in his hand. "If you could truly read my mind, you would know that I find you one of the most aggravating, perplexing, *intriguing* women I've ever encountered."

A rush of emotion shuddered through her as his lips covered hers. Almost of their own volition, her arms slipped around his neck. As her mind gave up its last feeble resistance, her body sought his, reveling in the hard strength of him crushed against her. How could she both detest and desire one man so?

His caresses both soothed and inflamed her, teaching her of an acceptance without qualifiers, and of an all-demanding passion. Even as she reveled in the gentle pressure of his lips on hers, she feared she might lose herself completely under the onslaught of his stroking hands. He traced the line of her backbone and the curve of her hip, his fingers finally coming to rest against the side of her chest, shaping themselves to the fullness of her breasts. She felt wanton and daring and more alive than she had since she'd crossed that raging creek as a child. If only she could navigate these shoals so well.

"Oh, my!"

The gasp that broke the afternoon stillness sounded loud as a gunshot. Lucy froze, suddenly aware of her surroundings. Her face burned as she realized she was standing at the front of the store, in a very unladylike embrace with a man she still could not declare fully as friend or foe—in full view of whoever had just walked in the door!

9

WRENCHING AWAY FROM TRACE, Lucy straightened her clothes and smoothed her hair, not daring yet to raise her eyes to see whoever had intruded upon the scene. The gasp bespoke a woman. If it was someone like Mrs. Early or Mrs. Scott, she might as well start packing her bags right now to leave town.

"Hello, Mrs. Pollard. You're looking very lovely today." Trace sounded as calm as a man greeting an acquaintance after Sunday church. He picked up his hat from the counter where he'd dropped it and nodded to Lucy. She could feel the heat of that look down to the base of her spine and quickly turned away from it. "Good day, ladies," he said, and left the store, taking all of her energy with him.

She forced herself to turn around.

The bruise along the side of Twila's face had faded to a faint yellow, which a new arrangement of curls and a wide-brimmed bonnet all but concealed. But no coiffure or hat could hide the weariness reflected in her eyes. "Good morning, Twila," Lucy said. "It's good to see you again."

She meant the words; Twila had been her closest friend for many years. After their conversation the morning after the party, she wasn't so sure. This was the first time they'd even seen each other since that awful day.

"It's good to see you, too." Twila glanced over her shoulder, at the closed door through which Trace had just passed. "Things seem to be going well with you and Mr. Abernathy."

Lucy's cheeks burned. How much had Twila actually seen from her position just inside the door? "Trace was just, uh, congratulating me," she stammered. "We've agreed to become, uh, business partners."

Twila raised one eyebrow. "I don't think I've ever seen a business agreement settled so *enthusiastically.*"

Her heart sank. "It's not what you think," she protested.

"I don't think anything. It's not my place to judge." She reached out and clasped Lucy's arm. "I want to be happy for you. If Trace Abernathy is the man for you, that's all that matters to me."

"Believe me, there's *nothing* between us." She eased her arm from Twila's grasp and turned away. Even as she spoke the words, her conscience nagged her. How could she kiss a man that way and declare it meant nothing? Trace had touched more than her body with his caress. Her heart still pounded with the fear of a rabbit who feels the snare drawing closed. It was all she could do to keep from running away before he captured her completely.

She pushed away such foolish thoughts and turned her attention to Twila. "Come in. What can I do for you?"

Twila followed her toward the back of the store. "I need a spool of black thread, a pound of coffee, a pound of sugar, and a can of baking powder." She consulted the list in her hand. "Oh, and some dried peaches, if you have them."

Lucy hoped the surprise she felt didn't show on her face. She didn't want to hurt Twila's feelings by saying anything, but baking powder and peaches were luxuries Twila had not been able to afford for some time, and until now her habit had been to buy only small quantities of sugar and coffee. She was even more astonished when Twila laid a gold coin on the counter to pay for the purchases.

"Mr. Pollard has found new work, hauling produce and such for several businesses in Birdtown," Twila said softly.

"That is good news." She dropped the coin into the cash box and began counting out Twila's change. Perhaps gainful employment and regular wages would ease Pollard's temper and improve Twila's situation. "I suppose that's why you're doing the shopping today, if he's at work."

Twila looked away. "He doesn't know I'm here. But, yes, he's working. He often leaves very early in the morning and comes home late at night. I worry the strain will be too much for him, but he seems to thrive on the activity."

Lucy thought having Pollard around less often would be a blessing to her friend, but she held her tongue.

"I was thinking, with Mr. Pollard away all day, I have plenty of time on my hands," Twila continued. "Perhaps you could bring your bridal quilt, and I'll help you finish it." She smiled. "Seems to me you might be needing it soon."

Lucy stifled a groan. "I am *not* going to marry Trace Abernathy!" she snapped. "He and Rye are just going to look after my cattle and drive them to market in the spring."

Twila looked doubtful. "And you think he's offering to do all that hard work just because he's so generous?"

"In exchange, I agreed to give up my claim to some land Mr. Gibbs has that Trace wants to buy."

Twila chuckled. "Some men court with flowers and candy—looks like Mr. Abernathy figures the way to your heart is with spurs and a lasso." She shrugged. "Besides, he probably sees it as a good chance to look after his own— if he marries you, those cattle will be his."

"They will not!" Lucy crossed her arms under her breasts in an effort to contain her agitation. "Those cattle are mine, and if Trace Abernathy thinks he's going to get his hands on them—or *me*—by making me beholden to him, he's got another think coming."

Twila's expression sobered. "Oh, Lucy. What's a few

head of cattle compared to the chance for a husband and family? Do you know how many women would give everything they own to be in your position, to have the attention of a handsome gentleman like Trace Abernathy?''

''Well, they can give all they want. I for one will never trade my independence for a wedding ring.''

''Those cattle won't keep you warm at night.'' Twila blushed, but continued. ''And they won't look after you in your old age.''

''No. I plan to be able to look after myself, thank you very much.'' She handed Twila her purchases. ''Don't feel sorry for me, Twila. I know exactly the kind of future I want, and Trace Abernathy isn't part of my plan.''

''What if you're part of *his* plan?''

''He'll have to change his mind—about my cattle and about me.'' A shiver raced down her spine as she said the words. It was one thing for her to speak so boldly here alone with Twila. Would she be able to remember her convictions when she was standing close enough for Trace to reach out and gather her into his strong arms? Or would his kisses erase her willpower and coax her to surrender?

∞

TRACE LASSOED HIS FIRST cow when the sun was scarcely over the horizon. At Rye's direction, he slipped behind the just-risen animal and dropped his loop of rope over the massive horns. Then, with the cow's bellows heralding sunrise, he dragged the animal to the newly built corral. Josh held the gate open wide, then slammed it shut as the cow ran past, whooping with glee at their first catch.

Trace savored the small triumph. ''Don't look so smug.'' Rye rode up beside him. ''You got lucky that time, but in this business, luck don't last.''

Their plan was to rope all morning and brand all afternoon, emptying the corral as they worked to start all over the next day. In a few weeks they'd move to another part of the ranch, build another corral and start again. In this way they hoped to amass a sizable herd before next spring.

Despite Rye's predictions, their luck held, at least for the morning. The cattle in this area hadn't been worked much since before the war, and every clump of trees seemed to shelter half a dozen or more rangy bulls or cows and shaggy calves. Though they lost half as many as they captured, between them Trace, Rye, and Josh managed to fill the pen by dinnertime. Rye was by far the best roper, but Trace and even Josh became adept at driving the cattle toward the corral, where Rye could help harry them into the pen.

Theresa arrived at noon with a kettle of beans and bacon for their dinner. Rye made a fire to reheat the meal and readied the branding irons. He had made the irons himself, simple bars of metal that could be used to write their chosen brands across the cowhide—a broken-arrow mark for himself and the Circle A for Trace. They'd also be marking out, or venting, Hiram Fischer's "fish" brand and branding those animals with the Circle A to show the change in ownership.

Trace watched the new irons smoke in the fire, and excitement gripped him. This was the start, the beginning of his climb back up in the world.

"Reckon we better get on with it." Rye slapped his gloves against his thigh, then pulled them on. "Much obliged for the dinner, Theresa. If you want to leave the kettle, I'll bring it on back to the house later."

She reached back and tied her apron more securely. "I wasn't planning on leaving. The baby'll be all right in the shade. Thought maybe I'd better stay and help."

Rye glanced at Trace. "What do you think? She could look after the irons."

Trace nodded. "All right. Do you have a pair of gloves?"

She picked up the piece of sacking she'd wrapped the kettle in. "I'll use this. Go on, now," She shooed him away. "I'll be all right."

Rye swung up into the saddle. "You ready, boy?" he asked Josh.

Josh puffed out his thin chest. "I'm ready." He ran to take up his post by the corral gate.

Trace hefted a metal prod in his hand and climbed up and straddled the corral fence. The plan was for Trace to pick out an animal, then drive it toward the gate. Josh would open it wide enough to let the cow through, and Rye would snag it with his rope as it ran past him and drag it to the fire to be branded. The calves wouldn't present too much of a problem, but some of these three- and four- and five-year-old mavericks easily weighed a ton. They were worth a lot to the man who could burn his mark on them, but one mistake and he might have a very short career as a cattleman.

At a signal from Rye, Trace dropped into the pen, into the milling mass of long-horned, sharp-hoofed beasts who couldn't by any stretch of the imagination be called tame. He found himself nose to nose with a flat-faced red cow with horns five feet across. He could smell the dust and sweat of her hide, see every scratch and scrape on those horns. Any one of these animals could run a man through quicker than a West Point sword, but that didn't bear thinking about right now. He squared his shoulders and shoved past the cow. A white-faced calf stood by her side, its high-pitched complaint adding to the moaning and lowing that reverberated around him.

He selected his first "victim," a midsized heifer with a mottled hide the color of caliche. With an occasional assist from the prod, he began driving the animal toward the gate, remembering Rye's advice to take things nice and easy. When they reached the gate, he leaned over and tapped on the wood three times with the prod. The gate swung open, and he swatted the cow's rump, sending her rushing out of the pen. He followed on her heels, blocking a half dozen would-be escapees in the process.

Rye already had his rope around the animal's back heels. With a sharp tug, she toppled forward. Trace slammed his body down on her in a wrestling hold. Dodging the slashing horns, he forced the animal's shoulders to the ground.

Rye leaped from the saddle to hog-tie the cow, one front leg bound securely to the back two. The animal's bellowing shook the air, but it ceased its struggle. Trace pulled out his pocketknife and nicked a deep notch in each ear. Rye grabbed a hot iron from Theresa and sketched Trace's Circle A brand into the cow's side. The stench of singed hair and hide filled the air. In this rush of sights, sounds, and smells, they staked their claim to the first of their herd.

Trace jumped out of the way just as Rye cut the piggin' string from the cow's feet. She scrambled up and trotted toward the shade of a tree about twenty yards away, where she stood watching them, a wary look in her eye.

"It's a good thing I showed up when I did."

Trace looked up and saw Lucy riding toward them. Her smile did funny things to his insides—not altogether unpleasant things. He walked forward to welcome her, thinking all the while that he might as well have welcomed a hanging party, or a bad case of swamp fever. Lucy O'Connor was at least as dangerous as those things. He'd been telling himself so ever since he'd lost his head the other day in her uncle's store and kissed her.

But then, he'd had plenty of experience tempting danger, hadn't he? It was becoming a bad habit, almost second nature by now, especially where Lucy was concerned.

"Looks like you could use some help," she said, sliding off her horse in front of him. She was dressed in almost military fashion, in a brass-buttoned jacket and man's flat-crowned, broad-brimmed hat, leather gauntlets, and brown leather boots. Despite its masculine styling, or perhaps because of it, the outfit made her look more feminine than ever.

He clenched his fists at his sides in an effort to keep from reaching out to touch her. He hadn't been able to put the feel of her, the scent of her—the taste of her—out of his mind, and here she was to remind him all over again of all the trouble he could so easily get himself into. "I think we're getting along just fine," he said.

She put her hands on her hips and grinned. "Were you branding that cow or wrestling it?"

Behind them, back at the fire, Theresa laughed. "I was thinkin' the same thing myself," she said, chuckling.

Rye rode toward them. "It ain't the most elegant operation I ever seen, but it gets the job done," he said.

Lucy tugged on her gauntlets. "Well, I'm sure another hand would be useful. What would you like me to do?"

Trace gaped at her. Obviously he wasn't hearing right. "Do?"

"I've come to help." She looked past him, toward the fire. "I'm sure I could handle the branding irons."

"Absolutely not. Those full skirts of yours could drag in the fire."

She stiffened and took another look around the clearing. "All right, then. I can handle the gate. Or I can drive the cows out for you."

"Are you crazy?" He grabbed her shoulder, forcing her to look at him. "You just saw how it took two grown men to barely control one cow—you'd be trampled into dust in no time."

She gave him a frosty glare. "Despite what you may think, I'm not an idiot. If Theresa and Josh can help, then so can I."

"She's got a point there," Rye said.

"You stay out of this," Trace snapped. He met her gaze with a stern look of his own. "Just what made you think you needed to ride out here and help us in the first place?"

She folded her arms across her chest. "You've agreed to look after my cattle—to allow them to graze on your land and to drive them to market next spring. It seems only right that I should do my part to help out."

"You already did your part—you gave up your claim to Sterling Gibbs's land."

"That one concession hardly seems a fair trade for all the work you're doing." She wrapped her horse's reins around her wrist. "Especially since I just doubled the size of my herd."

He stared at her, wary. "How did you do that?"

She brushed an invisible speck of lint from her shoulder, a very self-satisfied smile curving her lips. "I convinced Mr. Gibbs to sell me another ten steers."

"Writing pays that well, does it?" He couldn't keep the sarcasm from his voice.

She flushed in the aggravatingly pretty way she had. "Not exactly. I, well, I made a bargain with him."

"What sort of bargain?"

"I pay nothing for the cattle now, but after they're sold next year, Mr. Gibbs gets half." She glanced at him. "If I get a good price, we both come out ahead."

"And if you don't?"

She shrugged. "We'll get a good price. I'm sure of it. That is, if you're still willing to go through with our bargain."

He stared at her. She looked so calm, while he grew more exasperated by the minute. "I agreed to the bargain," he said stiffly. "I'm a man of my word, despite whatever else you might think."

"Still, I think it's best if I pitch in to do my part." She raised her chin, silently daring him to disagree.

"Boss, could I have a word with you a moment, private-like?" Rye called.

Trace whirled and stalked over to where Rye waited beneath a tree, out of earshot of Lucy. "Don't tell me you're on her side in this," he barked.

Rye looked thoughtful. "You ever heard the sayin' 'many hands make light work'? What's the harm in lettin' her pitch in if she's willing?"

"This is dangerous work. Don't you think we've got enough to do today without worrying about her getting hurt?"

Rye shrugged. "You could get your teeth kicked in by the next big heifer through that gate, or Josh could get stomped by a bull, or some cow on a tear might decide to gore my horse. The whole world's full of danger, and we can't always protect ourselves, much less anybody else."

"But she's a woman. It would be much more dangerous for her."

"I didn't hear you objectin' when Theresa offered to help."

Trace avoided his eyes. "It's different for Lucy. She's not used to hard work."

"You sure about that?" Rye rubbed his chin thoughtfully. "Not meanin' to be disrespectful, but I guess I just don't see it that way." He ran his thumb along the coiled rope in his hand. "The slave women work right alongside the slave men every day, so I guess I got used to thinking a woman could pull her own weight." He glanced at Lucy. "Besides, might be after she sees how rough the work is, she'll quit on her own. I'd say it's more likely that'll happen than you'll ever convince her to give up on your say-so."

Trace watched Lucy hobble her horse in the shade. The stubborn set of her shoulders was achingly familiar. Rye was right; he'd never beat that kind of conviction with words alone. He turned toward her once more.

"Take over the gate," he ordered. "Josh, you keep the irons hot and the piggin' strings handy. Theresa can notch ears." He handed his knife to the black woman. "Let's go. We've wasted enough time talking."

Lucy walked by him without a word, but he caught a hint of her soft fragrance as she passed. Somehow that soft odor cut through the harsher scents around him with an unexpected strength, like the woman who wore it.

∽

LUCY MANNED THE GATE for an hour, swinging it open at Trace's tapped command, rushing it closed behind him. It was easy, monotonous work. Trace probably hoped she'd be bored into quitting.

She watched him wrestle another calf to the ground. The muscles of his shoulders and back strained against his sweat-soaked shirt. One sleeve had been half torn off by

an angry cow. She doubted anything in his lawyer's training had prepared him for this kind of physical labor, yet
he never balked or complained about the work.

Rye used the branding iron like a pen to write his mark
across the animal's side—his broken-arrow brand this time.
While he worked, Theresa struggled to gouge the notches
in the calf's ears, her hands dripping with blood. No telling
how many times she'd cut herself in the process. At least
Rye had taken over gelding the bull calves, working with
amazing swiftness.

They released the calf and started for their places for the
next round. As Trace moved past Lucy, she saw he was
limping. "What's wrong with your leg?" she asked. "Did
that calf hurt you?"

He shook his head, a tightness to his expression as he
tried, and failed, to hide his pain. "It's an old wound, acts
up every once in a while." He pulled himself up and over
the wall one more time.

She bit back a caustic remark on the irony of being over-
ly concerned for others while failing to look after oneself.
Here they all were working themselves half to death, and
she was standing here unscathed and practically uninvol-
ved.

She leaned against the gate, watching Theresa, who had
sagged to the ground and looked as if she'd gladly never
get up. Suddenly she knew exactly what she had to do.

She hurried to the black woman's side. "You take my
place at the gate while I spell you here," she said, easing
the knife from Theresa's grasp.

Theresa's eyes widened. "I don't think Mr. Trace would
like that."

"Maybe not, but I won't let that stop me from doing
what's right."

To her surprise, Theresa grinned. She rose and wiped her
hands on her apron. "Yessiree, Mr. Trace has done met his
match this time." Still smiling, she hurried to the gate.

Lucy had little time to puzzle over Theresa's comment.
She had barely fitted the knife to her hand before the gate

burst open and the biggest bull she'd ever seen came charging straight toward her, Rye and Trace in pursuit, ropes swinging.

Rye lassoed the bull around the neck, but the bull paid no more attention than if he'd been stung by a gnat. Head down, bellowing like a freight train, he stormed toward Lucy. She was dimly aware of Theresa's high-pitched wailing and Josh's excited shouts, but her own voice was silenced, screams clogging her throat.

Trace's rope caught the bull around the heels. The animal stumbled, then righted itself and kept coming, dragging the man behind it. "Run, Lucy!" he shouted.

His shout pulled her from her trance. She turned to flee, almost falling into the fire in her haste. The sight of the glowing coals sent a flash of inspiration through her mind. Snatching up one of the branding irons in one gloved hand, she wrapped its end in the burlap Josh had used to handle the heated irons. She worked quickly, ignoring the shouts of those around her and the pounding in her heart, which sounded to her ears almost as loud as the thundering hoofbeats of the approaching bull.

She plunged the iron into the fire and the burlap-wrapped end burst into flames. Brandishing this torch, she whirled to face the bull once more. It was close enough now for the flames to singe its nose.

With an enraged moan, the bull slowed, then stumbled as Rye hauled back on his rope. Theresa rushed forward to help Trace pull his end taut as well. Suddenly the clearing was silent, the bull stretched out beside the fire. On shaking legs, Lucy stepped forward and, knocking the last of the burning burlap away from the iron, inscribed Trace's Circle A on the animal's hide.

Trace was the first to break the silence. "What in the devil did you think you were doing?"

"Looks to me like she done branded your bull." Rye swung down off his horse and walked to the animal's head. "You done a good job there, Miss Lucy," he said as he knelt to notch the ears.

She dropped the iron and turned away, still shaking, fearful of embarrassing herself by either bursting into tears or throwing up. Trace's hand on her shoulder stopped her. She tensed. By heaven, she was tired of defending herself to him. "I wasn't hurt, all right?" she snapped, not bothering to look at him. It pained her too much to see those warm blue eyes turned cold to her. "I told you I could take care of myself and I did. I won't let you put me in some nice safe place out of the way. I came here today to help, and that's exactly what I intend to do."

"I wish I'd had a few like you beside me in battle."

He gripped her harder, almost hurting her, but his words shook her more. She raised her eyes to meet his gaze and saw not anger but . . . was that pride? "I don't know many men who would have been that brave and quick-thinking."

She opened her mouth to speak, but no words came. All she could do was stare at him in amazement as he handed her his knife. "Better get back to work."

∽

TRACE WALKED BACK TO the corral on legs that felt no sturdier than corn stalks. He'd cursed the bull six ways to Sunday when it dragged him down, then vowed to make it the guest of honor and main course at the biggest barbecue the county had ever seen. But his curses had faded away, and his heart had stopped beating when he looked up and saw the beast headed straight for Lucy.

One minute he'd been sure she'd be trampled to dust—the next she'd been brandishing that torch as if she didn't know the meaning of fear. Even Marion hadn't had that kind of sheer nerve in her. His wife had flouted convention for the sake of gaining attention or for the pleasure of having her own way, but obstinacy like that wasn't a substitute for courage.

He could admire Lucy's bravery, but he couldn't forget that battlefields were strewn with the bodies of brave men who'd had more courage than sense.

They finished up the last calf in gray twilight, then gathered around the dying fire, so weary they could hardly stand. Trace's leg felt as if someone had stabbed him in the thigh with a knife and left it there. He'd stopped even trying to hide his limp. The women had worked all afternoon without complaint, trading off between the fire and the gate, Theresa stopping from time to time to tend to the baby. They looked done in. Trace walked Lucy to her horse and boosted her into the saddle. Her hands lingered on his shoulder. He thought how easy it would be to hold her close and lose some of his weariness in her kisses.

Propriety and his own better judgment held him back. "You're too tired to ride home in the dark," he said, stepping away from her. "Stay the night in the cabin with Theresa."

For once, she didn't argue. "Thank you. I think I'll do that."

They rode home in silence, Theresa and the baby riding behind Rye, Josh on Trace's horse with him. The boy fell asleep before they were out of sight of the corral. Trace held him against his chest and thought of those early days when he'd first left Virginia. He'd grown to welcome Josh's company on that lonely trip. Now it seemed his "family" was growing almost daily, with Rye and now Theresa added in. And Lucy. He looked ahead to where she rode, head down, her slight shoulders bent with weariness. Where was her place in all this? More than friend, less than lover, she valued her freedom above all else. And he valued his peace, a peace she was sure to disrupt.

They ate a cold supper together in the cabin, then Trace and Rye retired to the barn. Josh woke up enough to beg to go with them, and Theresa relented. The boy scampered into the loft and made his bed there, while Trace and Rye spread their blankets in the stall at the end. Trace fell asleep almost immediately, a deep sleep disturbed by sounds of running feet and shouting voices.

∞

"COME ON, WAKE UP!" Trace opened his eyes to darkness lit by wavery orange light. Rye shook him roughly. "Fire!" Rye shouted, tossing his boots to him. He grabbed up their blankets and plunged them in the horse's water trough. "Barn's on fire!"

10

SMOKE ROLLED IN WHITE clouds from burning hay-stacks, stinging Trace's eyes and obscuring his vision. He yanked on his boots, grabbed up his hat, and raced to help Rye free the horses. The frightened animals reared back as the men reached for their halters, shod hooves slashing the air. Shimmering heat made breathing difficult. Orange flames licked the dried-out walls, popping and crackling as they caught and spread.

Trace whipped off his shirt and fastened it around his saddle horse's head. Thus blinded, the animal ceased its struggling and allowed Trace to lead it through the smoke and flying ash to the yard, where he turned it loose.

He turned back toward the barn just as Lucy and Theresa came running from the house. "Is that all the horses?" Lucy shouted over the roar of the blaze.

He shook his head and started forward again. She rushed past him, shrugging off his efforts to restrain her. Before he could stop her, she'd plunged through the wall of smoke. "Come back here!" he shouted and raced in after her.

The air was like a heavy blanket, hot and too thick to breathe. He opened his mouth to take a breath and tasted smoke, bitter on his tongue. Clouds of ash made tears run down his face. He squinted, searching for Lucy in the chaos.

A figure stumbled past him—Rye, a bandanna tied over his nose and mouth, led his horse and Theresa's mule to safety.

Trace plunged farther into the inferno. Sparks stung his bare arms and chest, and heat made the hair on his arms shrivel. He shielded his eyes with one hand and tried to make out something—anything—in the dimness. "Lucy!" he shouted in a harsh, scratchy voice that didn't sound like his own.

No answer. He stumbled forward, fear like a belt tightened around his chest. She was in there somewhere. Like a fool, he'd let her run right past him. He should have known she'd pull a stunt like this. He should have stopped her.

By God, he wouldn't have another woman's blood on his hands. "Lucy!" He bellowed his rage and anguish into the smoke.

A shadow danced across his blurred vision. He blinked, and the shadow became the figure of a woman, bent at the waist, struggling with something.

He rushed forward, almost colliding with her in his haste. Lucy clung to the gelding's bridle with one hand. With the other she frantically beat at the flames licking at the hem of her skirt.

Trace joined her in trying to brush away the flames, but the lightweight fabric caught anew with every flying spark. Behind her, the horse whinnied and fought her hold. Trace grabbed the bridle and brought the animal under control. "Take it off!" he shouted as he watched her continue to battle with the singed skirt.

She looked up at him, face pale as milk in the firelight, eyes wide with fear.

"Take off your skirt!" He grabbed a handful of the smoldering fabric. "Dammit, take it off before I tear it off!"

Galvanized into action, she unbuttoned the skirt at the

side and stepped out of it, revealing the bottom half of a long nightgown beneath. "Let's go!" He grabbed her arm and held on tightly. She wouldn't get away from him this time. The horse in one hand and Lucy in the other, he bent his head and barged through the wall of smoke, gritting his teeth against the searing heat. The horse reared and bucked, threatening to tear his arm from its socket, but he held firm, to it and to the woman.

They burst through thick smoke into fresh air and gray dawn. He turned the horse loose, but kept hold of the woman, fearful she might go in after the remaining animal. They clung together, sucking in great lungfuls of fresh air, letting it flow into burning lungs like a cooling salve.

He was dimly aware of Rye, beating the ground around the barn with wet blankets, smothering sparks before they could spread to the house and beyond. He struggled to rouse himself to help the cowboy.

"Josh! Oh, my God, where's Josh?" Theresa's cry rose above the roar of the fire, jolting him from his stupor. "My boy! I thought he was with you!" She stared at Trace, hope and fear mingled in her expression.

He looked to Rye. The cowboy shook his head. Then he turned to Lucy. Her hair had loosened from its braid, and soot smudged one cheek. She looked young and vulnerable and sweeter than any woman had a right to look. He felt his anger slipping away like quicksilver in his hands. "Stay with Theresa. Please?"

She nodded, and he released her. Before fear or his own good sense could stop him, he fought his way back into the burning building.

Nothing looked familiar in the smoke-shrouded darkness. Already one side of the building, the side with the horse stalls, was near collapse. Josh had been asleep in the loft, on the other side of the building. The ladder was all the way back on the left. To reach the boy, he'd have to find the ladder.

Narrowing his eyes to slits, he struggled to walk a straight line toward the back of the barn. Flames erupted at his feet as the loose straw they'd used as bedding for the stalls caught fire. The ground grew hot enough to scorch the soles of his boots. He gritted his teeth and walked on, counting steps. Ten, twenty, thirty—the ladder should be about here, on his left.

He swung his arm out, groping in the darkness. His hand scraped against rough wood. He grabbed on to the ladder and shook it, testing its soundness. When it held, he began hauling himself upward.

The heat was more intense here, the smoke was thicker, stealing his breath. He tried to call out for Josh, but the words emerged as only a feeble croak. On hands and knees, he crawled across the floor of the loft, pausing every few feet to sweep the area around him with his hands. If he didn't find the boy soon, he'd have to turn back. His lungs burned, and he was already feeling dizzy.

A glowing line marked the back wall of the barn—flames climbing upward toward the loft. He tried to judge how much more time he had before the whole building collapsed—not long enough.

Panic squeezing his chest, he looked around the loft. Nothing looked familiar. None of the shadowy shapes resembled a sleeping boy.

Feeling sick, he began the slow crawl back toward the ladder. He was trusting instinct to find it. If not, he'd have to risk dropping to the ground. Whatever it took, he had to get out of here soon, before strength and breath gave out altogether.

His hand struck something soft, yet solid. He squeezed and was rewarded with a muffled cry. Josh—alive, though unconscious. He gathered the boy under the arms and dragged him to the edge of the loft. One hand gripping the edge, he inched along until he came to the ladder. Not much time left. He hefted the boy onto his shoulders and half climbed, half slid to the ground.

His legs moved as if they were encased in sand. His lungs felt as if he'd breathed in live coals. He couldn't see for the tears streaming down his face. *Count. Just count the steps to the door.* "One . . . two . . . three . . ." His voice was scarcely more than a whisper, but he made himself keep going. Ten . . . twenty . . . thirty steps. And then he was falling forward, into cool darkness.

∽

LUCY CRADLED TRACE'S HEAD in her lap. With shaking hands, she wiped the soot from his face with a rag dipped in lime water. He lay so still, his skin so pale. What if he never woke up? She bit her lip, forcing the thought from her mind. Trace would wake up. He had to.

When he'd stumbled out of the barn and collapsed at her feet, she hadn't been able to hold back the grief-stricken wail that tore from her throat. The thought that this strong man she'd grown to admire might be dead made her shake with fear. The knowledge that she cared so much made her tremble further.

She swept her damp rag across his shoulders, caressing the well-defined muscles. A shiver ran through her, and she held her breath, allowing her fingers to feather over his skin, down his chest, the hair crisp beneath her fingertips. She remembered how he'd looked the first night she saw him, drops of water in these curls, glistening in the lamplight.

"I made a poultice for that burn on his arm, and asafetida to try to bring him round."

Theresa's words startled her from her guilty pleasure. She snatched her hand away from Trace and looked up at the black woman. "How's Josh?"

"Scared. Hurtin'." Theresa smiled, a look of pure relief. "Thank God he's alive. And blessed with a strong constitution. He wouldn't be here now if it weren't for Trace. I left him inside to watch the baby—promised him homemade gingerbread after supper." She squatted down and laid the poultice across the blistered skin on Trace's arm, then glanced at Lucy. "Don't you worry, I ain't about to let this one sicken."

Lucy put her hands behind her back. "Why would I be worried?"

Theresa gave her a knowing look and waved the foul-smelling lump of asafetida under Trace's nose. He groaned and struggled to push her hand away. "That's more like it," she said and slipped one arm under his shoulder to help him sit.

"Maybe we should let him lie down for a while," Lucy said.

Theresa shook her head. "Got to get him up, moving around, to get the smoke up out of his lungs."

"Don't talk about me like I'm not right here," Trace rasped, then subsided into a fit of coughing.

Theresa pounded his back. "That's it. Cough it all up. I'll make you a chest plaster later to ease the ache."

"I'm all right." He pushed her away. "How's Josh?"

"He's gonna be fine." Her eyes sparkled with tears. "Thank you for savin' him."

Trace looked away. "Go on. Look after the boy. I can see to myself."

Theresa hesitated, then backed away. "All right. I'll be in the house if you need anything."

Trace waited until she was gone, then peeled back the poultice on his arm, wincing as he did so. He saw Lucy watching him and gave her a rueful look. "I suppose that's going to hurt like hell by tomorrow."

She wanted to offer some word of comfort, some praise of his heroism. Instead, what came out of her mouth was, "You're lucky you weren't burnt to a crisp."

He quirked up one corner of his mouth in a half grin. "You would have been if I hadn't gotten you out of that fool skirt." His gaze fell to her nightgown-covered thighs. "Too bad I didn't think of it sooner."

She knew her face must be bright red with embarrassment, but before she could speak, Rye approached. The cowboy's shoulders sagged with weariness. His clothes were gray with soot and ash, his eyes red rimmed from smoke. "Barn's burned out," he reported. "I don't think there's much danger to anything else." He glanced at the sky. "Looks like it might rain. That'll help."

Trace nodded. "We lost the one horse, but the others are okay?"

Rye nodded toward the corral, where the animals paced, tossing heads and twitching tails with skittish energy. "And Theresa's mule."

"Yeah, well thank God we saved the mule." His voice was heavy with sarcasm. He looked toward the smoldering ruin that had been the barn. "It'll take weeks to rebuild. And all the saddles and tack are gone." He slammed his fist against the ground beside him. "Dammit, we're barely started here and we're already behind."

Lucy looked away. It frightened her to see this strong man reduced this way. She'd begun to think of Trace as invincible. "How do you think it started?" she asked Rye.

He dug into his pocket and pulled out a battered tin box. "Found this a little ways from the barn." He handed it to Trace.

She looked over Trace's shoulder at the box. Embossed in the metal was some kind of design. "Crossed cannons," Trace said, smoothing his finger over the embossing. "Symbol of the Ninth Corps, Union Army." He lifted the cover and revealed a flint and a wad of cotton punk nestled inside. Lucy had seen such tinderboxes before. Travelers often carried them in lieu of more expensive matches. By striking the flint against a stone, one could strike sparks and set fire to the punk, which could be used to light dry leaves and twigs and thus a campfire.

The wind picked up, filling Lucy's nostrils with the smell of fresh smoke and plastering her nightgown against her legs. The thought drifted through her mind that she should go inside the house and change clothes, but she could not find the strength to move.

Trace closed the tin and turned it over and over in his hand. "Whoever set fire to the barn must have dropped this."

"A Yankee?" Lucy nodded toward the box. "Someone from the Ninth Corps?"

Trace shook his head. "I don't know."

"I looked for tracks," Rye said, "but with all the running back and forth, putting out the fire, any sign that might have been there is long gone."

Trace struggled to his feet. His face was pale, but his mouth was set in a hard line. "We'll go after them. Track them down."

Rye shook his head. "It's been hours. They'll be long gone. You're in no shape to ride." He looked down at his ash-covered clothing. "Neither am I."

Trace clenched his fist around the tinderbox. "If I find the man behind this, believe me, he'll pay."

Lucy hugged her arms across her chest and shivered, but not from cold. "Maybe the Buckboard Bandit did it," she said out loud.

The two men stared at her with puzzled expressions. "The Buckboard Bandit?" Trace asked.

"That's what the paper calls the man who's been holding up people in the area. He usually leaves notes behind with his victims."

Rye shook his head. "No note. Or if there was one, it most likely burnt up."

"I don't think the Buckboard Bandit is a Yankee, though," she said. "In fact, he seems to have a particular hatred for them, along with federal agents and carpetbaggers . . . anyone he sees as against the South."

"What does this Buckboard Bandit look like?" Trace asked.

She shook her head. "I don't know. The paper said he wears a long coat and pulls a handkerchief over his face so that no one can recognize him. He travels in a wagon and leaves messages about how the South won't be beaten down."

Trace frowned. "Sounds like the kind of common thief who gets made into a hero."

"That's what Uncle Nate said, too. The paper says people are refusing to reveal his identity out of sympathy for his cause. They're calling him a Southern Robin Hood.''

''His cause! Stealing and tearing down what other men have sweated to build up isn't a cause, it's a crime.'' A fit of coughing interrupted Trace's outburst. Lucy squeezed her arms more tightly across her chest to keep from going to him. He didn't want her help, any more than she wanted him to know how deeply he had touched her.

''Could be that's the same fellow who tore down our corral,'' Rye said when Trace's coughing had subsided.

''Tore down your corral?'' She stared at the cowboy.

He nodded. ''We found wagon ruts in the ground where they'd pulled down the pickets.''

''Maybe it's about time I rode into town and talked to a few people.'' Trace started for the corral. Thunder shook the air, stopping him in midstride.

''Ain't nobody goin' nowhere right now,'' Rye said, looking up at the sky.

Fat raindrops hit the ground like gunshot pellets, scattering dust. Then water began to pour from the heavens in sheets. Lucy turned and raced for the cabin, Trace and Rye close behind her. Theresa held open the door and ushered them inside. ''Praise the Lord. He gonna make sure that fire is out for good,'' she said as she handed around towels and dry clothes. ''Josh, you put the kettle on, and I'll fix us a pot of sassafras tea.''

Half an hour later, Lucy sat at the kitchen table, dressed in one of Theresa's dresses, her wet hair hanging in a single braid down her back, her hands cupped around a mug of sweet, spicy tea. Rain beat steadily against the cabin, sending an occasional hissing drop into the fire, and the aroma of baking gingerbread filled the air.

The rhythmic rainfall, the sweet tea, and the morning's trauma combined to blanket her with a numbing lethargy. She stared at the screen of clothes gently steaming before the fire, her mind blank.

''Don't sound like it's about to let up anytime soon.''

Rye spoke from his seat by the hearth, where he sat whittling.

"You'll have to spend another night here."

A long moment passed before Lucy realized Trace was speaking to her. He sat at the table across from her, his eyes, bright and feverish, fixed on her. She shifted in her chair, trying to shake off her weariness. "I should be able to leave once the rain passes."

"Comanche Creek will rise. It won't be safe to cross."

His objection was reasonable, but paled beside her sudden overwhelming desire to be back at home—in her own room, wearing her own clothes. She needed to be away from Trace, from his piercing gaze and his unsettling nearness and the memory of his skin beneath her fingers. She could not draw breath in this small room without being aware of his own even breathing beside her. The very air in this place was saturated with his subtle scent, and everywhere she looked was some reminder of the man who lived here. That one man could so dominate her thoughts disturbed her. "I've swum the creek before," she said, chin raised in defiance. "Amigo's a strong swimmer. I won't have any trouble."

He set his cup down on the table hard enough that the crockery teapot rattled. "Have you crossed riding bareback? Your saddle burned up in the barn, remember? Besides, in another few hours it will be dark. It'll be safer in the morning."

She looked away, her only acknowledgment of defeat. She didn't want to quarrel with Trace. She didn't know what she wanted, only that she was afraid of the tangled emotions that pulled at her like a strong current, threatening to sweep her away from her carefully planned future.

She could feel Trace watching her still, but she refused to look at him. She searched the room for some diversion. Theresa sat on the side of the bed, sewing. Behind her, Josh and the baby slept, curled together like furled leaves.

She stood and went to sit beside Theresa. "What are you making?" she asked.

"I found a whole bunch of tobacco sacks up under the eaves, like somebody'd saved 'em up for a long time," Theresa answered. "I undid the seams and ironed them out flat. Then I dyed some with onion skins and some with pokeberries. Now I'm sewin' 'em into a quilt." She spread the half-finished quilt top across the bed between them. The approximately five-inch-square pieces of cotton marched in neat lines across the quilt, arranged in diagonal stripes from the natural unbleached muslin of the original tobacco sacks through the light brown of onion skins, to the wine-red of pokeberries.

"It's beautiful." Lucy smoothed her hand across the neatly joined squares.

"You left your sewin' behind when you was here the day I come." Theresa nodded toward the sewing basket, which now sat on the floor by the bed. "Show me what you're makin'."

Reluctantly Lucy retrieved the basket and opened the lid. Her heart gave a lurch as she stared down at the jumble of colorful fabric inside. Was it possible she'd actually missed this quilt? She drew out the half-finished coverlet and smoothed it across her knees. "It's my bridal quilt," she said softly and waited for the usual taunts about her lack of progress on the quilt.

Theresa traced the outline of a brown gingham heart. "I like it. It's colorful. When you get ready to quilt it, send for me, and I'll come help."

"Oh, I won't be ready for that for a while yet." She started to refold the quilt but changed her mind. Maybe keeping her hands occupied with sewing would help to pass the time and lessen her uneasiness. She drew out two pieces of calico and her needle and thread and began to stitch.

"I used to sew dresses for Miz Marion, but I like makin' quilts best," Theresa said after a while.

"Marion—she was Trace's wife, wasn't she?" She glanced toward Trace. He sat staring at the tinderbox, seemingly unaware of them.

Theresa nodded and pulled her thread through the layers

of fabric. "When she and Mr. Trace said their vows, she had a baker's dozen of quilts in her dowry chest." She smiled. "I stitched every one of 'em." She gave Lucy a sharp look. "How many quilts you have in your dowry chest?"

Lucy flushed. "Not any. Well, this one. Of course, it isn't finished." She lifted her chin. "But I've made other quilts. I just haven't kept them."

"Uh-huh." Theresa's needle never slowed. "Seems like a gal your age needs to be thinkin' on keepin' a few quilts, so's you'll be ready to set up housekeepin'."

"I'm not in any hurry. I don't plan to marry for years yet."

"For true?" Theresa looked amused. "Well, maybe next time you at a quiltin', you should have a cat-shakin', see if you're right."

"A cat-shaking?" Lucy frowned. "What's that?"

"You ain't never heard of a cat-shakin'?" Theresa snapped off her thread and smoothed out the seam she'd just sewn. "A cat-shakin' is where you take the finished quilt out of the frame, and all the single gals at the gatherin' hold the quilt by the corners. Then you put a cat in the middle of the quilt and the girls commence to shakin' it. When the cat jumps out, the girl closest to where the cat jumped is gonna be the next to marry."

"I don't believe it."

Theresa nodded. "You just try it and see."

"It doesn't matter." Lucy shook her head. "I'm not going to marry until I'm rich enough to buy all the quilts I'll ever need."

Theresa chuckled. "Miz Marion didn't have time for such doin's, either. She'd rather be out ridin' horses or dancin' at parties." She picked up another square of fabric and smoothed it across her thigh. "What makes you so certain you won't be marryin' anytime soon?"

Lucy clenched her fists in her lap. "I plan to make my fortune before I'm wed. That way, no man will be my master."

All the mirth faded from Theresa's face. "Oh, child, it makes my blood run cold to hear you say that."

"Why? Do you think it's wrong for a woman to want to be independent?"

Theresa shook her head slowly. "Nothin' wrong with a man or woman bein' free. But don't nothin' in this world come without a price. Miz Marion was always goin' on about havin' her freedom. In the end, I think it killed her."

Lucy swallowed hard, cold to the pit of her stomach. She started to ask Theresa what she meant by that, but Rye's approach silenced her. "How you comin' with my soogan?" he asked, smiling down at Theresa.

Theresa gave him a haughty look. "A fine quilt takes time, Mr. Rye Booth."

He laughed. "It's not a quilt. It's a soogan. That's the proper name for a cowboy's bedroll." He fingered the edge of the fabric. "This'll make up into a sturdy, warm bedroll, all right."

He opened his hand and let half a dozen carefully carved clothes pegs tumble into her lap. "There's the first payment for the work you're doin'," he said.

Theresa's eyes sparkled. She looked as if she was trying not to smile. "Won't nobody sleep warmer than you under this quilt."

"Maybe. Maybe not. Might depend on if I have the right woman to sleep under it with."

The hint of a smile tugged at the corners of Theresa's mouth. "Oh, you are a fine talker," she said, shaking her head.

"I can do more than talk. Wait and see." He grinned and walked away, back to his place by the fire.

The smile blossomed fully on Theresa's face. "Ain't he walkin' tall? A woman could do worse than to spend time with a man like that."

She looked at Lucy, who glanced away, embarrassed to have been caught staring at what seemed a private exchange. "How old are you?" Theresa asked suddenly.

"Twenty-two. Almost twenty-three."

''Too young to be gettin' foolish ideas into your head, sayin' you won't marry until you're rich. A body could work their whole life and never have more than two spare coins to rub together. If a good man asks you to be his wife, you say yes. A good man is sure enough hard to find.''

Lucy turned her head and saw that Theresa wasn't watching her anymore. Her eyes were fixed on the man by the hearth, who sat with his back to the fire, shaving thin curls of wood from an oak twig. ''Yessiree, there's too many bad men in this world,'' she said softly. ''You find a good one, you better hang on tight.''

TRACE LISTENED TO THE murmur of the women's conversation. Their voices, soft and velvet edged, rose and fell, the words indistinct, like distant music.

He watched Lucy out of the corner of his eye. She smoothed her palm along the quilt top, and he remembered the feathery touch of her hand across his chest. He'd been only half-conscious at the time, sure he was dreaming that gentle caress. When he'd opened his eyes and seen her face, filled with worry, bent over him, he'd breathed a prayer of thanks that he'd made it through the fire to be with her.

He looked away, his fingers clenched around his now-cold cup. He and Lucy weren't with each other. They never would be. She'd made it plain she'd like nothing better than to be away from here and gone, even if it meant swimming her horse across a flooded creek.

Even when she knew he was right about something, like not wanting her to ride home tonight, she had to argue with him. Something in her nature compelled her to defend her own views so stubbornly, even when they were wrong.

She is independent to a fault. Those were the words his father had used to describe Marion. Even a blind man could see Lucy had the same failing. And *his* failing was letting himself fall under the spell of a woman whom he could never truly protect from herself.

He shook off the maudlin thought and turned his attention to the tinderbox on the table before him. Did the box belong to Pollard? Or had some other bitter Southerner like this Buckboard Bandit targeted him? He picked up the box and ran his thumb across the raised impression of the crossed cannon. Whoever owned this box would have worn the same insignia on his uniform, with the color of the patch indicating which division he belonged to.

Dropping the box seemed a careless mistake for someone eluding discovery. Of course, a man in a hurry, working in darkness, might drop the box and not realize it.

But what if the box had been left behind on purpose? Lucy said the Buckboard Bandit left notes with his victims. This tinderbox might be a note of another kind. The idea hit him with a fierce certainty. Whoever had set the fire had wanted him to know it was deliberate. He stared at the Union insignia on the front of the box, and the hair on the back of his neck stood on end. They'd been wrong to think a Yankee would be the only one to possess such a box. A Southern soldier might just as well own one. It was the type of thing men collected after a battle, out of necessity or sometimes out of a perverse desire for a souvenir from a vanquished foe. The longer he stared at the box, the more certain he was that this was the case. Pollard, or someone like him, had stolen the tinderbox from a dead Yankee soldier and left it behind today as a warning.

A warning that Trace, or someone he cared about, might be the next to die.

11

LUCY LEFT EARLY THE next morning, while dew still dripped from the trees. The sharp odor of smoke stung her nose as she stood watching Trace lead Amigo out of the corral. The man's footsteps and the horse's measured plodding echoed in the predawn stillness. They had spoken little during a breakfast of coffee and cornbread, as if with silence they might hold back any further argument over her returning home this morning.

Trace fastened the corral gate behind him and pulled an old quilt from where he'd tossed it across the top rail of the enclosure. He folded the coverlet in quarters and draped it across the horse's back in place of a saddle, then turned to her. "You'll have to ride astride."

She nodded. "I can manage."

He held her gaze a long moment, as if trying to determine truth or lie in her words. Tiny lines etched the skin around his eyes, evidence of a restless night. From her place in the cabin's only bed, she'd heard him cry out once, a muffled groaning that tore at her. She waited, prepared for more protests, but the fire or his weariness or her own stubbornness made him let go of his objections unsaid. "All right, then. I'll help you mount." He draped the reins across the horse's neck, then knelt, one knee in the dirt beside the horse, hands cupped to make a step.

It was a humbling position, yet he had never looked stronger. Lucy hesitated, feeling strangely vulnerable as she faced him. "Don't you trust me?" he asked, one eyebrow raised in challenge.

She shook herself. "Of course." She set aside her sewing basket, then put her foot in his hands and grasped his shoulder to balance herself. His warmth radiated to her, banishing the early-morning chill. His muscles bunched, and he lifted off the ground. For a moment she was suspended, helpless in his embrace.

And then she was on the horse, skirts hiked around her thighs. She shifted and tugged at the fabric, acutely aware of his gaze on her. She looked up, expecting to find him pleased with her discomfort or amused by her awkwardness. Instead, she saw a naked longing that made her tremble. She gripped the horse with her thighs, trying to ease the sudden ache deep within her. He reached for her, and she held her breath, afraid of the fierce desire that possessed her, making her lose her will.

In the blink of an eye, the moment passed. Trace reached up and jerked her skirt down over her knees, his movements brusque, dismissive. He handed up the basket. "You'd better go," he said curtly, looking away.

She dug her heels in the horse's flanks, anxious to flee from here and from these confusing emotions that she had perhaps after all imagined.

She reined in the horse when she was out of sight of the cabin, near the creek. Mist hung like cotton lint in the trees along the water. She breathed deeply of the damp air, trying to slow her racing heart. Amigo, as if sensing her uneasiness, danced sideways at the slightest noise in the underbrush. It took all her skill to keep from being unseated.

The creek still ran high, her usual crossing slick with mud. She stared down at the steep bank. If she dismounted to walk the horse down to the water, she'd have no way of getting back onto the horse to cross. But with no saddle or stirrups could she keep from falling off on the steep climb down one side of the bank and up the other?

She looked up and down the bank, but no better crossing presented itself. "All right, Amigo, what's the worst thing that could happen here?"

The horse snorted and shook its head in answer.

She looked down at the path. "I could end up sitting in the mud and then I'd have to walk home." She threaded her hands through the horse's thick mane. "Or we could turn around and listen to Trace Abernathy say 'I told you so.' " She smiled. "I think I'll risk the mud." She threaded one arm through the handle of the sewing basket and grasped Amigo's mane with both hands. She nudged the horse in the sides, and they started down the steep bank.

They began the slow descent, Lucy balancing carefully on the horse's back. Halfway down, Amigo's hooves skidded on the slick surface of the path. She squealed and gripped the animal's sides until her thighs burned and throbbed. They half slid the rest of the way down, stumbling into the water with a mighty splash. She ignored the water that bubbled up to soak her shoes and stockings and leaned forward to rest along the horse's neck. The pounding of her heart and the animal's wet slurping of creek water were the only sounds beside the gentle lapping of the water around them.

Then another sound reached her ears—the creak of a wagon wheel striking rock. She raised up and craned her neck to scan the road behind her, but the rutted caliche track sat empty.

Amigo twitched his ears and snorted. A chill ran up Lucy's back. Was someone hiding up there on the road, watching her? She felt terribly exposed here in the middle of the creek. She didn't relish the idea of someone from town seeing her like this, riding bareback with her skirts hiked above her knees, her shoes and stockings soaked. Wouldn't the gossips have a field day with her then?

She shuddered at the thought and jabbed her heels into Amigo's sides, sending him vaulting up the bank. She re-

gretted the move almost as soon as it was made. She slipped
sideways on the horse's back and had to fight to hang on.
The basket knocked against her side, the handle cutting into
her arm. By the time they reached the top, she clung to the
animal with one knee hooked over its back, her arms
around its neck. Feeling as if her limbs were about to be
pulled from their sockets, she hauled herself upright and
sat there, panting, totally spent.

She heard splashing behind her, and looked down to see
a wagon rolling through the crossing. A solitary man
guided the team. He wore a long coat that hung past his
knees, a broad-brimmed hat pulled low over his face.

The Buckboard Bandit! She stared at the figure, heart in
her throat. Someone from town would have surely hailed
her from above, but this man, for whatever reason, had kept
silent.

She urged Amigo forward, into the trees. She was suddenly acutely aware of her defenseless position. The gun
she usually carried for protection had been in her saddlebags, destroyed in the fire. Scarcely daring to breathe, she
craned her neck for a better look at the mysterious traveler
as he slowly moved toward her hiding place.

His concealing dress left him unrecognizable. Likewise,
she couldn't recall seeing his team before. Certainly the pair
of sleek bays were not Pollard's swaybacked hacks. The
nondescript farm wagon was like dozens in the area: a
plain, serviceable vehicle, with no markings to tie it to any
particular owner.

Nothing about this stranger called forth any spark of recognition. And nothing, truly, suggested that he was indeed
the Buckboard Bandit. She relaxed a little, beginning to feel
silly about hiding in the bushes like this. Besides, she reminded herself, even if this was the Buckboard Bandit, he
would have little interest in her; she wasn't a Yankee or an
employee of the federal government.

She guided Amigo back onto the path. She had nothing
to worry about. She sat very erect, head held high, and
forced herself to look straight ahead. She could hear the

steady clop of horses' hooves and the jingle of harness behind her, but still the man in the wagon said nothing.

She imagined she could feel his gaze boring into her. Were her ears playing tricks, or had he increased his speed, drawing ever closer to her? A thin whistling reached her ears. The familiar tune made her blood run cold. How many times had she heard "Dixie" sung or whistled? Today it sounded sinister. Was the man trying to tell her something?

She glanced over her shoulder and saw him sitting there, collar pulled up close around his chin, hat tugged low over his face. He was staring right at her now, she was sure, though she couldn't see his eyes. Still he said nothing, just whistled, turning the normally cheerful anthem into a haunting dirge.

Was this the Buckboard Bandit or another sort of bad man, one without a preference as to his next victim? It was no secret some men had grown too fond of the rape and murder they'd learned during the war. A young woman out by herself would prove a tempting target to that sort. Though she'd often resented Trace's warnings of danger on the road, his words came back to haunt her now.

She heard the reins pop across the horses' backs and the wagon traces rattle as the wagon sped up. What would happen when he overtook her?

Heart pounding, she searched for some avenue of escape. Trees lined the road closely on both sides, hemming her in. A hawthorn branch scraped her shoulder, knocking her bonnet awry. She reached out and snapped off the spindly branch, the rough bark snagging her gloves. The wagon was close enough now that she imagined she could hear the horses' labored breathing.

She started to throw the broken branch to the ground, then inspiration struck her. Bending low over Amigo's neck, she used the branch as a whip, sending the horse hurtling forward, racing for home.

The wind whipped her hair into her eyes, and with every jarring movement she thought the horse's backbone would cut her in two. But she wouldn't slow down. The one sound that reached her over the thunder of the horses' hooves drove her onward: the sound of a man's laughter, wild and evil like the voice of the devil himself.

∞

TRACE STARED AT THE pile of blackened timbers that had once been his barn. The smell of wet ashes left a sour taste in his mouth and filled his head with bitter memories.

Hand in his pocket, he turned the watch over and over in his palm, fighting a flood of memories. This same stench had hung over Belle Haven when he'd returned there after the war. All the scents he'd long associated with his wife's home—the perfume of magnolia blossoms, the tang of curing tobacco, the heady aroma of baking bread—had been overwhelmed by the charred smell of death and destruction. Yesterday's fire brought it all rushing back to him with sickening clarity.

He heard footsteps and turned to see Theresa picking her way through the rubble toward him. "You all right?" she asked, glancing up at him.

He looked away. "Why wouldn't I be?"

"You been standin' out here a long time with that backwards look on your face."

He frowned. " 'Backwards look'?"

"You're looking forward, but you're seein' somethin' that's behind you—somethin' in your past." She stopped beside him and surveyed the ruins of the barn. "When they burned Belle Haven, Marse Alan cried and cursed the Yankees." She glanced at him. "He cursed you most of all."

Trace nodded. "Alan Sutton cursed me from the day I first stepped over his threshold."

"Miz Marion never cursed you."

He turned to her. "Don't lie, thinking to ease my conscience. Marion cursed me the day I left. The last thing she ever said to me was to wish me in hell."

Theresa looked sad. "That was the pain in her talking.

She didn't want you to go. After you left, she locked herself in her room and cried for three days.''

This news startled him, like a hammer blow to his chest. He glared at her. ''No more lies, Theresa.''

She traced an X over her heart. ''God's truth, she did. After she come out, she never talked about you again, until the day of the fire. Then when her daddy went to cursing you, she turned on him, tol' him he better not speak ill of her husband ever again.''

He closed his eyes, trying to take it all in. He wanted to believe Marion had not died hating him—wanted to, but the picture that formed behind his closed eyelids was Marion screaming at him from her bedroom window as he rode past. ''What happened to all your promises to stay and take care of me?'' she shouted. ''Is the precious Union more important to you than your wife? Damn you to hell, Trace Abernathy!''

Marion had got her wish, if three months in a field hospital, surrounded by the screams of the dying, could be thought of as hell. And her parting words tore at him still. If he'd stayed, would it have made any difference? Could he have kept her from riding the stallion that killed her? Not knowing was the worst punishment of all.

''Now, what do you think he been up to?''

Theresa's words recalled him to the present. He looked up and saw Rye Booth riding into the yard at a gallop. Trace's stomach clenched. Rye had a grim look on his face, as if the news he had to bring wasn't good. ''What is it?'' he asked when the cowboy reined in beside them.

''Saw some buzzards circling the ridge and went to investigate. Found one of the cows we branded day before yesterday. Some son of a bitch put a bullet in her skull and stripped off her hide.''

Trace nodded. ''Some local in need of a little cash decided to help himself.''

Rye folded his hands atop the saddle horn. ''A lotta folks'll tell you all these wild cattle are good for are sellin' to the hide-and-horn man. Struck me as peculiar, though, that they'd kill one with a fresh brand like that. Lots of others up on that ridge with no brand or Fischer's old mark."

The knot in Trace's stomach tightened. "You think it was deliberate?"

Rye shrugged. "Can't say. Might pay to be extra careful for a spell."

Trace turned away, back to the charred rubble. "I thought when they mustered me out of the army my fighting days were over."

"You don't think ever' person on God's earth ain't got they own battles to fight?" Theresa gave him an indignant look. "The day we quit fightin' 'em is the day we lay down an' die."

He rolled his shoulders, as if shrugging off his gloom. "I never said I was giving up." He leaned down and took hold of the end of one fallen timber. "Let's start clearing up this mess."

They had been working steadily for an hour when the door to the cabin flew open and Josh came running from the front of the house. For a boy who had been near death only the day before, he had bounced back remarkably well. Seeing him made Trace's own pain hardly noticeable. "Wagon comin'!" he shouted, leapfrogging over the chopping block and skidding to a halt in front of Trace.

Trace tossed aside the remnant of a metal feed bucket and stripped off his filthy gloves, then led the way to the front of the house.

"Might be you got a few more friends than you give yourself credit for," Theresa observed as they watched the wagon roll toward them. Nate O'Connor drove a double-ox team, Lucy at his side. She sat perfectly upright, hands in her lap, the picture of decorum in her simple bonnet and modest calico dress. He felt the now-familiar rush of pleasure at the sight of her, his feelings made all the more acute by the memory he had of how she'd looked when he'd last seen her: astride her horse like some warrior maiden, skirts hiked up to reveal long, firm legs. He'd longed to run his hands along her satiny thighs. He had known when their eyes met that his face revealed his desire for her too clearly, and had forced himself to turn away.

She shattered her pretense at decorum when the wagon stopped before the gate. Before he could step forward to help her, she'd leaped from the spring seat and begun pulling the tarp from the wagon load.

"We've brought lumber and tools to help you build a new barn," she said, her face aglow with enthusiasm. "And look. Saddles to replace the ones that burnt up."

Hands in his pockets, he surveyed the bounty spread out in the wagon bed. From here it looked as if Nate had cleaned out half the store. Sawn lumber, a keg of nails, hammers, shovels and rakes, even two fifty-pound sacks of oats shared space with the saddles. The two plain, workmanlike rigs were sturdy and not inexpensive. Everything was exactly what he needed. And exactly what he couldn't afford. He took a step backward. "I appreciate the thought, but I can't pay you for this and I can't take charity."

"I didn't say you had to pay for it right now, did I?" Nate clapped him on the shoulder. "I reckon your credit's good."

Trace swallowed hard. No one else in town would have extended help to him this way. Why was Nate different? Was it because of Lucy? He watched her as she bent over the wagon, rummaging among the goods there. "I don't know what to say."

Lucy raised her head and met his gaze. "Say thank you and help us unload everything."

The saucy gleam in her eye made him want to kiss her again. Her very presence was like a fresh breeze reviving him. "Thank you. I'll open the gate, and you can drive the wagon around back."

Working together, the wagon was soon emptied, its contents stacked neatly near the site for the new barn. Then Theresa passed around coffee and gingerbread as they rested in the shade of an oak. "It's been a long time since

I've been out here,'' Nate said. He nodded in approval. ''You've got a nice place here.''

''Thanks,'' Trace said. ''I hope to make it nicer.'' He waved his hand toward a clump of trees up on the rise. ''I'd like to build bigger corrals up there, and maybe some pens for training horses. One day I'd like to add on to the house, too.''

Nate nodded. ''A man with a family would need a larger house.''

Trace stiffened. Was this a subtle hint? Was O'Connor that anxious to be free of his responsibility for Lucy? ''I don't plan on starting a family for a long while yet,'' he said firmly.

Nate seemed undisturbed by this announcement. ''Lucy thinks the Buckboard Bandit followed her home from here this morning.''

Trace almost dropped his coffee cup at this startling announcement. ''She what?''

Nate half turned to face him. ''She says a man in a wagon, dressed in a long coat with a hat pulled down low over his face, followed her this morning. He wouldn't speak, but kept driving closer. When she ran away, he laughed.''

Trace gripped the china cup until he thought it might shatter in his hands. ''I should have insisted on escorting her home myself,'' he said. ''I promise you it won't happen again.''

Nate shook his head. ''I'm not blaming you. After all, Lucy isn't your responsibility, and I know how stubborn she can be. I just thought you'd want to know.''

''Want to know what?'' Lucy sashayed over to them. For a woman who had supposedly had a bad scare, she looked annoyingly vivacious.

''I was just telling Trace here about your run-in with the Buckboard Bandit,'' Nate said.

She grinned. ''Well, I'm not sure it was him, but I think so.''

''You shouldn't make light of what could have been a

dangerous situation." Trace set his cup aside on a stack of lumber. "I can't believe now that I let you ride off alone like that."

She shrugged. "Nothing happened. I don't really think he intended for it to. He tried to intimidate me, perhaps, but I'll have the last word." She grinned.

Warning bells sounded in Trace's head. "What are you talking about?"

"I'm writing a story for *Leslie's* about the notorious Buckboard Bandit!" She rubbed her hands together. "I intend to expose him for the cowardly petty thief he is. He's hiding behind some 'noble' idea of 'defending' the South, when really all he's doing is lining his own pockets. People won't be so willing to support him if they see him for what he is."

Trace stared at her, his alarm growing. "Aren't you worried a story like that will only make him angry? Next time he might do more than just intimidate you."

She laughed. "The man's a coward! I'm sure of it. I'm only sorry now I didn't turn and confront him when I had the chance."

"You got a good look at him? What did he look like?"

"Not Bill Pollard, if that's what you're thinking. At least, I know the horses weren't his. This man was driving a matched pair of bays."

Trace frowned. "Unless Pollard stole new horses."

"You think Pollard's behind this?" Nate asked.

Lucy shrugged. "I don't *think* that's who this was. It was hard to tell really. That long coat and the slouch hat pretty much hid everything from view." She shook her head. "Still, I don't see how a man with one leg could do some of the things the papers say the Buckboard Bandit has done."

"Don't believe everything you read," Nate said.

"If it's not Pollard, it's someone like him," Trace said. "Someone made bitter by the war, who wants to make the Yankees and the federal government pay for his sufferings."

"That could be half the men who fought," Nate said. "On either side for that matter." He brushed gingerbread crumbs from the front of his shirt. "I say we ignore men like Pollard and this bandit and get on with the work of putting our lives back together. Lucy tells me you've started branding your herd."

He nodded. "Yes, sir. We'll set to work again tomorrow." He turned to Lucy. "I want you to be in charge of my brand book."

"What's that?" she asked.

"It's the book where I keep track of all the cows I come across that have brands other than yours, mine, Rye's, or Hiram Fischer's. Any calves found with those cows I have to brand with the mother's mark. If I take those animals to market, I owe the brand owner the selling price of the animal, less a handling fee. Other owners will do the same for me."

"How will they know the Circle A brand is yours?"

"I registered it at the courthouse in Blanco on my way here last month." She had a puzzled look on her face. "Don't tell me you didn't register your brand?"

She shook her head. "I didn't know I had to."

"I don't suppose you really have to yet. The cows you bought from Sterling Gibbs will all still have his mark."

"But what if I decided to brand *other* cows—mavericks?"

He raised one eyebrow at the thought of Lucy roping and throwing a wild cow, then branding it with her mark. But he wisely kept silent. "Then you'd need to have your brand and earmarks on file at the county courthouse. Otherwise they aren't legal marks."

She turned to her uncle. "I have to go to the courthouse."

He nodded, his expression amiable. "We'll take care of it soon enough, dear. In the meantime, maybe you'd better leave the mavericking to Trace."

Her green eyes sparked with displeasure at this vague dismissal. Trace bit his lip to keep from laughing. It seemed he wasn't the only man to stand in the way of Lucy's carefully laid plans.

12

LUCY LEANED HER HEAD on her hand and studied the line she'd just written in the wavering lamplight. *Jake Forrest glared at the so-called Buckboard Bandit. "You're a poor excuse for a man, hiding your petty thievery behind Southern loyalty. No true Southerner would behave in such a dastardly manner."*

Smiling, she dipped her pen in the inkwell and added another line. *The bandit cowered in Jake Forrest's brawny shadow.* She frowned. Could a shadow be brawny?

"Time to douse the light and come to bed, child." Uncle Nate called down the stairs.

She yawned and stretched. "I'll be right up." The brawny shadow could stay until tomorrow. She was too tired to wrestle with the question tonight. She capped the inkwell, then carefully blotted her page, closed the notebook, and slid it into the drawer. With luck, she'd finish the story by tomorrow. The editor at *Leslie's* would surely be pleased and want to buy this piece.

She blew out the lamp and stood for a moment, letting her eyes adjust to the dim light cast by the moon streaming through the open front windows of the store. She started to step out from behind the counter, on her way to the living quarters at the back. The scrape of footsteps on the front porch stopped her. She stood frozen, ears straining. What was someone doing out there this time of night?

Noiselessly as possible, she crept forward, ears straining. The sound came again, a muffled shuffling on the wooden floor of the porch. She stopped beside the window and pressed her nose to the screen. The town lay still as a tomb. Not even a stray cat roamed the street. The only noise to reach her ears was the heavy drumming of her heart.

"Lucy!"

Her uncle's shout made her jump, gasping. She turned and Nate clumped into the room, guided by the light of a sputtering candle. He wore a pair of wrinkled trousers over the top of his long johns, one of his suspenders twisted around backward. "What are you doing all the way over there by the window?"

"I thought I heard something."

Nate smiled indulgently. "It's just that imagination of yours working overtime. All this talk of bandits and such has you nervous as cat. Come on, now, or you won't be fit for anything tomorrow."

"All right, Uncle. I'm sorry I got you out of bed."

"I wasn't sleeping anyway." He wiped the sweat from his brow, causing his hair to stand on end. "Too hot."

"It's cooler down here." She grinned. "I was thinking about spreading a pallet on the floor."

"What, and startle Sandra Early's teeth out of her mouth when she comes to sell eggs?" He shook his head. "Upstairs with you, girl. I let you run wild enough as it is." He stepped aside to let her pass through the door to their quarters, then followed her in. "I sometimes wonder if I've been wise to let you have your own way so often."

"You didn't have any choice," she teased him. "I was this way when you got me."

He set the candle on the little table at the bottom of the stairs leading to their bedrooms. "Sometimes I think you were born that way. You get that from your father, I suspect."

"Really?" She turned, curious as always about the man she could remember only vaguely. "Did people say he was headstrong, too? Or is it all right to be that way if you're a man?"

"It's easier if you're a man, I reckon." He paused, as if choosing his next words carefully. "You know how he died, don't you?"

She nodded. "He contracted blood poisoning."

"Yes, but do you know *how* he contracted blood poisoning?"

She shook her head.

"He was shifting some boulders out of a field. These were really big rocks, and rather than wait until someone could come and help him, he decided to tackle the job himself. One of the boulders shifted and crushed his foot. He might have been all right even then, if he'd stayed off his feet like the doctor said, but he was too restless. He insisted on carrying on with his work even then. The bones didn't knit right, infection set in, and the next thing we knew, he was dead." He patted her shoulder. "There's such a thing as being too independent, child. Doesn't matter if you're man or woman." He started past her up the stairs. "Good night. Bring the candle with you when you come up."

She nodded, only half hearing. The faint and wavery picture she had of her father, a handsome man with thick brown hair and a ready smile, filled her mind. Her heart ached with a grief that surprised her. Killed because of his own impatience and independence. What a waste. Uncle Nate's story explained so many things—her mother's sometimes sudden anger whenever her late husband's name was mentioned, and even Lucy's own incredible urge to stand on her own two feet, without depending on anyone else.

She picked up the candle and began climbing the stairs to her room. Where was the line between self-reliance and foolishness? Had Trace Abernathy's warnings just been attempts to keep her from crossing over that line?

She stepped into her bedroom and set the candle on the

dresser. The light reflected in the mirror filled the room. She removed her dress and hung it on a peg by the door, then slipped on her night rail. She was tired, but too restless to sleep. Thoughts of Trace Abernathy pricked at her like cactus thorns under her skin.

She didn't want his opinion to matter so much to her. The moment she let someone influence her that way, he had an enormous power to wound her with a sharp glance or an unkind word. Though the brief moments in Trace's arms had been a kind of heaven for her, she wasn't sure they were a fair trade for the kind of hell he might put her through later.

She turned to blow out the candle, and her gaze fell on the incomplete quilt top draped across the chair by the dresser. Green and red and yellow triangles formed a saw-toothed path around each quilt block in a pattern her mother had carefully labeled rocky road to California. Lucy had found the paper pattern pinned to a stack of neatly cut triangles near the bottom of the hope chest. For the past week, she'd been assembling them into a quilt top.

She picked up the quilt top and a stack of cut triangles and sat in the chair. She'd work on it just a little while before she went to bed. The soothing rhythm of weaving the needle in and out of the layers of fabric would calm her mind and allow her to sleep easier.

Using the blocks she'd completed earlier as a guide, she began to assemble a new block. She'd been nervous at first about piecing this quilt almost from scratch, fearful it wouldn't measure up to the other two, which Mrs. Sorenson had pronounced true works of art. But as she'd sewed, she'd gained confidence. Assembling the pieces was like working a puzzle, each triangle fitting to the next in a pleasing design.

She needed a green triangle next. She searched through her stack of pieces and selected a triangle of dark green cambric with a background pattern of black leaves and vines. A sudden image flashed into her mind of her mother wearing a dress made of this fabric, sitting before a mirror and doing up her hair. She closed her eyes, remembering the feeling of awe she'd had as a very little girl, wondering if she would ever be as beautiful as her mother.

She hadn't thought of her mother that way, as beautiful, and happy, for a very long time. She held the handful of quilt blocks to her nose and inhaled the aroma of lemon verbena, her mother's scent. If only she could capture these memories and use them to blot out the more recent images of all the bad times in her life, those times when her mother had been all but lost to her.

She swallowed a knot of tears and opened her eyes. *No sense wishing for the impossible,* she told herself, stabbing the needle into the fabric. *You can't go back and change the past, so best to just get on with the future.* That meant finishing this quilt to sell to Mrs. Sorenson. She still owed Mr. Gibbs money for cattle, and after that she'd have supplies to buy for the cattle drive next spring. She'd need money for land, too. And even after that, she wanted money to set aside in the bank, as a kind of safeguard for emergencies. She'd have to sew a lot of quilts and write a lot of stories to get everything she needed to be truly independent.

She fit the green triangle next to a piece of yellow. No, that wasn't right. Frowning, she consulted her mother's pattern and her neatly scripted instructions. Ah, yes, now she could see it. She flipped the triangle around, and it fit perfectly.

Strange, Mama writing everything out like that, Lucy mused as she sewed the two pieces together. *I've never known a quilter to do that before. It was almost as if she knew I'd need these instructions one day.*

She froze, needle in hand, and stared down at the bright fabric triangles, their sharp outlines blurred by tears that wouldn't be held back this time. She'd long ago convinced herself that her mother had been too burdened by her own suffering to give more than brief thought to her daughter's needs. She'd even grown to feel thankful that she'd learned independence at such a young age.

Could she have been wrong? Maybe her mother had tried to take better care of her headstrong daughter, but Lucy had been too busy going her own way to notice. Now when she needed her guidance, her mother was here, in these colorful scraps of fabric, and in the neat lines of writing on an old piece of brown paper.

As the thought took shape in her mind, she felt something loosening in her chest, like a tight fist opening to release a long-held grudge. She smoothed her hands across the neatly stitched fabric and smiled, filled with gratitude and wonder too great for words.

∞

THE SHOTGUN BLAST TORE through the store, loud as a cannon. Lucy was up, standing in the middle of her room before she even realized what had awakened her. She blinked into the darkness, ears ringing with the echo of gunfire.

"Lucy!" Uncle Nate's voice strained with alarm.

She groped her way to the door and jerked it open. "I'm all right, Uncle," she called. "What happened?"

A circle of light appeared at the end of the hall, followed by her uncle. He carried a lit candle in one hand, a rifle in the other. "Sounded like someone fired into the store. I'm going down to check it out."

"No!" She raced to him and grabbed his arm, the one cradling the gun. "They might still be down there. You could be hurt."

He shrugged her off. "I heard them ride away. Besides, anyone who wants me dead knows where to find me. They don't have to go wakin' up half the town in the middle of the night."

"Then I'm coming with you." She straightened and crossed her arms over her chest.

Nate sighed. "Suit yourself."

They crept down the stairs, pausing every few steps to

listen. The ticking of the clock in the hallway above them echoed loudly in the absolute stillness.

In the kitchen, Nate paused to light a lantern. He turned down the wick, then frowned at Lucy. "Try to stay in the shadows when we go in there, just in case someone's still hanging around." He pulled his overcoat off the peg behind him and shoved it toward her. "Put this on. That white night rail stands out like the moon at midnight."

She shrugged into the coat, then tiptoed behind him into the front room. The lantern spilled its light over a sickening sight. Shards of window glass sparkled like dew amid a sea of molasses oozing from a busted keg. Flour sifted like dust from broken bags and toppled cans of peaches rolled in every direction. The smell of vinegar from a pellet-pierced keg hung sharp in the air.

"Why would anyone do this?" Lucy whispered.

"O'Connor? You all right in there?" She cringed as someone pounded on the door and shouted. Nate shouldered his rifle and strode to the door. "We heard the shots." Zeke Early stepped into the room, followed by Dr. Lambert and several other men. Zeke stopped just inside the door and surveyed the destruction. "Looks like they did a lot of damage."

"Nothing that can't be replaced." Nate rested the shotgun against the wall. "Did anybody see anything?"

The men looked at each other and shook their heads. "I was sound asleep," Dr. Lambert said. "When that shot went off, I thought I was back at Antietem."

Nate nodded. "I heard horses galloping away right after the shot went off."

"Whoever did this probably fired through the window, then vamoosed it out of here," Zeke said.

"But why?" Lucy stepped forward. All the men turned to stare at her. "This is the only store in town," she said. "Why would anyone want to do this kind of damage?"

"Can't any of you people read?"

The harsh voice made goose flesh rise on her arms. She

wrapped Uncle Nate's coat more tightly around herself as Bill Pollard appeared in the doorway.

"What are you talking about, Bill?" Zeke asked.

He jerked his head toward the street. "Come out here and see."

They filed out onto the porch, Nate in the lead, Lucy last. By the time she stepped through the door, they had all turned to face the building. She gasped at the horrible image that held their attention. Someone had written in foot-high letters across the front of the store: A TRAITOR AND A YANKEE-LOVER LIVE HERE. The words, painted in broad strokes of white paint, glowed in the moonlight, a ghostly epitaph.

"It's about time somebody spoke the truth around here," Pollard declared.

Nate turned on his former friend. "How do you know so much about it?" he demanded. "Are you the one who did this?"

Pollard shook his head and spat tobacco juice onto the porch boards between his feet. "I was comin' home from Birdtown when I heard all the commotion over here. Besides, it says right there who did it." He pointed to the end of the message.

Lucy leaned forward with the rest to squint at the letters scrawled there. " 'B. B.' " She looked up. "The Buckboard Bandit!" She pushed her way through the press of men until she stood in front of Pollard. "Why would the Buckboard Bandit attack Uncle Nate? He's not a Yankee or part of the federal government."

Pollard scowled at her. "Maybe he got wind of the help you and your uncle have been giving that thievin' Yankee Abernathy. The worst kind of traitor is one who aids and abets the enemy."

"That's enough!" Nate's cutting tone silenced Pollard. "The war's over," he continued. "The only enemy is men like this bandit, who think they can bully others in the name of their distorted ideas about right and wrong."

"You're the one with the wrong ideas," Pollard growled.

"When that Yankee grenade took your leg, he must've took half your brains, too!" Nate retorted.

The two men faced each other, shoulder to shoulder, hands knotted at their sides. Lucy feared at any minute one would strike out at the other.

"The middle of the night is no time to stand around arguin'." Zeke Early put a hand on each man's shoulders. He looked at Pollard. "No matter what you think about Abernathy or anybody else, Bill, it ain't right for a man to go around bustin' up another man's property in the middle of the night. Nate here has always stood by the folks in this town, givin' us credit when we needed it. While we were off fightin', he made sure our women and children always had groceries, even when times were tough for him. If he's chosen to extend to Trace Abernathy the same Christian charity, I reckon that's his business."

"He sure as hell won't have anymore of my business." Pollard jerked away from Zeke and staggered backward. "My wife and I will be takin' our trade elsewhere from this day on." He turned hate-filled eyes toward Lucy. "And I forbid my wife to have anything more to do with you, missy."

"Quit talkin' and get the hell off my porch!" Nate said. He made a shooing motion with his hands. "Go on. If I never see you again, it'll be too soon."

Pollard whirled and stalked off the porch to the wagon that waited in the shadows at the end of the building. He hauled himself awkwardly into the driver's seat, relying on his one good leg and his powerful shoulders to swing into position. "Hyahh!" The command to his horses sounded angry. Lucy shivered and turned away. For years she'd found Bill Pollard irritating; since the night he'd tried to harm Trace, his hatred had truly frightened her.

Nate sagged against a porch post and stared after the retreating wagon. In the silvery moonlight, his face looked bleached of all color, haggard and old. Lucy came and put her arm around him.

Zeke clapped his friend on the shoulder. "Me and some of the others'll post a watch until morning," he said. "Make sure whoever did this doesn't cause any more trouble tonight."

Nate shook his head. "I doubt he'll be back. He stirred up trouble and left his message. That's all he wanted. This time, anyway." He turned back toward the store. "I appreciate your offer, though. Now, if you'll excuse us, I guess we'll try to get some sleep."

Zeke nodded. He hooked his thumbs in his suspenders and stared off in the direction Pollard had driven. "Don't seem like nobody come out of the war without changin' some way," he said. "Some folks came through it with a kind of gentleness, a better regard for life. Others just got all hardened up inside."

Lucy stared down the street, the sound of the retreating wagon fading in ears. To her way of thinking, Bill Pollard had been a mean, petty man before the war. Battle and the loss of his leg had only made him meaner. Uncle Nate had suffered right along with everybody else, but suffering only made him try to do that much more good. It seemed whatever a man started out with, goodness or meanness, that was what he ended up with when he came through trials.

Trace had fought in the war, too. He had lost his home and family somewhere along the way and had been wounded in battle. How had the war whittled his personality down to its essence? He wasn't saintly, like Uncle Nate, or evil like Bill Pollard. He was just an ordinary man, trying to live his own life. She took comfort in his commonness, his balance of strength and vulnerability. In a world turned topsy-turvy by strife too long, Trace was the kind of man she could trust—the kind of man she could fall in love with, without half trying.

∞

TRACE STARED AT THE note in his hand and read through it again. The neat, feminine handwriting seemed more suited to addressing an invitation to tea than to writing the disturbing message he found instead: *I regret I cannot come and help with the branding today as promised,* Lucy wrote. *Uncle Nate's store was attacked last night by the Buckboard Bandit. We are unhurt, but there is quite a mess, and Uncle Nate needs me here.*

He looked up at Zeke Early, who had delivered the message. "What happened?"

Zeke slouched in the saddle and scratched his chin. "Well . . . along about midnight, somebody rode up and fired a shotgun blast through the front window. Busted up a bunch of stuff."

"She says here it was the Buckboard Bandit. How does she know?"

"He left a note." Zeke shrugged. "I guess you could call it that. Painted across the front of the store. Signed 'B. B.' We figured it had to be the Buckboard Bandit."

Trace gritted his teeth. Zeke seemed determined not to tell him any more than he had to. "What did the note say?"

Zeke looked uncomfortable. "It said, 'A Traitor and a Yankee-Lover Live Here.' "

Trace suddenly had trouble catching his breath. His vision blurred in a haze of anger. "So help me God, he'll pay for harming those innocent people. And if any of you Texans are conspiring to hide his identity out of some misguided Southern loyalty, I'll make you regret the day you ever laid eyes on—"

"Hold on a minute there." Zeke glared down at him. "Don't you go gettin' wrathy on me. Who said anything about hidin' anybody?"

Trace steadied himself on the gatepost and took a deep breath. "I apologize. It just makes me see red to think this—this *thug* attacked Lucy and her uncle because of their friendship with me." He gave Zeke a searching look. "You're sure they're all right?"

Zeke nodded. "Shook up, I reckon, but fine. Folks

around here are made of pretty stout stuff, even the women.''

He had a sudden flash of memory: Lucy brandishing her makeshift torch in the face of the charging bull. The recollection almost made him smile. It also made him feel better about Lucy's welfare. If a charging bull didn't reduce her to hysterics, a nighttime gunshot blast wasn't likely to upset her for long. As his anxiety eased, he remembered his manners. ''Thanks for bringing the note out,'' he said. ''Will you come in for a minute, have a cup of coffee or a drink of water?''

Zeke shook his head. ''Reckon I won't. I only brung the letter as a favor to Miss Lucy.'' He nodded, then turned his horse around and set off down the road.

Trace's irritation returned as he watched Zeke ride away. He drew out the watch and clutched it in his hand, as if holding on to this remnant from happier times could help him rise above Zeke's scorn. To men like Early, he'd never be anything but the enemy. They might tolerate his presence, but they'd never accept him.

He turned away and stared at the note once more. Nate O'Connor had accepted him, welcomed him even. Because of that, his store had been damaged, his livelihood threatened, his pride assaulted.

He stuffed the note into his pocket with the watch and started for the corral. He'd saddle up and ride hell-for-leather into town and . . . and do what? He stopped in the middle of the yard, common sense catching hold of him like a hand grasping the back of his shirt. His presence couldn't bring Lucy and Nate anything but trouble right now. Because of their friendship with him, they'd been attacked in their own home.

Logic told him staying away was the best course of action right now, but instinct rebelled at the thought. The very qualities in Lucy that frustrated him the most—her pride, intelligence, determination, and independence—also drew him to her, arousing his strongest protective instincts. He wanted to fight for her, defend her against anyone who would speak ill of her or try to harm her. When they'd first met, he'd thought it best to keep his distance from Lucy to protect himself from the frustration and hurt she was certain to bring into his life. How ironic that now he was forced to stay away in order to protect *her*.

The situation was nearly intolerable. If he didn't find some way to work off his frustration, he was liable to do something rash. Continuing toward the back of the house, he called up to Rye, who was straddling a roof timber of what would one day be the new barn. "That can wait until later," he said. "Let's take a ride over back of Anderson Hollow and see if we can round up some mavericks."

Rye laid aside his hammer and slid down a corner post to the ground. "What's got into you?" he asked. "Yesterday you was all fired up to get this barn dried in."

"We'll get it dried in soon enough." He started toward the corral once more. "I came here to raise cattle, so let's get to it."

Rye shrugged and untied his nail apron. "Reckon I'd rather be out ropin' cows than driving nails any day."

AN HOUR LATER, TRACE and Rye stopped atop a high ridge and stared down into a nearly dry creek bed that formed a narrow canyon. "If we herd a bunch of cattle into there, we can block the entrance with brush and hold 'em while we brand 'em," Rye said. "We won't have to drive 'em all the way back to the corral."

Trace nodded. The barren creek bank was steep and rocky, pocked with shallow caves and animal dens. Even the most surefooted Longhorn would be hard-pressed to escape from that prison. A pool of water at one end would be handy for the cattle and horses, and a thick growth of trees at the back would provide shade and shelter. The mouth of the canyon was maybe twenty feet across, with enough dead trees and brush nearby to block this avenue of escape.

"That looks a likely spot for some old mossyhorns to be hanging out with their calves." Rye pointed toward a brush-choked gully across the hills. "What say we go roust them out?"

They rode toward the gully at an easy pace, keeping downwind of their destination. Rye's keen eyes spotted the cattle first, the twist of a horn mimicking the curve of a bare branch. Trace squinted and was able to make out a pair of cows and their calves settled in the deep shade. A few feet from them, another cow and calf rested with two half-grown bulls.

Trace looked at Rye, then nodded. "Hyahh!" They charged the gully, shouting and waving their hats, circling the animals, intent on driving them from their cover and herding them toward the canyon. The young bulls gave up their hiding places first. Then a frightened calf darted into the open. Rye lassoed it and dragged it away. The mother trotted after it.

Trace plunged into the brush after another calf. Thorns tore at his leather leggings and scraped his horse's hide. At last he managed to force the animal into the open and cut off its return to its hiding place. The cow rushed out to protect her offspring, and he blocked her escape also.

He swung his horse around and rode into the brush once more, in search of the remaining cow and calf. Horns flashed before him. He spurred his horse forward and came face-to-face with a massive bull. Its horns were compact, sharp tipped, just beginning to show the wrinkles of an animal in its prime. The broad nose bore the scars of other battles, but the ears were smooth and uncut. This was a prize—a bull who'd escaped the branding fire before the war, property of whoever could be the first to claim him.

The bull was so close, Trace could see the lashes around his eyes. The animal blinked, then turned, diving for cover. Trace was a step ahead, shouting and waving his hat in the bull's face, driving it out into the open. The bull's confusion and surprise worked in Trace's favor. He knew if the animal ever suspected it had the upper hand, it could turn and rip him open with one thrust of those rapier-sharp horns.

They came blasting into the open almost side by side. Rye took up the chase then, steering the bull toward the rest of the milling herd. The animal trotted in amongst the cows and calves, then stood, sides heaving, head up, eyes scanning its surroundings as if looking for a route to freedom while the men continued circling the group at a trot, lassoes ready to snag any would-be fugitive.

When the animals had grouped into a compact herd, Trace and Rye took up positions on either side and began to drive them over the ridge to the canyon. In about an hour, they drew in sight of their destination. Trace began to relax a little. They were almost there, with as fine a collection of animals as any they'd yet branded. Except for two old cows that bore Hiram Fischer's brand, all the animals were mavericks—a good day's payment for their hard work.

At the top of the hill, the animals picked up speed. "They smell the water in the creek," Rye said. "They'll practically drive theirselves there now."

Trace thought later that the old bull must have sensed their complacency. Whatever the reason, as they headed down into the canyon, the animal raised his head, stretched his neck out, and galloped away. The ground shook at his passing. Rye's rope sailed toward him and missed completely, landing in a tangle in the dirt.

Trace swore under his breath and turned his attention to the remaining animals. They shuffled around nervously, tails and ears twitching. "Bunch them up, and let's get them inside before all hell breaks loose," he said.

They closed ranks behind the herd and drove them forward. Drawn by the promise of water, the cattle flowed into the canyon and ran toward the pool at the end. A covey of quail exploded from the brush as the cattle surged forward, the rush of their wings like a long sigh of complaint at having been disturbed from their resting place.

Rye lassoed a fallen cottonwood and dragged it into the

opening. Trace dismounted and added brush to the pile. "Looks pretty good." Rye surveyed their work. He glanced up the hill. "I'd like to go after that bull. A maverick like that'd be worth a lot."

Trace nodded. Without having to say the words, he knew Rye was asking his permission to claim the animal. As landowner and boss, Trace had the right to take the maverick as his own. "If you can catch him, he's yours." He hauled himself back into the saddle. "Go on. I'll wait here and keep an eye on this bunch."

Rye pulled his hat down on his head, then turned his horse and raced up the hill. Trace watched him disappear over the top, then rode over to check out the herd. They milled about at the shadowed end of the canyon. One old cow had already settled down on her haunches to chew cud. She studied Trace with a baleful eye. Satisfied, he sought out a patch of shade of his own and drew out his canteen.

The water was warm and metallic tasting, but refreshing just the same after the hard riding he'd done for the last couple of hours. He wet his handkerchief and mopped the dust and sweat from his face, wishing for a breeze. But not so much as a leaf stirred.

Now that he had time to study it further, he was struck by the forbidding nature of this corner of his property. The land bore signs of a recent fire, patches of blackened rock, dead trees stretching bare limbs skyward like reaching skeletons.

And silence. Even the cattle had grown still. After the fury of their chase, the place seemed blanketed in an unnatural calm.

He shook himself. He was imagining things, letting his worry over Lucy and Nate get the best of him. He'd do better to focus his energies on stopping the Buckboard Bandit from hurting them again.

If he could figure out the identity of the bandit, he'd put a stop to the man's terrorism at once. He settled himself more comfortably in the saddle. What did he know about the bandit?

From what Lucy had told him, all the crimes attributed to the man had taken place in the immediate area, no farther away than Birdtown. The man drove a wagon and disguised himself. He apparently didn't say much to his victims, preferring to leave notes. He had a particular hatred for Yankees, Negroes, and the federal government. He claimed to be defending the South against his enemies.

Trace weighed these facts in his mind. Together, they painted a picture of a man who was bitter about the outcome of the war, someone who felt he'd been cheated out of what was rightfully his—money, status, power. He was probably someone local, a literate man who tried his best to hide his identity.

Bill Pollard fit the description, but so did a dozen or more others who had been at Pollard's party the night Trace was threatened. Any of those who gathered around Trace that night could be the Buckboard Bandit. Or it could be someone else entirely.

The distant sound of falling rocks disturbed the stillness. He looked toward the creek bank to his left and watched a tiny avalanche of gravel skitter and bounce down the slope, as if dislodged by a horse, or a man's footstep. The hair on the back of his neck rose, and he reached for the pistol at his side. "Who's there?" he called.

A flash of light blinded him, then the roar of gunfire thundered in his ears. His horse reared, pawing the air and crying out. Trace struggled to hang on, but was thrown from the saddle. He hit the ground hard, a burning pain in his thigh and the hot stickiness of his own blood soaking into his trousers.

13

ANGER SQUEEZED TRACE'S CHEST, a white-hot rage at whoever had shot him and frustration at himself for allowing this to happen. The silence alone should have tipped him off that something wasn't right. Hadn't his encounter with the sniper taught him anything?

He shook his head, trying to clear it of the gray fog that engulfed him. Muscles tensed, scarcely daring to breathe, he rose up on his elbows, searching for cover. Whoever had shot him might still be out there, waiting.

The piled brush at the mouth of the canyon offered the best promise of refuge. Clenching his jaw against the dizzying pain, he dragged himself toward the mound of tangled brush and dead trees. Every inch of ground he covered seemed a mile. Gravel tore at his shirt and scraped the palms of his hands. Pain stabbed him every time he so much as bumped the injured leg. He tried to hurry, aware of how vulnerable a target he was out in the open. He waited for a second flash of light and thunder of gunfire, and the slam of bullets into his body that would surely kill him.

He reached the bottom of the brush pile and rested, gathering his courage for the climb to the other side. A wide

smear of blood and dirt marked his progress so far. Whoever was out there would have no problem hunting him
down and finishing him off.

A fresh surge of anger swept through him at the thought.
By God, he wouldn't just lie here and die. With a grunt,
he hauled himself upright, over the tree trunk that formed
the base of the brush fence. His shirt snagged on a jutting
branch, and he jerked it away, ripping the fabric. His boots
slipped on the smooth trunk, and pain shot through his injured thigh like a lightning bolt, reverberating in dizzying
waves. He clenched his jaw and kept moving, up to the top
of the barrier, then over, rolling and falling down the other
side.

He hit the ground hard, the breath knocked out of him.
Pressing his cheek into the gravel of the creek bed, he listened for the approach of his attacker. But the heavy thump-
ing of his own heart blocked out all other sound. He
clutched the pistol in his right hand, weariness dragging at
him like an anchor. He closed his eyes. If only he could
rest awhile, sleep. . . .

No! He forced his eyes open and shoved himself up until
he was sitting, his back to the brush pile. His leg throbbed.
When he could finally bring himself to look at it, all he
could see was a bloody mess. He took his handkerchief
from around his neck and tied it above the wound, hoping
to slow the bleeding. Then he lay back, pistol cradled on
his chest, and waited.

Rye would have heard the shot. He'd be here soon. Is
that why his attacker had not yet returned fire? Was he
waiting to kill them together?

Pain pulsed through his leg. Had it hurt this bad before,
at Appomattox, when the sniper shot him and Hiram Fischer?

The specter of that day filled his senses like a waking
nightmare. The sniper's fire had hit the horses first, and
while the men dashed for cover, Hiram caught a ball in his
shoulder. Trace hurried to help his friend, only to find his
leg cut out from under him by a bullet through the thigh.

They barricaded themselves behind their dead horses, off
to the side of the road. Weapons drawn, they waited, scanning the trees overhead for some sign of the marksman who
had almost killed them both. The sounds of battle echoed
around them, the air saturated with the stink of smoke and
powder, and the cries of other wounded. A rebel yell echoed through the trees, an eerie cry that seemed to go on
and on.

They tore their uniforms and bound up their wounds as
best they could. Hiram's injury was the most serious of the
two, his shoulder shattered to hell, white bone showing
through ragged bits of skin. Trace's leg wound had seemed
minor in comparison, though he suspected the shot had
fractured the thigh bone.

Fear and the threat of death was like a third being hiding
behind that barricade with them. They distracted themselves
with talk of Texas. Trace asked question after question to
keep Hiram talking. What does the land look like? How
many cows do you think you have? What does your brand
look like? What do you think will happen after the war?

That conversation must have been on Hiram's mind later,
in the hospital, when he pressed the land deed on Trace
and told him to "take his frau to Texas."

Damn Texas! He'd come here and had nothing but trouble ever since. He shook his head, trying to rid himself of
the dizziness that swept over him in waves. His leg was
bleeding again. What was keeping Rye? Maybe whoever
had shot Trace had found Rye and killed him, too.

Had the killer left him here to die slowly this way? He
tried to stand, thinking he'd somehow drag himself onto his
horse and ride for help. But the horse had run off, and just
sitting up straighter plunged him into nauseating blackness.

He sagged back against the brush and fumbled for the
watch in his pocket. Raising it to his eyes, he studied the
inscription on the back, "Daniel Abernathy."

If all men were just, there would be no need of valor.

The watch was all he had left of his father, the only thing

he'd carried with him from the remains of the home they'd
shared. He clung to it now like a talisman, as if his father's
own brand of justice and valor could somehow seep from
the metal into him.

Daniel Abernathy wouldn't have given up, and neither
would his son. He slipped the watch back into his pocket
and sat up a little straighter. He had too many reasons to
keep living. He had work to do, building up the ranch.
Theresa and Josh and little Mary depended on him. And
Lucy—

He closed his eyes and swallowed hard. Lucy was counting on him to get her cattle to market next spring. And
whether she was willing to admit it or not, she needed him,
to protect her from her own recklessness.

No, that was wrong. She didn't need him. But maybe he
needed her, to prove to himself that he hadn't left the best
part of himself back there in Chancellorsville and Williams-
burg and Antietem and Appomattox.

Was he in love with Lucy, or did the nearness of death
just make a man want to hold on to someone—anyone? Or
maybe he just wanted his death to mean something to
someone. Practically every man on the battlefield had
someone he wanted to send last words to—a wife or sweet-
heart or maybe a mother. They all wanted someone to care
what those last words had been.

He wanted Lucy to care, wanted it desperately. The
fierceness of that desire overwhelmed him. He'd lied, telling himself he should stay away from her because of the
guilt he'd feel if he failed to protect her, the way he'd failed
to protect Marion. Here, lying in a pool of his own blood,
the truth weighed heavy. He'd been a coward, afraid of
falling in love with Lucy and having her reject him, the
way Marion had rejected him. He couldn't die with that
fear gripping him.

Where was Rye?

∞

LUCY SMOOTHED THE QUILT top across her bed. The bright red and green and yellow triangles zigzagged against the white background in a path that resembled railroad tracks or, she supposed, a mountain road. She felt as if she'd taken her own kind of journey putting this quilt together. Almost every piece of fabric recalled some long-forgotten memory. And every stitch she sewed bound up another old wound.

Of all the quilts she'd made so far, this one was her favorite, perhaps because she'd done most of the work herself. It was going to be hard to sell this one, but sell it she would. She couldn't afford to miss a payment to Mr. Gibbs. This time next year, she'd have more than enough money to buy fabric and make another rocky-road-to-California quilt, using her mother's pattern and her mother's guidance.

As for this one, she only had half of the border left to piece, then she'd be ready to quilt the whole thing together.

And then what? She sighed and began refolding the quilt top. The easiest thing would be to hold a quilting bee and let the other women in the community help her finish the work. That would be the conventional way, the accepted way. She'd show them all that she was as accomplished as the rest of them. The women would make comments like "Better late than never" and "Maybe there's hope for the girl yet."

Of course, she could always finish the quilt alone, as she had the other two. It would be easier that way. She wouldn't have to waste time explaining her motives to people who wouldn't understand anyway. She slipped the folded top inside a pillowcase to keep it clean. She'd decide what to do later.

A knock on her door made her jump. "Lucy? You'd better come down here."

A shiver of apprehension chilled her. Uncle Nate sounded worried. "What is it?" she asked, pulling open the door. "Is something wrong?"

He didn't say anything, just took her gently by the arm and led her downstairs. She gasped when she saw Rye

Booth waiting just inside the kitchen. The cowboy stood in the doorway, hat in hand. "Afternoon, ma'am," he said, nodding to her. "I come with bad news, I'm afraid."

She swayed and might have fallen if Uncle Nate hadn't been holding her. "What's wrong?" she demanded. "Where's Trace?"

"He's back at the cabin. Somebody shot him."

She gasped and covered her mouth with her hand, as if to hold in her cry of anguish.

"But, ma'am, he's alive," Rye hastened to add. "I come to town to fetch the doctor and thought I better let you folks know, seein' as how you're his friends and all."

The words stunned her. She had a hard time even believing they were real. "Who shot him? Why?"

Rye shook his head. "Don't know, ma'am. We was out near Anderson Hollow roundin' up cattle when I heard the shot." He put his hat back on. "I better not stay any longer, ma'am. I need to get the doctor."

"I'll go with you to fetch Dr. Lambert," Nate said, reaching for his jacket. "Lucy, you pack some bandages, laudanum, iodine, and whatever else you think we might need. We'll pick you up on our way back out of town."

Moving in a daze, she hastily assembled whatever medicines and bandages were within easy reach and stuffed them into a picnic basket. Then she added a jar of beef tea, the prescribed nutrition for bedridden patients. Packets of sugar and tea and a box of ginger cookies filled most of the rest of the space in the basket. She looked around, frantically trying to think of anything else she might need. A bottle of Besom's Best brandy caught her eye. She tossed it in and fastened the picnic basket lid.

She wished Rye had told her more. Was Trace conscious? Where exactly was he shot? Had he been asking for her? She raced up to her room and combed her hair and put on a clean apron. Then she stuffed a night rail and a clean bodice into a pillow slip, along with her hairbrush and clean stockings. Trace might need nursing through the night. She could stay and help.

On her way out of the room, she spotted the quilt top and added it to her load. If she did sit up with Trace, sewing on the quilt would help her stay awake.

Downstairs again, she put on her bonnet and waited by the door. What was taking Uncle Nate and Rye so long? Had they been unable to find Dr. Lambert? She paced back and forth, wringing her hands. *Oh, God, please let him be all right.*

At last the doctor's buggy appeared, escorted by Rye and Uncle Nate. "You can ride with me, Lucy, dear," Dr. Lambert said, jumping down to help her with her parcels.

Once they were on the road, the doctor quizzed Rye about Trace's injuries. Lucy listened with growing fear as the cowboy told of finding Trace unconscious, bleeding from a wound in his thigh. Once they'd reached the cabin, Theresa had been able to stop the bleeding, but Trace had yet to awaken.

"Which leg was shot?" she asked.

The two men looked at her, as if they'd forgotten she was there. "The right one," Rye answered.

"That's the one that was hurt before, in the war," she said, her stomach clenching at the thought.

Rye nodded. "He never said much about it, but he limps on it sometimes."

The doctor frowned. "Depending on his injuries before, it could complicate matters now."

Lucy gripped the edge of the buggy, wishing the doctor would shut up and drive faster. He hadn't even laid eyes on Trace yet and already he was making dire predictions.

Uncle Nate and Rye rode on ahead to the cabin, leaving Lucy to guide the doctor. She wished she'd thought to bring her own horse. She could have been there by now!

At last Lucy and the doctor came in sight of the cabin. Rye ran out to see to the horse and buggy. "He come to once, Theresa said, but he's talking all crazy-like."

Uncle Nate sat on the front porch, holding Josh and Mary on his lap. Josh looked as if he'd been crying. "Theresa's in there with him," Nate said.

Lucy rushed inside, Dr. Lambert on her heels. She stopped at the foot of the bed and stared at the man stretched out before her. His face was white as the bed linens beneath a dark shadow of beard. His leg was swathed in bandages, propped on a bolster of blankets. Dr. Lambert took a pair of scissors from his bag and began cutting away the bandage. "Tell me what you've done for him," he said.

"I applied pressure to stop the bleedin'," Theresa said. She hovered at the head of the bed, worry lines creasing her brow. "Then I cleaned the leg best I could." She shook her head. "It don't look like a regular bullet wound, but some kinda little pellets, scattered around."

The doctor pulled away the last of the bandage. Lucy put her hand to her mouth to keep from crying out. Trace's thigh was as pale as his face, dusted with dark hairs. A single deep scar, twisted and shiny, ran from the top of the thigh almost to the knee, and a pattern of small wounds pocked the rest of the leg.

The doctor let out a low whistle. "How did he ever keep from losing that leg in the war? If he'd been in my hospital, I'd have sawn it off rather than risk infection." He pulled out a scalpel and probed one of the new wounds. Trace flinched and flailed his hand about. Theresa captured his fingers in her own. Lucy chewed her knuckle, determined not to leave until someone made her. It wasn't proper for her to be standing here, staring at a man's naked leg, even an injured one, but she didn't care. She wanted to see for herself what the doctor would do, and not rely on someone else's version of the truth.

Dr. Lambert held up a piece of lead shot on the tips of his tweezers. "Bird shot. The pellets themselves did a lot of damage, but not as much as a larger caliber bullet might have done. He's lucky whoever shot him didn't have a rifle." He dropped the pellet into a shallow bowl that sat on an upturned crate beside the bed and went after the next one.

Trace groaned and opened his eyes. He stared at Lucy, his eyes bright and feverish, their normal blue darkened almost to violet. He raised his head and opened his mouth as if to speak. She leaned closer. His voice was rasping, but strong. "Thank God you came." And then he collapsed against the pillow once more, eyes closed, his face paler than ever.

"What are you doing standing there?" Dr. Lambert demanded. He turned to Theresa. "Take her out of here. She shouldn't be watching this."

"It's all right. I'll leave now." She turned and walked out onto the porch. She had heard all she needed to know.

∽

TRACE FELT SOMEONE STABBING him, like red-hot needles digging into his thigh. He groped for the pistol he kept under his pillow. He'd told the doctor he'd shoot him before he'd let him take his leg. What kind of a doctor was he if he couldn't cure a man without cutting him all to pieces?

While Trace had held the gun on him, the sawbones split his thigh to the knee and sewed everything up inside him. He soaked everything in alcohol, including himself, but even drunk the man could stitch better than a Chinese tailor. When he'd finished, he'd told Trace he'd probably die anyway, and if he lived, he'd never walk.

Well, he wasn't dead yet, and today wouldn't be the day they got to him with their saws. But he couldn't find the pistol. A hand captured his, gentle and cool. He struggled to open his eyes, and stared at the shadowy image of a woman. Her lavender perfume drifted to him, stronger even than the death stink that hovered over the hospital tents. He didn't remember Marion wearing lavender before. . . . It didn't matter. What mattered was that she was here. He'd begun to give up hope. The hospital was scarcely two days' journey from her father's plantation, and yet for weeks he had heard nothing from her. He imagined she was still cursing him, holding on to her anger as stubbornly as she ever defended her decisions.

She didn't look angry today. His vision blurred, but he thought she was smiling. "Thank God you've come," he croaked, and collapsed against the pillow, worn out with the effort of speaking. It didn't matter. He could sleep now. Marion had forgiven him. She had come.

∞

LUCY'S NEEDLE FLASHED IN the lamplight as she sat beside Trace's bed, sewing the last strip of fabric for the quilt's border. The hum of cicadas through the open windows provided the rhythm for her sewing. She could feel the tension ease from her shoulders as she worked, the monotonous movement of the needle in and out of the layers of fabric and the nighttime stillness filling her with peace.

Trace was peaceful now, too, his deep, even breathing assuring her that he slept well. Uncle Nate had taken Trace's place in the barn with Rye, and Theresa and the children rested on pallets on the floor. Only Lucy was awake, too restless to lie down, glad to keep this watch over the man who only hours before had seemed near death.

She paused in her sewing to look at him. His cheeks had lost their waxy paleness, burnished gold by the lamplight. One lock of dark hair fell across his brow. She resisted the urge to brush it aside. *Thank God, you've come.* The words echoed in her head. Her throat tightened whenever she thought of them, and longing filled her until she thought she'd burst. But longing for what? What did all these strange feelings mean?

Was she in love with Trace? The thought frightened her. Could you love a man and keep from losing all of yourself to him? Could a man love you and not want to rule over you?

He stirred in his sleep, and she gave in to the urge to reach out and push the errant lock of hair off his forehead. He opened his eyes, velvet black in the lamplight. "Oh!" She gave a small cry and jerked her hand away.

"No, don't stop." He spoke in a harsh whisper. "Feels good."

Hesitantly she reached out to him again. He rested his cheek against her palm. His beard rasped against her skin, and the heat of him melted something inside of her, making her tremble. She pulled away again, afraid of these intense emotions that coursed through her. "How are you feeling?" she asked.

"Like a fool."

She looked puzzled. "Why do you say that?"

He looked toward the ceiling. "That's the way a grown man feels when he's got no more strength than a baby."

"Would you take some broth? It'll help you get your strength back."

He nodded. She rose and took the pot of broth from the back of the hearth, where she'd been keeping it warm on a bed of coals. She poured some into a tin mug, then fetched a napkin and went to help him sit up.

Even in his weakness, his body was solid, his muscles firm beneath the linen of his shirt. Lucy put one arm behind his back, and the contrast between the hardness of his body and her own softness struck her. Her nipples rose and tightened as her breast pressed against his side, and she longed to press herself closer to him still.

He smiled, a roguish gleam in his eyes. "I see there are certain *enjoyable* things about having you for a nurse."

She turned away to hide the heated flush that rose to her face, and retrieved the cup of broth from the crate by the bed. "Drink this," she said, pressing it into his hands.

He sipped from the cup and made a face.

"Drink it all," she said. "You need to build back all the blood you lost."

He nodded and tipped the cup to his lips again. When he handed it back to her, it was empty. "What happened?" he asked, lying back once more. "The last thing I remember I was sitting in the middle of nowhere, bleeding like a stuck pig."

"Rye returned with the bull he'd been after and found

you and brought you here. While Theresa looked after you, he rode to town and fetched us and Dr. Lambert.'' She took a deep breath to calm the shaking in her voice. ''Whoever shot you had his gun loaded with bird shot. It didn't do a lot of major damage, but you bled a lot.'' She picked up a small bowl from the crate and showed him its contents. Two dozen pea-sized pieces of lead rolled around in the shallow bottom. ''The doctor says he thinks he got them all, but he can't guarantee it.''

He studied the pellets for a long time. ''There was a covey of quail in the canyon. We flushed them when we drove the cattle in.''

''Then maybe this was just an accident.'' She idly stirred a finger through the pellets in the bowl. ''Maybe someone was aiming at the quail and shot you instead.''

He shook his head. ''The quail were long gone by then. But I suppose someone could have been angry we frightened the birds away.'' He collapsed back on the pillow. ''Or maybe he intended to shoot me all along.''

She shook her head. ''But why?''

He fell silent. He didn't say anything for so long that she thought he must have fallen asleep. She set aside the bowl of pellets and picked up her sewing once more.

''It looks as if you're almost finished.''

She raised her eyes and saw that he was looking at the quilt. She smoothed her hand over her work. ''It still has to be quilted.''

''What happens when a girl finishes her bridal quilt? I suppose you have to find a groom.'' His words were teasing, but the look in his eyes made her want to squirm in her chair. She fought the urge to flee him and his question.

''This isn't my bridal quilt,'' she said softly. She held it up so he could better see the design. ''It's called rocky road to California.''

''So you're working on a new one. Does this mean your bridal quilt is finished?''

She shook her head. ''I put that away for a while to work on this one.'' She hesitated, then added, ''A lady named

Mrs. Sorenson buys quilts from me. This is the third one I've made for her.'' The interest she saw in his eyes made her continue. ''I'm using the money to pay for my cattle.''

''I wondered how you were managing to pay for everything.'' His eyes glinted with amusement. ''I might have known you'd find a way, though I never would have guessed you'd choose quilting.''

''Just because I don't always act like every other girl doesn't mean I can't do the things they do just as well as they do them.'' She jabbed her needle into the edge of the fabric and folded the quilt top in her lap, then put it away under her chair.

''I never said you couldn't.'' His gaze darkened, searching. ''I don't doubt you're capable of pretty much anything you put your mind to.''

His intense gaze made her anxious to change the subject. She didn't care to have him know how much his opinion meant to her. ''Are you in much pain?'' she asked, standing. ''The doctor said you could have laudanum.''

He shook his head. ''They came near killing me with that stuff in the army. I'm lucky I didn't end up an addict, they pumped so much into me.''

She sat again, biting her lip. Curiosity got the better of discretion at last. ''What happened to your leg before—in the war?'' she asked. ''Dr. Lambert said by all rights, they should have amputated.''

''I wouldn't let them take it.'' Amusement crept into his expression. ''I can be as stubborn as you are when I put my mind to it.''

She laughed nervously. ''I'll consider that a compliment.''

He returned her smile. She looked into the dark pools of his eyes, and for a moment she forgot everything else. The whole world was reduced to whatever was in this circle of lamplight. The man in front of her had somehow found a way to breach the walls she'd so carefully built around herself. She had never felt as close to anyone as she did to him right now. Impulsively she leaned forward and kissed his cheek.

He looked startled. "What was that for?"

"For not dying on me."

He swallowed and turned away. "I was beginning to think you didn't care."

Fear latched on to her like a cat with sharp claws. "Well, of course I care," she said in a rush. "Who's going to get my cattle to market if you're not here to do it?"

She wanted to take back the words as soon as they were out. But how could she utter the alternative? *I care because I'm in love with you. And now* I'm *the one who feels like a fool.*

His face looked hard in the amber lamplight, like a bronze cast. He stared at the bowl of lead shot. "In the hospital tent, they told me I'd die. And then when I lived anyway, they told me I'd never walk. When I finally made it home after the war, my father-in-law told me I'd never be able to hold my head up again in Virginia, so I came to Texas to prove him wrong, too." He shifted his gaze to her. "I lay in that hospital tent every day for weeks, waiting for my wife to come and so much as lay a cool hand on my forehead. She never showed up, and then she died before I could get home to her."

"Oh, Trace, I'm sorry," she whispered, tears filling her eyes.

He reached out and captured her hand. "You came. You can say what you want about your feelings for me, but I'll always remember that you came."

She eased her fingers from his grasp and swallowed past the knot in her throat. "You should get some rest." She leaned over and turned down the lamp, but she could feel his gaze still on her in the darkness, strong as iron, and gentle as velvet.

14

TRACE SAT UP AND swung his leg over the side of the bed, grimacing as he did so. He hurt like hell, but he supposed that was preferable to the alternative—not feeling anything because he was dead. Grunting with the effort, he hauled himself upright, leaning heavily on the back of a chair, and reached for the pair of trousers draped over the foot of the bed.

He'd succeeded in pulling on the trousers and was looking around for his boots when Theresa came into the house, her apron laden with eggs from the hens she'd reestablished in the chicken house. "What do you think you're doing?" she protested, rushing toward him.

"What does it look like? Where are my boots?"

She put her hands on her hips and frowned at him. "I don't think you should be getting up just yet."

"I'll go crazy if I have to lie in that bed one minute longer. Now, where are my boots?"

Still frowning, she fetched the boots from beside the hearth and handed them to him. He sat on the side of the bed and pulled them on, grimacing only a little. Then he sat back, breathing hard, worn out from the effort of getting dressed.

"You've gone all gray as a goose," Theresa said. "If you go fallin' over, don't think I'm gonna risk my back pickin' you up."

A knock on the door saved him from having to reply. Theresa went to answer it and returned with Nate O'Connor. The storekeeper had exchanged his white apron for a suit coat and hat, but he carried the aromas of the store with him; the smells of coffee and tobacco, linseed oil, and shoe leather hung in the air around him the way bay rum and cigar smoke clung to a New Orleans gambler. "Up and about already, I see," Nate said.

Trace shook hands. "Hello, Nate. I'm up, but I can't say I'm about." He looked past him. "Is Lucy with you?"

"No. She didn't come with me today."

The gloominess that assailed him took him by surprise. He hadn't realized before this instant how much he longed to see Lucy again. So much had passed between them in the dark hours of last night. More still had been left unsaid.

Nate pulled out a chair and sat down. "Have you come up with any ideas about who shot you?"

He shook his head. "I never heard or saw anything."

"It might not be a bad idea for you to get out of town for a few days, lay low, in case whoever shot you is still hanging around."

Trace shook his head. "I've never run from a fight. I'm not about to start now."

"I'm not talking about some schoolyard squabble." Nate shifted in his chair, as if trying to gather his emotions. "Besides, leaving for a few days might be just the thing to flush this fellow out of wherever he's hiding."

"*If* he's hiding. *If* this wasn't just some crazy accident." He rubbed the top of his thigh, above the swaddling bandages, as if he could ease the ache.

"An accident?" Nate looked skeptical.

"I've had time to do a lot of thinking, lying here. If someone were determined to kill me, he'd have used a rifle. And I doubt he'd have missed." He glanced at Nate.

"From what I remember about the Texans we fought in the war, they were pretty fair marksmen."

"If it was an accident, why didn't whoever fired that gun go for help?"

He shrugged. "Maybe he got scared. Maybe he saw me, decided to take a pot shot for harassment's sake, and never really expected to score a hit. Then he ran off."

"It's attempted murder however it happened." Nate scowled. "The man who did it should pay for his crime."

"With all the trouble Bill Pollard and others have stirred up, and the rumors that have been going around about me, I suppose more than a few people would be glad to be rid of me."

"There are a few people around who are more than glad to see you're still here," Nate said gruffly.

Trace looked away, swallowing a lump that threatened to choke him. Nate's words ambushed him as fiercely as any gunshot. How could he answer that solid declaration of allegiance? His own feelings were too deep, his emotions too close to spilling over.

Nate cleared his throat. "It's not my intention to pry, but the thought crossed my mind, when Rye first told us you were shot, that there might be some family back East you'd want notified, in the event something, uh, unfortunate happened. But I can't help noticing you don't get any mail. . . ."

"There isn't anybody." The words sounded harsh in the afternoon stillness.

Nate looked at the floor. "I'm sorry."

The sympathy in that brief comment was so real, so different from the pity he'd dreaded. Trace bowed his head, the posture of a man in deep thought or prayer. When he finally spoke, the words came slowly. "My father died during the war. Cholera. My mother died when I was very young. I was married, but my wife died, too, while I was in the hospital after Appomattox."

Nate made no sound, just reached out his hand and grasped Trace's shoulder. Trace squeezed his eyes shut, afraid he might disgrace himself by breaking down and crying like a baby. He'd said little to anyone before about his losses. Strange as the idea was to him, talking to Lucy, and now Nate, had eased the pain a little.

"My own wife died a few years before Lucy came to live with me," Nate said. "We were each the only relatives the other had, so it was only natural that we help each other out. I never had children of my own, so Lucy has always been like a daughter to me. I'm proud of her, just the way I'm sure your father was proud of you. You say he was a lawyer?"

He nodded. "We practiced together." He cleared his throat. "When I came home and found him gone, I didn't have the heart to keep at it without him."

"You may change your mind one day." Nate shrugged. "Or maybe not. I can't see how an education like that could be anything but a benefit to a man. Could be your legal training will come in handy in dealing with whoever is causing all this trouble for you."

He shook his head. "I've puzzled over it for two days and I haven't come up with anything yet."

"Maybe I can help you out by keeping my ears open around the store, asking a few pertinent questions."

Nate's suggestion sent a jolt of alarm through him. "No. I don't want you risking any more trouble on my behalf."

Nate smiled. "It's no trouble. Pretty much everybody comes by my place sooner or later. I'll just make note of what's said and report back to you. If we put our heads together, we might see a pattern."

"All right," Trace reluctantly agreed. "But promise me you'll be careful."

" 'Watch and keep silent' will be my motto." He crossed his ankle over his knee and studied Trace for a moment. "I came by to see if you would do a favor for me."

"Anything." He could never do enough for this man who had befriended him when no one else would.

"Doc Lambert tells me it's going to be a few days before

you're up to any hard riding.'' Nate nodded toward the injured leg.

Trace grimaced. He hadn't told the old sawbones, but he had plans to get back in the saddle by tomorrow, at the latest. He had too much work to do to spend his days lazing around.

"I thought you could help me out while you're recovering," Nate continued. "Doc says there shouldn't be any problem with you riding in a wagon, as long as you take it easy.''

"What is it you need me to do?'' Nate wasn't looking him in the eye anymore. Trace suddenly felt uneasy.

Nate ran his hand over his jaw. "I thought you could take Lucy into Blanco so she could register her brand.''

Trace stared at him, openmouthed. "It's a two-day trip to Blanco.''

Nate leaned forward. "That's exactly why I can't go. I can't leave the store that long. You could go in my wagon, and you could take Theresa along as a chaperon.''

The trip would mean the better part of four days alone— or virtually so—with Lucy. A tempting prospect. His heart raced at the thought. "You're trusting me with an awful lot," he said.

Nate smiled. "I don't think I have anything to worry about.''

It occurred to Trace that Nate planned this trip as a way to force his hand. He'd made no secret of his desire to see Lucy happily wed. Apparently he'd decided Trace was a suitable husband for his headstrong niece. "What does Lucy think about this?''

"I thought it best to ask you first.'' He smiled. "I don't think she'll have any objections.''

Wouldn't she? For a moment last night, he'd felt closer to Lucy than he'd ever felt to anyone, as if he could look into her eyes and see the desires of her heart written there, in a code only he could decipher.

Then, just as quickly, that flash of understanding vanished, and her thoughts were once again hidden from him.

He no longer believed Lucy hated him, but he was far from sure she trusted him. Or maybe it was just that she didn't trust herself with him.

"It would help me out a great deal," Nate said.

He couldn't say no. Not after all Nate had done for him. And maybe this trip would be a good opportunity for him and Lucy to clear the air once and for all about their feelings for one another. He nodded. "All right. I'll do it."

Nate reached out and grasped his hand. "I knew I could count on you. Why don't you plan to start day after tomorrow?"

Both men stood, and Trace limped alongside Nate to the door. Outside, they met Rye and Josh riding in. Josh slumped in the saddle, scowling at some spot between the horse's ears. He didn't even look up when he rode past them.

Rye reined in beside them. "We rode over to Anderson Hollow to check on those cattle we penned yesterday." The saddle creaked as he half turned to face them. "Somebody done hauled all the brush out of the way, and the cows run off. We spent all day roundin' 'em up again and branding 'em."

"What's wrong with Josh?" Trace nodded toward the boy.

"Hmmmph. Dang young'un like to got hisself killed ridin' hell-for-leather after an old heifer. I thought I'd be scrapin' him off the ground and totin' him home in a saddle blanket. His mama'd never forgive me."

Josh jerked his head up and turned to look back at them. "I knew what I was doin'," he said heatedly. "I wasn't gonna get myself killed."

"Most folks don't set out with that in mind," Rye said. "You gotta learn to mix that nerve of yours with a little caution." He looked the boy up and down. "You do that, you'll make a halfway decent cowboy."

Josh gave him a wary look. "You mean it? You'll take me with you again?"

Rye nodded. "You done all right for a green sprout."

Josh straightened. He tugged his hat to a jauntier angle, and a smile split his formerly solemn features. "Next time I want you to teach me to rope like you do—catchin' 'em by the heels. And you could let me cut the ears, too."

Rye turned his horse and fell in step beside the boy. "Where'd you learn to talk so much? Didn't they ever hear silence is golden back in Virginia?"

Trace watched as the two rode toward the corral. Josh had set his hat at the exact angle Rye wore his, and he'd adopted the cowboy's habit of stuffing the legs of his overalls into the tops of his boots.

"Looks like Rye may have found himself a ready-made family," Nate observed. "A boy Josh's age needs a father."

Pain, as sharp and fresh as when his grief was new, stabbed at Trace as memory flashed a picture across his mind, an image of him following his father to court on a day when he was about Josh's age. He'd been allowed to sit up front beside his father and had almost burst his shirt buttons with pride when their side had won the case.

He reached for the watch in his pocket, soothing himself with the feel of it, heavy in his hand. Would he ever know that kind of closeness with a son of his own? When Marion had died, he'd given up hoping for a child, but now the desire returned anew, a longing for a boy with his dark curls . . . and eyes like moss-green emeralds and a spirit that wouldn't be trapped or tamed.

∞

LUCY CAREFULLY FOLDED THE completed top to her bridal quilt and stuffed it into the top of her sewing basket, surprised to find her hands were shaking. She tried to laugh off her nervousness. Why should her hands be shaking? She was just going to visit Twila, her best friend. She'd been to her house hundreds of times over the years.

But the memory of the last time she'd stood in Twila's kitchen, listening to her deny the cruelty Lucy had wit-

nessed with her own eyes, sent a shiver of apprehension up
her spine. Though they'd spoken in the store a few times
since, their old closeness had vanished, wiped out by those
awful moments in Twila's kitchen.

She fastened the lid on the basket and reached for her
bonnet. She didn't care what had happened before, she
needed Twila now. She needed another woman to help her
sort out the emotions that rose and fell within her like storm
swells. Were the feelings she had for Trace Abernathy pure
love, base lust, or some mixture of the two? And how could
she know for sure what was the right thing to do?

She tied the bonnet strings in a neat bow and draped her
shawl around her shoulders, then picked up the sewing basket and walked out the door. She'd seen Pollard drive by
the store on his way out of town this afternoon, a canvas
tarp draped over his wagon load of mysterious boxes and
kegs. In her imagination, the boxes and kegs had been filled
with gunpowder and blasting caps, or some other instru-
ments of mayhem. But her practical side told her Pollard
was more likely hauling a load of string beans and peaches
to Birdtown. In any case, he wouldn't be around to stop
her from paying a call on her old friend.

The flowers in Twila's garden had faded in the summer
heat, all but a few hardy blossoms reduced to drooping
stems and leaves. Lucy hesitated on the front porch, then
took a deep breath and knocked.

"Who is it?" Twila asked from behind the closed door.

"It's me, Lucy. I came to ask you to help me baste my
quilt together. You know it's such a big job for one person."

She heard a bolt turn, and then the door opened, just
wide enough for Twila to peer out. Her eyes looked huge
in her pale face, half moons of blue shadows beneath each
socket. "Hello, Lucy." Her voice was barely a whisper.

Lucy tried to smile, though she didn't know how long
she could hold the false expression. "Aren't you going to
ask me in?"

Deep lines creased Twila's forehead. "Mr. Pollard said

e ordered you not to come here anymore.''

Lucy's smile vanished. "So he did. But since when is
e my master?" *And since when is he yours?* she wanted
o add, but held her tongue.

Twila caught her bottom lip between her teeth, but made
o move to open the door.

"I promise he'll never know that I was here," Lucy said.
'What harm could come from us having a cup of tea together and sewing a while?" She swallowed past the lump
n her throat. "I've missed you so much."

Twila threw open the door and drew Lucy to her. "I've
nissed you, too," she said, her tears dampening Lucy's
shoulder. She pulled away and dabbed at her eyes with a
nandkerchief. "You'll have to forgive me. It seems my
condition makes me more emotional than ever."

Twila's condition was more evident than when Lucy had
ast seen her, though the loose wrapper she wore somewhat
disguised her advancing pregnancy. Despite her expanding
belly, Lucy thought Twila looked thinner and bone weary,
like an old woman worn to a frazzle.

"Come into the parlor. We'll push back the furniture and
put the quilt together there," Twila said, leading the way.

Lucy was surprised to see a new-looking sofa and match-
ing chair in rich red brocade in place of Twila's old faded
set. "When did you get this?" she asked.

Twila blushed. "Mr. Pollard has been quite spoiling me
since our finances are in better condition."

Lucy bit back a remark about Pollard's guilty conscience.
Together the two women pushed the furniture against the
wall. Lucy knelt and began to unroll the lengths of calico
she'd stitched together to form the quilt backing. She'd
managed the quilts for Mrs. Sorenson by herself, of course.
She'd completed the rocky-road quilt only last night. She'd
sent word to Mrs. Sorenson to expect her soon. But she'd
felt the need to see Twila first.

"I'll make us some tea," Twila said.

By the time Twila returned with the tea tray, Lucy had
spread the calico over the rug and was laying on cotton that

had been carded into thick sheets or bats. Twila set the tray on a side table and knelt awkwardly beside her. "You did a wonderful job with this batting," she said, fingering the fine tufts. "There's hardly a cotton seed in it."

"I can't take credit." She scooted backward, carefully unrolling the batting in front of her. "I paid Mrs. Scott to do it for me. I never could get the hang of carding cotton."

"Well, I'm sure a famous author like you can afford a little convenience like that." Twila's tone held a hint of her old teasing. Lucy looked over her shoulder and saw that her friend was smiling. She relaxed, feeling hopeful for the first time since she'd arrived. "Have you sold any more stories?" Twila asked.

"I just sold a new one. About a bandit." *Who might very well be your husband*, she added silently, then pushed away the thought. She wasn't going to think about unpleasant things this afternoon. She was going to concentrate on enjoying the company of an old friend.

"You'll have to let me know when it comes out so I can get a copy." Twila tugged a corner of batting even with the calico backing.

"I thought you had a subscription to *Leslie's*." The magazines were priced so cheaply that most people could afford them.

"We did . . . Mr. Pollard canceled it. He says reading such things is a waste of time better spent in other pursuits."

Lucy's stomach gave a nervous flutter as she looked at Twila's impassive face. "What do you do all day while he's gone?"

"Oh, I stay busy. I sew and write letters and clean the house." She sat back, her gaze on the quilt, avoiding Lucy. "I grow tired so easily these days; I usually lie down for a time every afternoon."

"Do you go out—pay calls?"

She shook her head. "Mr. Pollard says it wouldn't be proper for a woman in my condition to be seen in public."

Lucy felt cold. She reached out and grasped Twila's

hand, as if to pull her back from a deep pit. "Listen to what you're saying, Twila. Pollard won't allow you to go anywhere or to see anyone. He's cut you off from all outside contact—even from something as simple as a magazine. Can't you see what he's doing? He's making you a prisoner in your own home."

Twila pulled her hand away and laughed, the sound shaky and too high-pitched. "Nonsense. I'm not isolated. Mr. Pollard brings guests to our house often."

Lucy frowned, disbelieving. "Who?"

Twila looked away, still absently rubbing her wrist. "Men mostly. I . . . I don't like most of them, I must confess. They seem very . . . coarse." She took a deep breath and raised her head. "Mr. Pollard says they are men he met during the war. I imagine the fighting made them seem rougher than they really are."

Lucy stared at her friend's delicate profile and imagined her waiting on Pollard's rough friends. Twila—bright, witty Twila—would have no part of their conversations. She would be no more to them than a servant or a bright ornament, subject to their scorn. Her throat tightened with rage. But before she could give voice to her feelings, Twila turned to her once more. "I *am* glad you're here today, Lucy. Let's not quarrel anymore."

Struck mute, Lucy nodded and pulled the completed quilt top from her sewing basket. She handed one edge to Twila, and together they unrolled it over the prepared batting and backing. The green, brown, tan, blue, and red hearts filled the space between the two women, brightening the room with a cheerful glow.

"Lucy, it's beautiful." Twila traced her finger around a blue-flowered heart. "Just think how happy you'll be sleeping under it." She looked up. "Tell me the truth now— will you marry Trace Abernathy?"

Lucy looked away, even as a flutter of excitement made her catch her breath. The idea of sharing this quilt, and all of herself, with Trace made her skin tingle and her blood run hot. She wanted him to kiss her without stopping. She wanted to know the secrets of his body and of his soul. It seemed to her that marriage should mean that kind of sharing, that kind of freedom to wholly be yourself with another.

She smoothed her hand across the neatly pieced fabric. Maybe such ideas were just mere products of her wild imagination. Her mother had certainly never experienced anything like freedom in her marriage to Lucy's stepfather. And here was Twila, trapped by her wedding vows like a prisoner locked away for life. Trace was always trying to order her around as it was. Once he had a ring on her finger, would he take it as his right to be obeyed, and she would suffer the consequences if she did not?

She shook her head. "For one thing, Trace hasn't asked me to marry him. And I've made it clear to him I intend to make my fortune before I'll even consider a proposal from anyone." She raised her eyes to meet Twila's fearful gaze. "I want to have the money to look after myself if anything should happen. After all, even a good husband can die, or be injured so he's unable to work."

"We must trust the Lord to look after us in such circumstances," Twila said softly.

"Sometimes that means taking advantage of the opportunities set before us." Lucy pulled a spool of thread from her basket and unwound a length, then clipped it with a pair of scissors shaped like a stork. "If God gave me the talent to write stories and the desire to invest in cattle, I don't see why I shouldn't use those gifts."

Twila sat back and took up her own needle. "Perhaps you won't have to wait long," she said as she began taking long basting stitches from the center of the quilt toward the edges. "Those first cattle drivers should be back from Missouri any day now, shouldn't they? Next fall, they'll be able to take your cattle to market on the trails they blazed this year."

Lucy knelt across from Twila, concentrating on taking long, even stitches through the three layers of material. Twila's words sent a surge of hope through her. "Next fall isn't very far away,'' she murmured. Her profit from the sale of her cattle would be a tidy sum—enough to make her feel more secure about trusting her future with Trace. Provided, of course, he even proposed.

"I would imagine a man like Trace might appreciate a woman with some knowledge of his business—raising cattle, that is.'' Twila moved over and began to sew another ray in the sunburst pattern of stitches that would temporarily hold the quilt together. "You could probably help him a great deal.''

"Maybe *he* could help *me*.'' Lucy reached the edge of the quilt and snipped off her thread and crawled back toward the center of the coverlet. "I fully intend to keep my own brand and my own herds once we're wed.''

She waited for Twila's objection, but none came. Instead, Twila paused in her sewing and studied Lucy. "Mr. Pollard thinks Trace moved here intending to make trouble, but I can't believe you'd love him if he was truly a bad man.''

Lucy blinked. "When did I ever say anything about being in love with Trace?''

Twila smiled, a look of secret pleasure. "I can tell you love him by the way you look when you talk about him.''

Lucy shifted. How could Twila be so certain of her feelings when she wasn't even sure herself? "Do you love Pollard?'' she asked.

The smile vanished, replaced by a look of distress. "My situation is different,'' Twila protested. "I married Mr. Pollard for protection and security. In order to have children.'' She placed one hand on her stomach, a protective gesture.

"But you don't love him.''

Twila grew even paler. "I promised to respect, honor, and obey my husband and I intend to do so.''

Frustration rose in Lucy, fighting for release. "Why should you settle for less than love?'' She rose up on her knees and grabbed her friend by the shoulders, fighting the urge to shake her, as if shaking would drive some sense into her. "Don't you think you *deserve* better than a man who beats you and mistreats you?''

Twila shrank from Lucy's gaze, her head down, hands to her face as if to ward off the words like blows. "He doesn't mean to beat me. He's always sorry afterwards. He only does it when I do something to upset him. If I don't upset him, he treats me fine."

"Twila—it's not your fault. It's his. He's a bad man."

She shook her head. "I won't believe it."

"He tried to kill Trace. You saw it with your own eyes." She looked around the room and spotted the new furniture. "And you don't know what other wrongdoings he's involved in, he and his rough friends. Do you really think hauling produce pays well enough to buy new furniture and dresses and things?"

Twila wrenched away from her and staggered to her feet. "What are you saying?"

Lucy rose up in front of her. "I'm saying I think your husband is the Buckboard Bandit. If it isn't him, I'm sure he knows who it is. He's the one who's committing all these crimes in the area, preying on innocent people. He even attacked our store—and then had the nerve to show up afterwards and gloat about it to our faces."

Twila backed away, shaking her head. "No. No, he didn't do it." Her voice quavered. She swallowed hard, fighting for control.

"Yes, Twila. Can't you see it? Pollard's wrong, and you don't have to put up with his treatment. You can go home to your parents, and no one will think less of you."

"Leave me alone!" The choked plea tore at Lucy's heart. She reached for her friend, but Twila backed away. "You've said enough! Just go away and leave me alone!" She turned and fled from the room. Lucy heard her footsteps on the stairs, then a door slammed overhead.

She started out of the room after her, but stopped in the parlor doorway. Maybe Twila was right. Maybe she had said enough—too much, even. But she couldn't stand idly by and watch her friend's life ruined. Maybe some of what she'd said today would sink in. She sighed and turned back to gather up the quilt, not pausing to wipe the tears that fell to spot the fabric.

15

"YOU CAN'T BE SERIOUS." Lucy stared at her uncle, convinced she must have misunderstood. Surely he hadn't just told her she'd be traveling all the way to Blanco with Trace Abernathy.

"But of course I'm serious." Nate looked up from the display of tobacco he was arranging, the smile on his face entirely too smug to suit Lucy. "You need to register your brand, I have to stay here to look after the store, and Trace is available to escort you. It's the perfect solution."

A perfectly horrible solution, she thought. Four days alone with a man who never failed to upset whatever control she'd managed to maintain over her life. Four days with Trace, and she was sure to end up thinking, feeling—*doing*—things she'd never done before and never intended to do. She gripped the edge of the counter she was standing behind and took a deep, steadying breath. "I can't possibly go with him," she said. "It wouldn't be proper."

Nate elevated one eyebrow and pursed his lips. "Since when do you care so much about propriety? As I recall, you've steadfastly ignored every one of *my* lectures on the subject." He turned back to the tobacco. "Besides, the arrangement will be perfectly proper. Theresa is going along as chaperon.''

She flattened her hands on the counter and leaned toward him. ''But I'd really rather go with you,'' she pleaded. ''You deserve a vacation from all this hard work.''

He shook his head. ''I haven't taken a vacation in forty years. No need to start now. No, you'd best go with Trace.''

''Couldn't we find someone else?''

''Nope.''

Nate obviously wasn't going to listen to anything else she had to say on the subject. She knew when to give in. For now. She was a smart, creative person. Before she and Trace were scheduled to leave town, she'd come up with another solution. ''When are we leaving?'' she asked.

Nate glanced over his shoulder, toward the clock on the wall behind the counter. ''I'd say he ought to be along any minute now.'' He walked over to the foot of the stairs and pulled a carpetbag from behind the hall tree. ''I think you've got everything you need in here.''

She stared at him, openmouthed. ''You tricked me!''

Nate grinned. ''Let's just say I've come to know you a little too well.'' He handed her the carpetbag. ''You have a good time. I think I hear Trace now.''

Stunned, she followed Nate out to the front porch in time to see Trace pull up in Nate's wagon, Theresa beside him. ''Good morning,'' Trace said, tipping his hat to them both. He set the wagon brake, then climbed down to meet them. He moved stiffly, as if the leg still troubled him, but otherwise he seemed completely recovered. He took Lucy's carpetbag from her. ''I'll just put this in the back and we'll be on our way.''

She wanted to protest, but all of a sudden her mouth didn't seem to be working right. Everything was happening too fast. First her uncle's announcement, and then the sight of Trace himself, hale and hearty, in sharp contrast to the pale, wounded man she'd last encountered.

He helped her into the wagon, his hand on her elbow, radiating strength. Her spirits soared at seeing him so . . .

alive again. She curled her fingers against her palms, fighting the need to touch him. He settled into the wagon seat next to her, his thigh brushing hers, sending a jolt of awareness through her. Squeezing her legs together, she smoothed her skirts over her knees, hoping to hide her sudden trembling. How would she spend four days like this, sparked tinder on the verge of bursting into flame?

They said their good-byes to Nate, then Trace slapped the reins, and they started out of town. They were clear of the main street before anyone spoke. "Why are you so nervous?" Trace asked. "Don't you trust me?"

She was grateful for her sunbonnet to hide her burning face. She might be willing to trust Trace, but she couldn't say the same about herself. She pulled her shawl more tightly about her shoulders. "I resent you and Uncle Nate plotting against me."

"Your uncle asked me to do a favor for him, and I agreed. I don't see how that's a plot."

"Hmmph!" She raised her chin, determined to have as little as possible to do with him for the remainder of the trip.

As the sun rose in the sky, the heat grew more intense. Theresa raised a parasol and shared it with Lucy, but still she could feel perspiration trickling down her spine to pool in the small of her back. Surely there were few things more miserable than sitting in a rough-riding wagon on a hot day next to a man who looked altogether too comfortable in spite of the heat. If she was suffering, he at least ought to be, too.

"I'll say one thing, y'all ain't much for conversation." Theresa's observation broke their long silence. She adjusted the parasol over their heads. "Not that Trace there was ever much of a talker on his best days."

Lucy glanced at Trace, who remained expressionless, indifferent to the remark. "How long have you known each other?" she asked Theresa.

"Now, let's see. Nine . . . no, must be more than ten

years now. Since that first night he come to call on Miz Marion and she took a shine to him.''

Lucy turned to Trace once more. Was she imagining that flush of red up the back of his neck? She looked back at Theresa. ''I'm curious—why did you decide to come all the way to Texas by yourself?''

''My boy was here. I come to get him.''

''I know that.'' She shifted on the wagon seat. ''I guess a better question would be why did you decide to stay?''

Theresa shrugged. ''I wanted to be with friends. Besides, Trace and Rye didn't have no woman to do for them. I figured I'd better help 'em out before they starved to death or poisoned each other with their sorry cookin'.'' Her voice held a hint of laughter.

''It wasn't that bad.'' Trace spoke for the first time.

Theresa looked at him, then at her lap. ''You know the real reason I stayed. I owe you.''

''No, you don't.''

Lucy held her breath, aware of the tension radiating between them. Neither seemed conscious of her presence anymore. They both sat stiffly, not looking at each other or at her. The only sound was the steady *clop, clop* of the horses on the road.

''I do,'' Theresa said after a long while, her voice little more than a whisper.

Trace frowned and shook his head.

Lucy waited, afraid to ask for an explanation, though she was fairly bursting with curiosity. The wagon hit a bump, jolting them so that the women had to hold on to each other to keep from being thrown. Theresa came out of whatever trance she'd been in and acknowledged Lucy once more. ''You want to know why I say I owe him?''

She hesitated. Did she? Or was the truth of Trace's relationship with this woman something she'd rather not know? She thought of Josh, with his pale skin and white features, and little Mary, who looked so much like her brother. But how could she go on not knowing? She nodded.

"First off, he bought Josh from Miz Marion's father so he could come live with me."

"I only did what was right," Trace protested. He looked annoyed. "And it isn't as if Theresa hasn't already paid me back ten times over."

Theresa looked down and plucked invisible lint from her skirt. "Josh ain't all I owe you for, and you know it." Her voice was hard, tinged with anger.

Lucy instinctively put out her hand. It was too late to pretend she didn't care anymore. "What is it?" she asked.

"Trace kept Marse Alan away from me." She turned and met Lucy's puzzled gaze. "I know you been wonderin' if Trace was Josh's father."

She started to deny it, but the blush that engulfed her cheeks betrayed her. Theresa squeezed her hand. "It weren't Trace. Marse Alan was father to Josh. Mary, too. After Trace went off to the fightin', the old man come sniffin' around again just like the dog he was."

Relief flooded her, along with sympathy for what Theresa had endured. She wanted to thank her for easing her fears about Trace, but didn't know how.

"Did you really think I was Josh's father?" She could feel Trace's eyes boring into her as he spoke.

She shook her head. "I didn't know what to think. I could see he was half-white. And you and Theresa are obviously close . . ."

Trace slapped the reins across the horse's backs, setting them into a trot. "You're as bad as the Yankees I met who were convinced every Southern plantation owner had a black mistress on the side and half a dozen mulatto bastards."

Lucy ducked her head, shame washing over her. This must prove what she felt for Trace wasn't love—otherwise, how could she have ever doubted him?

"I say Miz Lucy is right not to trust a man until he proves hisself trustworthy." Theresa spoke up. "There's a lot of bad apples in that barrel."

"Is that what you think about Rye—that he can't be

trusted?'' Trace asked, his voice still sharp with anger.

Theresa's expression softened. "Maybe so. We'll see how he takes care of my babies while we're away."

Lucy latched on to this turn in the conversation. "You left Rye in charge of Josh and Mary?"

"He volunteered." She smiled. "I figured now's as good a time as any to see how he does at playin' daddy. He's comin' along slow with Josh, but makin' progress."

"Josh doesn't make it very easy for him," Trace said, relaxing some, obviously relieved to talk about someone other than himself.

"I'll admit the boy's a challenge," Theresa said. "He needs a strong man's influence. Maybe Rye is that man."

"Did you finish the soogan you were making for him?" Lucy asked, remembering the quilt Theresa had been sewing the night after the fire.

"Yes, I did. Now I'm making a Jacob's-ladder quilt. I had one like that back in Virginia. When Mary was born, the woman who helped birth her wrapped her in that quilt and marched her through all the rooms in the house."

"Why did she do that?" Lucy asked, puzzled.

"Why, so the baby'd be healthy. A baby done that way won't sicken and die—it's protected by the power in the quilt."

"I never thought about a quilt having power before," Lucy said hesitantly, remembering the closeness she felt to her mother whenever she worked on the rocky-road quilt.

"There's the power in all the pieces of fabric in the quilt. All the good memories from this party dress or that baby outfit or some comfortable wrapper worn until it was only good for quilt scraps. Even for a special quilt, where the fabric is bought new, it was all picked special for the quilt, so that gives it power, too."

Lucy nodded. Through her mother's quilts, Lucy had managed to learn new things about her mother, and about herself—things that couldn't be explained by mere bits of fabric.

"And then every woman that works on the quilt adds a

little bit of her power with the stitches,'' Theresa continued.
"You just think about when everybody come together to
quilt out a cover. They all talk and visit—it's a happy time,
and some of that happiness gets into the quilt.''

Lucy could feel her mother in every piece of the quilts
she'd cut out and never lived to sew. Was that what Theresa
meant by power?

"So you see, quilts is more special than any other kind
of bedcover,'' Theresa finished with a smile.

Lucy nodded. "I see what you mean.'' The thought occurred to her that she was putting her own power into the
quilts she sewed—the ones for Mrs. Sorenson and her still
incomplete bridal quilt. Would someone one day pick up
one of her quilts and sense her presence there? Maybe she'd
pass that gift down to her own daughter, the way her
mother had passed it on to her. The thought made her smile,
that something as simple and practical as a coverlet could
bind people and generations together.

∞

AT SUNSET, TRACE BROUGHT the wagon to a halt beside a shallow creek. He saw to the horses while Lucy and
Theresa gathered wood for a fire. "Feels good to get out
of that wagon and stretch my legs,'' Theresa observed as
she bent to add a stick to her pile of kindling.

"It does that.'' Lucy looked up at streaks of orange
etched across the graying sky. "You know, I've never
camped out before.''

"It's not bad. I wouldn't want to live this way, but when
you're travelin', sometimes you got no choice.'' She
paused and inhaled deeply. "The air smells sweet out here,
don't it?''

The air smelled of sun-warmed cedar and shady loam.
Their campfire added the scent of woodsmoke, and then the
aromas of coffee and crisp-fried bacon joined the rich pal-
ette of odors. As darkness closed in around them, Lucy sat
on a folded quilt beside the fire and stared into the flick-

ering flames, a feeling a contentment washing over her.

She wanted to savor this moment, to memorize every sensation—the taste of good food, the perfume of the outdoors, the soft carpet of fallen leaves beneath her feet, and the good company of friends around her. Someday she'd close her eyes, and it would all come rushing back to her, a perfect moment in time, captured forever.

She looked across the fire at Trace. He sat on a log, wiping his plate with a piece of bread, long legs stretched out in front on him. He'd removed his hat, revealing hair that needed trimming. It curled up at his collar, and one thick lock fell across his forehead. Firelight painted his face with shadows, erasing the fine lines carved by wind and sun. He looked almost boyish, as she imagined he might have looked before the war.

She knew she should look away, but she could not pull her gaze from him. He had attracted her from the first, not for his good looks alone, but for some inner quality of strength and stubbornness she now knew matched her own strong will.

Theresa rose and began gathering up the dishes. "I'll just take these to the creek and wash up."

"Let me help." Lucy started to rise, but Theresa motioned for her to remain seated.

"I'll get 'em myself. You stay here and keep Trace company."

How did you keep company with a man who seemed so complete unto himself? She smoothed her apron over her knees and tried to think of some topic of conversation. With Theresa gone, the woods closed in around them. The firelight trapped them in an intimate circle. In the silence, she imagined she could hear her heart beating.

Trace shifted, drawing his legs up and resting his elbows on knees. "We ought to be in Blanco by tomorrow afternoon."

"It's been a long time since I've been there," she said. "I'm looking forward to seeing it again."

He leaned forward and poked the fire with a stick, sending up a shower of sparks. The movement brought him closer to her. She scooted around the fire, to the edge of the quilt, wanting to be closer still.

"Are you cold? Here, take this." He removed his coat and leaned over to drape it around her.

She put her hand up to stroke the soft wool and savored the aroma of woodsmoke and leather and the subtle scent of Trace himself. Tingles danced up her arms. Closing her eyes, she thought of the way he'd once held her and wished he would hold her again. Such thoughts were wanton and dangerous, she knew, but she couldn't keep them from her head.

"Lucy."

She opened her eyes and found him studying her intently. "I told your uncle I didn't want to make this trip," he said, "but now I'm glad I did."

"Why didn't you want to make it?"

"I wasn't sure it was good for us to spend so much time together, practically alone."

"Why not?" She felt light-headed, breathless as she waited for his answer.

He moved toward her, until mere inches separated them. She could see the pulse softly beating at his temple, feel the warm exhalation of his breath. "Because of these feelings I have for you."

"What feelings?" she whispered.

"Feelings a man has for a woman."

She licked her lips and swallowed, trying to bring some moisture into her suddenly dry mouth. "Maybe I have the same sort of feelings."

"Do you?" He leaned forward and brushed his lips against hers in the briefest of kisses.

She smiled. "Can't you do better than that?" she teased in a voice that trembled slightly.

With a low sound in the back of his throat, somewhere between a growl and a moan, he pulled her into his arms. His lips found hers once more, caressing, suckling, *claiming* her. She lost herself in the sensation of *him*—the roughness of his unshaven cheek against her own softness, the thick satin of his hair against her hand as she stroked the back of his neck, the steel curves of his arms around her. She opened her mouth to the teasing dance of his tongue and reveled in the taste of him.

She pressed against him. "Hold me closer," she murmured. He pulled her nearer. His hands caressed her thighs through muffling layers of petticoats, then skimmed her corset-covered torso, coming to rest on the curve of her breasts as they swelled above the confining stays. She gasped as he deftly traced a path to her nipples, which rose at his touch, hard and aching. "Oh, Trace," she whispered, arching against him.

He tensed and grew still, then gently drew away from her. "We'd better stop," he said in a strained voice.

She stared at him, breathless and chilled in the sudden absence of his touch. "Why?"

She knew the answer even before he spoke. "It isn't proper."

"I never cared about propriety."

He frowned. "You should." He stood, his back to her. "Theresa will be back here soon."

She glared at him, opening and closing her fists. She hated the fact that he was right. She didn't want him to always be right.

"Lawdy, traveling all day sure do tire a body out." With a clatter of pots and plates, Theresa emerged from the trees. She carried the clean dishes to the wagon, avoiding looking at either of them. Lucy wondered if she had been watching them, waiting for the right moment to interrupt. She turned away, grateful the darkness hid her blush.

I'm not ashamed, she told herself. She wouldn't be ashamed of the feelings she had for Trace. She didn't know what she would do about them, but she couldn't see the shame in something that rose up from the depths of her soul, like poetry, or music—a gift of beauty she'd never known she possessed.

16

THEY REACHED THE TOWN of Blanco early the next afternoon. Lucy studied the modest collection of false-fronted buildings clustered around a shaded public square and tried to quell her disappointment. Somehow she'd expected a county seat to be bigger—almost a real city, even. Blanco was only a little larger than Elm Creek itself, its quiet streets scarcely a bustling metropolis. Still, they hadn't come for shopping or socializing, she reminded herself. This was a business trip, and she'd do well to keep her mind on business.

Trace found a place for their wagon across from the courthouse—a two-story frame building with a sign proclaiming the Masonic lodge met upstairs. "I thought we'd take care of filing the brand first, then find someplace to stay," he said.

"All right." She gathered her shawl and pocketbook and allowed him to help her from the wagon. As his hand closed around hers, she thought of the warmth and strength in his embrace, the heat and power of the man himself. All morning she had silently wrestled with her memories of last night. Those magical moments in Trace's arms were the stuff of dreams. Yet they troubled her as much as any nightmare, for in the end Trace had pushed her away. She stared at his back as he turned to help Theresa to the ground. Had propriety been all that motivated him, or did Trace in his wisdom sense they were not right for each other? Why else had he rejected the gift she would have so freely given?

"Right this way, ladies." He motioned them up the courthouse steps, through the double doors and down a long hallway. They found the wooden plaque proclaiming Clerk and stepped through the open door.

A white-haired man with a long face worked behind a tall desk. "Yes?" He looked up from his books and raised a questioning eyebrow at Trace.

"I've come to register my brand," Lucy said, stepping forward. "My cattle brand."

"Well, of course. What other kind of brand would you register?" He chuckled, delighted with his own cleverness. She fought down a flush of embarrassment.

The clerk left his work at the desk and turned to a wall of shelves behind him. He chose a large, leather-bound volume and carried it over to the desk. "What is the marking to be registered?" he asked in a flat voice.

She produced the folded sheet of paper from her pocketbook, with the drawing of the L-U perched atop a C. The brand was easily read as Lu-Cee, and she hoped not easily altered.

The clerk studied the drawing over the top of his wire-rimmed glasses and grunted, then opened the book and began to run his finger along the columns of letters and numbers there. Even upside down, Lucy recognized some of the markings—the Lazy K, Double Diamond, and Mr. Fischer's fish, for instance. She thought she spied Trace's Circle A, too. The question was—was anyone else using *her* brand? She watched the clerk's ink-stained forefinger travel down the ledger columns, scarcely daring to breathe until he closed the book with a solid *thump!* and looked up. "Nothing like that here," he said. "You're free to use it." He took a pen from a tray in front of him and removed the cap from an inkwell. "And the name in which this brand is to be registered?'' Once again, he addressed Trace.

''Lucy O'Connor.'' She stepped between Trace and the clerk, forcing the old man to look at her. He frowned, then bent his head to write. She gave him her address, date of birth, and information on the size and location of her herd, then paid her filing fee. Thus duly registered and recorded, with a paper in her bag to prove it, she left the courthouse ready to celebrate yet another important step on her road to independence.

She paused on the courthouse steps and took a deep breath. ''Thank God that's over with.''

Trace laughed. ''I guess that clerk doesn't get too many women coming in to register their own brands. He didn't appreciate the novelty of the situation.''

She stiffened. ''I'm not doing this as a lark. This is a business for me, just as it would be for any man.''

He nodded, solemn once more. ''Of course. And I've no doubt you'll beat many a man at the game.''

She studied him out of the corner of her eye. Had he just given her a compliment? Before she could decide, he interrupted her thoughts. ''Why don't you ladies have a look around, maybe do some shopping, while I find a place for the horses and rooms for the night?''

''There are a few things I'm needin'.'' Theresa patted her pocketbook. ''Come on, Miz Lucy, let's see what the stores in Blanco have to offer.''

They headed first to the general mercantile, a place much like Uncle Nate's store, only a little larger and, they hoped, stocked with a better variety of goods. The same familiar aromas of roasted coffee and vinegary pickles and leather harness greeted Lucy as they stepped through the door, so that she felt almost at home among the displays of shoes and yard goods and canned vegetables.

''I need some quilting thread and a packet of pins,'' Theresa said, steering them toward the sewing supplies.

''I need to find a wedding gift for Elizabeth Ferry,'' Lucy said. ''She and Dudley Southworth will be married next Saturday.'' She trailed her hand over a bolt of plum-colored satin, the kind of fabric one would use to sew a beautiful wedding gown.

"You don't sound exactly overjoyed at the idea." Theresa glanced back at her. "Is it Elizabeth, or Dudley, or just marriage in general you don't like?"

Lucy jerked her hand away from the fabric. "I never said I had anything against marriage. *I* just don't intend to marry too soon." Even as she spoke the words, she felt a pain in her chest. Was she making a big mistake to pass up what might be her one chance for happiness, all because she was afraid of the distant possibility that things might not work out as wonderfully as she wanted? She shook her head and followed Theresa down the aisle. Nonsense. She was just being practical, planning for her future.

From the sewing aisle, they drifted to the front of the store, where a display of ceramic teapots attracted Lucy's attention. "I think Elizabeth would like one of these," she said, holding up a black glazed pot decorated with painted red poppies. She turned to the store clerk behind the counter. "Could you wrap this up for me, please?"

"I'll just get some candy for the chil'ren." Theresa moved toward a display of horehound and peppermint sticks, but stopped short in front of a stack of magazines. "Isn't this the paper you write for?" she asked, picking up the copy of *Leslie's Illustrated Weekly*.

"Yes, it is." Lucy smiled and took the magazine. She opened the cover and scanned the table of contents, her heart beating faster as she read the title of her latest story, "Defeat of the Buckboard Banodit: A Ranger's Triumph."

"You write for them, huh?" The clerk leaned over to study the magazine.

"I wrote that story right there." She pointed to the bandit story.

The clerk nodded. "You know, I always wanted to be a writer," he said. "In fact, I have the perfect idea for a story. I just haven't had time to write it down yet, but when I do, hoo boy, them New York fellas better watch out."

Lucy somehow managed to keep her smile in place as

she folded the magazine and laid it on the counter. Of course, everyone thought they could be a writer. Good thing for her not everyone got around to doing it. Oh, well, even if she wasn't getting famous, at least she was putting money in the bank. Between the checks she got from writing stories and the money she made quilting for Mrs. Sorenson, she was well on her way to being able to look after herself.

"Say, Al, any word yet from Dutch and the boys?" The floorboards shook as a beefy man in chaps and a buckskin vest strode up to the counter. He nodded to Lucy, one hand politely tugging his hat brim, then turned to address the clerk once more. "They ought to be back from Missouri any day now, hadn't they?"

The clerk shrugged and wrapped another sheet of newspaper around Lucy's teapot. "Reckon a lot of folks are anxious to hear how things went." He handed Lucy her teapot. "Will there be anything else, miss?"

She cradled the teapot in one arm and turned to the man in buckskin. "Excuse me, but these men you're referring to—are you talking about the ones who drove a herd of cattle north to sell in Missouri?"

He grinned. "That's the ones, ma'am. Talk was they could get as much as forty dollars a head up there, for cattle worth only four dollars in Texas. Considerin' the cattle I sent with 'em, I'm due a tidy sum."

The man's excitement was contagious. Lucy could feel it swelling within her. "Good luck to you, sir," she said. "This first success is bound to mean good things for everyone who owns cattle in Texas."

"Yes, ma'am, I reckon it does. Once the Yankees get a taste of good Texas beef, they'll be hollerin' for more. Next year, we'll send 'em twice as many—and make twice as much money."

Lucy's thoughts were a blur as she quickly computed the value of her herd. *Let's see, that's twelve steers at forty dollars each, minus twenty dollars to Mr. Gibbs, then twenty cows at forty dollars each, minus the seventy-five dollars I paid for them, plus the fifty dollars I still owe . . . no, wait—*

if those cows had one calf each, that would make forty-eight . . . or what if some of them had two *calves . . . .*

Whatever the total, it would give her a tidy sum to put in the bank for the future. She'd have the money she'd always wanted, and then she could marry Trace.

Her hands shook as she opened her pocketbook to pay for the teapot. *Marry Trace.* Like some magical incantation, the words sent a flood of feeling rushing through her. Now that the prize was within her reach, she could admit that all along she'd harbored a secret desire for it. In spite of her efforts to resist the powerful emotional pull, she'd fallen in love with Trace, and now she allowed herself to fall equally in love with the idea of being his wife.

"While we're here, I'd better get these." Theresa placed a card of bone buttons on the counter. "Nearly all of Rye's shirts are missing buttons."

Lucy smiled. She couldn't keep from smiling, she was so happy. And she wanted everyone to be as happy as she was. She waited until they stepped out onto the sidewalk to ask, "So when are you and Rye getting married?"

Theresa glanced at her. "What makes you so sure I'm marryin' him?"

"Don't lie and tell me you don't want to. He's all you ever talk about. My goodness, you left your children with him this weekend. You'd be crazy not to marry—"

"Ain't you the one to talk?" Theresa stopped and put her hands on her hips. "I thought you didn't hold with women marrying and giving up their freedom. Changed your tune now, have you?"

"I never said marriage wasn't a good thing," she protested. "For some people, anyway. I even plan to marry one day, after I've made enough money to ensure a secure future. Maybe even as soon as next year." She couldn't keep a hint of a smile from slipping back to her face.

"A year's a long time. That man ain't gonna wait for-ever, you know."

Lucy stiffened. "What man?"

"You know what man." Theresa lowered her voice. "I

saw the way Trace was kissin' you last night. A man with those kind of feelings ain't gonna put himself aside like that for too long. You keep makin' him wait, he'll go find somebody else.''

Lucy was sure that for a moment her heart stopped beating. She stared at Theresa, acute embarrassment and the compulsion to know more doing battle within her. "How do you know what kind of feelings Trace has for me?" she blurted at last. "If he loves me, a year isn't that long to wait.''

Theresa gave her a pitying look. "It is if he don't think you love him back. The way you been actin', how's he supposed to know?''

She turned and walked away, leaving Lucy to stare after her. *You're wrong!* she wanted to shout, but she couldn't believe the words. How could Trace *not* know she loved him? Hadn't her actions last night told him as much? Or did he think her affection was insincere, some wayward girl's attempt to pass the time enjoyably?

She'd fought all her life to be practical, not to allow her emotions to interfere with her plans for the future. Had she been so singleminded, so focused on what she wanted, that now she risked losing what she needed most of all? She hugged the teapot to her chest and straightened her shoulders. She was *not* going to let Trace slip away from her so easily. All she needed to keep him was a new plan.

TRACE PARKED THE WAGON behind the livery stable and buried his head in his hands. What was he going to do about Lucy? He found it harder and harder to control his feelings for her. Being near her, even sitting beside her in the wagon, was torture. He had almost asked Theresa to trade places with her today, except he wouldn't have been able to bring himself to confess why he wanted her to do so. Instead, he had spent the day in a state of misery. Every movement he made seemed to bring him in contact with her. Every breath he took filled him with the soft scent of her. Yet she appeared oblivious to his torture, calm as a still pool, perfectly in control.

Only last night, when he'd finally given in to the need to kiss her, had her careful reserve slipped. For a moment he'd glimpsed once more the passion buried beneath her studied control. In his arms she transformed like mercury, what appeared to be cold and indifferent dissolving at a touch to burning heat and light. Like a man lost in darkness, he craved that light—craved it too much. Anything you wanted so badly had the power to control you, to hurt you. Hadn't he learned that lesson with Marion?

He raised his head and tried to shrug off these feelings. What did it matter? Lucy didn't love him. Oh, she might think of him as a friend; she'd certainly cared enough to nurse him when he was hurt. But maybe he'd been mistaken about her motives there, too. Maybe she was just acting out of Christian charity, the way she would have for any wounded neighbor. It didn't mean she'd ever want to marry him.

He climbed down from the wagon and began to unfasten the horses from the traces. Marriage! He grunted in self-disgust. He might as well get that word out of his vocabulary. He needed a wife—especially a wife like Lucy—the way he needed another hole in his leg.

But the old arguments didn't have the same power in the face of his strengthened feelings for the woman who challenged both the best and the worst sides of his character. *It's just plain, old-fashioned lust,* he told himself as he led the horses to stalls in the stable. *You've been without a woman too long, and Lucy happens to be the one who appears most available.* But she was not available, and he knew it. He fastened the doors of the stalls, then measured oats into the feed bins. "The thing to do is just keep as much distance as possible from her and allow time for these feelings to pass," he said aloud as he watched the horses bury their noses in the fragrant feed. For a man who'd faced down charging rebs at the Wilderness and outlived a sniper's bullet at Appomattox, how tough could it be to outlast one little woman?

∞

"MY, AIN'T WE DRESSED up nice?" Theresa chuckled and shook her head as she surveyed the outfit Lucy had chosen for dinner. "Miss Lucy, this is Blanco, Texas, not the grand ballroom in some Richmond hotel."

Lucy tugged on the low bodice of her gown, wondering if she'd gone a little overboard. She'd had Theresa cinch her corset so tightly her breasts swelled above it in what she liked to think of as a very womanly show of bosom. She fanned her suddenly too-warm cheeks. "I thought it would be nice to dress for dinner. It's not as if I get to eat in a real restaurant every day of the week."

"I think Mr. Trace would have been just as happy to have supper here at the boardinghouse." Theresa began tidying the dressing table. "You had to practically beg him to take you out to eat."

"I'm sure he'll enjoy himself once we're there." She looked at Theresa over her fan. "I'm sorry you can't go with us."

Theresa shrugged. "No, you ain't." She gave Lucy a sharp look. "Don't think I don't know you're up to something."

"What makes you say that?" She couldn't keep from blushing.

"I recognize all the signs." Theresa shook her head. "You just be careful. And don't be thinkin' you know everythin' there is to know about a man like Trace."

"We're just going out for a nice supper." She looked away. "I wish he'd hurry up and get here. I'm hungry."

"Hmmph! You got your stays so tight, it's a wonder you can breathe, much less eat."

Lucy ignored the remark and perched on the edge of the bed, waiting for Trace's knock. What she proposed to do tonight was outrageous, daring, and more than a little foolhardy. But then, writing stories and buying cattle weren't exactly conventional behaviors for a young woman, either, and she'd survived both those endeavors nicely. Who was to say tonight's plans wouldn't turn out just as well?

A single knock on the door made her pop up like a jack-in-the-box. Theresa frowned and motioned her to sit again while she opened the door. "It's a good thing you got here when you did," Theresa said to Trace as she ushered him into the room. "She says she's about to faint from hunger."

Trace nodded to Lucy. Theresa was right; he didn't look pleased about the prospect of dinner with her. In fact, he looked almost angry, his mouth fixed in a stern line, his face pale. Lucy straightened her shoulders, and he blanched even paler. Maybe he was just tired from their long journey. A leisurely dinner, perhaps a drink of wine, would help him relax and unwind.

Lucy picked up her wrap and offered it to him. He hesitated, then took the shawl and draped it around her shoulders, his frown more severe than ever. At least he'd dressed up for the occasion. His coat was freshly brushed, and the starched white shirt he wore looked brand-new.

"I'd still prefer to eat right here at the boardinghouse," he said as they stepped out onto the sidewalk.

She frowned, picturing the traveling drummers, government officials, and other boarders crowded around the long plank table in the dining room downstairs. No, that wouldn't do at all. "Let's go to the hotel instead," she said, naming the only other dining establishment in town. She and Theresa had glimpsed inside the front doors on their walk through town. The small square tables, each with its own fresh linen cloth and bud vase, would provide the perfect setting for a romantic evening.

He hesitated, as if about to protest.

"If it's the expense you're worried about, I'll pay," she said. "I mean, this was my idea after all. . . ."

Too late, she realized she'd offended him. "Money is no object, Miss O'Connor." He offered her his arm.

Ouch! She winced as she placed her hand in the crook

of his elbow. The "Miss O'Connor" hurt. So far her plan was progressing badly. And her tight stays hurt!

They walked in silence to the hotel. Like almost every other building in town, the Metropolitan Hotel had a tall, square false front, making it appear much larger than the two-story structure behind the imposing facade. The dining room occupied the front half of the ground floor. A well-dressed young woman welcomed them inside and took Trace's hat, then escorted them to a table by the front window. Trace held Lucy's chair for her while their hostess lit the single candle in the center of the table. Lucy smoothed the linen napkin in her lap, avoiding his gaze as he settled across from her.

"Tonight's special is chicken and dumplings," their hostess announced.

Lucy bit the inside of her cheek to keep from laughing. "That sounds . . . fine," she managed to stammer.

"I'll have that, too." Trace waited until the young woman had walked away before he leaned across the table and spoke in a low voice. "Are you all right? You look as if something went down the wrong way."

She couldn't keep a chuckle from escaping her then. "It just struck me as . . . humorous that such a fine and fancy place would serve something as plain and ordinary as chicken and dumplings."

He shook his head, apparently not sharing her humor. She dropped her gaze and pleated her napkin in her lap. "I suppose I was just expecting something . . . fancier, that's all." She started to say "more romantic," but stopped herself. Maybe men didn't think about things that way at all.

"I like chicken and dumplings," was the only answer he gave.

She stared out the front window, fighting back her growing frustration. Nothing was going the way she'd planned. The hostess hadn't even offered them wine—not that she could imagine drinking some fine vintage with everyday chicken and dumplings.

The hostess returned with their meal, two china plates

filled with fragrant pieces of chicken and pillowy dumplings in a rich broth. In spite of her earlier reservations, Lucy had to admit they were delicious.

Darkness fell outside the window, transforming the glass into a mirror reflecting the dancing candle flame and their own solemn faces. She watched Trace in the glass. He ate with all the determination of a man preparing himself for a forced march. Her stomach clenched with desperation. If anything useful was going to happen tonight, it was up to her.

She pasted a pleasant expression on her face and turned to face him. "I heard some men in the store today talking about the cattle drive. They expect the drovers to return home soon with the money from the sale."

He nodded. "I imagine a lot of people are anxious to see what kind of profit they made."

"The man in the store said cattle up North are selling for forty dollars a head. That's ten times what they'll bring here." The thought buoyed her. "Next year we'll have a market ready and waiting for us. We could both be rich." *There won't be anything to keep us from marrying.*

He picked up his fork and turned it over and over in his hand, then laid it aside and looked directly at her. "Why is money so important to you?" he asked. "It's not as if you've ever really wanted for anything, is it? Or have you?"

She shook her head. Her family had never been wealthy, but neither had they been poor. How could she make Trace understand? "I don't care so much for the money itself. Not to spend on fancy clothes or jewelry or *things*." She shifted in her chair, wishing she could find some position where the rigid boning of the corset didn't jab her ribs. "I just . . . well, a woman with money is never truly helpless."

He frowned. "Helpless? Since when were you ever helpless?"

"Not me, but . . ." She licked her lips, searching for words. "When I was very little, my father died and left me and my mother alone. Uncle Nate hadn't moved here yet, and Mama . . . well, Mama wasn't like me. She couldn't see any way for her to support the two of us by herself. She was scared we'd starve to death, so she set out to find a husband and she accepted the first man who proposed to her.'' She stared down at the table, her mother's words ringing in her memory. *I had to marry him. There was no other way.* ''My stepfather . . . well, he wasn't a very nice man.''

The unexpected brush of Trace's hand against her own startled her. She jerked her head up, and he pulled his hand away. ''Did he . . . hurt you?''

She flushed. ''Not physically. But he was cruel to us, just the same.'' She lifted her chin. ''I swore I'd never put myself in that position again. I'd always make sure I had choices in my life.''

''Not every man is like your stepfather,'' he said slowly.

''No. But accidents happen. Men die. Or go off to war.'' She made her hands into fists in her lap. ''Women have to be able to look after themselves. And they have to be able to look after their children, too.''

He looked doubtful. He was a man—how could he know the terror of being trapped in a life he didn't want?

''I just—I remember hearing my mother crying late at night, when she thought no one would hear. It scared me so much. And I see Twila now, married to a man like Pollard, expecting a baby.'' She looked at him, pleading for him to see things through her eyes. ''Haven't you ever been scared that way?''

He looked away. ''Everyone in a war is scared. If they tell you they're not, they're lying.''

''I just want to do this,'' she said, ''to put money aside for my future. A year isn't so long to wait, is it?''

He stared at her. ''To wait for what?''

Her face burned with embarrassment. She hadn't meant to say those words at all. After all, *he* was supposed to propose to *her*, not the other way around. It was bad enough that she'd already trampled his pride by offering to pay for supper. And what if marriage was really the farthest thing from his mind? "To wait . . . to make any plans . . . for the future . . . *my* future," she stammered.

They finished the meal in silence. Trace paid the bill and retrieved his hat, then escorted her out into the street once more. She pulled her shawl tight around her shoulders, desperation building with each step that brought them closer to the boardinghouse. She'd planned to captivate Trace this evening with all her feminine charm. Instead, she'd only shown him once more what a headstrong, independent female she was. Why should he love her?

Her agitation grew until she could hardly catch her breath. Her plan to woo Trace had failed; suddenly all she wanted was to get back to her room and get rid of this cursed corset! She tried to hurry up to the steps at the side entrance to the boardinghouse and stumbled on a loose board.

"Careful now." Trace caught her, his arms around her securely, reminding her again of all her foolish behavior had cost her. She choked back a sob of frustration. "Are you all right?" In the dim light of a lamp that sat on the railing to guide the late boarders home, he peered at her, his eyes dark with concern. "You look like you're having trouble getting your breath."

"It's this wretched corset! I laced it too tight."

"I wondered."

She gave him a sharp look. "I thought you didn't notice."

A hint of a smile flicked across his face for the first time that evening. "A man would have to be dead not to notice." His gaze dropped to her breasts. "I was quite, um, distracted, all evening."

Heat curled up through her, sharp and sudden as lightning. All hope of calming her erratic heartbeat or recapturing her breath lost, she leaned heavily on his arm as he escorted her into the house. They halted just inside the door, at the bottom of a set of stairs. Trace's room was on this floor, just down the hall. Lucy and Theresa shared quarters on the second story. "Shall I help you up the stairs?" he offered.

She looked up the steep, narrow flight of steps and felt like sobbing. "I'll never make it up there," she gasped.

He frowned. "I could try to carry you."

She had an awful picture of Trace finding her too heavy and dropping her halfway up the steps. "No! I mean— you'll have to loosen my stays. Then I can make it on my own."

"What?"

She could hardly believe she'd said the words herself. She swallowed hard. "I can't walk another step. In fact, I feel quite faint." She leaned her head against his shoulder, fighting dizziness. "Let's just step into your room, and you can loosen the tapes enough so I can breathe."

He looked doubtful, but after a moment's hesitation, he agreed. He helped her to his room, and they quickly darted inside, anxious to avoid any unexpected encounter with their landlady or other boarders.

She leaned back against the door while he walked to the dresser and turned up the lamp. This room was much like hers, small and simply furnished with a single bed, dresser, and chair, the air heavy with the hotel scents of stale tobacco and floor polish. She closed her eyes and smiled as she caught the familiar sandalwood and leather aroma of Trace himself.

"Turn around."

Her stomach trembled at the simple command. She opened her eyes and swiveled to face the door. His shadow loomed, then covered her completely, even as his hands began to fumble with the row of buttons down the back of the dress.

He moved slowly, awkwardly. She could no longer catch her breath, not just from the tight stays, but because of his closeness. She could feel the heat of him, hear his labored breathing. Her earlier desperation returned fourfold. She didn't want to lose Trace, but how could she ever make him see the true nature of her feelings for him?

At last he parted the back of her dress, cool air rushing in, raising gooseflesh on her shoulders. He reached in around her, his hands warm against her ribs, and struggled with the tapes. At last the hooks gave way, and relief flooded her, along with despair, as his hands retreated. She whirled to face him, words tumbling from her lips as scattered as her thoughts. "I want to stay. Don't send me away." She pressed herself against him, as if to communicate with her body what she couldn't find words to express. "I love you. Please don't make me go."

17

LUCY STARED UP AT Trace, her heart in her throat. He put his hands to her shoulders, as if to push her from him. "What did you say?" he whispered.

"I . . . I love you. And . . . I want to stay with you. Tonight." She stood on tiptoe and pressed her lips to his, wrapping her arms around his neck.

He went as still as a statue. Her heart sank, and she braced herself for his rejection. Then with a groan, he pulled her near, his mouth seeking hers hungrily. She reveled in the sensations flooding her. *I love you, I love you, I love you,* she chanted over and over in her head, the words keeping time with her beating heart.

Trace's lips against her own were in turn fierce and gentle, demanding and pleading. He teased, taunted, and cajoled without ever saying a word. She was dizzy with love for him, breathless with delight. She had never dreamed a kiss could be so many things. Just when she was sure he had amazed her beyond belief, she felt his tongue against her lips, coaxing her to open to him.

Her whole body delighted in this new intimacy. She arched against him, anxious to be closer still. Timidly at first, then with more assurance, she made her own teasing, tasting explorations of his mouth.

At last he raised his head, and she felt bereft. She never wanted him to stop kissing her. But when he began trailing kisses down her throat, she sighed and surrendered herself to a wordless passion that sang through every part of her.

He feathered kisses along her collarbone, then paused to lavish attention on each breast in turn. "These beauties have been painfully distracting me all evening," he murmured as he peeled away the layers of fabric covering them. "Now I'll give them just what they deserve."

He made ever smaller circles with his tongue around each bared breast in turn, suckling at each taut nipple, drawing it between his teeth until she was moaning for release, fearful she might faint from delight.

When he finally released her, she cried out in despair. "Hush. I'm not done with you yet." He swept her into his arms and carried her to the bed, where he laid her carefully atop the covers. She watched as he stepped back and began to remove his own clothes. Some small part of her told her she ought to have more care for her own half-naked condition, but she was intoxicated with love for the man who revealed himself before her, his body as beautiful to her as any Greek statue glimpsed in some schoolbook.

He knelt beside her on the bed and helped her out of the rest of her clothes, then lay down beside her and gathered her into his arms once more.

Trace held her as if she might vanish into the night, the product of some fevered dream. She could not really be here in his bed, naked against his own flesh. But, no—she was real, soft and warm and more beautiful than all his imaginings. He could not get enough of touching her, or of having her touch him. He shuddered as she reached out and stroked her hand across the scar on his thigh, tracing the bullet's path along his skin. He should have known that even in this she would be bold. Always Lucy had insisted on going after what she wanted; his spirits soared at the thought that tonight she wanted him.

He skimmed his hands along her back, feeling the sharp ridges of her backbone, the indentations where the corset had bitten so cruelly into her flesh. He wanted to cradle and protect her always from ever hurting again.

The memory of her in the restaurant returned to him, her face contorted with pain as she talked of her mother's tears. He'd wanted to tell her of his own fear, when he'd lain in that field hospital, too terrified even to fall into a deep sleep, dreading waking up without a leg, his whole future ruined with a few strokes of a surgeon's saw. But he hadn't found the words to dig that deep inside him, to share that much of himself even with her.

He tried now, to give himself completely to her and for her. No words could begin to express his feelings, but he hoped to succeed in showing her his love for her. He felt the pull of his calloused hands across the skin of her stomach, and watched the pupils of her eyes widen and darken as he found the sensitive secret hidden in the mound of curls at the juncture of her thighs. He began to stroke her, gently at first, then with more insistence. Tomorrow morning, first thing, they'd walk over to the courthouse, and he'd make her his legally. No more talk of money or waiting until next year. She'd never have cause to worry again once she was his wife. He'd make sure of that.

Her breath caught, and her muscles tensed. Joy filled him, and he brought his mouth to hers to capture the cries of her climax. Then he lowered himself over her and slid inside her, hesitating only a moment before breaking the barrier that changed her from bride to wife. His wife. He'd protect her and keep her, always. The words echoed in his head as he found his own release. ''Lucy, I love you,'' he whispered against her lips, and rested his head between her breasts. He meant the words as a promise, more powerful than any repeated vows, and just as binding.

∞

TRACE WOKE TO THE unaccustomed chill of cool air across his naked skin. Opening his eyes, he stared at the shallow indentation in the pillow where another had lain beside him. Ah, Lucy, he thought, reaching out to twine his finger in the single brown hair that glistened on the pillow slip. *You won't have to slip away in the darkness ever again.* As soon as the courthouse opened this morning, he planned to be there, to make her officially his forever.

Filled with energy, he untangled himself from the sheets and dressed quickly. The new shirt he'd purchased yesterday and his clean suit would do for wedding garments. Maybe he could find someone to sell him a bouquet of flowers for Lucy to carry. Imagining her pleasure at this gesture, he smiled. And to think he'd once objected to the idea of marrying again!

Breakfast was already under way when he arrived downstairs. He took a seat across from Lucy and smiled at her. She blushed and quickly looked away. No wonder she was shy this morning. Perhaps she was worried, too, that he wouldn't do the right thing and marry her.

He hastened to set her mind at ease, stopping her in the hallway at the bottom of the stairs. "Find Theresa, and we'll go to the courthouse right away," he said.

She gave him a puzzled look. Before she could speak, Theresa emerged from the kitchen at the end of the hall. "What do we need to go back to the courthouse for?"

He took Lucy's hand. "So that Lucy and I can get married."

"Married?" Theresa began to chuckle.

Lucy gasped and jerked her hand away. "I can't marry you *today*!" She flushed a deep red. "I mean, well, I'm very flattered and . . . oh, I thought we were going to wait."

He put his hands on her shoulders. "Wait for what? I love you and I want to marry you. And I understood that you wanted to marry me, too."

"I do!" The words sounded more desperate than happy. She looked up at him, obviously struggling to control her agitation. "I'll be happy to marry you—in a year, when we've sold the cattle and I've secured my future.''

"Your future is with me." He took a deep breath, re-minding himself that he needed to tread carefully here. He didn't want to upset her any further. "You'll still have the cattle," he said. "I'll even let you keep your own brand and herd—separate from mine, to do with as you please."

She stared up at him. "Didn't you listen to *anything* I said last night?"

He frowned. "I listened when you said you loved me. I didn't think I needed to hear anything else."

With an anguished wail, she wrenched from his hands and fled up the stairs. Trace felt as if he'd been kicked in the gut. He didn't know whether to run after her and try to force some sense into her, or to let her go until she calmed down. Theresa gave him a pitying look. "I'll go talk to her," she said.

"What am I supposed to do in the meantime?"

Theresa shrugged. "You might try buyin' a weddin' li-cense."

∞

BY THE TIME THERESA walked into their room, Lucy had thrown everything they'd brought with them into their bags and was trying to force the largest carpetbag shut by sitting on it. "What do you think you're doing?" Theresa asked, walking up behind her.

"I'm getting ready to go home." She stuffed the trailing edge of a skirt, the one she'd worn last night, back into the bag.

"Uh-huh. And just how do you think you're going to get there?"

She inhaled sharply. "Trace will drive us."

Theresa crossed her arms over her chest. "What makes you think he's gonna want to have anything to do with you now that you stomped all over his heart like that?"

The words were as ugly as she felt right now. She gave

up on the carpetbag and sank down onto the bed. "I didn't mean to hurt him. I really do love him."

"Then what's the problem?"

"I spent an hour last night at supper explaining to him how important it was for me to wait to marry until next year, when I had my own money in the bank. I thought he listened and understood." She gave Theresa a pleading look. "What's wrong with waiting a year? Lots of people have engagements that long and longer."

Theresa frowned. "Most of those people don't jump the gun with the wedding night."

She felt her face flame. "How did you know?"

"What was I supposed to think when you come creepin' in here after midnight last night?"

"We stayed up talking?"

"You were carrying your corset in your hand. Must've been one heck of a conversation for it to come off like that."

Lucy buried her face in her hands, shame and confusion overwhelming her. "I l-love him," she sobbed. "I didn't want to l-lose him. Why won't he w-wait for me?"

Theresa sat down beside her and gathered her close. "There, there, child. Don't get in such a state. I'll talk to Trace."

She looked up through a haze of tears. "You will?"

Theresa nodded. "It wouldn't be a good idea to start off a marriage with the bride in tears. He's a sensible man—most of the time. He'll eventually see the wisdom in waiting."

"Oh, Theresa, thank you! I will be a good wife to Trace, if he'll just give me a little more time."

Theresa smoothed Lucy's hair back from her forehead. "I reckon a strong man like Trace just naturally needs a strong woman to keep him in line. It won't hurt him to wait a little for you, though I'd wager neither one of you will last a year."

Lucy straightened and blotted the tears from her cheeks. "I've got everything all figured out," she said. "A year from now I'll walk down the aisle to become Mrs. Trace Abernathy.''

Theresa chuckled. ''Since when do love work on a time-table, Miss Lucy?'' She shook her head. ''Oh, child, you have a lot to learn. You and Trace both.''

Lucy stared after Theresa as she slipped out of the room. Of course, she didn't pretend to know everything about Trace, or about love. But she knew herself well enough. She'd promised herself she'd wait a year to wed, and come hell or high water, that's exactly what she intended to do.

∞

THE JOURNEY FROM BLANCO to Elm Creek was con-siderably more solemn than the trip out. Somehow Theresa had convinced Trace to agree to postpone their marriage for a year, though the grim expression on his face made it clear he wasn't happy with the arrangement. Still, he hadn't broken the engagement off altogether, so that was some-thing. She could only hope that given time to cool off, Trace would be a little, well, friendlier to her once more.

Anxious not to aggravate him further, she rode gripping the edge of the wagon seat, struggling to sit very still, with-out touching Trace. He held himself just as rigid, eyes fo-cused straight ahead, jaw fixed in a hard line. Still, in the swaying, bouncing wagon, they could not keep from mak-ing contact from time to time. Whenever their shoulders or arms brushed, Lucy felt a jolt of heat run through her, like the aftershock of the tremors that had begun when they'd come together last night.

When they stopped for the evening, Trace was polite but distant. He gave short, clipped answers to Theresa's at-tempts at conversation, until even she gave up and retired to bed early. Lucy lay awake a long time, staring at the dying campfire and blinking away tears. If the day had been difficult, tonight was sheer torture. She ached to feel Trace's arms around her, to hear sweet words of under-standing from his lips.

He said he loved me, she reminded herself. *Why would he lie? And I love him. In time he'll see this is the right thing to do. This will give us time to set our affairs in order.*

For one thing, she'd finally finish her bridal quilt. Maybe she'd even have time to make another, as a wedding gift for Trace. They could both build up their herds and plan a nice wedding.

Most important of all, Trace would never have to wonder if she'd married him for money or security. He would always know theirs was a union built on love and respect for each other.

She pulled her blanket closer about her and squeezed her eyes shut, trying to force sleep where none would come. Respect was a mighty poor companion under the covers. The year couldn't be over fast enough to suit her.

∽

BY THE AFTERNOON OF the second day, Trace had reconciled himself to waiting for Lucy to come to her senses. He'd discarded his first instinct to drag her in front of the judge and make her agree to the marriage, knowing this would only make her dig in her heels more. Theresa had wisely pointed out to him that perhaps all the excitement of a trip out of town, not to mention guilt over her rash decision to spend the night with him, might be working together to make Lucy nervous about any more changes in her life just now.

The long drive home gave him time to think. His relationship with Lucy had been, to say the least, unconventional. Maybe she just needed a little old-fashioned wooing. A few weeks, or at most a couple of months, of gentlemanly calls and spooning on the back porch, and she'd be racing him to the altar. At least he hoped so. He was learning that Lucy O'Connor was anything but predictable.

They reached Trace's cabin in late afternoon. As he turned the wagon into the yard, the first thing he noticed was the completed barn. The unpainted wood gleamed in the setting sun, and the smell of fresh sawdust filled the air. He pulled the wagon to a halt in front of the new building and looked around. By all rights, someone should have come out to greet them. Josh's and Rye's horses whinnied to them from the corral, so he knew the two were not out riding.

"Where is ever'body?" Theresa asked as Trace helped her and Lucy down to the ground.

"I'm up here, Mama!"

They followed the sound of Josh's voice and found him grinning at them from atop the barn. "Joshua Washington, you get down from there this instant!" Theresa ordered.

His grin broadened. "I'se just keepin' a lookout for you." He slid down the long slope of the roof and hopped to the ground.

"Where's Rye?" Trace asked as Josh hugged his mother.

The boy's smile vanished. "He's in the house."

Puzzled, Trace turned toward the cabin. Lucy and the others followed. He pushed open the door and peered into the dim interior. "Rye?"

"Over here."

Behind him, he heard Theresa gasp as they looked toward the bed and saw Rye laid out there, his foot swathed in bandages and propped on a stack of folded quilts. Mary sat next to him, chewing on a little rag doll. The baby gurgled happily and reached for her mother.

"Laws, what happened to you?" Theresa scooped her daughter into her arms and studied Rye's bandaged foot.

Rye sighed. "It's kind of a long story."

"I'll put the kettle on for tea," Lucy offered, untying her bonnet. "Then you can tell us all about it."

While Lucy prepared the tea, Theresa changed the baby. Josh made a show of arranging the pillows behind Rye's back. "I got the last of the shingles nailed up," the boy said. "Tomorrow maybe I can start nailin' the stalls together."

"You let Trace help you with those, now," Rye cautioned.

Wondering at the new closeness between these two, Trace went to see to the wagon horses. When he returned, Lucy was handing out cups of tea. Theresa sat on the end of the bed by Rye, and Josh settled on the floor with the baby. Trace and Lucy pulled up chairs and waited.

Rye took a long sip of tea. "This tastes real good, Miz Lucy."

"Thank you, Rye."

He looked at Trace. "You made good time from Blanco. I reckon you didn't have no trouble or anything."

Trace frowned. "Not the kind of trouble you seemed to have had. Quit stalling, Rye. Tell us what happened."

The cowboy let out a heavy sigh. "Josh and I had just about finished the barn." He looked at the boy. "He's a good hard worker once you get him goin'."

Josh continued to play with Mary, as if he hadn't heard this praise. But Trace noticed the way he straightened his shoulders, which seemed broader than before. Almost overnight, he appeared taller, more filled out. While Trace wasn't looking, the little boy who'd followed him west had turned into a young man.

"We come out one mornin' and commenced to shinglin' the roof," Rye continued. "I went over to the woodpile to fetch the ax to trim some o' the shingles and stepped right into one of them leghold traps, like folks set out for muskrats or foxes."

"Oh!" Lucy gave a small cry. Theresa reached out and grasped Rye's uninjured leg.

"How did the trap get there?" Trace asked. "Josh and I cleaned up this whole place when we moved in, and I never remembered seeing one."

Rye scowled at his bandaged foot. "I don't think it was there then. This weren't some rusty old trap somebody had forgotten in the weeds. It were new lookin', oiled up good."

"I saved it for you, Trace. Hung it up in the barn," Josh

said. "I figure whoever dropped it by our woodpile deserved to lose it."

Trace nodded, determined not to let his agitation show. He and Rye both knew no one had "dropped" the trap accidentally. Someone had deliberately set it to hurt Trace or someone living with him. Theresa or Josh could just as easily have been injured when they went to fetch wood. If he'd brought Lucy back here to live as his bride, she might have been the one wounded or even crippled. The thought shook him so that for a moment he couldn't even speak.

"What did you do about your foot?" Theresa asked.

"Josh heard me holler, and he come down from the roof and helped me spring the trap." Sweat beaded on Rye's forehead as he related the ordeal. "I was bleedin' considerable, but my boot saved the bone from bein' crushed. Josh cut a stick for me to lean on, so's I could hobble back to the cabin, then he cleaned me up and doctored the foot with some of your herbs." He smiled at the boy. "He knew just which ones to use, too."

The man who'd planted the trap—his nameless, faceless enemy—knew just how to strike at Trace's most vulnerable areas, his already wounded leg or his friends and family.

"What you gonna do about this, Trace?"

He looked into Theresa's questioning brown eyes. He was supposed to be the man with the answers, wasn't he? How could he tell her he didn't have any? He shoved himself out of his chair. "I'm going to get to the bottom of this." He turned to Lucy. "But right now I'm going to take you home."

On the ride into town, they were alone again for the first time since that night at the boardinghouse. A certain awkwardness remained between them, but the attack on Rye had given them other things to think about, a new basis for conversation.

"Who do you think set that trap?" she asked as they pulled away from his cabin.

He shook his head. "Pollard? Or somebody else altogether. Maybe there's a group of 'em, determined to run me out of town.''

''I visited Twila the other day. She said Pollard has a group of friends he entertains at the house.'' She shook her head. ''I got the impression she didn't like them much.''

He gave her a sharp look. ''I thought Pollard ordered you to stay away from his place.''

She straightened her shoulders. ''I'm not afraid of him.'' Her expression softened. ''I'd hoped I could talk Twila into leaving him, into going to live with her parents.''

''She wouldn't listen to you.''

She dropped her chin to her chest. ''No.''

''Some people might say you're interfering where you don't belong,'' he observed.

''What do you say?'' She gave him a challenging look.

He wanted to reach out and grasp her hand but dared not risk touching her again. His feelings for her simmered too close to the surface, raw passions barely contained by common sense. ''I'd say you're a good friend to be so concerned about the welfare of another. Twila's lucky to have someone like you on her side.''

She fell silent. He wondered if perhaps she was crying. When she spoke, her voice was soft, raw-edged. ''You won't let whoever's doing this run you off.'' It wasn't a question, just a statement of fact. He loved her more for her faith in him.

He glanced at her, wishing that damned sunbonnet didn't hide her face. He would have liked to see her eyes just now, to read the expression there. ''I know one thing. I'm glad now we didn't get married in Blanco.''

She made a little choking sound, and he fought back a smile. She hadn't expected that, had she? ''Y-you are?''

''If we were married now, you'd come to my cabin to live. Then you'd be a target, too, for whoever's after me. At least at the store I know you're relatively safe.'' He leaned forward, elbows on his knees, and contemplated the road ahead of them. ''I think it'd be best if we kept quiet about our engagement for a while, too. At least until this trouble dies down or blows over.''

She was silent for so long, he wondered if she'd even heard him. The steady *clop, clop* of the horses and the creaking of the wagon sounded loud in his ears. When she did finally speak, her voice sounded small. "All right."

He frowned. He hadn't meant to hurt her feelings. "I'm just thinking of what's best for you," he said. "After all, you're my responsibility now. I can't be watching over you twenty-four hours a day."

"I didn't agree to marry you because I wanted a bodyguard." She turned toward him, face alight with anger. "You know I'm perfectly capable of looking after myself."

"I know you like to think that."

"Trace Abernathy! You take that back! Since when have I needed you to *rescue* me from anything? I fended off that charging bull, didn't I? I outran the Buckboard Bandit the day he was following me, didn't I? *I'm* not the one who almost killed himself charging into a burning barn, am I? And I'm not the one people are shooting at and setting traps for."

He didn't know whether to laugh at her or scold her. He knew for sure arguing wouldn't work. Better to let her think she'd won this skirmish. "All right. I'm willing to agree you're very capable of looking after yourself—most of the time."

"I want a husband, not a caretaker," she said stiffly, facing forward once more. "I want you to *promise* me you'll let me decide for myself when I need your help and when I don't."

He ground his teeth together. Whoever heard of such a crazy promise? It was his duty to protect Lucy, and nothing she said was going to change his mind about that. "I promise I'll let you look after yourself," he said. *But that doesn't mean I won't be looking out for you, too,* he silently added.

"Well, I'm glad that's settled."

He looked away. Nothing was settled, really. Nothing

could be settled until he was sure it was safe to bring Lucy to the cabin as his wife.

As usual, Nate's store was the busiest place in town. Several people greeted them as they pulled up. Was it his imagination, or did people seem friendlier to him today? Maybe some of them, at least, were coming to accept him. Or maybe it was only his attitude that was changing. Lucy was helping him to feel a part of this place, a true neighbor to these people.

Nate hurried out from behind the counter to wrap Lucy in a hug. "How was your trip?" he asked. "Did you have a good time?"

"A very good time, Uncle."

Trace wondered if he had anything to do with the blush that flooded her cheeks as she answered her uncle's innocent question.

"Our shipment of *Leslie's* came in while you were gone." Nate took Lucy's hand and pulled her toward the front counter, where a stack of the magazines waited. "Everyone's been reading your story."

"That's wonderful." She grinned and picked up the magazine, flipping right to her story about the Buckboard Bandit. "Maybe the real bandit will read it and see that people are starting to turn against him.

"And how are you, Trace?" Nate shook his hand. "I trust everything went well."

"Just fine." He leaned closer to his friend and lowered his voice. "You haven't sold a leghold trap to anyone lately, have you? One about the size you'd use to trap a fox?"

Nate pursed his lips in thought, then shook his head. "Nope. It's not trapping season. Those traps are more of a winter item."

"So anybody buying one would stick in your mind?"

"Yes." Nate frowned. "What's this about?"

"Somebody set a trap like that by my woodpile. Rye stepped in it. He's just lucky he was wearing heavy boots."

Nate gave a low whistle. "I'll ask around. Maybe somebody's heard something."

"Uncle Nate, why didn't you tell me I had a letter?" Lucy emerged from behind the counter, waving an envelope.

"It just came this morning." Nate looked over her shoulder at the envelope. "I didn't recognize the handwriting."

She grinned. "Maybe it's a letter from one of my readers." She broke the seal and unfolded the single sheet of paper. As she read, her smile vanished, and her face paled.

"What is it?" Trace asked.

"Oh. Nothing." She tried to stuff the letter in the pocket of her skirt, but he stepped forward and captured it. Nate moved to his side to read with him.

If you know what's good for you, you'll leave off writing your lies in that magazine. You and your friends won't be safe till I rid the country of vermin. If you try to stop me, you'll be sorry.

                                                    B. B.

Lucy snatched the letter away from them and shoved it into her pocket. "It's just idle threats," she said. "It doesn't mean anything."

"How can you say it doesn't mean anything?" Trace glared at her. "This is the same person who fired a shotgun into the store here. It might be the same person who shot me and set the trap that injured Rye."

"But why would he want to hurt me?" She tried to smile, but the expression wavered, and her voice shook.

"This isn't some harmless prank." He took her by the shoulders. "Don't you see—he's getting bolder. He might just decide to kill anyone he thinks is in his way."

Her eyes widened.

"I want you to agree not to write any more stories about him," he said. "Stick to Russian princesses and run-down plantations. And don't go out riding alone anymore, either."

"No!" She wrenched away from him. "I won't let this—this *coward* tell me how to live my life. And I won't let *you* tell me what to write and what not to write."

"This is not a game." Trace spoke through clenched teeth.

"And you are *not* my master!" she snapped.

They faced each other across three feet of floor, but it might as well have been three miles. All the arguments he'd ever had with Marion flooded his memory. Why was it so important for her and Lucy to win—even when they weren't right? It was as if once they'd had a taste of power, they didn't have sense enough to relinquish it when necessary.

He opened his mouth to tell her as much, but the door to the store burst open, and Zeke Early rushed in. "Rider just came by my place on his way to Blanco," he gasped. "One of the drovers back from up North."

"What did he say?" Lucy grasped his arm, eyes aglow with anticipation. "Did they sell all the cattle? Did they get a good price? How much?"

Zeke removed his hat and twisted it in his hands. "The man said it was a total disaster. They lost everything."

All the light went out of Lucy's expression. She looked stunned, the way Trace had seen men look on the battlefield when they'd received a mortal wound and hadn't yet fallen. She'd never struck him as the fainting kind, but he moved around behind her, ready to catch her, just in case. "What happened?" he asked.

Zeke looked up at the crowd that was fast gathering to hear the news. "Man said men with guns met them at the Missouri border, told 'em they weren't going to let no tick-infested Texas cattle into the state to infect Missouri cows."

The news outraged the crowd. "Lies!"

"All cows got ticks!"

"Do that Missouri stock good to mix with some decent bloodlines for a change!"

Nate held up his hand for quiet. "Go on, Zeke. What else?"

He shook his head. "Apparently they tried to move west, to find a place to get in, but folks with guns were waitin' every step of the way. They couldn't find water, and the cattle started scattering. Some of the Missourians started shootin' the cattle. He said before it was over, the Texans were lucky to get out of it without bein' shot themselves. They lost pretty much everything but the clothes on their backs."

"Everything?" Lucy's voice was barely a whisper above the commotion in the store, but it echoed like thunder in Trace's ears. He reached out and touched her shoulder in a gesture of comfort, but she wrenched away and raced for the door into the kitchen. In a moment he heard her footsteps pounding up the stairs to her room.

Trace started to go after her, but Nate's hand on his arm stopped him. "Give her a little time to settle down," Nate said. "She's not ready to listen to anybody just now."

He looked after her, knowing Nate was right, but aching to be with her just the same. Maybe he was the only person who had an inkling how much this first cattle drive had meant to Lucy. He'd have to help her see the good that could come out of this. Now they wouldn't have to wait on her cattle money to marry. As soon as it looked as though she'd be safe at his cabin, they could find a preacher and say their vows.

Right now Lucy probably felt like this was the end of the world. He'd have to help her see it was just the beginning.

18

LUCY LEANED AGAINST THE closed door of her bedroom and shut her eyes. If only she could have shut her ears as well to the awful news Zeke Early had delivered. Oh, God, it couldn't be true, could it? With no market up North, all those cattle she'd bought weren't worth much more than she'd paid for them. She'd never make her fortune this way, never be free to marry Trace.

Trace. The ache in her heart grew at the thought of her erstwhile bridegroom. How could she feel so close to him one moment and so far apart the next? She'd spent all that time explaining to him why she *had* to have that money in the bank before they could wed, and he still didn't understand. One minute he was promising to let her make decisions for herself, and the next he was ordering her not to write this and not to do that. She clenched her fists at her sides and groaned. She didn't need a crystal ball to look into the future and see things wouldn't get any easier once they married.

Opening her eyes, she began to pace. For all his sweet talk about letting her keep her own cattle and do as she pleased, Trace didn't really believe she had as much sense as he did. He wouldn't have the ring on her finger two days before he'd be ordering her around like a lord of the manor.

Well, she wasn't having it! With money of her own in the bank, at least she would have had the satisfaction of knowing she didn't have to stand there and take anything he cared to dish out. That money would have given her the security to stand up and say her piece, whether he liked it or not.

Without that money, she and any children she might have would be totally dependent on the generosity of a man who might grow to resent her stubborn independence. Tears stung her eyes at the thought; could Trace really lose his love for her that way? She wanted to think his feelings for her were as strong as her own love for him. But what woman could predict the mind of a man?

She stopped her pacing and inhaled deeply, determined to take control of her shaky emotions. Better to stand alone, responsible for only her own happiness, than risk losing everything at the mercy of another. She'd have to break off her engagement to Trace. It wasn't fair to keep him waiting who knew how long while she saved her money and looked for other ways to make her fortune.

She walked to the dresser, intending to take out a sheet of paper and write Trace a letter. Then her gaze fell on the unfinished bridal quilt in the chair against the wall. One edge of the coverlet trailed to the floor, one red calico heart pierced by her needle. She closed her eyes against the sight, squeezing back tears. Her own heart felt pierced, wounded beyond repair. How could she go through with this?

She shut the drawer and sagged into the chair, gathering the quilt around her, seeking comfort in its folds. She would never look at this cheerful pattern of hearts and not think of Trace. She would never lie in his arms beneath this coverlet, would never bear his children in a bed warmed by it. Instead of a thing of beauty and joy, the quilt would always be for her a reminder of the grief she felt today.

She sobbed her sorrow into the quilt's soft layers until the edge of the fabric was soaked, and no more tears would come. Then she stood and carefully folded it away. All her life she'd been practical, planning and saving, wasting neither money nor effort. But in this one thing, she would not be practical. She would put the quilt away, unfinished. If she could not share it with Trace, she would not share it with anyone else.

"Lucy?"

The tap on her door startled her. Frowning, she scrubbed tears from her eyes and straightened her shoulders. If Uncle Nate thought he was going to talk her into coming back downstairs and talking to Trace, he was wrong. She had nothing to say to that man right now.

"Honey, Mrs. Sorenson is here to see you. I thought it'd be all right if she came on up."

Mrs. Sorenson! Of all times for the Swedish woman to show up! "J-just a minute." She raced to the washstand and splashed cool water on her face, hoping to erase the evidence of her tears. Then she smoothed her hair and, struggling for more calmness than she felt, went to admit her visitor.

Mrs. Sorenson swept into the small bedroom like a woman on a mission. "Vhere is it?" she asked eagerly. "Vhere is my new quilt?"

She spotted the bridal quilt on the chair and pounced on it, unfurling it with one snap of her wrists. "Exquisite," she exclaimed. "And such an unusual design."

"That one's not for sale." Lucy reached out and gathered the quilt protectively against her. "Besides, it's not even finished yet." *And never will be*, she silently added.

"Oh." Mrs. Sorenson frowned. "But you sent word that you haf another quilt for me."

Lucy knelt and pulled a cloth-wrapped bundle from beneath her bed. "Here it is," she said, stripping off the protective muslin cover and revealing the bright red and yellow and green triangles. "It's called rocky road to California."

Mrs. Sorenson fingered the edge of the quilt. "Yes. I haf seen this pattern before. Very nice." She whirled to face Lucy once more. "Now, about this other—"

Lucy hid the bridal quilt behind her back. "I'm sorry, but it's not for sale."

"Vhy not?"

She flushed. "I . . . because it's my bridal quilt." Never mind that she intended to put it away, unfinished. It didn't seem right to let someone else have it.

The lines on Mrs. Sorenson's forehead deepened. "I haf no idea you are to be married."

Lucy shifted from one foot to the other. "I'm not . . . exactly."

"Then we haf no problem." Mrs. Sorenson brought her hands together with a resounding clap. "You vill be having plenty of time to make another bridal quilt before you are to marry." She reached around behind Lucy and caught the trailing edge of the quilt between her fingers. "And for your trouble, I vill pay you double for this quilt."

Lucy gasped. "Fifty dollars?" She could think of a dozen ways to use such a sum. She dropped her gaze to the bright arrangement of hearts and felt a sharp pain in her chest. "That's very generous, but no." She tightened her grip on the quilt as Mrs. Sorenson tried to tug it away from her.

"Nonsense." Mrs. Sorenson glowered. "You think I do not know vhat you are about? But I vill humor you. Seventy-five dollars for this quilt with the hearts."

Lucy's stomach knotted. Seventy-five dollars would be a good sum to have in the bank. Perhaps she could find some way to invest it. . . . She closed her eyes and shook her head. "No. I won't sell."

"You are a greedy, stubborn girl." Mrs. Sorenson let go of the edge of the quilt and crossed her arms over her chest. "One hundred dollars. This is my final offer."

One hundred dollars for a quilt? Lucy stared at Mrs. Sorenson in disbelief. She wet her lips. "Perhaps I can make you another quilt like this one."

"No. This is the one I vant. You must sell it to me."

Lucy brought the quilt around in front of her and folded it over her arm. She remembered sewing every heart in place. Over the year she'd worked on the quilt, she'd planned and dreamed and learned more about quilting, and about herself, than she'd ever imagined she could know. She sighed and shook her head. ''I'm sorry, Mrs. Sorenson. I can't sell this quilt to you.''

Mrs. Sorenson snatched up the rocky-road quilt and pulled a wad of bills from her pocket. ''There is the payment for this one. I vill give you some time to think over your rash decision about the other. When you haf come to your senses and decided to sell, you may bring it to me.'' She tossed the bills onto the dresser and huffed out of the room, slamming the door behind her.

Lucy sank down onto the edge of the bed and hugged the patchwork-hearts quilt to her. Maybe Mrs. Sorenson was right. What was a quilt but scraps of cloth—leftovers, really? She could make another one, a different one without the painful memories this one brought to mind.

She smoothed her hand over a heart-filled square and remembered the quilting bee at Twila's, when she'd accidentally sewn the quilt to her skirt. She'd danced with Trace that night and kissed him for the first time. She'd begun to fall in love with him then, to secretly think she might need a bridal quilt after all.

This quilt was so much more than mere scraps of cloth. Selling it would be like selling a dream. Even though she knew the dream could never come true, she wasn't ready to let go of it yet.

∞

HALF A DOZEN TIMES over the next few days, Trace started to saddle up and ride into town to speak with Lucy. He couldn't decide whether he wanted to apologize for ordering her around the other day or argue with her about her foolishness in thinking she was invincible. Considering the state she'd been in the last time he'd seen her, argument seemed the most likely outcome of a visit. He decided it was wiser to let her come to him.

In the meantime, he threw himself into his work, rounding up and branding mavericks with Josh and Rye. The hard, dirty labor kept his mind off his troubles, at least during the daytime.

At night, memories and fantasies of Lucy plagued him. The very scent of her haunted his dreams. They had spent only one night together, and yet she seemed imprinted on his flesh. The satin texture of her skin was as real to him as the calloused roughness of his palms. He had only to close his eyes to recall every detail of her appearance and the fevered cries she'd made in the throes of passion echoed in his brain.

His chaotic emotions made him question his sanity sometimes, and he thought he might be hearing things the day Lucy finally did show up at his place.

"I don't know why you're bothering to brand those worthless animals," a familiar voice called out as he and Rye struggled to mark a half-grown calf.

Trace narrowly missed cutting his thumb off, Lucy's arrival caught him so off guard. But he managed to collect himself enough to finish with the calf and send it on its way before walking over to her. He fought back a smile, not wanting her to think him too eager. Yet he couldn't keep his happiness and relief at seeing her again from ringing in his voice. "What brings you out this way?" he asked, reaching up to help her down from her horse.

She put her hands on his shoulders, and it seemed the most natural thing in the world for him to sweep her down off the horse and into his arms. His mouth found hers, hungry for the taste of her. Yet he forced himself to hold back, aware of Josh and Rye watching. The kiss was warm, but all too brief.

Even that was enough to leave her flushed and gasping for breath. He couldn't hold back his smile any longer. So she had been eager for him as well. He liked that. Maybe they wouldn't have to wait so long to marry after all. "It's good to see you," he said.

She looked away. It amused him to think she was still

so flustered by one kiss. "Theresa told me you were up here," she said. "I'm surprised to see you going to all the trouble to brand more cattle."

He looked toward the corral, where half a dozen mavericks scraped their horns and swished their tales, anxious for freedom. "I haven't given up on them yet." He turned his gaze back to her. "I spoke with Zeke again after you left the other day. He says there's talk of a bunch of investors building stockyards in Abilene, Kansas. Some of the big livestock owners propose to blaze a trail up that way next year."

"I . . . I hadn't heard that."

"I think there's money to be made in cattle yet."

She nodded, still not looking at him. She looked so pale. "Are you feeling all right?" he asked.

She jerked her head up. "Of course. Why do you ask?"

He shrugged. "You just look a little peaked."

She squared her shoulders and inhaled deeply. "I'm perfectly all right."

He couldn't help noticing what a nice effect this posture had on her chest and started to tell her so, then held his tongue. In the right setting, a woman would know that sort of remark was a compliment; he didn't think a cow camp was the right setting. "So, are you still in?"

"In what?"

"Are we still business partners?"

Her shoulders sagged a little. "I suppose so. It's either that or lose my investment."

"You don't sound too happy about that."

"I'm . . . just tired, that's all."

She looked tired. When she turned toward him, he noticed the shadows under her eyes and the tightness around her mouth. He wanted to gather her close and lay her head on his shoulder, to tell her to rest in his arms.

Of course, maybe she'd been having the same kind of dreams about *him* that he'd been having about *her*. Probably the sooner they were married the better. At least then they could sleep *part* of the night. "Rye has decided to lease part of my land and build his own cabin,'' he said, hoping this news would cheer her.

''Oh?''

''As soon as it's done, he and Theresa can marry and move in there. I'll have my house back to myself—at least until our wedding.''

She stared over his shoulder. He looked back, following her gaze to Rye and Josh, who were pretending to practice roping a cedar stump. He had a feeling Josh at least was hanging on their every word. ''Can we talk somewhere more . . . private?'' she asked.

He took her elbow and guided her a little way up the hill. A welcome breeze hit them as they topped the rise, bringing the scent of fresh grass and sun-warmed cedar to wash away the stench of manure and singed cowhide. They stopped in the shade of a spreading live oak. He started to take her in his arms, but she stepped away, avoiding his grasp. ''There's something I have to tell you.'' She folded her arms across her stomach and turned away from him.

Despite the heat of the day, he suddenly felt as if he'd stepped off into an icy stream. Was it the tone of her voice or the fact that she refused to meet his gaze that warned him the news to come wouldn't be good? ''Now, Lucy—'' he began.

''I've decided it's best if we break off the engagement.'' He stared at her, and she rushed to fill the sudden, awkward silence. ''It doesn't matter anyway, since Theresa is the only one who knows we were ever officially engaged. I mean, there won't be a public disgrace or anything.''

He wished now he'd made a point of telling Nate, or maybe even announcing the news in the middle of the store the other day. Maybe she wouldn't be so eager now to end things before they'd really begun. Then again, she'd obviously made up her mind.

''Just tell me why?'' His voice sounded gruff, harsh. He struggled to temper it. ''I told you I was willing to wait.''

''That's just it!'' She whirled to face him. ''It's not fair of me to ask you to wait, with everything so uncertain. Who knows how long it will be before I can sell my cattle and get the money I need?''

You don't need that money, he thought, but he didn't say it. She wouldn't hear the real meaning behind the words. "I said I would wait for you. I meant it."

She looked so sad. "Maybe I'm just not cut out for marriage." She shook her head. "I don't think I can bend my will to someone else's. I have to write what I want to write, go where I want to go, think for myself."

He took a step toward her, wishing he could find a way to close this gap between them that had nothing to do with physical distance. "I'm not asking you to stop thinking," he said. "Just . . . I want you to realize you're not immortal. You have to take care of yourself. And if you won't, then I feel obligated to do so."

She went very still. He stared at her, willing her to look up at him, to look into his eyes and tell him she didn't want to be his wife. But she never raised her head. "I can't let you do that," she said after a moment of silence.

He took the last step to bring him to her side and laid his hand on her shoulder. She felt as delicate as a bird, her bones fine and fragile beneath the soft fabric of her dress and her even softer skin. "I love you." His voice rasped, dredging the words from deep inside him. "I can't stand by and see you hurt."

She shuddered, as if with unvoiced sobs. "If you love me, you'll let me make my own mistakes." She made an effort to smile. "It's the only way some of us learn."

He grasped her shoulder, as if he could hold on to her soul as well as her body. "I said I would wait for you. Now I'm asking you to wait for me. Don't break off the engagement now. We'll see what happens next summer. In the meantime, we can work together." He took a deep breath. "And I'll respect your ability to make your own decisions."

She hesitated, then nodded. He longed to pull her close but instead released her, to turn to him or not as she wished. She chose not. He followed her back down the hill, where the heat and dust and stench of branding assailed him once more. Rye looked up, eyebrows raised in question. Trace shrugged. What could he say?

Lucy stopped beside her horse and turned to him once more. "I almost forgot. Uncle Nate said to tell you he hasn't been able to find out about anybody who bought a trap like the one you found. But a friend of his over in Birdtown had one stolen not too long ago."

He frowned. "Pollard goes to Birdtown several times a week, doesn't he?"

"Yes, but that might not mean anything."

"No, it might not." He bent and with his hands made a step for her to mount. Once she was settled in the saddle, he started to tell her to be careful, then bit his tongue. Of course she would be careful. He could only hope so, anyway.

He remembered his decision to court her properly. "I'd like to come calling Friday evening."

"Calling?" She looked amused.

He rubbed the back of his neck. "Yeah, well, you know. I stop by. We sit in the parlor and talk." Talk—he'd much rather let their lips have a conversation without words. The thought made him flushed and hard. He shifted, trying to get comfortable again.

She nodded. "All right."

"I'll see you Friday, then." He watched her ride away. Something didn't feel right. Some sixth sense of his was sounding alarm bells in his brain, the way it had the day the sniper had shot him.

He waited until Lucy was out of sight, then turned and started for his horse. "You and Josh finish up here," he called to Rye. "I've got something I need to do."

⚭

"YOU'RE NOTHING BUT A coward, Lucy O'Connor." Out of sight and hearing of the camp, Lucy softly scolded herself. She'd spent three days working up the nerve to speak with Trace in person, and somehow he'd managed to talk her out of breaking off the engagement.

Despite her resolve, she'd been lost almost from the first, when he'd gathered her into his arms and given her that head-spinning kiss, not caring who saw. Her heart still pounded from the memory of his lips, warm and insistent against her own yielding mouth.

She steered Amigo along the creek bank, toward the cut where she always crossed. She'd wanted a nice, clean break. Instead, she'd agreed to no telling how many months of silent torture. Her stomach fluttered, hope testing its wings before soaring aloft. She had never stopped loving Trace. She'd like to think things could still work out for them.

Obviously he'd done a lot of thinking since she'd seen him last. She nodded. He'd realized how wrong he'd been to try to boss her around. She was proud of him for that. It had to be difficult for him to let her go her own way. She supposed instinct drove a man to want to protect a woman. It wasn't really the protection she minded so much, just the assumption that she didn't have enough sense to look after herself most of the time. After all, she'd been pretty much taking care of herself for years now, and doing fine. Maybe Trace just needed more time to get used to the idea that she wasn't like most women, used to depending on others for everything. She preferred to do for herself when possible.

Just like her quilts. People thought she was odd, not wanting anyone to help her with her bridal quilt. They'd think her even odder if they knew about the others she'd sewn by herself. But really, she just found it easier to work alone. That way she was sure of getting exactly what she wanted.

She started down the steep creek bank, thankful once more that Amigo was so surefooted. This time of year, the creek was almost dry, with just a shallow trickle in the bottom of the bed. She let Amigo stop and take a drink, then tapped his flank with her quirt and started him up the other side.

The woods on either side of the creek were quiet. Too quiet, really, as if everything was sleeping.

Or holding its breath, waiting.

A shiver danced down her spine. Feeling a little foolish, she reached back and unbuckled her saddlebag. Groping inside it, she found the heavy, cloth-wrapped bundle and pulled it out.

The pistol was man sized, a Colt revolver like the one she'd lost when Trace's barn burned. She'd learned to fire it using both hands. "If you're going to insist on galavantin' all over the county, you're going to learn to use this," Uncle Nate had ordered. So she had, though she'd never hit anything more threatening than a bottle propped on a fence rail.

She unwrapped the gun and laid it across her lap, taking comfort from the size and weight of it. *It's silly to be afraid, anyway,* she thought. *You're letting Trace's worrying rub off on you.*

"Hold it right there, missy."

She gasped and reached for the gun in her lap, but the distinctive sound of the hammer of a rifle being pulled back made her freeze.

"Slow and easy, now. Drop that gun."

She did as he asked, heart pounding in her chest. Harness chains jingled and wheels creaked as a wagon rolled out of the deep shadows by the side of the road. A pair of matched bays stood in the traces, and a man wearing a broad-brimmed hat and a long canvas duster, with a handkerchief pulled up over his face, held the wagon lines with one hand. With the other hand, he steadied a rifle against his chest.

"Now," he said, his voice a low growl, muffled by the handkerchief. "I reckon you're gonna come with me,"

☙

RACE COULDN'T LET GO of the feeling that something
asn't right. He followed Lucy at a distance, staying far
ack so she wouldn't be suspicious. He'd have hell to pay
` she caught him trailing her. All the same, he wouldn't
est easy until he knew she was home safe.

At the creek bank, he waited, letting her cross first. Then,
vhen he was sure she was on down the road on the other
ide, he started to follow. At the bottom of the trail, he
topped in the creek bed to let his horse drink, then dis-
nounted and walked a little way upstream to slake his own
hirst. The water tasted gritty, but felt good going down all
ne same. He sat back on his heels and looked over his
houlder, up the bank Lucy had climbed a couple minutes
efore. His uneasiness grew. Everything was still, not even
he cicadas buzzing in the afternoon heat.

The jingle of harness chains and the crunch of wagon
vheels on the caliche road up ahead jolted him to his feet.
Ie squinted up the bank, but trees blocked his view. With
our strides he was on his horse, charging up the bank with
iis heart in his throat. The sane part of his mind told him
ie was being foolish. There was nothing sinister about a
vagon on a public road. But the part of him ruled by in-
.tinct and passion told him he had better catch that wagon.

By the time he reined in at the top of the embankment,
a dusty haze hanging over the road was the only evidence
of the wagon's passing. "Lucy?" He spoke the name softly
at first, then louder, more insistent, "Lucy!"

The words were swallowed up by the trees crowding the
oad on either side. He looked down the road toward
own—nothing. How had he lost her? He peered at the dust
at his feet and made out the faint imprint of a horse's shod
oot. He followed these off the road and into the under-
rush.

Amigo was contentedly munching a mouthful of bear-
grass, Lucy's sidesaddle on his back, empty.

Maybe she just had to relieve herself and was hiding,
mbarrassed at being caught in such a delicate position, he
old himself, scanning the surrounding brush. His heart beat

so wildly he had trouble getting his breath. "Lucy!" H
shouted this time, not caring who heard. But the word onl
echoed back at him.

He left Amigo grazing and backtracked to the road. H
couldn't stop thinking about that wagon. *Wagon. Buck
board. The Buckboard Bandit.* He stared at the pattern o
wagon wheels in the dirt, then something metallic glinte
at the edge of his vision.

He swung off his horse and bent down to scoop up th
revolver from the weeds at the edge of the road. A foot t
the left of it lay a sacking towel, carefully embroidered wit
a row of daisies. He stared at the delicately stitched flowers
and fear clawed at him. Lucy had dropped this gun—th
one she'd told him she carried in her saddlebag.

He checked the cylinders. The gun was loaded, no smel
of powder clinging to its barrel. It hadn't been fired today

Whoever had taken Lucy had done so without gunfire
She'd never even cried out—why should she? As far as sh
knew, no one was nearby to hear her.

He rose and stuffed the towel and the gun into his saddle
bag, then mounted and spurred his horse down the road
following the pattern of wagon tires in the dust. Lucy truly
needed him now; he wasn't about to fail her.

19

LUCY LAY FACEDOWN IN the bed of the wagon, wedged between a crate of onions and a bushel basket of turnips. A scratchy wool blanket that smelled of horse shut out the daylight and hid her from view. The bandit had ordered her into the wagon at gunpoint, then bound her hands behind her and lashed her feet together at the ankles. She was helpless even to brace herself against the bouncing and rocking of the wagon. Every jolt over the rough road added another bruise.

She tried to estimate how long they'd been traveling, and how far, but in the musty darkness, she'd lost all sense of time and direction. The best she hoped for now was to recognize their destination whenever they did arrive.

She was uncomfortable, frustrated, and enraged, but she refused to allow herself to be afraid. All she had to do was keep her wits about her and she could come out of this all right. She was young, intelligent, and used to looking after herself. She'd been doing so since her father's death. At first, her mother had been too distracted by grief and worry to do more than go through the motions of looking after Lucy. Later, when she'd remarried, Mary O'Connor had been too beaten down to take care of herself, much less her daughter. Lucy had learned early in life that the only person you could truly depend on was yourself.

She had gotten into this by herself; she was going to have to get out of it alone as well.

She concentrated on remembering everything she could about her attacker. He'd worn the same concealing clothes described in the newspaper articles she'd read, so she couldn't see his face or even much of his body other than his hands, and even they were gloved. His voice, muffled by the handkerchief, hadn't sounded familiar, but he could have been deliberately disguising it. All in all, he'd struck her as ordinary, except for one thing—why didn't he get out of the wagon to tie her? Of course, once she was in the wagon, she'd been at his mercy. She wished now she'd turned Amigo and raced away, taken a chance that his shot would miss her. But staring down the barrel of that gun she'd been paralyzed into doing anything he wanted.

"Whoa, there!" The wagon jolted to a stop. She strained her ears to identify the noises around her. There was the scrape of the wagon brake being set into place, the jingle of harness, the stamping of horses' hooves. The wagon seat creaked as the bandit shifted his weight, and one shoe shuffled against the wagon floor, then came in contact with the step. She waited for the other foot to follow; instead came the solid thunk of wood against wood. A hollow foreboding formed in the pit of her stomach.

Her captor moved slowly around the wagon, then the blanket was thrown back, and cool air washed over her. A strong hand grabbed her by the collar and jerked her back up onto her knees. "I'm gonna cut loose your feet now, but don't try anything."

The voice, unmuffled now by the handkerchief, confirmed what she had already reasoned. She glared over her shoulder at Bill Pollard. "So it was you all along. You really are the Buckboard Bandit." He used the rifle like a cane to brace himself and reached down and severed the rope around her ankles. The sharp blade of his knife grazed across her skin, sending shivers up her spine. "People never suspected me. 'The old cripple can't even ride a horse,' they said. They thought I was no use to anybody.''

He grabbed the waistband of her skirt and dragged her backward, out of the wagon. She stumbled, barely saving herself from falling. He sneered at her. ''You thought that, too.''

''You were never any use to me, leg or no leg!'' she snapped.

He slapped her hard, so that her eyes watered and her head rang. She fell against the wagon, bruising her hip. Before she could fully regain her senses, he grabbed her arm and pushed her toward an army tent half-hidden by a grove of trees.

As her vision cleared, she took quick stock of her surroundings. They were in a box canyon where a narrow creek petered out to a gravel bed. Half a dozen cottonwoods and a thick undergrowth of yaupon screened Pollard's camp from the casual observer. In this hideaway he'd erected a surplus army tent, the once-white canvas darkened with mud and mildew. The fetid, earthy smell of mud and decay hung heavy in the air.

Shouldering the rifle, he pushed her into the tent, then followed her inside and fastened the flap behind them. The tent was large, furnished with a metal cot, a single wooden chair, and a scarred table. An oil lamp sat on the table, casting a feeble yellow light over the dim interior of the tent. Barrels and crates were stacked around the walls. U.S. was stamped on the side of several boxes. Bolts of cloth tumbled from one crate; Lucy thought of Twila's new dresses.

Pollard motioned to a wooden barrel that sat across from the single chair. ''Sit down.''

She glared at him, making no move to obey.

''I said *sit*!'' He made a move toward her, as if to slap her again.

She sat, awkwardly perched on the barrel. Making an effort to hold her shoulders absolutely still, she twisted her wrists against their bindings. He had tied her tightly, but perhaps not so tightly she couldn't work her hands free, given enough time. She needed to stall. "So how did you do it?" she asked. "How did you prove everyone wrong?"

"I may have lost my leg at Gettysburg, but I didn't lose my mind, not like some." He tapped the side of his head. "I could still outwit most of these high-falutin' Yankees." He lowered himself into the chair across from her and rested the rifle in his lap, the barrel pointed at her. "I've had federal agents *beggin'* me for mercy. I let them know the South was a long way from cowed." He leaned forward, eyes dark, glittering with hatred. "I'm a *hero* to true Southerners."

You'll never be a hero to me, she thought, but this time held her tongue. The evil in his eyes sent an icy chill through her. She struggled to keep her voice from shaking as she asked, "What do you want with me?"

His eyes narrowed. "You deserve to be taught a lesson for interferin' where you don't belong. You wrote that fool story to turn people against me, and now you ought to be punished."

Like an accused prisoner waiting for the verdict, she said nothing. He studied her, the tension building between them. She held her body rigid, poised to run, to scream, to hurl herself at him—anything but sit idly and let him shoot her.

He smiled, an expression full of malice. "I reckon I'll wait, though, until Abernathy gets here. It'll be more . . . satisfyin' to make him watch." He nodded. "Yeah. I reckon I've finally figured out the best way to get to him."

Her stomach clenched at the mention of Trace. "I—I don't know what you're talking about," she stammered. She sucked in a deep breath and raised her chin, trying for a look of disdain. "Trace Abernathy couldn't care less what happens to me." She had to force the lie from her throat. Trace *did* care for her. The thought gave her courage.

Pollard shook his head. "No sense tryin' to lie to me. I saw him followin' you, watchin' out for you."

"When?" she said with a gasp.

"Just now." He shrugged. "I kinda got the impression

he didn't want you to know about it. He was hangin' back, which is just as well for me. It gave me plenty of time to get you into the wagon. But I reckon he'll trail us here eventually. Then I'll have him right where I want him.'' He reached out and pulled the lamp closer to him. He turned up the flame and lit the end of a twig. When he had a glowing coal, he applied this to his pipe.

Her heart sank at the news. If Trace followed her here, he'd walk right into Pollard's trap. If only she had some way to warn him! But close on the heels of this worry came the thought that if he hadn't gone against her wishes and followed her in the first place, he wouldn't get into any trouble.

Trace had lied to her! The knowledge shook her more than the sight of Pollard's rifle pointed right at her. He'd made a promise to allow her to make her own decisions, to live as she chose without his help. But as soon as her back was turned, he'd abandoned his promise and trailed after her. He couldn't have known Pollard was after her, so why had he followed? Could she ever trust anything he said again?

∞

TRACE FOLLOWED THE WAGON tracks as they turned off the road. The heavy wheels had crushed the summer-dry grass as they rolled along, marking a trail plainly across the prairie. He rode his horse at a fast walk alongside the tracks, reining in his own impatience, resisting the gnawing urge to set off at a gallop. Traveling too fast, he might lose the track, and thus lose valuable time.

The wagon recrossed the creek, and he thought he'd missed the trail. Then a broken branch pointed him in the right direction once more. Whoever was driving the wagon hadn't taken much care to hide his tracks. It was almost as if he *wanted* him to follow. The hair rose up on the back of his neck. He thought of the sniper and the trap that had been laid for him that day.

But he couldn't turn back. He couldn't abandon Lucy.

The trail headed up a ridge, and his sense of foreboding grew. He'd been shot not far from here, the day he and Rye had been rounding up mavericks. That had been, what—two weeks ago? Since then, he'd come close to dying, made a trip to Blanco he hadn't wanted to take, finally owned up to the fact that he was in love, won Lucy, and almost lost her again. She'd captivated him, infuriated him, and elevated him to heights he'd never known. His father used to say a little emotional upheaval was good for a man; it guaranteed he'd never be bored to death. With Lucy by his side, Trace expected to live a long and anything but boring life—he wasn't about to let anyone take her from him now.

By the time he rode the length of the ridge, he was not surprised to see that the trail led right to the canyon where he and Rye had penned the cattle the day Trace had been shot. He was sure now that the man who had fired on him and the one who'd taken Lucy were one and the same. He'd probably shot Trace to keep him away from the outlaw's hideout.

He dismounted and tied his horse in the shade of a scrub oak, then crept along the creek bank until he reached the far end. Kneeling down, he pushed through a thick stand of yaupon and stared down on the outlaw's camp.

He spotted the wagon first. It sat empty, save for a few baskets of vegetables and an old blanket. The horses, a sleek pair of bays, were tethered nearby, dozing. As his eyes adjusted to the surroundings, he discovered the tent tucked back in the trees. The once-white canvas had been smeared with mud so that it blended perfectly with the creek bank behind it. He stared at the tent, his stomach tightening. Lucy had to be in there. Whoever had captured her was likely there with her.

He debated leaving and going for help. At his fastest, it would take two hours to ride to his cabin and return with Rye—another two hours still to make it to town. More

manpower would make it easier to subdue Lucy's captor,
but could Lucy wait that long?

The answer came in the form of a scream that shattered
the afternoon stillness, and pierced Trace with the deadly
accuracy of a sharpshooter's ball. He vaulted over the
screen of yaupons and hurtled into the canyon.

∞

LUCY BLINKED BACK TEARS and struggled to regain
control of her stampeding heartbeat. She hadn't meant to
cry out like that. She'd always been proud of the fact that
she wasn't given to hysterics. But instead of shaking out
the twig when he'd finished lighting his pipe, Pollard had
leaned over and touched the lighted end to her arm. The
gesture had shocked and hurt her.

"Why did you do that?" she blurted, leaning as far away
from him as possible.

He sat back. "Maybe to put you in your place. You
always did think you were too good for any man. 'Course,
I noticed you run after Abernathy soon enough."

She glared at him, while behind her back she continued
to worry the rope that bound her. She was sure she could
eventually free her hands, but did she have enough time?

Pollard rose and moved toward her. Terror gripped her,
making it difficult to breathe, but she refused to give in to
the fear. She flexed her foot and wondered how hard she'd
need to kick Pollard's good leg in order to knock him over.

She never had a chance to find out. The door flap of the
tent exploded inward, and Trace rushed toward them, gun
drawn. "Let her go, Pollard!" he shouted.

Her heart leaped at the sight of him. He was the hero of
all her stories—the avenging knight, the Texas Ranger
fighting for justice. How could evil possibly prevail against
him?

"One more step and I'll scatter her from here to Birdtown." The sharp jab of the rifle in her side took her breath
away, reminding her this was no made-up story, but real

life, where men like Pollard often triumphed, even though they were wrong.

Trace looked from her to Pollard. Pollard pulled the hammer back on his rifle; she couldn't keep from flinching at the sound.

"Let her go." Trace let his gun fall. It hit the ground with a heavy thud. "You've got me now."

"I've got both of you." He motioned Trace to move farther into the tent.

Trace came to stand beside Lucy. He touched her lightly on the shoulder in a gesture of comfort. "Get your hands away from her!" Pollard barked.

Trace took a step back, but his eyes remained locked on hers. She turned away, despair weighing on her like a heavy pack. Why had he come? Things would only get worse now that he was here. Pollard disliked her, but to him she was just a woman. He was used to women like Twila, who didn't know how to fight back. He was bound to underestimate Lucy. She had only to wait for the opportune time and she would have her chance to get away.

Pollard's expression when he looked at Trace spoke of hate mixed with a measure of wariness. Pollard would never underestimate Trace. He would never let down his guard around him.

"I knew you'd fall into my trap." Pollard leered at Lucy, which made her shudder. "I just had to use the right bait."

"What do you want with me, Pollard?" Trace held his hands behind his back, as if they were already bound. Was he hoping Pollard would forget to tie him?

Pollard cradled the rifle in his arms and leaned against the table, all his weight on his good leg. "You never should have left Virginia, Abernathy. Or did you run away, one step ahead of the hanging party? That's what they do to traitors, you know. They hang them." He nodded. "Maybe that's what I ought to do with you, too."

"You're the one who set fire to my barn," Trace said, "and you put out the trap that injured Rye. Why?"

Pollard scowled. "Why should you have what I didn't—

a good farm and two good legs? You deserved to know what it's like to be the one burned out and crippled, everything you ever wanted gone just 'cause you were on the side of the defeated.'' He shoved himself away from the table and began to pace in front of them, the rifle across his shoulder like a sentry on picket duty. Step, *thump*. Step, *thump*. The uneven cadence jarred Lucy's nerves. Did Pollard notice that irregular rhythm, one more reminder of what he'd lost?

''You shot me the day Rye and I were penning cows here,'' Trace continued. Lucy cringed. What did Trace hope to accomplish by forcing Pollard to admit to his wrongdoing? Wouldn't that give the old man that much more reason to kill them both?

Pollard nodded. ''I was huntin' quail for supper when you showed up. I couldn't let you find my hiding place.'' He scowled. ''I should have killed you, but a dead body might have led folks to snoop around too much. Wounded, I figured they'd be in a hurry to get you back to town, and they wouldn't bother to search the canyon too closely. That gave me time to hide the goods.''

Trace looked around. Lucy followed his gaze to the stacked crates and barrels. ''How much of this did you steal?'' he asked.

''I wasn't stealing. I was taking back what rightfully belongs to the Confederacy.'' Pollard stopped pacing and turned to face them. ''Every time I make a fool of another Yankee, I win more people over to my cause.''

''What cause is that?'' The question burst from Lucy. How could the man believe his crimes would benefit anyone but himself?

He narrowed his eyes. ''The Confederacy is my cause!'' He leaned forward, his gaze burning into her. ''Don't you understand? We should have won!'' He turned to Trace. ''We had the better fighters. We had General Robert E. Lee himself on our side.'' He spoke the name in that reverent way Lucy had heard so often, as if only Jesus Christ himself could command more respect than the Confederate general.

"We were fighting for home and honor," Pollard continued. "Our men were committed to their cause. We should have won! We were cheated of a victory that was rightfully ours."

"Maybe so."

Trace's words shocked Lucy. She turned and found him watching Pollard with hooded eyes. "I never met fiercer fighters than some of those rebel brigades," he said softly.

"Nobody was better," Pollard affirmed. "Why, our boys could shoot the eye out of a squirrel at fifty paces." His expression had a distant look. She had the sense he was looking inward, at a vision that replaced the horror of war with glory.

Trace turned to Lucy, his expression sharp, filled with warning. *Be ready,* he seemed to say. She worked furiously at the ropes around her wrists. "Have you ever heard a rebel yell?" he asked.

She shook her head. She'd heard talk, of course, of how the Confederates would charge the enemy, screaming a bloodcurdling war cry.

"I'll never forget that sound as long as I live," Trace said. "I've seen men paralyzed in their tracks by the rebel yell."

"The Yanks knew they better start sayin' their prayers when we charged down on 'em, hollerin' that war cry." Pollard smiled faintly, as if at fond memories.

"Do you still remember how to do it?" Trace asked.

Pollard snorted. "As if I'd ever forget!"

Trace glanced at Lucy. "I've never heard it," she said, taking her cue. "Could you do it for me . . . now?"

Pollard drew himself up to his full height and puffed out his chest. Shoulders squared, he squinted his eyes shut, threw back his head and began to yell.

The scream was like nothing Lucy had ever heard. It undulated through the air, sending shivers through her body. Her ears rang, and her mouth went dry. She jerked her hands from her bindings just as Trace launched himself at Pollard.

The two men fell back against the table with a hard thump. The oil lamp slid to the edge, coming to a stop with the flame sputtering. Trace and Pollard struggled, Pollard's hands locked around Trace's throat. "I'll kill you!" the old man shouted.

Trace shoved hard, and Pollard lost his balance, pulling Trace to the floor with him. They rolled, wrestling for the rifle between them, all their energy focused on the fight, too absorbed for words now, only their labored grunts testifying to the fierceness of the battle.

Lucy stared at them, her heart in her throat. Pollard's face was red and contorted with rage. With strength she would not have guessed he possessed, he shoved Trace away. With an animal groan, he tried to bring the rifle up to use like a club. But Trace held the advantage of youth. He parried Pollard's thrust and wrapped his hands around the older man's throat.

Lucy spied Trace's pistol lying in the dirt near the entrance to the tent. She stepped around the wrestling men and retrieved it. It was heavy, the large grip awkward in her hand. She sighted down the long barrel, carefully aiming toward Pollard, but just as she readied to fire, he rolled over, and Trace's head swung into the line of fire. Exasperated, she took a deep breath and grasped the gun by the barrel. Stepping carefully to avoid losing her balance, she leaned over the two men and brought the butt end of the gun down hard on the back of Pollard's balding head. Without so much as a grunt, he collapsed.

Trace squirmed out from under his now unconscious foe and quickly bound Pollard's hands and feet. "That ought to hold him until we can get him to the sheriff," he said, stepping away from him.

He turned to Lucy, and without a word she moved into his arms. She was weak-kneed with relief, too moved to speak. Trace skimmed his hands over her back, her head, her arms, as if reassuring himself she was healthy and whole. She flinched as his hand brushed the place where Pollard had burnt her.

"What's this?" He pulled away to examine the burn. "Did Pollard do this?"

She nodded. Before she could speak, he turned to glare down at the older man. "I ought to beat him within an inch of his life—"

She grabbed his arm. "No. Leave it for the sheriff. There's been enough violence."

The tension went out of his shoulders, and he nodded. "You're right." He gathered her close once more. She closed her eyes, relaxing into the comfort of his embrace. She had never felt more safe in her life than when she was in Trace's arms. Even though he'd been wrong to follow her, she was glad he was here now.

"I should have known you'd know exactly what to do," he murmured, stroking her hair.

"Yes, you should have." She looked up at him. Better to let him know how she felt. Once he saw how serious she was about being allowed her independence, he'd apologize. Next time, she might not have to remind him. "You shouldn't have come here at all."

He frowned. "Why would you say that?"

She took a deep breath. Had she ever done anything this difficult? All she really wanted was to snuggle into his arms once more. But if they were to forge a happy future together, she had to make her feelings plain to him now. "You promised me you'd let me make my own decisions— live my own life, without interference. And yet the words were scarcely out of your mouth before you were trailing after me." She clenched her fists at her sides and spoke past choking tears. "Did you think you could just tell me what you thought I wanted to hear, and it wouldn't matter how you acted?"

His face clouded with anger. "I knew it wasn't safe for you to be out riding alone. And you see I was right."

"Oh, you were, were you?" She raised her chin, defiant. Is that what mattered most to him, being right? Never mind that he'd broken a promise and trampled her feelings. "How do you know Pollard didn't take me prisoner precisely because he knew you were following me? He said he wanted to use me to get to you. If you'd have left well enough alone, we could both be home and safe right now.''

He shook his head. ''I couldn't take that chance.''

''And *I* can't take the chance of marrying a man who would lie to me!'' The words were out of her mouth before she could think. She put her fingers to her lips. But hadn't she spoken the truth?

''Lucy, don't say that.''

He reached for her, but she turned away, wrapping her arms around herself as if she could somehow squeeze out the ache inside her that pained her far more than Pollard's burn. ''Take me home,'' she whispered.

He left the tent without answering. She followed and found him hitching Pollard's horses to the wagon. ''We'll carry Pollard into town and send someone to Birdtown for the sheriff,'' he said, not looking at her.

Pollard was coming around by the time they went in to fetch him. ''What the hell do you think you're doing!'' he shouted. ''Damn you, Abernathy, you'll pay for this!''

''Be quiet, or I'll gag you.'' Trace reached for the handkerchief at his throat, and Pollard fell silent, though his hate-filled stare burned into them, sending shivers up Lucy's spine. His silence was more unnerving than his curses. Looking at him now was like staring at the devil himself in the guise of an old acquaintance.

She helped Trace lift Pollard into the wagon. They sat him up against the side and she wedged blankets around him to cushion him. She could have punished him, she supposed, but she hadn't the will in her. She felt drained, her emotions muffled as if by a layer of cotton wool.

Trace tied his horse on behind the wagon, and they set off toward town. They rode in silence. She glanced at his profile, at the hard line of his jaw, the proud tilt of his chin. Would it always be like this between them, this brittle politeness that teased her with the hope that one day they might be friends again?

And if friends, then lovers. No. Never that. She couldn't

risk that. No matter how much she loved Trace, she couldn't change him. If he wasn't willing at least to consider her side of this, and to apologize for the wrong he'd done her, how could they ever be happy together?

People turned to stare as they pulled into town. By the time they reached the store, a crowd had gathered. Uncle Nate came out on the porch to greet them. "What's going on?"

The crowd stared up at them, eager for news. "We caught the Buckboard Bandit," she announced.

Trace frowned at her. Was he angry because she'd stolen his thunder, announcing the news first? Well let him scowl all he wanted. She'd made the discovery first, hadn't she? Didn't that give her the right to share the news?

"Pollard? It was Pollard all along?" In one form or another, these words rippled through the crowd.

Nate cast a sorrowful look toward his former friend. "I suspected as much, but I never wanted to believe it," he said.

Trace climbed down from the wagon while Uncle Nate stepped forward to assist Lucy. "He's got a camp in a canyon over by Anderson Hollow where he's hidden the stolen goods," Trace said. "He captured Lucy and took her there." He glanced at her. "I followed her, and he threatened to kill us both."

"Lies, all lies!" Pollard bellowed.

"I can take you to the canyon, prove it to you," Trace said.

"No—*he's* the bandit!" Pollard shouted. "*He* stole the goods and hid them there. I surprised him and the girl there, and they took me prisoner."

The crowd murmured, eyeing Pollard the way one regards a lunatic. Whatever credibility he had once had with them, it was gone now.

"How did you get away?" Nate asked.

Trace looked at Lucy again. She slipped her arm around her uncle. "It's a long story," she said.

"Is there someplace you can hold him until the sheriff comes?" Trace asked.

"One of the saloons has a back room where they lock up rowdy drunks," Dr. Lambert said. "I reckon that would do."

Lambert and Zeke Early climbed into the wagon and prepared to drive Pollard to his makeshift cell. But before they could do so, a woman's cry of distress stopped them. White-faced, her bonnet askew, Twila pushed her way through the crowd. "Mr. Pollard, what is happening?" she asked.

"Your *friends* attacked me!" He spat the words, as if he held her equally responsible for his fate.

She shrank back, her expression clouded with confusion. She spotted Lucy on the porch and turned to her. "What is going on?" she asked.

Lucy smoothed her apron, fumbling for words. "I'm sorry, Twila," she began.

"Your husband is the Buckboard Bandit." Patricia Scott's voice dripped with disdain as she delivered the news.

Twila put a hand to her chest and swayed. Lucy feared she might faint. "No!" Twila gasped. She looked at Lucy again, eyes pleading.

Lucy nodded. "I'm afraid it's true," she said softly. "He admitted as much to me, and he hid the stolen goods in a canyon."

Twila looked down at her dress. "All my new things . . ." she whispered. She clutched at the brown print fabric as if she feared it might suddenly dissolve. Lucy thought she would cry, but she inhaled a shaky breath and rallied. "I . . . I'm sure there must be some mistake," she stammered.

"Go home, woman!" Pollard ordered. "Quit makin' a spectacle of yourself in the street."

Lucy willed her to defy him, but instead Twila mutely turned and walked back down the street. The crowd parted to let her pass; no one moving to follow her. She shuffled away, shoulders bent like an old woman, or like someone trying to make herself smaller, invisible.

Lucy's throat clogged with tears, and her vision blurred. Where was the beautiful, proud young woman who had laughed and teased with her? Where was her friend, who had looked for the best in everyone and fashioned gardens from junk and beautiful quilts from tattered rags?

The wagon rolled past, carrying Pollard to the saloon. He sat upright in the back, glaring defiantly at all who looked his way. She wished now she had made him suffer more. Of all the crimes he had committed, stealing Twila's friendship from her had been the worst.

The crowd followed the wagon toward the saloon. Nate went back inside the store to wait on a few remaining customers, leaving Lucy and Trace alone on the porch. "We need to talk," Trace said.

"What is there to talk about?" She waited, hoping against hope that now he would apologize. He would listen to what she had to say.

Instead he glared at her. "Most women would be grateful to have a man who wanted to look after them."

"Most women are used to being looked after. I'm not!"

"Then you'd better get used to it," he growled.

The words made her sick inside. Why had she ever thought things could be different for them? She looked up at him, into a handsome face she would never forget, into eyes that burned with twin flames of anger and love. "No. I've made up my mind. I know what I have to do." She swallowed tears and forced the words from her throat. "Good-bye, Trace," she said softly. "I think it's best if we agree never to see each other again."

She didn't wait for him to answer, but turned away and walked through the store, not looking back, afraid he would read the misery in her eyes and convince her to reconsider. She could not reconsider. This is what she had to do, and there was no sense crying over it, she told herself, even as tears filled her eyes.

"Lucy? Lucy, we need to talk."

A hand on her arm halted her escape. Dazed, she looked up at Mr. Gibbs. "I . . . I'm not feeling very well," she stammered. "Maybe some other time . . ."

"Sorry, hon, but I only come to town for a little while." Mr. Gibbs let go of her arm and tugged at his beard. He looked unhappy. "I need to talk to you about that contract we made for those ten steers."

She blinked, trying to clear some of the fog from her brain. As her senses returned, the numbness was replaced by stomach-clenching dread. "Wh-what about them?" she asked.

He shook his head, eyes sorrowful. "Well, the contract's no good now, don't you see? Those old boys went up to Missouri and didn't sell a single cow. The market's just not there."

Her mouth went dry. She opened her mouth to speak, but words deserted her.

"I'm gonna have to take the cattle back or have payment," Mr. Gibbs rushed on. "If you can't pay me, I'm better off selling 'em for their hides and horns."

"How much?" Her voice sounded very small.

"A hundred dollars." He squared his shoulders. "It's a fair price."

It might as well have been a thousand dollars, for all the cash she had on hand. "I—I can't give you the money right away."

"I can give you a few days. Let's say a week. If you can't pay me by then, I'll send a boy over to get the cattle." He nodded and turned away.

She stared after him, anger and despair washing over her in dizzying rage. Why did her whole life have to fall apart at once? Shaking, she made her way through the store and up the stairs to her room. Only in that refuge, behind a locked door, did she allow herself to give in to the flood of tears that swept over her. As the flood subsided, she tried to consider her situation with more calm. What were her choices here? She could try to convince Mr. Gibbs to keep to their original agreement. She could talk to him about the plans to take the cattle to new stockyards in Kansas next year.

She sighed. In Mr. Gibbs's eyes, those cattle were good for nothing but the few dollars they'd bring from the hide and horn man.

"He'll be sorry next year," she said petulantly. She sniffed and dashed a stray tear from her eyes. Next year, she'd be the one reaping the profit in Kansas, while narrow-minded men like Mr. Gibbs wrung their hands over the poor choice they'd made. This could even turn out to be a *good* thing for her. If she bought the cattle from Mr. Gibbs outright, she wouldn't have to share her profit with him. All she had to do was come up with a hundred dollars.

As if drawn there, her gaze shifted to her bridal quilt draped across the chair by the dresser. Mrs. Sorenson had offered a hundred dollars for the quilt. If she sold it, her problems would be over.

The solution seemed so simple. After all, she wouldn't be needing the quilt anymore. Other women could devote themselves to domestic duties. She'd put her energies into building up her fortune. Wasn't this just how she'd pictured things would be? She stared at the tumbled cloth and felt as if a giant fist squeezed her heart. If this was the right choice to make, why did it hurt so much to make it?

20

TRACE RODE HIS HORSE into a lather on the way back to his cabin. Lucy was crazy, that was all there was to it! Any other woman would have thrown herself into his arms, weeping for joy over the fact that he'd raced to rescue her. But *she'd* scolded him for interfering. Her confounded *independence* was more important to her than her own safety even.

"I should have paid attention to my instincts," he grumbled as he turned the horse onto the path leading back to the new barn. "I knew the moment I laid eyes on that woman she'd be nothing but trouble."

He unsaddled the horse and wiped him down, then left him in a stall with a measure of oats. "If she doesn't want to see me again, that's *fine*. I don't need her." His gut twisted as he said the words. Maybe he didn't need Lucy, yet part of him still wanted her. But was it too much to ask for her to at least be *sensible* about things?

Shoulders slumped, he made his way into the cabin. With barely a nod to Theresa, who sat by the window sewing, or Josh, who played on the floor with Mary, he poured himself a cup of coffee, then began searching through their stores, opening trunks and sorting through the canned goods. Theresa looked up and gave him a questioning look. ''Where are you hiding the whiskey?'' he asked.

She laid aside her needlework. ''What's the matter with you?''

''Nothing. Now, where's that whiskey? I know you keep some for 'medicinal purposes.' ''

She came and elbowed him out of the way and unearthed a brown glass bottle from the depths of her trunk. He grabbed it and poured a generous slug into the coffee cup. Getting drunk wasn't going to solve his problems, he knew, but it might ease the pain for a little while.

She snagged the bottle from his hand before he could pour any more. ''That's enough 'medicine' for now.'' She took a seat at the table and set the bottle in front of her. ''Josh, you take Mary outside and play. Mr. Trace and I are going to have a talk.''

Josh opened his mouth to protest, but a warning look from his mother silenced him. He hoisted his little sister onto his hip and disappeared out the door. When he was gone, Theresa turned to Trace. ''Now sit down here and tell me what's gotten into you.''

''Dammit, I am *tired* of women telling me what to do.'' But he sat down at the table anyway. He told himself it was more tiring to get drunk standing up. Besides, at the table he'd be within easier reach of the bottle.

''You and Miss Lucy had a little dustup.'' She nodded, a wise look on her face.

''No. We had an out-and-out *fight*. She thinks she can take care of herself so well, then just let her.'' He took a long drink of the coffee and whiskey mixture. The ''medicine'' burned going down.

Theresa sighed. ''Tell me what happened.''

He wouldn't have talked to anyone else, but with Theresa, the words came tumbling out. How many times before had they sat like this around the kitchen table at his home in Virginia, while he raged about Marion's latest wild scheme, and his inability to control her? Theresa said the same thing now she'd said then. ''You're not a man made for some meek little mouse of a woman. You'd be bored to distraction with a clingy woman.''

"Why does she have to be so stubborn? Can't she see I just want what's best for her?''

Theresa sat back and studied him a moment. "I reckon you'd know all about stubborn.''

He took another drink. "What's that supposed to mean?''

"I remember the day you and Miz Marion got married. I was helpin' serve at the reception and I remember seein' you standin' there with her, back so stiff it's a wonder you could bend.''

He grimaced. "All her relatives were staring at me like I was something the cat dragged in.''

She smiled. "Oh, but you were determined to show them, weren't you?''

"Her father told me to my face I wasn't man enough to handle his daughter.''

She leaned forward. "Sometimes I think the only reason you tried so hard to control Marion is to prove that you could.''

"And I couldn't, could I? She died having her own way.'' He drained the cup and reached for the bottle, but Theresa held it out of reach.

"She died because she was a foolish, reckless woman.'' She grabbed his hand and held it. "Lucy isn't like that. And she *loves* you. You don't have to prove anything to her or to anyone else.''

He sagged back against his chair. "I just . . . don't want to lose her. She doesn't see the danger in all these things she does—riding alone and working cattle and taunting bandits in her stories.''

"Maybe she sees the danger but thinks freedom is worth the risk,'' Theresa said quietly. She released his hand. "Are you really so worried about her getting hurt, or are you just trying to save yourself from that pain?'' She shook her head. "You can't do it.''

He closed his eyes, not wanting to see the truth in

Theresa's eyes. Her words stabbed him, like arrows sinking into a target. He couldn't stand the thought of Lucy hurt—for her own sake and for his. He'd loved Marion, and when she'd died, he felt the loss keenly. But Lucy—Lucy had taken possession of him heart and soul. To lose her would be to lose himself.

Theresa stood and stowed the bottle of whiskey back in the trunk. "You gonna spend the rest of your life alone instead of riskin' a little hurt?" she asked.

He opened his eyes. "It doesn't matter. She never wants to see me again."

"And you think she really meant it?" She put her hands on her hips. "There's a time to be stubborn and a time to give in. It's a wonder the Yankees ever won a battle, with you so quick to surrender."

He tried for another drink, but his cup was empty. Theresa's lecturing was really getting on his nerves. "So now I'm a coward, am I?"

"No, you're just a man." She snatched the cup away from him. "And it's time you remembered that some things are *really* worth fighting for."

"That's enough!" He shoved back his chair and stood.

"Where are you going?" she asked as he grabbed his hat from the peg by the door.

"Some place with no *women* around to nag me!"

⚭

LUCY SLEPT FITFULLY, DREAMING of Trace. She woke early and lay staring up at the watermarked ceiling, her mind still full of half-formed dreams and snatches of yesterday's conversations. Why had things ended so badly between them? All she'd wanted was for him to apologize, to acknowledge that he was wrong. Was that really asking so much, even of a man as proud as Trace?

She threw back the covers and climbed out of bed, driven by a nervous restlessness. If there was only something she could do to make things right again, or to make this suf-

fering pass. *I've got to keep busy,* she thought as she pulled
on her stockings. I *won't think about Trace at all.*

She might as well have told herself to stop breathing.
Reminders of Trace seemed hidden everywhere—in her
dress, which was the one she'd worn the day after she and
Trace had made love in Blanco; in the burn on her arm,
which snagged against the sleeve of the dress as she pulled
it on; in the sandalwood soap she used to wash her face;
and in her bridal quilt, which she had never been able to
bring herself to put away, despite her earlier vows. It still
lay across the chair beside the dresser, a reminder of unfinished dreams.

"I'm through with this now," she said aloud, and gathered the quilt in her arms. She'd wrap it up and later this
week she'd carry it to Mrs. Sorenson. Then she'd take the
one hundred dollars she'd get for it to Mr. Gibbs. Everything would be settled.

The appliquéd hearts brushed against her cheek, pillow
soft and bright as flowers against the white background of
the coverlet. What warmth and comfort this quilt would
have given her. She traced her finger around the hearts,
moving from one to another. Individually, each was beautiful, but together they formed a different picture, grander
and more lovely than any one heart alone.

She and Trace were like those separate hearts—able to
stand alone, but oh, how much stronger and more beautiful
would they have been together. *You can't always do everything by yourself,* he'd told her. She closed her eyes,
squeezing out tears. She'd been looking out for herself for
so long, she wasn't sure she knew any other way to act.
She'd said she wanted to be independent; she'd never
meant that she wanted to be alone.

*Most women would be grateful to have a man who
wanted to look after them.* Trace had said that, too. She'd
been so upset, she hadn't really listened to his words or,
more importantly, listened for the meaning behind them.
Could it be that, like her, he'd wanted something from her
that he couldn't bring himself to ask for?

She'd wanted his apology. Maybe he'd wanted her to acknowledge his help, his bravery and concern. She felt as if she'd swallowed rocks. Maybe Trace just wanted to be *needed*—by a woman who pretended never to need anyone.

She sank down onto her bed, the quilt gathered into her lap. If only she had someone she could go to for advice. Uncle Nate did his best, but he was a man. She needed a woman, a sister or friend or . . . mother. If Mary O'Connor had lived, would she have been able to help Lucy sort out her tangled feelings and make the wise decision?

She hugged the quilt to her chest, comforted by its softness. She'd spent a lot of time with quilts these past few months. She'd felt closer to her mother while working on the quilts, closer even than when Mary was alive. Every time she ran into difficulty with a pattern or a set of stitches, her mother's clear instruction and example had been there to help her.

Could her mother somehow help her now? Had she left anything behind that might offer her daughter guidance?

Feeling slightly foolish, but desperate enough to try anything, Lucy put aside the quilt and headed for the attic. She climbed the narrow stairs and pushed open the trap door, then lit the single candle and made her way to her mother's trunk in the corner.

The large chest was almost empty now. A few scraps of cloth, perhaps set aside for future quilts, lay in the bottom of the trunk, along with some lengths of muslin. Lucy unpacked each item and spread them around her on the attic floor, as if she might derive some message from these scraps of her mother's life.

She lifted the muslin out last, only then realizing that something was wrapped in the cloth. Scarcely daring to breathe, she unwound the material to reveal an elaborately pieced quilt. Fruit and flowers, and delicate leaves and buds sprouted from the twining branches of a graceful tree. Birds roosted in the branches and flew overhead. Protected all these years, the brilliant reds and greens, indigos and yellows remained bright. Heavily quilted, the design had a luxurious texture. It was a quilter's masterwork. *Her mother's bridal quilt.*

Lucy traced the outline of a fanciful blue bird. She had vague memories of her mother telling her about this tree-of-life quilt. Mary had made it to celebrate her engagement to Matthew O'Connor and had made him wait to wed her until it was complete.

Why had she kept this quilt, even after all her other work had been lost? Had she ever taken it from the trunk and looked back on happier days? Or did she hide it away because to see it made her unhappiness unbearable?

Maybe Mary kept the quilt because she wanted to remember—or she wanted her daughter to remember—that this kind of love was still possible.

Lucy's tears made wet circles around the singing birds and watered the tiny cloth flowers. She lay down and pressed her cheek against the quilt's soft surface, like a child cuddling up to her mother's lap. Mary's body had left a long time ago, but her spirit lingered here, in the lemon-verbena-scented folds of her bridal quilt. Once again, when Lucy needed her most, she'd delivered the right answer to the questions in her daughter's heart.

"Lucy! Lucy, where are you?"

The muffled cries roused her from her reverie. Reluctantly she dried her eyes and retraced her steps to the trapdoor. She snuffed out the candle and descended the stairs. "Here I am, Uncle Nate. I was just looking for something in the attic."

"What are you doing up there, child?" Nate hurried down the hall toward her. "There's somebody here to see you."

Her heart leaped at the words. Was it Trace? What would she say to him? She forced herself to walk slowly down the stairs behind her uncle. She didn't want Trace thinking her too eager. She was willing to talk to him, to try to hash things out between them; that didn't mean she was going to give in completely.

But her visitor wasn't Trace. Instead, Twila and her

mother sat at the kitchen table, staring into untouched cups of tea. Twila looked up at Lucy's approach, her face pinched and fearful, her eyes alight with hope. "Hello, Lucy," she said softly.

Lucy wanted to run to her friend, to throw her arms around her, but she held herself back. "If you've come to defend Pollard to me, I won't talk about him anymore."

Twila flushed and looked away. "No, I won't defend him. What he did . . . was wrong."

Ada Russell leaned forward and put her hand on her daughter's arm. "Twila has left Mr. Pollard," she said. "She's moving back home."

All caution deserted Lucy then. She rushed forward to fling herself on Twila. "I'm so glad to hear it," she said, arms around Twila's neck. "I've been so worried about you, living there alone with him."

Twila sniffed and dabbed an embroidered handkerchief to her red-rimmed eyes. "I tried so hard to make it work, but, like Mama said, both people in a marriage have to do their part."

Lucy looked at Ada Russell in silent thanks across Twila's head. The older woman nodded. "Twila did all she could, but you can't have a happy home when one person does all the giving, and the other only takes."

Lucy slid into a chair and held both Twila's hands in her own. "Now, you let me know if there's anything at all I can do to help you."

Twila gave a wan smile. "Oh, Lucy, you're so quick to offer to help others, but you won't ever accept help from us." She sniffed. "You won't want to hear it, but you and Mr. Pollard had that in common, at least."

Lucy stiffened. How dare Twila compare her to that bullying, mean-spirited *thief* she'd been married to! Twila's smile expanded, a hint of the old teasing look Lucy had seen so often. She relaxed, but her friend's words still nagged at her. Was Twila right? In her push for independence, did she drive others away? Had she driven Trace away?

Had she been doing all the taking—expecting him to make every concession to her wants and will—without making the same sacrifices for him? She thought back over her behavior with him, her stubborn insistence on always having her own way, and blushed with shame. "I guess I've worked so hard to get what I want, I've forgotten how important compromise can be," she said softly.

Twila squeezed her hand. "I didn't mean to hurt your feelings. I only meant for you to remember that *I* might be able to help you sometimes, too."

"You've already helped me, Twila. More than you can know." She looked at them both. "In fact, I'd be much obliged if you'd help me right now."

Twila glanced at her mother. "Of course we'll help you."

She smiled. "All right. Then come upstairs. I've got something I could never do justice to by myself."

∞

TRACE TURNED BACK THREE times before he was able to ride toward town. He'd spent the better part of the past two days riding and thinking. Theresa's words burned on his conscious, like the sentence of a hanging judge. *He was stubborn.* Guilty. *He was proud.* Guilty. *He was a coward.* That charge stung most. He'd never run from a fight or turned his back in battle, but he feared the pain of losing a part of himself in love more than he'd ever feared forfeiting his life in battle or surrendering his leg in that field hospital.

But like the sniper who'd fired on him at Appomattox that day, Lucy had caught him unawares, and felled him as surely as that sharpshooter's bullet. She'd captured his heart despite the battles he'd fought to keep it. All his struggling had only served to increase his pain. All that was left to do now was surrender. Let her ride alone, or write inflammatory stories, or learn to lasso wild cattle. Only let her do it at his side, wearing his name.

He slowed his horse at the sound of a rider approaching. Someone else was in a hurry as well, galloping down the road toward him in a flurry of dust. His hands tightened on the reins. Was there some trouble in Elm Ridge? Had Pollard escaped?

He was startled to see Lucy racing toward him, a muslin-wrapped bundle draped across the saddle in front of her. She reined in Amigo beside him and looked up at him, cheeks flushed as if she herself had been running. "Hello, Trace."

"Hello, Lucy." He couldn't stop looking at her, at the wild wisps of hair escaping from under her bonnet, at her eyes, feverish with a mysterious excitement. "Is something wrong?" he asked. "Why were you riding so fast?"

She smiled, an expression that made his catch his breath. Surely he had never met a more beautiful woman. "I was coming to see you," she said.

"You were?" Then he remembered his own mission. He cleared his throat. "I was coming to see you."

"You first."

They both spoke at once. She laughed and ducked her head, a demure gesture made more charming by the fact that it was wholly out of character for her. "I came to thank you—for rescuing me from Pollard."

He arched one eyebrow. "Even though you didn't really *need* rescuing?"

She tossed her head. "Well . . . it's the thought that counts, right?" She sighed. "It's just . . . I'm not used to having anyone so . . . *concerned* for me. So I guess I don't quite know how to take it sometimes. I . . . I apologize if I seem ungrateful."

He didn't know whether to groan or laugh. Ungrateful didn't exactly describe the way she'd castigated him. Still, he recognized the effort she'd made. "I owe you an apology, too," he said.

Her expression softened. "You do?"

He nodded. "I broke my promise, and that was wrong . . . even though I did it with the best of intentions." He hreaded the reins through his fingers. "And I can't claim hat I'm not used to stubborn, independent, women. It's just aken me a while to learn I can't out-think them." He ooked her in the eye. "I'm in no way a perfect man, but f you can put up with a stubborn, proud, imperfect one, hen I'd like to give us another try."

She looked away, smiling at the cloth-wrapped bundle across her knees. "What's that?" he asked to fill the sudden, frightening silence between them.

She folded back the muslin cover to reveal the bright hearts of her bridal quilt. "Twila and her mother spent all yesterday helping me finish it." She looked up, joy dancing in her eyes. "Everybody knows a woman needs a bridal quilt if she's going to be married soon."

She laughed and held out her arms. He pulled her close, almost dragging her off her horse. The quilt bunched up between them, soft as down. He imagined the nights they'd spend beneath it, wrapped in each other's arms, separate but together, stitched down tight with love.

TIME PASSAGES